"WILL YOU FORCE SOME MAN TO MARRY A WOMAN JUST BECAUSE YOU WANT TO PAIR THEM ALL UP?" SARA ASKED.

Gideon stalked toward her, finding a grim satisfaction in the sudden wariness that leapt into her face. "My men have spent the last eight years at sea with only an occasional night in port to satisfy their need for female companionship. Your women could be horse-faced and snaggle-toothed, and my men would *still* want them, I assure you!"

She backed away from him until she came up against the door to his cabin. "I hardly believe that your men would want a wife who's—"

"Enough!" He planted his hands against the oak door on either side of her, pinning her between them. He raked his fingers through her thick, silken hair and twirled one coppery lock around his finger. Soft, so soft.

"Stop that," she whispered, and gasped when he stroked one finger along her neck. "It's not . . . proper."

That made him smile. "Proper? You're on a pirate ship, remember? You're alone in a cabin with a notorious pirate captain . . . and I'm about to kiss you."

Other **AVON ROMANCES**

A DIME NOVEL HERO *by Maureen McKade*
THE HEART BREAKER *by Nicole Jordan*
HER SECRET GUARDIAN *by Linda Needham*
THE MACKENZIES: DAVID *by Ana Leigh*
THE MEN OF PRIDE COUNTY: THE OUTCAST
by Rosalyn West
THE PROPOSAL *by Margaret Evans Porter*
A ROSE IN SCOTLAND *by Joan Overfield*

Coming Soon

KISS ME GOODNIGHT *by Marlene Suson*
WHITE EAGLE'S TOUCH *by Karen Kay*

And Don't Miss These
ROMANTIC TREASURES
from Avon Books

DEVIL'S BRIDE *by Stephanie Laurens*
THE LAST HELLION *by Loretta Chase*
MY WICKED FANTASY *by Karen Ranney*

The Pirate Lord

SABRINA JEFFRIES

AVON BOOKS ◆ NEW YORK

This is a work of fiction. Names, characters, places, and incidents either are the product of the author's imagination or are used fictitiously. Any resemblance to actual events, locales, organizations, or persons, living or dead, is entirely coincidental and beyond the intent of either the author or the publisher.

AVON BOOKS
A division of
The Hearst Corporation
1350 Avenue of the Americas
New York, New York 10019

Copyright © 1998 by Deborah Martin Gonzales
Inside cover author photo by René William Gonzales
Published by arrangement with the author
Visit our website at **http://www.AvonBooks.com**
Library of Congress Catalog Card Number: 97-94324
ISBN: 0-380-79747-X

First Avon Books Printing: April 1998

AVON TRADEMARK REG. U.S. PAT. OFF. AND IN OTHER COUNTRIES, MARCA REGISTRADA, HECHO EN U.S.A.

Printed in the U.S.A.

WCD 10 9 8 7 6 5 4 3 2 1

To Emily Toth, my favorite feminist,
and to my parents,
who taught me to stand up for my rights

Chapter 1

How much it is to be regretted, that the British ladies should ever sit down contented to polish, when they are able to reform. . . .

—HANNAH MORE
ENGLISH WRITER AND PHILANTHROPIST
ESSAYS ON VARIOUS SUBJECTS . . . FOR YOUNG LADIES

London, January 1818

Miss Sara Willis had known a great many awkward moments in her twenty-three years. There was the time as a seven-year-old when her mother had caught her filching biscuits from the grand kitchen at Blackmore Hall, or the time shortly afterward when she'd fallen into the fountain at her mother's wedding to her stepfather, the late Earl of Blackmore. Then there was the ball last year when she'd unwittingly introduced the Duchess of Merrington to the duke's mistress.

But none of those compared to this—being physically accosted by her stepbrother as she departed from Newgate Prison in the company of the Ladies' Committee. Jordan Willis—the new Earl of Blackmore, Viscount Thornworth, and Baron Ashley—wasn't the sort of man to mask his disapproval, as so many members of Parliament had learned to their detriment. And now he took charge of her person with a shameless lack of propriety, propelling her toward the waiting Blackmore carriage as if she were the merest child.

She could hear the choked laughter of her friends as Jordan jerked open the door of the carriage and glowered at her.

"Into the carriage, Sara. Now."

"Jordan, really, such dramatics are not neces—"

"Now!"

Swallowing her dismay and embarrassment, she climbed into the well-appointed carriage with as much dignity as she could muster. He followed her in, slammed the door, then threw himself onto the seat across from her with such force that the carriage rocked on its springs.

As he ordered the coachman to drive on, she cast an apologetic glance out the window toward her friends. She was supposed to join them at Mrs. Fry's for tea, but they must realize that was impossible now.

"Deuce take it, Sara, stop making sad faces at your friends and look at me!"

Settling her slender frame against the damask cushions, she faced her stepbrother. She opened her mouth to chastise him for his untoward handling of her, then closed it when she saw the ominous furrowing of his brow. Though she was used to Jordan's formidable temper, she didn't at all like being the recipient of it. Most of London society joined her in that particular dislike, for Jordan was frightening indeed when he was angry.

"Tell me, Sara," he bit out, "how do I look today?"

If he could ask a question like that, she thought, perhaps he wasn't so very angry after all. Folding her hands in her lap, she surveyed him. His cravat was crookedly tied, most unusual for him. His auburn hair was in its natural unruly state, and his frock coat and trousers were rumpled. "Rather mussed, to be truthful. You need a shave, and your clothes are—"

"Do you know why I look this way? Do you have any

idea what brought me racing from the country without taking time to sleep or groom myself properly?" His scowl forced his dark auburn brows into a solid line of disapproval.

She tried to match it but failed miserably. Scowling wasn't her forte. "You were eager for my company?" she ventured.

"It's nothing to joke about," he growled in that warning tone he used to cow the matrons at the marriage marts who attempted to introduce him to their daughters. "You know quite well why I'm here. And no matter how charming you make yourself, I won't overlook this latest mad scheme of yours."

Good heavens. He couldn't possibly know, could he? "Wh-what mad scheme? The Ladies' Committee and I were merely distributing baskets of food to the poor unfortunates at Newgate."

"Don't lie, Sara. You do it badly. You know quite well that's not why you were at Newgate." He crossed his arms over his snug-fitting frock coat, daring her to contradict him.

Did he know the truth? Or was he bluffing? It was always hard to tell with Jordan. Even when he was eleven and her mother had married his father and brought Sara to live at Blackmore Hall, Jordan had been completely inscrutable, especially when trying to worm something out of her.

Well, she could be just as uncommunicative. Crossing her arms over her chest to mimic him, she asked, "So why *was* I at Newgate, Mr. All-Knowing?"

No one could get away with mocking Jordan. The only reason he endured it from her was because he truly considered her his sister, despite the lack of blood between them. Still, judging from the glint in his brown eyes, she was trespassing farther than he liked on his goodwill.

"You were at Newgate meeting the women who are being transported to New South Wales on the convict ship that leaves in three days, because you have some fool idea about sailing with them." When she opened her mouth to protest, he added, "Don't try to deny it. Hargraves told me everything."

Oh, bother it all. The butler had told him? But Hargraves had always been loyal to her. What had made the wretch betray her confidence?

Feeling defeated, she slumped against the seat and stared out at the sky, which was thick as clotted cream with heavy fog and dew. They were traveling along Fleet Street now. Usually the grubby bustling of its ink-stained denizens cheered her, for it showed that someone at least was trying to make a difference in society. But nothing could cheer her now.

Jordan went on, his voice clipped. "When I received Hargraves's letter, I left a great deal of unfinished work at Blackmore Hall so I could rush to London to talk some sense into you."

"That's the last time I trust Hargraves," she muttered.

"Don't be like that, Sara. I've told you before, while you may ignore the dangers you encounter with that Quaker woman Mrs. Fry and her Ladies' Committee, the servants and I do not." The note of concern in his voice grew more pronounced. "Even Hargraves, who approves of your reform efforts, is no fool. He recognizes how risky your new scheme is. He merely did his duty by telling me. If he hadn't, I would have sacked him, and he knows it."

She stared at her handsome stepbrother, whose auburn hair and chestnut eyes so resembled her own that people often mistook her for his real sister. Sometimes his attempts to protect her were endearing. Mostly, they were tedious. If not for his time-consuming duties as the new earl, she would never be able to engage in the pursuits she deemed more important than safety or propriety.

At her silence, Jordan added, "Look here, Sara, it isn't that I disapprove of reform. I heartily applaud the ef-

forts of the Ladies' Committee. Without them, there
would be more orphans in the street, more babies gone
hungry—"

"More hapless women forced into virtual prostitution
for daring to steal bread for their children." She leaned
forward, stirred by moral outrage. "These convict
women are being sent to a foreign land for the slightest
of offenses, merely because Australia needs more
women."

"I see," he said dryly. "So you're saying none of them
deserves incarceration."

"Don't put words in my mouth," she snapped. She
thought of the women she'd met today. "I'll admit that
many are thieves and prostitutes . . . or worse. But at
least half are women whose poverty compelled them to
steal. You should hear their 'heinous' crimes—stealing
old clothes to exchange them for meat or taking a shil-
ling from the till. One woman was sentenced to transportation for stealing four cabbages from a field. Four
cabbages, for goodness sakes! Why, a man would hardly
have his hand slapped for such a crime!"

His expression grew solemn. "I know there are mis-
carriages of justice, moppet. But one must deal with
those through Parliament and the passing of laws."

He *would* call her "moppet" now. He only did that
when he wished to soften her. "Parliament has relin-
quished its responsibility for transported convicts to the
Navy Board, which is oblivious to what goes on."

The cold dampness of the Blackmore carriage couldn't
compare to the bitter cold those women suffered at
Newgate and would suffer on the voyage. And they
would suffer worse things. Her voice hardened at the
thought. "The minute those women enter the ships, the
crew make advances to them. The ships become floating
brothels. That is, until the women reach their destination, where they are handed over to even worse masters.
Don't you think that too harsh a punishment for a
woman who stole milk for her baby?"

"Floating brothels. And telling me this is meant to convince me to let you travel in one of those hellholes?"

"Oh, the men won't bother *me*, you understand. They only take advantage of the convict women because the women can't fight back."

"They won't bother you," he repeated with sarcasm. "If that isn't the most naive, ridiculous—"

He broke off when she glared at him. "Sara, a convict ship is no place for a—"

"Reformer?" The carriage jolted as it hit a pothole. When it moved more smoothly again, she added, "I can think of no place that needs a reformer more."

"And why the devil do you think your presence on that ship will change a deuced thing?"

She winced at his profanity. Unfortunately, this was no time to give him her usual lecture about it. "The grand lords of your Parliament have ignored the protests of the missionaries who accompany the ships. But they *won't* ignore the sister of the Earl of Blackmore if she presents them with an honest account of the deplorable conditions, both on those ships and in Australia."

"You're right." He leaned forward, bracing his gloved fists on his knees. "They won't ignore you—*if* you go. But since there's no chance in hell that I'll let you—"

"You can't stop me, you know. I'm old enough to go where I please, with or without your permission. Even if you lock me in my room, I shall simply find a way to escape—if not in time for this voyage, then in time for the next."

Jordan looked so livid she feared he might ignite before her very eyes. Good heavens, he was volatile. Lord have mercy on the woman who married *him*.

"If you didn't think I could stop you," he bit out, "then why did you put this scheme into execution while I was away?"

"Because I wanted to avoid this discussion. Because I

care about you enough to dislike arguing with you, Jordan."

He muttered a curse that could barely be heard over the rumbling of the carriage. "Then why don't you care enough to stay here?"

She sighed. "Come now, Jordan, my absence may actually enhance your life. Won't it be easier for you to run your estates if you don't have me around to worry about?" The voyage to New South Wales took nearly six months each way, so she could be gone as long as a year.

"Don't have you to worry about? What do you think I'll be doing all that time?" He pounded his fist against the side of the carriage. "My God, Sara, ships go down! There are epidemics, and there's always the possibility of mutiny—"

"Not to mention pirates. We'd certainly present a fine prize for *them*." She suppressed a smile. He always did prepare for the worst, even when it was absurd.

"You find this very amusing, don't you?" He ran his fingers through his hair, mussing it even more. "You have no sense of what you're risking."

"I do, truly I do. But sometimes one must face a little danger to do a great deal of good."

A wistful look entered his eyes then. With a sigh, he shook his head. "You are very much Maude Gray's daughter."

Mention of her mother sobered her completely. "Yes, I am. And I'm proud of it, too."

Her mother had fought hard for reform, starting on the day Sara's father, a soldier out of work, had been cast into debtor's prison. It had continued even after his death there. Indeed, Sara was convinced that her mother's altruism was what had attracted the late Earl of Blackmore to her. Her mother had met the earl, a very progressive man, while soliciting his aid in getting members of the House of Lords to listen to her plan for prison reform. They'd fallen in love almost at once. Even after marrying him, she'd stayed active in her reform work.

Until she'd died two years ago after a long and wrenching illness.

Tears came to Sara's eyes, and she brushed them away, then dropped her fingers to stroke the etched silver of her mother's locket, which she always wore.

"You miss her still." Jordan's soft comment broke the silence in the carriage.

"Not a day passes that I don't think of her."

The telltale tapping of his fingers on his knee showed how uncomfortable her depth of emotion made him. "I cared for your mother, too, you know. She treated me like a son at a time when . . . I was cynical about being mothered."

Sara had always sensed there was something peculiar about Jordan's relationship to his own mother, who'd died only a year before her mother had met and married his father. But Jordan and his father had always refused to speak of the first Lady Blackmore in any depth, and Sara had never pressed them.

"In any case," Jordan hurried to add, "I miss your mother, too. And I honor her zeal for reform."

"So did your father, if you'll recall."

"Yes, but even Father would have been against this. He would have said you should stay here and—"

"And do what? Feed the poor? Make occasional visits to the prison while dodging your matchmaking efforts?"

She regretted those last bitter words the minute she saw him flinch. She hadn't wanted to upset him, not when she was leaving London in only a few days.

"My matchmaking efforts! What the devil do you mean?"

"I'm not an idiot, Jordan. I know why you insist that I attend those fashionable affairs." Leaning forward, she clasped his hands, which felt stiff and cold even through the supple kid leather of his gloves. "You think if you throw me at enough eligible bachelors, one of them will take pity on me and marry me."

"Take pity on you!" He jerked his hands from hers with a sound of disgust. "How can you talk like that? You're beautiful, intelligent, and witty. If you were to meet the right man—"

"The right man doesn't exist. Can't you get that through your thick head?"

"You're still punishing me for Colonel Taylor. That's what it is. You're refusing all other men because I wouldn't let you have that one."

"Of course not! That was five years ago, for goodness sakes. And it's not as if I couldn't have had him if I'd wanted." When he cast her a quizzical glance, she hesitated, torn between her pride and her need to make him understand her feelings. The latter won out. "I ... I never told you this before, but do you remember the night you revealed all you knew to your father? The night he called me in and threatened to cut off my portion if I married the colonel?"

"How could I forget it? You were furious at me."

"Well, I sneaked out later that night to meet with Colonel Taylor in secret."

True shock showed on his handsome face. "The devil you say!"

"I went to him and ... and offered to elope." She turned away, the mortifying memory making it impossible for her to meet her brother's gaze. "He refused. It seems he was exactly the bounder you said he was. He *did* want me only for my inheritance. And I was too foolish to see it."

She waited for him to pounce on her confession as a way to demonstrate that she'd made rash decisions in the past. When he patted her knee kindly instead, she had to bite back more tears.

"Not foolish, moppet." His voice was husky with caring. "You were merely young. Women follow their hearts at that age, and as they say, love is blind. You couldn't see his character as truthfully as the rest of us."

"Oh, but I *should* have! Everyone else could see it— you, Papa, even Mama. I was the only one who couldn't."

"Is that why you won't countenance other suitors? Because you think they'll deceive you?"

She worried one of the ribbons on her blue levantine morning gown, twisting it round and round her gloved index finger. "While Mama was ill, I couldn't think of suitors. After she died, I guess I . . . lost my nerve. I chose so badly the first time, and now I don't know if I can distinguish the fortune hunters from the reliable men."

"You can't accuse any of my friends of wanting you for your fortune. Take St. Clair, for example. I'll admit his fortune is small, but then wealth doesn't matter to him. And he often comments on your beauty."

"St. Clair would never countenance my work. He wants a mistress of the manor, not a reformer." She added in a teasing tone, "Besides, he likes salmon, and I simply can't abide a man who likes salmon."

"Be serious, Sara. There are plenty of men who would suit you perfectly."

She twisted the ribbon tighter. "Not as many as you'd think. Men beneath my station are attracted by my fortune, and men above my station need not saddle themselves with a wife who'll plague their friends about reform."

"Then find someone in the middle."

"There's no such creature. I'm a commoner adopted by an earl, but with no lineage to speak of. I'm neither fish nor fowl. I don't belong in your world, Jordan. I never have. The only place I'm comfortable is with the Ladies' Committee, and there are no potential suitors among them, I assure you."

What she left unsaid was that she'd never found a man of any station with whom she could imagine spending the rest of her life. Jordan's friends were all very nice, but they would rather play at life than do anything useful. And none of them understood her. Not a one.

"Deuce take it, Sara, if I thought it would keep you from going, *I'd* marry you. We're not blood relations. We *could* marry, I suppose."

She laughed. "I *suppose*? Such enthusiasm!" Knowing how he felt about marriage, she was surprised he'd even suggest it. She tried to imagine being married to Jordan and recoiled at the thought. "What an idea! It's impossible and you know it. We may not be siblings by blood, but we're siblings in every other way. We could certainly never consummate a marriage."

"True." He looked vastly relieved that she'd refused his hastily spoken offer. "Besides, it wouldn't keep you from going, would it?"

"I'm afraid not. Come now, Jordan, this convict ship won't be as awful as you imagine. Most of the women were convicted of non-violent crimes. The surgeon will have his wife aboard, and missionaries have brought their wives with them in the past. I'll be perfectly safe."

They'd passed into the Strand, and he glanced out the window as if seeking for answers in the glittering shops that catered to the aristocracy. "What if you took a servant along for protection?"

She cast him a shrewd glance. He was weakening, she could tell. She chose her words carefully. "I can't take a servant. We're keeping my relation to you a secret. I'm supposed to be a spinster schoolteacher. I'll be running a school for the convict women and their children, as the missionaries have previously done."

"Children?"

The very thought of all the children who ended up traveling aboard those ships made her see red. "Yes, a transported convict woman is allowed to take with her any male child under six and any female child under ten. If you think I'll be exposed to terrible sights, think of those poor children," she said grimly.

He was silent a moment, as if envisioning it. "Why must you be incognito?"

"I'm keeping a journal chronicling the abuses. If the captain and crew know I'm your sister, they'll hide what they're doing. We want an honest assessment of conditions on the voyages, which is why we can't tell them of my noble relations."

"That doesn't mean I can't send someone—"

"Sara Willis, schoolteacher, wouldn't travel with a servant, I assure you."

"Wonderful," he said with considerable sarcasm. "You won't even have a servant on your side."

"I won't need one." She tried for a lighter tone. "Do you think me so inept I can't do without a maid for a while?"

"You know quite well that ineptness has nothing to do with it." He paused. "So you think to set sail on the *Chastity*, do you? Devil take it, that's an inappropriate name for the ship if I ever heard one."

When she shot him an irritated glance, he turned his face from her to stare out the window. They were already driving up in front of the Blackmore townhouse on Park Lane, an impressive Palladian villa meant to intimidate any of the lesser mortals who ventured into its lofty halls.

Sara could remember how its towering pillars and myriad windows had awed her when she and her mother had first come to dinner there. But her stepfather hadn't let her feel intimidated. He'd offered to show her the new litter of puppies in the kitchen, and that had endeared him to her forever.

Sometimes she missed him as much as she missed her mother. She'd never known her real father, and the earl had filled that position so admirably that she could never think of him as anything but a father. He'd loved her mother dearly. Though his death a year after her mother's had devastated both her and Jordan, it had come as no surprise. Lord and Lady Blackmore had never liked to be parted.

The carriage shuddered to a halt, and Jordan climbed down onto the frost-crusted driveway, turning to help her out. He didn't release her hand at once, but took it in both of his. "Is there nothing I can say to talk you out of this?"

"Nothing. It's something I must do. Really, Jordan, you shouldn't worry. Everything will be fine."

"You're my only family now, moppet. And I have no wish to lose you, too."

A lump formed in her throat as she squeezed his hand. "You won't lose me. You're just lending me out for a while. The year will fly by, and I'll be back before you know it."

A year. It sounded like forever to Jordan. Although he said nothing as she tucked her hand in his elbow and let him lead her into the house, he wanted to rant and rave and shake her senseless. A woman of her station on a convict ship! It was insanity!

But there was little he could do to stop her. Perhaps if Father were alive. . . .

No, even Father had been unable to curb Sara when she was determined upon some course. Her tale of sneaking out to meet Colonel Taylor proved that.

The devil take Taylor! If it weren't for that deuced colonel, she might even now be settled with a husband and two babes, instead of gallivanting off to Australia on a fool's errand.

He watched as Hargraves came out to take her cloak and she cast the man an accusing glance.

Poor Hargraves colored to the roots of his thinning hair. "I'm sorry, miss. Truly I am."

As usual, Sara softened at the sight of the servant's remorse. Patting Hargraves's hand, she murmured, "It's all right. You were just doing your duty."

As she left them both to climb the thickly carpeted stairs, Jordan stood there staring after her. The woman was too kind and generous by half. How on earth would she survive on a convict ship? Her work with the Ladies' Committee had given her a taste of human misery, but she'd never been immersed in it. Once aboard that ship, she'd be stuck there a year or more. Unprotected. Alone.

He looked at her slender back, at the wisps of auburn hair escaping her chignon, at her unconsciously feminine walk, and a sigh escaped his lips. Sara was oblivious to her own attractions. She might feel awkward in society, but that had never kept men from desiring her. Quite the contrary. He'd spent her first season quelling the untoward advances of her more eager suitors.

It wasn't that she was especially pretty, though her looks were certainly presentable. She drew men to her with her intelligent manner and her frank kindness toward everyone, regardless of their station. A sour, pinch-faced spinster teacher might have nothing to fear from the sailors aboard the *Chastity*, but that wouldn't be true of Sara. How could he let her go off on that ship with no protection whatsoever?

He couldn't. And since forbidding her to go was useless, he had only one alternative. He must make other arrangements for her protection.

As soon as Sara was out of earshot, he faced Hargraves. "Do you know any sailors?"

"Aye, my lord." The middle-aged servant took his great coat and beaver hat, his face carefully expressionless. "My youngest brother, Peter, is a sailor."

A plan was forming in Jordan's mind. "Is he capable of defending himself? Or defending someone else?"

Hargraves shot him a shrewd glance. "He served in the navy for six years before he signed on with a merchant ship. He's good in a fight, as I recall. I don't see him much, you realize, since he's at sea most of the time."

"Is he at sea now?"

"As it happens, my lord, he sailed into port a fortnight ago."

"Excellent. Do you think he'd be willing to go to sea again in a few days' time? There's a handsome sum of money in it for him."

The servant nodded. "I'm sure he'll be willing. He's got no wife to worry about. Besides, he owes me a favor or two."

"Have him come here tomorrow at ten. And be sure Sara doesn't see him. Do you understand?"

"Indeed I do," Hargraves said with a conspiratorial air. "And may I say, my lord, that I'm sure Peter will suit your purpose."

"I hope so." With a smile, Jordan dismissed Hargraves, pleased to have found a way to keep an eye on Sara while she was on that dreadful ship. He would reserve judgment until he met Peter Hargraves, but if the man proved suitable, Sara would have a companion on the *Chastity*. Whether she wanted one or not.

Chapter 2

Nobody should trust their virtue with necessity, the force of which is never known till it is felt, and it is therefore one of the first duties to avoid the temptation of it.

—LADY MARY WORTLEY MONTAGU
ENGLISH SOCIETY FIGURE, LETTER, 22 JUNE 1752

A week after Sara's discussion with her stepbrother, she stood on the decks of the *Chastity*. It was early morning, when the ocean looked like a fluid carpet. It was such a marvel. She'd never even glimpsed it until two days ago when they'd passed out of the Thames into open water, but already she loved its changeable nature.

The first day it had been like a spirited dragon carrying ships on its sharply undulating back. Its breath had sprayed mist over the rails into their faces, and its watery claws had slapped furiously against the hull, forcing the three-masted frigate to roll and pitch on each fresh swell.

Today, however, it was gentler, more like a rocking horse thumping the ship along in a pleasing motion. She breathed in the salt-drenched air, so different from the cloying stench in London. Thank goodness she'd escaped the seasickness that plagued some of the convicts. It was as if she'd been meant to sail.

"'Tis a lovely day, ain't it, miss?" said a voice at her side.

She whirled to find one of the sailors standing beside her at the rail. She'd noticed him before, looking at her as if trying to make her out. Something about him struck her as familiar, but she couldn't figure out why. He looked like nobody she knew. A wiry man of about thirty years, with big ears and skinny limbs, the only thing he resembled was an organ grinder's monkey. Though he seemed harmless enough, the intensity of his interest disturbed her.

And he was standing far too close. "Yes," she murmured, edging away from him along the rail. "It is indeed a lovely day." Turning her face back toward the ocean, she pointedly ignored him, hoping that would make him leave her alone.

But he only moved closer. "You're the one what's teaching the convicts, ain't you? Your name's Miss Willis?"

"Yes, we begin our classes this morning."

When he leaned toward her, her heart began to pound, and she scanned the ship for some sign of rescue. But despite the sailors scrambling about the spider's web of rigging above her, no one was within hailing distance. Not that she would hail any of the twenty-two crewmen. She didn't trust them one jot. Already she'd had to chastise a sailor she'd found sneaking into the ship's prison quarters late at night when she'd left her tiny cabin, unable to sleep.

But where were the captain and the ship's officers this morning? Or the surgeon and his wife?

"I been wanting to speak to you—" the man began, and she braced herself to give him a sharp set-down. Then the ship's bell rang, signaling the beginning of the next watch.

As the men scurried down from the rigging and others came on deck, she used the ensuing bustle to escape the strange sailor. But her blood thundered in her ears as she hurried to the saloon where she and the ship's officers breakfasted. Perhaps Jordan's concern for her had been warranted, after all.

Don't be silly, she told herself as she entered the familiar saloon. *There are plenty of people around. Just don't stroll about the deck alone anymore.*

But that wasn't easy to do. She couldn't bear to stay in her cabin or below decks all the time, and there was no one to stroll with her on deck. She watched glumly as Captain Rogers entered and took his seat at the opposite end of the breakfast table. The good captain would never escort her. A blustering, gruff man in his fifties, he was more interested in sailing his ship than in talking to the troublesome woman the Ladies' Committee had sent aboard.

She glanced around the table at her other companions. The officers were all too busy to walk with her. And although the surgeon and his wife would probably accompany her, she'd prefer complete solitude to any conversation with them. She'd never seen such a somber pair, full of dire predictions about storms and shipwrecks. Why, the surgeon had already terrified one of the convict women's girls by claiming that her protruding forehead proved she would lead a life of crime, like her mother. The girl had calmed down only after Sara had pointed out that the surgeon's wife had a similar forehead, though it was hidden by corkscrew curls.

The ship's cook thrust a bowl of oatmeal in front of Sara, and she grabbed the edge to keep it from skittering along the table with the movement of the ship. No, finding a companion was not the answer. She would simply have to content herself with her work. Thankfully, there was plenty to keep her busy, what with the eight children of school age aboard the *Chastity*, in addition to the fifty-one convict women and the thirteen younger children. She suspected that everyone—except the two babies, of course—would need some sort of schooling.

Thus, an hour later when she went below to the prison cells on the orlop deck, she found herself eager to begin. Oddly enough, she felt safer with the convict women than she did with the sailors.

With the cell doors open and the women milling around preparing for the day, she could almost forget they were criminals. They were divided loosely into eight messes. At night, two messes of women and their children were locked in each of the four nine-by-twelve-foot cells, but during the day, they had more freedom. As they moved in and out, stowing their belongings on one of the three levels of berths and washing up at a barrel of sea water, they looked remarkably like any other traveling women.

Well, except for the tattoos, of course, that peeked out from beneath some of the women's coarse cuffs. What possessed a woman to adorn her body so permanently? Probably the same thing that drove civilized women in past decades to wear powdered wigs and hoop skirts. Convict fashions were probably no more bizarre than any fashion.

In truth, only the most hardened criminals wore tattoos, the women who'd been in gangs of burglars or who'd mixed prostitution with thievery. The dairy maids and shopgirls who'd been sentenced to exile for stealing pies and used clothing would never dream of defacing their bodies.

Grabbing onto a post when the ship dipped, Sara surveyed the lot of them with a critical eye. Their clothing was pitiful. As usual, the Navy Board's regulations were idiotic. Some fool had dictated that wool and flannel carried disease and thus were unacceptable materials for convict uniforms. As a result, the sad wretches wore cotton gowns that proved no protection at all against the wintry air of the North Atlantic. Even the children were allowed only cotton garments.

Something must be done about that at once. In addition to the summery muslins she'd packed in anticipation of warmer climes, she'd also packed five inexpensive wool gowns. But she didn't need all of them. Two would suffice, though it meant washing every day. The others could be made into warmer clothing for the little ones. As for the women, perhaps she could prevail upon the captain to allow a stove to be placed in the hold, at least until they neared the tropics.

But that could be dealt with later. Now it was time to set her little school in motion. Releasing the post and spreading her feet wider to allow her a better balance on the rolling bottom of the ship, she clapped her hands to gain the women's attention.

As soon as they settled down and faced her, she ventured a smile. "Good morning. I trust you slept well." When they murmured responses, she went on. "Many of you already know me as one of Mrs. Fry's ladies who visited at Newgate. But for those of you who don't, I'm Miss Sara Willis. I'm your teacher."

The women began muttering. They'd been told they'd receive instruction, but the idea clearly didn't appeal to some of them. After much prodding and whispering, one of the women stepped forward from among the others.

The poor dear's face and gloveless fingers were chapped and reddened from the cold. Nonetheless, she wore a haughty air quite at odds with her situation. "Some of us know our letters and sums already, miss. We won't need instruction."

Sara didn't take offense at the woman's insolent tone. The convicts had gone through many disturbing changes recently and were bound to be suspicious of her. She'd just have to allay their suspicions as much as possible.

She smiled at the woman. "Very well. Those who already have an education can help me with the ones who don't. I'll be pleased to have your help, Miss—" She broke off. "What is your name?"

Her amiability seemed to take the woman aback.
"Louisa Yarrow," she blurted out, then scowled as if
she'd been tricked. She tossed her head, making her
cropped-short blond hair bounce. "I don't know if I
want to help you."

"That's purely your decision, Miss Yarrow. Of course,
it'd be a shame if the children went the entire voyage
without any instruction. I was so hoping someone could
deal with them while I tend to the women who *are* interested in furthering their education." She gave an exaggerated sigh. "But if no one wants to help—"

"I'll help, miss!" called a voice from the back of one
of the compartments.

Sara looked toward the timid young voice, but when
the black-haired girl stood, clutching at the iron bars of
a cell to steady her balance, Sara realized she wasn't a
girl at all, but a doll-like creature of womanly propor-
tions.

Sara cast her a reassuring smile. "And your name is—"

"Ann Morris. From Wales." The woman's heavy
Welsh accent made that quite clear. "I don't know my
English letters so good, but I know the Welsh ones."

"What the bloody hell good will that do where we're
goin'?" a harsh voice cried from one of the berths. "Just
because it's called New South Wales don't mean it's got
Welshmen!"

Everyone laughed uproariously at that sally. Little
Ann Morris looked stricken, which made some in the
crowd only laugh harder.

With a frown of disapproval, Sara clapped her hands
until she got silence again. "You can help me anyway,
Ann." She ignored the snorts of the others. "You don't
need to know your English letters to be able to help the
children while I teach the women. You and the children
can learn together."

Another woman might have been insulted to be
lumped in with the children, but Ann Morris flashed

Sara a grateful smile before she sat down again. Clearly she liked children, and Sara intended to take advantage of that to help the girl learn.

When Sara returned her attention to the others, she was surprised to find that some of their hostility had abated. "Now, then, the Ladies' Committee has provided us with a hundred pounds of cloth scraps and sewing materials for making patchwork quilts. Each of you will receive a packet of materials and two pounds of cloth. You may sell whatever quilts you complete and keep the proceeds for yourself."

That proposal met with more approval from the women. Though the money the quilts brought in might not be much, Sara knew it would be welcome in a strange land. This was the first time providing materials had been tried. On previous journeys, ship's crews had complained that the restless convict women caused trouble. Of course, anyone with an ounce of common sense could have seen that the women needed something to do, but common sense had been scoured out of the Navy Board members at an early age, so it had taken Mrs. Fry to point out the obvious. Once she'd gained the Navy Board's approval, the Ladies' Committee had convinced several textile factories to donate cloth scraps. The ladies had bought the thread, needles, and other tools on their own.

"I'll distribute the packets in a moment," Sara informed the women, "but first, I want to determine what sort of education all of you have. Those who already know their letters, please raise your hands." An uncomfortable silence ensued, full of wary glances and shifting feet. When nothing happened, Sara added, "I assure you, ladies, I simply want information. I promise not to hold your ability to read or your lack thereof against you."

That seemed to reassure them. About half of the women lifted their hands, including Louisa Yarrow. When they started to put their hands down, she said,

"Wait. Those of you who know your letters well enough to read a page of type, keep your hands up. The rest may put theirs down."

Half of those with their hands up lowered their hands. Sara estimated there were about thirteen women who professed to be able to read. She did a similar division for those who could write and ended up with seven women who could both read and write. After some discussion, she succeeded in assigning two of the women to help Ann with teaching the children and the other five to teach small groups of women, divided according to their level of skill.

One of the women who claimed to both read and write, a saucy tart by the name of Queenie, refused to do any teaching, stating that she'd rather spend her time in "other" pursuits. When she lifted her skirts and swished them about her calves, several women laughed and Sara knew at once what Queenie meant.

Mrs. Fry had warned Sara that the problem of the sailors consorting with the women wasn't always the men's fault. Some of the "soiled doves" among the convict women were more than happy to continue their profession on the voyage.

Sara refused to tolerate such behavior. It took only one woman engaging in such illicit acts to provoke the men into forcing the others to do so, too. She'd seen it happen in Newgate, and it would surely happen here. Besides, she wanted these women to see their own value—and they wouldn't do that by selling themselves.

But she couldn't very well say that to Queenie, could she? Instead, she took a different approach. "That's fine, Queenie. If you're incapable of teaching, then by all means, do something else. I want only those with true ability. If you're inadequate for the position, I certainly wouldn't want you ruining the other women's chances to better themselves."

At the titters of those around her, Queenie lost her

smirk. "See here, I wasn't saying I couldn't do it, just that—"

"I'll be perfectly happy to take Queenie's pupils," Miss Yarrow cut in, much to Sara's surprise. When Sara shot her a questioning glance, the well-spoken young woman stuck out her chin and added, "*I* don't have any other pursuits, not of Queenie's kind, at any rate. I'm not letting any filthy man put his paws on *me*."

Her words were spoken with such vehemence that Sara couldn't help wondering about it. She stared at Louisa Yarrow, straining to remember what she'd read about her in the list of convicts and their crimes. Ah, yes, Louisa was the one who'd been a governess to the Duke of Dorchester's daughters until the night she'd stabbed the duke's eldest son and nearly killed him. Now the gently bred woman was serving a sentence of fourteen years' transportation.

Louisa's angry words had silenced the women, and Sara didn't know how to respond. Suddenly, a soft voice spoke up. "Beggin' yer pardon, Louisa, but it ain't like we'll have a choice when we reach New South Wales." It was Ann Morris speaking, her girlish brow creased with a frown. "I've heard tell of what they do, how they send the women off to serve the colonists. There's too many men, I heard. They'll make fallen women of us whether we want it or no."

The blood rose in Sara's veins at the thought that even a sweet young woman like Ann could feel so helpless. "No, they won't. I'll do all in my power to keep that from happening. Once we reach New South Wales, I'll see to it you receive decent assignments where you'll be treated with respect."

Moving to the burlap bags filled with the packets of sewing materials, Sara took a handful and began to pass them out. "But before you can gain respect from others, you must learn to respect yourselves. You must strive to improve your other feminine strengths and make

yourselves proud. Then you'll have a chance at escaping
your former lives."

There were some who scoffed. They gathered to form
knots of grumbling voices in the cells. But others looked
to her with renewed hope. They took the packets from
her, staring down at them with curiosity.

Soon she was joined by Ann Morris, who shot her a
shy smile as she helped pass out the packets. Then some
of the ones Sara had chosen as teachers joined her, and
before long the women were thoroughly engrossed in
looking at their materials and talking about quilts.

When all the packets were distributed, Sara stood
back to observe her charges. So many of these women
had never been given a chance. No one had ever told
them they were worthy of saving, and they'd been
taught to believe that they were forever lost to a world
of thievery, prostitution, and murder.

But it wasn't true. They were capable of more. She
could tell from the way some of them helped each other,
the way others sat down at once to begin sewing, the
way Ann took aside one of the little boys and patiently
showed him how to pick a pocket—

"Ann Morris!" she exclaimed, hardly able to believe
her eyes. She walked up to the petite Welsh woman just
as the little boy whisked a packet of sewing materials
out of Ann's apron pocket with a giggle. "What in
heaven's name are you doing?"

Ann looked up, a wide, ingenuous smile on her face.
" 'Tis a magic trick, Miss Willis. Queenie showed it to
me yesterday. You can take a body's things off him
without him even noticin'." She turned to the boy.
"Hand it back, Robbie. You can't keep it. That would
be stealin'."

Suppressing an irritated sigh, Sara shot a stern glance
beyond Ann to Queenie, who suddenly became very engrossed with organizing her cloth scraps, mumbling all
the while about "naive country girls."

Sara softened her tone as she returned her attention

to Ann. "Yes, well, I suggest you avoid using such 'magic tricks' from now on. They're liable to get your sentence lengthened."

When Ann merely looked at her questioningly, she shook her head. She certainly had her work cut out for her, trying to keep the incorrigibles from corrupting the innocents.

Some of these women could become contributing members of society. It just wouldn't happen in a day.

Night had fallen by the time Sara ended her first day with the women. Though lessons had long been over, she'd lingered below decks, trying to find out as much as she could about the convicts. They'd hesitated to tell her much at first, but after some coaxing she'd gleaned a few tidbits about them and their children.

There was Gwen Price, a Welshwoman like Ann, except that she spoke so little English Ann had to interpret for her. There was squirrelly Betty Slops, who seemed a slave to her wretched surname, for she constantly sported the remains of her last meal on her coarse cotton gown. And there was Molly Baker, who'd been convicted of selling stolen goods and was pregnant with her second child. Her first child, Jane, was the daughter of her husband, but the baby had been conceived in Newgate after she'd been "seduced" by a guard. More like rape, it was. And it was infuriating to think that the very same system that had gotten her with child had punished her for something that wasn't her fault by following through with the sentence of transportation despite her very advanced pregnancy.

Sara had tried to spend a few moments with all of them. By the time the women were locked in for the night and she'd climbed the steep steps from the hold to the 'tween decks, her head ached and all her muscles were sore. She'd left the prisoners only twice to take her meals in the galley, and now all she wanted was to climb into her berth and sleep.

Then she opened the hatch to find a sailor standing beside it in the cramped 'tween decks. Bother it all. It was the same sailor who'd sought to go down to the women the night before, and he looked as surprised to see her coming up as she was to see him standing there.

Taking advantage of his surprise, she clambered up quickly and closed the hatch behind her. "Good evening," she said in her sternest voice. He was alone, of course. The 'tween decks were used as storage. Seldom did anyone come down in them, which meant he was probably there for all the wrong reasons.

Feeling a tremor of uneasiness, she sought to hide it by glowering at the sailor. "What are you doing down here?"

The sailor was of the most unsavory sort. His beard was unkempt and he stank of stale sea water and grog. Too much grog. "Look here, missy," he retorted. "Queenie's expectin' me, so don't you be interferin'."

The thought of this man having relations with a woman in front of everyone in the prison appalled her. Donning her most severe expression, she crossed her arms over her chest. "Surely you realize I can't allow you to expose young children to such debauchery."

He scowled. "Young children? Nay. I'll be bringin' her up here with me, I will." He drew out a ring of keys that had been tucked into his grimy breeches and dangled them in front of her. "I'm sure the lass and I c'n find a private spot to do our business, not that 'tis any of yer concern."

She stared at the ring of keys he was twirling round and round on his grubby forefinger. "Who gave you those keys?" she demanded.

"The first mate. Tole us men that as long as we don't bother nobody, he don't care wot we do with the women."

The very idea! She would certainly record *that* in her journal. The Ladies' Committee would be apprised that

this travesty extended all the way up to the ship's officers.

Quickly, she stepped on the hatch, blocking his way
to it. "I'm afraid I can't allow you to go down there."

"You ain't got any say in it, missy." He stepped closer
and grinned, exposing a gap between two of his rotting
teeth. "You best be gittin' out of me way, before I
change me mind about who it is I'm wantin'."

She colored as she realized what he meant. The audacity of the man! Oh, she would speak to the captain
about him at once! Surely the captain wouldn't countenance such overtures made to a perfectly respectable
woman!

"I'm not moving until you vacate this deck," she retorted. "Leave now or I shall tell the captain what
you've been up to!"

An ugly frown beetled his low brow. He set down the
candle he'd been carrying, then clasped her arms with
two hammy fists and lifted her off the hatch. "You ain't
tellin' nobody nothin'. I'll say you lied and the first
mate'll back me." He dropped her behind the hatch like
a sack of meal, then bent to open it.

She refused to give up, especially with Ann Morris's
mournful words about forced whoredom still ringing in
her ears. After regaining her balance on the rolling deck,
Sara shoved the hatch door closed again with her foot.
This time the wretched sailor drew back his hand as if
to slap her.

But a voice from the steps behind him arrested him.
"Lay a hand on her, matey, and you'll see stars, you
will!"

Both Sara and the sailor turned to the steps in shock.
They hadn't noticed the man who'd climbed down from
the top deck and was now rounding the steps, his flattened hands held in front of him like knives.

Sara groaned. It was the monkeyish sailor who'd spoken to her on deck this morning. Wonderful. Now she
had two oafs to deal with.

"This ain't none of y'r business, Petey," the sailor with the rotting teeth spat. "You go back up where ye came from, and leave me and the miss to settle our tiff."

The man named Petey drew circles in the air with the edges of his hands. "Get away from her or I'll lay you out."

"Lay me out? A scrawny little thing like you?" The sailor shook his fist in the air. "Get on with you, and leave me and the chit be."

What happened next came so quickly that Sara could scarcely believe it. One minute the two men were facing each other. The next minute the sailor who'd accosted her was flat on his back unconscious, and Petey was standing over him, locked in a strange stance.

When Petey lifted his gaze to Sara, she whispered, "Good heavens, what did you do to him?"

He relaxed his peculiar stance, his face shadowed in the candlelight as he scooped up the keys that had been thrown clear of the other man. "I learned a few tricks about fightin' when I was in Chinese waters, miss. With me bein' a little man an' all, I figgered I'd best learn what I could. A little man can fight the Chinese way as easy as a big man."

She shut her gaping mouth, a sudden fear overtaking her. If Petey could send a hulking sailor unconscious in two seconds flat, what could he do to her?

Still, he *had* come to her rescue, hadn't he? She forced a cordiality into her tone that she certainly didn't feel. "I see. Thank you, sir, for using your . . . unusual tactics on my behalf. And now, if you'll excuse me—"

She moved toward the steps, hoping to get away before he decided to claim some unsavory reward for his help.

But she wasn't fast enough. "Wait, miss, I gotta have a word with you. I been tryin' to talk to you all day—"

"I can't imagine what you could have to say to me," she muttered as she hurried up the steps to the main deck. Oh, if only she had some sort of weapon—a knife, a pistol . . . anything.

To her alarm, he stepped over the inert sailor and clambered up the steps after her. "Please don't worry yerself. I ain't gonna hurt you." He caught her by the ankle, and when she looked down to fix him with a frosty glance, he added in a lower voice, "Name's Peter Hargraves, miss. I'm Thomas Hargraves's brother. I'm in the earl's employ."

Everything changed in that one moment. A rush of relief hit her, so intense she felt faint from it. If he was Thomas Hargraves's brother and in the earl's employ, that could only mean one thing: Jordan had hired him. Thank heavens for her meddling and overprotective stepbrother.

She should have known Jordan would never give up so easily. When he hadn't gotten what he'd wanted from her, he'd simply found another way to make sure she had protection. She ought to be furious with him. Instead, she was thanking her good fortune that he'd decided to ignore her wishes.

"I understand." She glanced around, hoping no one else had heard his words. "Perhaps we'd better discuss this in private. In my cabin." Then she climbed up to the main deck and waited for him there before heading toward where her cabin was situated beneath the quarterdeck. "Come with me."

As soon as they'd entered her modest cabin, she turned to survey the sailor, who'd removed his broad-brimmed hat. Now she understood why he'd looked so familiar. He resembled Hargraves quite a bit. He had his brother's ginger-colored hair and deep-set hazel eyes.

She couldn't, however, imagine Hargraves attempting to lay a man low with fancy Chinese maneuvers. She smiled at the man. Jordan had chosen well. "Would you like a jot of wine to warm you before you return above decks, Mr. Hargraves?"

"Nay, miss, I'm on night watch. I ain't got much time. But thank'ee kindly."

"If you don't mind, I shall take a little myself." The encounter with that wretched sailor had left her cold to the bone. Opening one of the oak compartments that contained her utensils and meager private stores, she removed a bottle of burgundy and a glass. "So my stepbrother hired you to look after me, did he?"

"Aye. He said I was to make sure nobody harmed you."

She poured a generous amount of burgundy into the glass. "And I suppose I was not to be informed of this arrangement."

"Actually, yer stepbrother told me to wait until we were well out to sea, then let you know I was here to watch out fer you. I meant to tell you sooner, but y've been down in the prison all day."

"I see." At least Jordan hadn't intended for her to spend the entire voyage oblivious to the fact that help was available if she needed it.

"As for you stayin' down in the prison till all hours of the night," he added, "you really shouldn't be below decks after dark, you know. 'Tis dangerous."

After replacing the wine bottle in its compartment, she took a sip from her glass. "So I gather." She couldn't prevent the accusing note that entered her voice. "But somebody has to keep these men from molesting the convict women."

He turned his hat round and round in his hand, scrutinizing her with curious eyes. "You care about these women, don't you, miss? Tom told me you were a soft touch, but I didn't think you'd be riskin' yerself for a lot of bloomin' whor—I mean, ladies of easy virtue. You mustn't take such chances no more. Next time, I mightn't be around to see that you come to no harm."

Bother it all. She could see this protector of hers could be a nuisance. "I won't let the sailors have their way with the women," she warned. "There are children down there, and girls who are no more than fourteen. If the crew are allowed to come and go as they please—"

"Don't you worry none about that, miss. If you want the women looked after, I'll make sure the men don't go down there no more, even if I have to speak to the cap'n about it meself." He scratched behind one ear. "But you got to promise me you won't stay below decks after dark no more, you understand? It ain't safe."

She took another sip, eyeing him warily. "You mean that? If I promise to halt my work after supper, you'll protect the women from the sailors, Peter?"

Though he reddened at her use of his Christian name, he bobbed his head. "His lordship paid me well to look after you. And if lookin' after you means lookin' after a bunch of convict women, I suppose I can manage it."

She took one look at his stoic expression, so like his brother's, and she relaxed. It was exactly the sort of thing Hargraves might have said . . . and done. "All right, it's a bargain. But I'm going to hold you to your end of it, Peter."

He gave a solemn nod as he clapped his hat back on his head. "Long as you hold to yer end, miss, I'll not fail you. You'll see."

When he headed for the door she said, "Peter?"

He paused. "Yes, miss?"

"It seems to me that Jordan bought the very best man he could find."

Peter's ears pinkened. "Thank you, miss. I'll do my best by you, I will."

After he left, she dropped into a chair, relief coursing through her. Now she wouldn't have the entire burden of worrying about the women.

Suddenly, the trip that lay before her seemed a little less daunting, a little less grueling. Maybe everything would be fine, after all, thanks to Jordan's forethought. And if she and Peter could keep the ship from becoming a "floating brothel," who knew what they could accomplish in New South Wales?

Chapter 3

Go tell the King of England,
Go tell him thus from me,
If he reigns King of all the land,
I will reign King at sea.

—ANONYMOUS
"A FAMOUS SEA FIGHT BETWEEN
CAPTAIN WARD AND THE *RAINBOW*"

The tropical sun dusted the palm trees with its fading light as Captain Gideon Horn of the *Satyr* and the ship's cook, Silas Drummond, climbed up the path through the crowded market of the town of Praia, which was carved in Santiago's mountainside. Santiago was the last and largest of the Cape Verde Islands that Gideon and his men had visited. They'd gone to the smaller islands first, thinking they'd have better luck finding what they wanted, but they'd been wrong. And now Gideon feared they wouldn't find it even on Santiago.

So he'd decided instead to buy provisions to carry back to Atlantis Island. If Praia couldn't provide them with what they really needed, there was no point in staying here any longer.

He scanned the nearest stall, where a grinning native

33

woman wearing a crumpled straw hat offered bolts of dyed cotton and called out to passersby in the bastard Portuguese the islanders used.

"How much?" Gideon asked in English, then waited while Silas, who spoke a little Portuguese, translated.

The woman shifted her eyes to him, her grin fading at once. First she rubbed the sweat from her brow with indigo-stained hands. Then she let forth a veritable torrent of words, gesturing to Gideon with jerky motions.

His burly translator chuckled. "She says if the 'American pirate' wants the goods for his lady, he'll have to pay dearly for 'em."

Gideon scowled. "Tell her I don't have a lady and am not likely to have one soon." Then, before Silas could get out a word, he added, "How did she know who I am, anyway?"

Silas talked to the woman animatedly for a few moments. Apparently she found Gideon's presence at her bamboo stall alarming.

When at last Silas faced Gideon, he was tugging on the ends of his heavy brown beard. "Word travels quickly on the islands, Cap'n. It seems they all know that the notorious Pirate Lord and his crew are here. She took one look at that saber tucked in your belt, and figured you were him." He looked thoughtful. "Maybe that's why we've had little luck gettin' what we want from these damned islanders. When they found out who we were, they started hidin' their young women."

"Maybe." Gideon shot the stall-keeper an ingratiating smile that didn't seem to mollify her one bit. "Confound the woman! Tell her I don't want her cloth after all. What good does it do us if we can't get any women?"

Silas nodded solemnly as Gideon spun on his heel and headed for the docks. After muttering a few words to the stall-keeper, Silas hurried after Gideon, moving with surprising speed on his wooden leg. "So what do we do now, Cap'n?"

"I don't know. We'll have to talk to the crew. Maybe

some of them have had better luck today than we have."

"Maybe," Silas said, though he didn't look hopeful.

They strode down the rock-strewn paths of Praia in silence. Gideon was barely conscious of the scowling man at his side. This whole scheme was pointless; he should have seen that from the beginning. It just couldn't work.

He was still telling himself that when Barnaby Kent, his first mate, rushed up the mountain path toward them. "You'll never guess what's come into port!" he cried.

Barnaby was the only Englishman Gideon had ever allowed to join his crew, but he'd never regretted it. The man was a gifted seaman, even if he dressed like a dandy.

"What is it?" Gideon asked as Barnaby drew to a halt in front of them, gasping. It must be something fantastic to excite Barnaby enough to hurry. The man generally strolled languidly about, surveying everything and everybody with a jaundiced eye.

Barnaby bent over and planted his hands on his thighs as he sought to catch his breath. "A ship . . . has come into port . . . one that might interest us."

Gideon groaned. "We've been through all that, Barnaby. We've got enough blasted jewels and gold and silver to fill a warship. It's women we need, not more prizes."

"Aye, sir." Barnaby straightened, then took out his handkerchief and mopped his face. "And this ship has women. Lots of women. All for the plucking."

Gideon and Silas exchanged glances. "What do you mean?" Gideon asked.

Barnaby had finally caught his breath and now he spoke quickly. "It's a convict ship from England—the *Chastity*. It's carrying women to Australia. There's fifty or more women aboard, from what I could gather, and they might just fancy being rescued, if you know what I mean."

Glancing down toward the crowded harbor, Gideon rubbed his chin. "Convict women, you say? *English* convict women?"

"I know what you're thinkin', Cap'n," Silas put in, "but it don't matter if they're English. English women will do as well as any others. The men don't all hate the English as much as you do, you know."

When Gideon glowered at him, he added hastily, "Not that I don't understand why you hate 'em. I do. Truly, I do. But these here women . . . they ain't like the kind of English you don't like. They're just poor sods like the rest of our crew, who got handed a raw deal from the first. They'll suit the men just fine, much better than these uppish island girls who think themselves too good for a bunch of pirates."

"But we don't have much time," Barnaby said, wisely staying out of the entire discussion about the English. "The *Chastity* sets sail in the morning. She only put in here tonight for provisions."

Ignoring Barnaby, Gideon focused on his normally grumpy cook, who had no personal stake in the scheme. Silas disliked women and had sworn never to take up with one. "Do you really think this will satisfy the men?"

"Aye, I do," Silas said. "I truly do."

Barnaby straightened his cravat with a knowing look. "It'll certainly satisfy *me*."

Gideon hesitated. But he really had no choice. This was the best opportunity to come along in the past few months. And a convict ship would be easy to take at sea. Convict ships were never well armed.

"All right." When his two closest friends looked relieved, he went on. "Barnaby, find out all you can about the ship—what guns it carries, its dimensions . . . anything we need to know to take it. And for God's sake, try to be subtle about it. Luckily, we're moored in another harbor, but do what you must to keep the *Chastity*'s crewmen from hearing that a pirate ship's in port.

Keep them drunk, even if you have to pay for their drinks the whole night. We don't want to spook the prey."

As Barnaby hurried back toward the docks, he turned to Silas. "Round up the crew. Tell them we sail at first light, and I want them on board tonight." When Silas bobbed his head and started off down the rock-strewn path, Gideon called out, "And make sure they know why, so they don't curse you for it."

After they were gone, he gazed down at the harbor to where a ship with a demurely draped female figure-head squatted in the water. The *Chastity*. It had to be. Though he saw no sign of the women, he imagined they were kept in chains below when they were in port.

The *Chastity*'s crew was scrambling about, obviously eager to finish furling her sails before they went in to Praia to drink and gamble and whore. Good. With any luck, they'd play right into Barnaby's hands.

He assessed the ship as best he could from the distance. Square-rigged, three-masted . . . and obviously sitting heavy in the water. He didn't see many guns from here, and he counted twenty-odd crewmen, far less than the sixty-three men in his company. He couldn't ask for an easier prize.

Ah, yes. A smile touched his lips. *You're a beauty, my dear, and carrying a very valuable cargo. It'll be like plucking grapes off a tree.*

He could hardly wait for tomorrow.

Petey climbed out on the royal yard, his body performing the task of furling the sky sail. But his mind lay elsewhere, on the puzzle that was Miss Willis.

Two weeks had passed since his conversation with the little miss, and she still insisted that he look after the women every night. She'd even convinced the captain to put him on duty there permanently. He'd hoped he could stop once the men realized he meant business, but Miss Willis didn't trust anybody, that one. She wanted him there every night.

Wiping sweat from his brow with the back of his hand, Petey threaded the line through the block and inched back along the royal yard. It wasn't as if his lordship hadn't warned him that the miss would be a mite troublesome. Petey had known to expect that. At least she'd held to her part of their bargain. There'd been no more confrontations between her and the sailors, thank God. It almost made up for the sleepless nights he spent, watching after the women on the orlop deck.

Actually, it hadn't been so bad, leastways, not after the first night. The first night, the women had been a mite wary of him, and the children had stared through the bars, all goggle-eyed to see a sailor hook his hammock up betwixt the cells. It hadn't been a quiet night, neither. Sailor after sailor had stuck his head in at the hatch, though the captain had commanded them to stay above decks unless they had business below. Once they'd understood that Petey intended to make them follow captain's orders, they'd stopped trying.

After that night, the women had suffered his presence in silence. Some had even ventured to thank him. Indeed, there was one little lass, a sweet young thing named Ann, who'd offered him some of her supper. Considering that the women made better use of their rations than Cook did, he'd been happy to take a bit.

Of course, the crew resented his interference, but he didn't care. His real employer, the earl, was paying him three times his pay as a sailor. For that sum he'd fight the lot of them if he had to.

Thankfully, he'd only had to trounce one man, and the man had been drunk. Though the other sailors had tried to make his life a misery, what they thought would be misery to him wasn't. The first mate sent him up to the royal yard as often as he could, thinking to punish him. Petey was a logical choice, of course, because of his small frame, but furling the sky sail wasn't a happy task for most sailors, seeing as how it was so dangerous.

What the first mate didn't know was that Petey liked being up in the rigging, where he could feel the fine salt wind dust his ears and see the grand ocean spilling out around him on a fair day like a fortune in sparkling diamonds. Now that they'd left the cold drear of England far behind, he was more than happy to sweat beneath the tropical sun. Besides, he'd rather do dangerous tasks than dirty ones like tarring the lines.

Looking down, he spotted the small group of women scrubbing the decks. The convict women had been put to work in shifts, and they didn't seem to mind, since it meant being allowed above decks. He watched a moment. They were really putting their backs into it. At least it was them and not him.

He glanced around at the other men, who watched the women with only a bit of interest. After spending last night in port at Praia, the men were still sated enough from whoring not to feel an urgent need come upon them when they looked at the convict women.

But it wouldn't last. Petey knew that only too well. And strangely enough, two weeks of protecting the convicts had made him regret that soon they would have to suffer the sailors' advances again.

"Hey, matey," called the sailor who was posted as lookout in the crow's nest. "I gotta take a piss. Will you relieve me for a minute?"

Nodding his agreement, Petey clambered along the rigging to the mast. He took the spyglass from the sailor and replaced him in the crow's nest. He scanned the horizon, then surveyed Santiago as the *Chastity* cleared the last outcropping of rock. It was a perfect day for sailing. Though the *Chastity* would reach the deadly calm of the Equator in a day or two, today a playful wind filled her sails, pressing her south along the coast of Africa.

He settled back against the wood curve of the crow's nest, his thoughts returning to little Ann. Welsh, she was, judging by her speech. And a pretty Welsh woman, too, with creamy skin and teeth white as ivory. He wondered what she could've done to end up with that crowd of criminals. It didn't seem right.

Maybe it was because of lasses like Ann that the earl's sister risked so much to help the convicts. She tormented the captain something sore to improve their conditions, and she spent every waking moment down in the orlop deck, learning them their letters. Only two weeks out of London and the women already talked about Miss Willis as if she were a bloody saint. He sighed. Maybe she was.

Picking up the spyglass, he searched their surroundings again, taking in the sweep of water and benign clouds with a practiced eye. He'd just made a complete span of the ocean and was scanning the islands they were leaving behind when something arrested his gaze. Focusing the spyglass in closer, he drew a sharp breath.

A ship had emerged from the windward side of Santiago. She'd come out of nowhere, and the sight of her gave him an uneasy pang. It was as if she'd been lying in wait for them. To be sure, it looked as if she were approaching the *Chastity*. His heart beat faster. A sailor knew to be wary of meeting another ship at sea, especially one that slid out from behind an island.

"Ship to starboard!" he called down to the first mate.

The first mate sauntered beneath the mast. "What sort of ship?"

Petey trained the spyglass on the ship. He watched until the distant blur of sail and timber separated itself into a right good schooner, bristling with guns. The sight of so many guns alarmed him. This was no merchantman, to be sure. He scanned the outline for a flag but could see none.

"Well, Petey?" the mate called up impatiently. "What do y' see?"

"I'm tryin' to make it out. 'Tis a fast schooner. Two masts. Lots of guns."

The first mate scowled, obviously all too aware of what that might mean. "The flag. What's the flag?" His cry was seconded by the captain, who'd already been called on deck by the bosun.

Petey swung the spyglass along the ship's fearsome flanks again, until finally he saw a flag being hoisted. "Hold a minute! They're hoistin' the flag now!" That in itself was a bad sign, for most ships sailed with their flags hoisted.

"God protect us all," he muttered when he caught sight of the flag. It was black as tar, with a grinning white skull and crossbones.

"Pirates!" he shouted. "Pirates approachin'!"

"All hands on deck!" cried the captain as the bosun scurried to ring the warning bell. "Get the women below, and tell the lads to show a leg!"

Never had the ship's crew moved so quickly into action, swinging into their duties like marionettes at a county fair. Ignoring the questions of the women, two of the sailors hustled them down the hatches as the captain barked commands, and other sailors rushed to unfurl the top sails and man the ship's few guns.

"Full sail!" the captain shouted to the first mate, who repeated the order. "We'll outrun them!"

Petey thought that unlikely. He kept the spyglass trained on the ship, looking for any signs of weakness and finding none. The schooner was American made by the look of her, and her light draught made her faster than any English frigate. Schooners manned by American privateers had been a sore trouble to English merchant ships during the War of 1812. Though the war was long over, many privateers had turned to pirating, and he feared that was the case with the ship that dogged them.

Perhaps when they saw there was no booty to be gained from the capture, they'd let the *Chastity* go. It had happened before, or so he'd heard.

"They're gainin' on us!" Petey called down to the captain, who in turn worked the sailors into a frenzy to get the ship moving faster. But there wasn't much they could do. The same wind drove both ships, but the other ship was lighter and thereby faster.

Petey leveled the spyglass again. They were closer now, close enough that he could see the flag in great detail. He squinted to get a better look at the skull. This skull looked different, not like the usual skull and crossbones. Something about the shape of the head . . .

Horns. The skull had horns. His heart sank. Only one pirate ship bore that flag—the *Satyr*.

To make sure, he looked for the figurehead. When he saw the telltale carving of the mythological half-goat, half-man, he groaned aloud. Then he lifted his glass and saw the black-haired man standing in the bow. It was the *Satyr*, all right. And its demon owner, Captain Gideon Horn.

" 'Tis the Pirate Lord himself!" he called out as he tucked the spyglass under his arm and began to shimmy down the main mast. " 'Tis Captain Horn of the *Satyr*! And we'll not outrun him! He's got the fastest ship on the seas!"

As he reached the deck, the captain hurried to his side, his face white beneath his muttonchop whiskers. "Are you sure, man? The Pirate Lord? Why would he be after us? Our owner ain't no nobleman, but a tradesman!"

The Pirate Lord's peculiar choice of targets had given him his nickname. The first ship he'd attacked had been carrying its owner, a stupid earl who'd foolishly warned the pirate not to show such disrespect to "a member of the House of Lords."

The witnesses to that first capture had immortalized the pirate's retort: "In America, all men are equal, and even a pirate is a lord. So I bow to no one but God, sir, especially not a dandified English noble." Captain Horn had stolen everything the earl possessed, down to the clothes on his back. And he'd stolen a kiss from the man's own wife as well.

All of the *Satyr*'s targets since then had been ships owned by English nobility or those carrying noble passengers, and it was rumored he took great delight in fleecing them. Some of the nobility had even taken to traveling incognito and hiding behind other partners to protect themselves and their ships.

With an uneasy lurch, Petey thought of Miss Willis. Surely the man wouldn't attack them solely because of her. Though she was the adopted daughter of an earl and the stepsister of the new earl, she wasn't truly a lady. Besides, no one associated with the ship knew of her noble connections.

"Are you sure the ship's owner is a tradesman?" he asked the captain. "Are you sure?"

"Aye. 'Tis a cousin of mine. There's not a hint of nobility aboard this ship, I tell you."

Except Miss Willis. Petey had better get to her and warn her to say naught of her brother if they were taken. *When* they were taken, that is; the capture seemed inevitable.

"P'raps the Pirate Lord will let us go when he sees we got no booty," Petey murmured.

"He'll slaughter us, that's what he'll do!" The first mate was at the helm, and tossed the words back at them as if Captain Horn himself had made the threat. "I heard tell he can flatten a man with one blow of his fist!"

Petey swallowed. He wasn't afraid of many things, but the Pirate Lord was one of them. Far as he knew, no one had ever accused the pirate of the kind of murthering and mayhem that some pirates were wont to engage in. But that didn't mean Captain Horn mightn't strike out in anger when he discovered the lack of booty on the *Chastity*.

"P'raps we should fight," Petey suggested.

Captain Rogers snorted. "Fight? Are you bloody

crazy? That's the *Satyr*, man, with thirty guns if there's one! They'd blow us to pieces! We don't have the guns or manpower to fight off a well-armed pirate ship. Besides, if we fight, they'll think we have something worth fighting for, and that'll make it worse for us."

"You can't outrun 'em," Petey repeated, "not with the weight on us." As if lending credence to his words, the *Satyr* surged forward, hounding them like a demon on the heels of a sinner. In moments it would overtake them.

The captain glanced at his crew, then back to his first mate and Petey. "That's our only choice, lads. Run or be taken. And I much fear that 'tis taken we'll be unless a miracle come to save us."

The miracle never came. Scant minutes later, the other ship hailed them, threatening to fire their guns if the *Chastity* didn't halt to be boarded. And it was only as Captain Rogers gave the order to his crew to surrender that Petey remembered he hadn't warned Miss Willis.

Chapter 4

Until today Sara had found the voyage fairly uneventful. True, she'd had trouble squelching the gambling of the more hardened women who liked to fleece the country maids of their rations. And she'd given many a lecture on the inappropriateness of swearing. Still, her classes had gone well, and she and Petey had succeeded in keeping the women separate from the men.

Now, however, confusion reigned around her. The women who'd been above decks had been sent below, and they gathered around Sara, panic-stricken and babbling. It took some minutes before she could make sense of what they were saying. A pirate ship approaching? Surely not. Pirates grew scarcer with every year as the British and Americans sought to clear the waters of the nasty pests. And what would they want with a convict ship that carried nothing of value?

Of course, they didn't know that the *Chastity* carried

only women. She froze, a sick fear settling into the pit
of her stomach. Women. Everyone knew what pirates
did to women. And if these men found no gold to sate
their savage appetites, they would surely turn to other
terrible pleasures.

"They'll kill us!" Ann Morris cried above the clamor
of voices, speaking aloud Sara's worst thoughts.
"They'll rape us and then kill us! Oh, Miss Willis, what
are we to do?"

Sara wanted to scream that she didn't know, that
she'd never faced pirates before. Only by great force of
will did she keep the words to herself.

At Ann's cry, the others had fallen silent, and now
they watched her expectantly, as if they thought she
could somehow conjure up an army of protectors to
save them. Oh, if only she could.

She forced a calmness into her voice that she didn't
feel. "There's no need to panic. The sailors will fight
them off. The ship is armed and—"

"Armed?" Queenie grumbled. "A few guns is all, not
enough to fend off pirates."

"The sailors won't fight," came Louisa's familiar cynical voice from behind Queenie. "That puling bunch?
Why should they? They'll jump ship before they lose
one finger for us."

Panicked voices rose again around Sara. She felt an
unfamiliar helplessness surge in her. Louisa was right.
The sailors wouldn't fight for a shipload of convict
women.

The milling voices in the hold became oppressive, and
she had to struggle to keep from forgetting all her ingrained control and letting loose in a panic as the other
women were doing.

Suddenly Louisa cried in a loud voice, "Listen, everybody!"

One by one the women heeded her words until only
the sounds of babies crying and the children's plaintive
voices broke the silence. They listened but could hear

nothing from above, except perhaps a faint muffle of voices. The ship seemed to have stopped, although it was hard to tell in the hold.

Suddenly there was a rumble as of several men jumping on the decks. Then the ship swayed ever so slightly to one end, causing the women to grasp at the bars for balance, before the ship righted itself.

"They've come aboard," Queenie pronounced.

"Perhaps if we stay very still, they won't know we're here," Ann Morris whispered timidly. "Perhaps Captain Rogers will tell them the hold is empty, and they'll leave."

"Leave?" Though Louisa's pretty features were ashen in the lantern light, she'd lost none of her dry tone. "With just a word from our good captain? I think not. Besides, he won't tell any lies on our behalf. We're the only thing of value he can throw as a sop to the pirates."

The chilling words made all the women shudder, even Sara. Never had she dreamed, when she'd jested with Jordan about being accosted by pirates, that such a thing could occur. There shouldn't be pirates in these waters, and they shouldn't have stopped the *Chastity*. This couldn't be happening!

There must be some other explanation for the other ship's appearance, she thought desperately. In a moment the crew would come down and inform them that it was merely a British navy ship that had boarded them, wanting supplies. No, that made no sense. They were still within a short distance of Santiago, where anyone could get supplies.

If only she and the others could fight. If only they could keep the pirates from entering the hold. But they had naught with which to defend themselves, for the women had been given nothing that could be used against their captors.

No one seemed capable of movement. Every creak of the ship added to the tension in the hot, stifling air of the hold. Even the children seemed to be holding their breaths, waiting for what would become of them.

"Oh, how I wish Petey . . . I-I mean, Mr. Hargraves . . . was down here to protect us," Ann burst out into the ominous silence.

"Even your Mr. Hargraves cannot stop a band of pirates, Annie," Louisa retorted. "He's not God, you know. This time all the Miss Willises and Mr. Hargraves of the world cannot stop us from being forced into unspeakable acts—"

"That's enough, Louisa," Sara said sharply. "You're scaring the children. And it's not as if we all need to hear—"

She broke off at the telltale sound of the hatch door opening. The women all turned as one toward the stairs, their eyes gleaming with fear in the poorly lit cells.

It wasn't a pirate, however, who descended the steps, but Captain Rogers's nimble-footed cabin boy. As soon as the women saw him, they let out a collective sigh and surged toward the stairs.

Cries of "What's going on?" and "Is it truly pirates?" filled the air as he stopped halfway down the steps.

"I been sent to tell you to gather your things and come on deck," the cabin boy said. His skin was pale beneath the grime on his cheeks, and his skinny legs were shaking.

"Sent by whom?" Sara came forward to ask.

"Captain Horn, miss. Of the *Satyr*. 'Tis his ship that has taken us."

The *Satyr*. She thought perhaps she'd heard of it, but she couldn't remember what she'd read. "This Captain Horn is a pirate?"

The boy looked at her as if she were mad. "Aye, miss. Everybody knows that."

It didn't cheer her to have her fears confirmed. "And why has he asked that the women gather their things?"

"I don't know, miss, but—"

"Come on, lad, that's enough prittle-prattle," shouted a coarse voice from above, cutting him off. "Tell them to be up here at once. Captain Horn wants the lot of them to present themselves on deck now or risk his wrath!"

The sound of that menacing voice sent the women into a frenzy. They dashed this way and that, gathering their meager possessions, cautioning the children, and drawing on their shoes, for many of them had begun going barefoot once they'd reached warmer waters.

Soon they were heading toward the stairs with rough canvas bags clutched in their hands. Most of them even carried the makings for their quilts. Before they could climb the steep ladder stairs, however, Sara moved in front of them. She wouldn't let them go into this alone. Someone had to speak for the women, and it might as well be her.

"Listen to me, ladies. Remember all we've been talking about. No matter what they do to you, your soul is your own. They can't touch it if you hold it safe within you."

Her words seemed to give them courage, though it was a somber group who followed her up the stairs through the 'tween decks and then up to the top deck. The sight that met Sara's eyes as she emerged into the brilliant sunlight was a sobering one. The *Chastity*'s crew lined the sides of the ship, guarded by the most presentable bunch of pirates she'd ever expected to see.

For one thing, they were clean and orderly, quite the opposite of Captain Rogers's none too fastidious crew. How could these men be pirates? Why, there wasn't an eye patch or a hook among them! And as the women massed on the deck, they didn't hoot or grab at them or make any lewd remarks.

But their indecent attire certainly befitted pirates. Leather vests predominated, often without so much as a scrap of a shirt. She'd never seen so many bare-chested men in her life . . . nor so many heads of shoulder-length hair.

Then she caught sight of their weapons and her blood

froze. Knives with carved bone handles gleamed in their hands, and a few had pistols tucked into their belts. They might be clean and orderly, but those weapons made it clear what they were here for. All too clear indeed.

Before she could brood further on it, however, a stocky, bearded man with a wooden leg ordered the women to proceed along the deck to the bow. There they found more pirates, a crowd that far outnumbered the *Chastity*'s crew and even perhaps the women themselves.

Then the crowd parted, and she was given her first glimpse of the man who could only be the *Satyr*'s captain.

He stood with his legs splayed apart and his arms crossed over his open-necked white shirt and leather vest, a serious expression hardening the already harsh angles of his face. With narrowed eyes, he watched the women crowd onto the decks.

She didn't know how she knew he was the captain; she just did. There was a certain haughtiness in him that was lacking in the others. There were other things, too, like his great height. And his clothes, which were as fine as any she'd seen. The dove-gray breeches hugging his muscled legs were of an excellent cut and quality, and his belt was crowned with a jeweled buckle.

His ship's name suited him perfectly. Even though he wore weathered black boots where hooves should be, and there were no horns peeking out above his unruly shoulder-length black hair, his expression bore such mocking satisfaction that only a real satyr could have matched it. His brutally thorough gaze assessed the women, as if to ferret out their every weakness.

And his face! Though clean-shaven, it was also that of a satyr's—blatantly masculine, coldly handsome despite its thick brows and crooked mouth . . . and frighteningly menacing. What was it that made him seem so fearsome? Perhaps it was his scars—the crescent-shaped one that bisected his wind-reddened cheek, and the tiny slash along the outer edge of his eyebrow that seemed narrowly to miss his eye. Most assuredly, the huge saber he wore tucked in his wide leather belt had something to do with it.

But it was more than that. She suspected this man would be alarming even if devoid of scars and saber and dressed in frock coat and beaver hat.

"Good day, ladies," he said with a distinctly American accent when all the women were above decks and the hatches closed. With a grin that took some of the edge off his fierce looks, he surveyed the crowd and added, "We've come to rescue you."

His words were so unexpected, so completely self-assured, that Sara bristled. After all his blatant methods of intimidation, after he'd stood here surveying the women like cattle before the slaughter, he had the audacity to say such a thing!

"Is that what they're calling thievery, pillage, and rape these days?" she snapped.

As a murmur of shock passed through the *Chastity*'s crew and the women moved back from her as if to distance themselves from their mad companion, Sara cursed her quick tongue. Oh, but she was done for now. She might as well have begged him to slice her in two with that wicked saber. This was no civilized lord or blustering sea captain whom she could lecture with impunity; this man had no morals, no scruples, no hint of mercy about him.

And he had now turned his complete attention on her.

She held her breath as he cast an insulting glance over her, seeming to take in every inch of her somber attire, from her lacy mob cap to the tips of her scuffed kid slippers. Then, to her great shock, he let out a mirthless laugh. "Pillage, thievery, and rape? And who might you be, my brave little woman, to speak to me so?"

Her stomach lurched. Fear made her want to beg his pardon, to protest that she was naught but a fool. But pride overrode that. He hadn't killed her yet, and perhaps that meant he was amenable to reason. "I am Miss Sara Willis, sir, instructor and protector for these women."

The wind lifted his raven hair away from his face, exposing the small gold hoop he wore in one ear. With a nonchalant air, he leaned back against the bow. "I see. You intend to protect them from our 'pillage, thievery, and rape,' do you?"

When a rumble of laughter erupted from the pirates surrounding them, she colored. "You know quite well I can do no such thing. I have neither a sword nor the strength to wield it." She couldn't help adding with a trace of irony in her tone, "Perhaps that's why I don't find the situation as amusing as you and your bloodthirsty companions."

The humor in his face faded abruptly. "Then it should please you to hear, Miss Willis, that my men and I aren't here for that. Thievery would be useless, since I doubt there's so much as an ounce of gold or jewels on this ship. As for pillage, that's an occupation I find pointless and wasteful, don't you?"

When he paused, a knot of fear formed in her belly. "That only leaves rape, doesn't it? A ship full of women . . . a ship full of pirates—"

"We're not here to commit rape either," he growled, pushing away from the bow with an unaccountable expression of anger. "What we have to offer your . . . pupils is anything but that."

"Offer?"

Striding up to her, he planted his hands on his hips. "Yes, offer. We're here to offer these women rescue. Freedom."

He was close enough she could see the color of his eyes, a vivid blue-green that mirrored the tropical sea. It was far too attractive a color for a murderous pirate.

"And you offer this without expecting anything in return," she remarked coldly.

The merest hint of a smile tipped up the edges of his mouth. "I didn't say that."

Her heart plummeted. "Of course not. Pirates aren't known for their altruism, are they?" She didn't know what possessed her to speak to him so boldly. Perhaps fear had driven her insane. But if he was going to kill her anyway, she might as well make her death count for something.

"Then what do you want?" she went on. "A few nights of pleasure before you dump them on the coast of Africa to fend for themselves? You want to use them as whores, but pay them in dubious freedom instead of in coin?"

"Nay." He leveled on her a thunderous scowl. " 'Tisn't whores we want, Miss Willis. 'Tis wives. Wives for me and my men."

Sara gaped at him. A confused murmur rose up from the women behind her, but all she could do was stare at him, trying to fathom what he was saying. She glanced around at the pirates' faces, surprised to see the truth of Captain Horn's words mirrored in their expressions.

"But you're . . . you're pirates! What would you want with wives?"

His expression grew shuttered. "That's no longer your concern, Miss Willis. We're taking these women whether you approve or not." He scoured her with an insultingly impudent gaze. "Don't worry. We're not taking you along. The last thing we need is a tight-lipped spinster giving us trouble."

With that final insult hanging in the air, he ordered a few of his men to take the women and children aboard the *Satyr*. He commanded the others to confiscate the *Chastity*'s stores.

She watched in disbelief as the men scurried to do his bidding, and the *Chastity*'s crew glumly stood by. How could they? This wretched scoundrel was kidnapping an entire shipload of women for his own nefarious purposes, and the crew intended to let him!

"You can't do this!" she told the pirate captain. " 'Tis unconscionable!"

Ignoring her, he turned to Captain Rogers. "I'm leaving you no water and no food. Your only choice is to return to the port at Santiago. From there, I don't give a damn what you do, as long as you don't try coming after us. When we sail away, if you so much as attempt to follow, I swear I'll blow you out of the water."

When he pivoted and started to brush past her, she caught his arm. "I won't let you do this!"

He cast her a mocking grin. "As you said before, you can't stop me."

The futility of it all enraged her. She'd worked so hard to help these women to a better life, to see that they found the good within themselves. And now he planned to wreck it all in one fell swoop.

Well, if he wouldn't listen to Miss Sara Willis, then perhaps he'd listen to someone of higher station. "No, but my brother can," she said, with as haughty a tone as she could muster. "And I'll make sure he searches you and your men out, if it takes every breath in my body!"

He shrugged off her hand with a laugh. "And who might your brother be that he'd take on a pirate? Some merchant's son? A clergyman perhaps?"

"The Earl of Blackmore." She wielded the title like a weapon. "He'll come after you if I ask him to."

There was a chorus of groans from the crew and captain of the *Chastity*, though why they were so dismayed by her revelation now, when it no longer mattered, she couldn't possibly imagine.

Unfortunately, the pirate captain's reaction was more alarming. Instead of the fear she had hoped for, a cold light glittered in his eyes as he clutched her arm in a painful grip, then fixed Captain Rogers with a fierce look. "Is this chit telling the truth? Her brother is an English earl?"

Out of the corner of her eye, she could see Petey Hargraves flashing her a dire look of warning, but she ignored it. If revealing her true identity might save the women, then surely she must do it.

Captain Rogers had gone pale as death. "Not that I ever heard, sir. If her brother's an earl, 'tis news to me."

"The woman's crazy," Petey called out. "Got grand ideas about her position and all. She ain't no earl's sister, Cap'n Horn, you can depend on it."

How dared Petey lie! Didn't he see how important this was? "I most certainly am the Earl of Blackmore's sister!" she protested. "I've been traveling incognito, to report to the authorities in London about the treatment of convict women aboard these ships!"

Wrenching free of the pirate, she fumbled in the pocket of her apron until she found her journal, which she kept with her at all times. She slipped a fine sheet of vellum from between the pages, then handed it to Captain Horn.

Jordan had insisted that she carry some identification with her in case of emergency. Accordingly, he'd written a letter proclaiming that Miss Sara Willis was his sister and had pressed the Blackmore seal at the bottom. Thankfully, he hadn't called her his "stepsister." Jordan had meant her to use the letter if she had difficulty gaining passage home once she reached New South Wales, but this seemed a far better use for it.

The pirate captain scanned the letter, his expression darkening as he read the signature and saw the seal.

"If you insist on taking these women," she told him in her loftiest tone, "I'll make sure my brother does all in his power to thwart you. I won't rest until he sends ships to search the seas for you and your men. I'll—"

"Enough," he growled, folding the letter and tucking it into his belt. He cast her a wholly unnerving smile.

"You've made your point, Miss Willis . . . Lady Sara. This changes matters entirely."

A wave of relief swept over her. Her bluff had worked. He would let the women go and find someone else to torment.

But his next words utterly shattered her assurance. "It seems, my lady, that you'll be going with us after all."

Chapter 5

If the abstract rights of man will bear discussion and explanation, those of women, by a parity of reasoning, will not shrink from the same test: though a different opinion prevails in this country.

—MARY WOLLSTONECRAFT
ENGLISH FEMINIST WRITER
A VINDICATION OF THE RIGHTS OF WOMEN

Gideon Horn paced the decks of the *Satyr* in a fury, trying to blot out the sounds of weeping coming from the hold as he ordered his men to remove the grappling hooks that kept the *Chastity* moored to the *Satyr*.

Confound those women and their wailing! Didn't they know they were lucky to escape the *Chastity*? He'd been to New South Wales. It was a lawless colony filled with murderers and thieves and no place for a woman, even a woman convict.

As the *Satyr* edged away from the *Chastity*, Barnaby approached him, an ironic smile on his lips. "Well, Captain, I'd say that went smoothly."

"Keep your blasted English humor to yourself, Barnaby. I'm not in the mood for it."

"The noise the women are making below decks is unsettling the men."

"They've heard women cry before," Gideon retorted

57

with a shrug. He had to admit, however, that the keening coming from the hold was markedly worse than the sound of a woman crying over the loss of her jewels. He shouted an order to the bosun, then turned back to Barnaby. "Tell the crew to stop up their ears if they have to. We've got some hard sailing ahead of us if we're to be out of sight before the *Chastity* returns to Santiago and sends a ship after us."

Barnaby nodded, but didn't leave his captain's side. "The trouble is, these aren't just any women. They're prospective wives, and the men don't like it that they're so upset. It's not what they expected."

"It's not what I expected either, believe me. It's that blasted Lady Sara. They were quiet until I threw her in the hold with them. I should've known she'd stir them up. She's a troublemaker if I ever saw one."

"Aye." Taking out a cheroot, Barnaby lit it and drew deeply on it. "Maybe you should have left her behind. All her threats were pointless. Even if she could have convinced her brother to go in search of a few convict women, he couldn't have found us. Our island is uncharted and—"

"I didn't want to take the chance. If we're to do what we plan, we must have peace. We can't always be looking over our shoulders for some confounded earl."

"Bringing her along didn't prevent that. If anything, it's made the situation worse. Do you think this earl will let his sister simply disappear without looking for her? Not bloody likely."

Gideon stared back at the quickly receding *Chastity*. The fact that Barnaby was right didn't make the man's words any easier to stomach. "As you said, who will find us? Besides, the woman would be more of a threat back in England, inciting her brother. Without her around to goad him, he might not bother. If you had a sister like that, would *you* want her back?"

"I don't know. Maybe." Barnaby let out a puff of smoke, his expression thoughtful. "Are you sure you didn't have . . . um . . . other reasons for bringing her with us?''

With a scowl, Gideon strode to the quarterdeck. "What's that supposed to mean?''

Barnaby followed him. "She's an earl's sister, and you *have* been known to do things simply to tweak the noses of the nobility, captain.''

Gideon remained silent as he climbed up to the quarterdeck and took the helm from the bosun. He couldn't honestly say what his reasons had been for bringing Miss Willis—Lady Sara—aboard. Except that when she'd thrown her brother's title at him, he'd seen red.

The British nobility always made him see red. Those mincing fops were a bane on the civilized world. If not for people like the Earl of Blackmore and his sister, there'd be less oppression and heartache, less cruel separation of lovers . . .

He cursed as the old pain hit him anew. No matter how many times he'd made fools of those blasted dukes, marquesses, and viscounts, no matter how often he'd taken their property and scoffed at their warships, it hadn't driven out the pain or changed the British system that had destroyed his father and had convinced his mother to do the unthinkable.

His mother. He fingered his jeweled belt buckle. It had once been a brooch, but he'd had it made into a buckle as a constant reminder of his mother's treachery. Maybe Barnaby was right. Maybe he *had* brought Lady Sara aboard because he'd wanted to torment her for being nobility.

"If you didn't bring her aboard because of who she is,'' Barnaby added, as if he'd read Gideon's thoughts, "then perhaps it was because of what she is. I'm sure you noticed she's a very pretty young woman.''

"She's one of *them*,'' he spat. "It outweighs everything else.''

When Barnaby laughed, Gideon tightened his fingers on the wheel. Yes, he had noticed Lady Sara's pleasing figure and winsome face. He'd seen only a bit of her hair, a lock or two peeping out from beneath that prudish cap, but it had been a rich, dark red. He found himself wondering what it would look like blowing loose in a fine tail wind or even wet and streaming down her slender back.

Her *stubborn* back. Confound it all, he couldn't be thinking of the chit in *those* terms, could he? She was a quick-tongued nuisance, for God's sake. Enticing though she might be, she couldn't tempt him. He had different requirements for a wife, and she fit none of them. He wanted a sweet-tempered maid who'd give him peace and comfort during the long nights, not a defiant noblewoman who'd plague his days as well as his nights.

"Never mind my reasons for taking her off the *Chastity*," he growled at Barnaby. "She's on board now, and it's too late to send her back." When there was a surge of sound below decks, Gideon scowled. " 'Tis a shame, too. Those women won't stop their caterwauling as long as she's down there stirring them up."

"She seems to think that if the women make enough noise, you'll change your mind and return them to the *Chastity*."

"Return them to the *Chastity*, hah! Those women are lucky to be saved from what awaits them in New South Wales, not to mention the journey ahead."

"Yes, but they don't know that, do they? And you didn't tell them much about what we intended."

Gideon rubbed his stubbled chin. "You're right. I was in such a hurry to get them aboard without any bloodshed that I didn't tell them anything except that my men wanted wives."

He steadied the wheel. Perhaps he ought to set their minds at ease. If he made it clear they weren't going to be harmed, then they'd be more likely to cooperate. That is, if he could force that Lady Sara to stop riling them.

She seemed to have appointed herself their spokes-woman.

A half-smile touched his lips. Their spokeswoman. Might as well go directly to the source of the problem. "Barnaby, go below and bring Lady Sara to my cabin. Then come take the helm."

"Now?"

"Now. I think it's time that vexing woman and I had a little discussion."

Sara stood in the cramped hold, so filled with right-eous indignation that she could scarcely contain it. How dare that wretched pirate kidnap them! How dare he carry them all off like this!

"Come now, ladies, I know you can make more noise than that!" Sara cried above the heads of her charges, who were wailing and carrying on as if their children had been torn from their breasts. "We'll get them to turn this ship around if we have to scream ourselves hoarse!"

"They might murder us instead!" Queenie shouted above the din. She'd been the only one to disapprove of Sara's plan for annoying the pirates, but she'd been out-numbered by the other women, who'd thought it as good a plan as any. Besides, it had given them some-thing to do instead of lying in the dark waiting to be parceled out to the men like so many provisions.

"If they wanted to murder us, they'd have done so by now!" Sara shouted back. "They said they wanted wives! Let's show them that we'd make terrible wives, and maybe they'll let us go!"

The words were leaving her mouth as the hatch to the hold opened, and one of the pirates came halfway down the narrow stairs. Instantly he grinned, making her wonder if he'd heard her words.

She motioned to the women to be quiet as she sur-veyed their new assailant. His elegant attire made him look remarkably different from his companions. Indeed, in England he might have been considered a dandy with his silk stockings, striped waistcoat, and cravat tied in a Bergami knot.

As the women fell silent, he tipped his head toward Sara. "The captain wants a word with you, Lady Sara, if you'd be so good as to come with me."

Why, the man was English! Amidst all these barbarian colonials, at least there was one Englishman, one man who might have some moral scruples.

Might. He was still a pirate, after all.

At his words, the women had crowded around her as if to protect her. Though the gesture touched her, it hardly made any difference. They couldn't even keep themselves safe, much less her.

"It's all right, ladies." She forced a reassuring smile to her face. "I shall go speak to the captain if he wishes. Who knows, perhaps he has come to his senses."

The women's skeptical looks did nothing to lift her spirits. The last thing she wanted was to enter the private cabin of a self-proclaimed satyr. But she put a brave face on her terror as she set her shoulders and wove her way through the crowd to the stairs.

When she reached the pirate, he stood aside, gesturing to her to ascend the stairs first. She hesitated only a moment before doing so. It was difficult to keep her skirts close about her as she climbed the steep stairs. Why she was bothering to be so modest, she didn't know. The odds were that she wouldn't be allowed to retain her virtue much longer. Still, such habits of gentility were too ingrained for her to relinquish them easily.

As soon as they were both on deck, the pirate took her arm in a surprisingly gentle grip and stopped.

"I'm Barnaby Kent, the first mate. And before I take you to meet the captain, I wish to caution you about your behavior in his presence."

She forced all the haughtiness into her tone that she could muster. "My behavior? Are there rules of pirate etiquette that I'm unaware of?"

His lips twitched as he stared at her. "No. But you could benefit from some advice concerning our captain." He jerked his head in the direction of the stern. "I wouldn't make too much of your relations to the Earl of Blackmore, if I were you."

"Whyever not?"

"Haven't you heard of the Pirate Lord? I know he's been much spoken of in the London papers."

For some reason the words "Pirate Lord" rang a bell where the words "*Satyr*" and "Captain Horn" had not. Her heart began to pound. "The Pirate Lord. You mean that . . . that awful man who makes it his practice to attack noblemen whenever possible?"

"Yes," he said dryly. "That 'awful man' is Gideon Horn. Your captor."

She swallowed convulsively. Good heavens. So that's where she'd heard of the *Satyr*, from the papers. No wonder the pirate captain had been so furious when she'd thrown Jordan's title at him. She'd thought to help them all by telling him about Jordan, and she'd worsened the situation instead. "I-I see."

"No, you don't see. Captain Horn hates the nobility, so you should refrain from reminding him of your noble blood if you want to stay on his good side."

"He has a good side?"

A slow smile spread over the English pirate's face. "He does." His gaze trailed down her length, and his smile widened to a grin. "Especially where a woman as pretty as you is concerned."

She jerked her gaze from his, the color rising in her cheeks. "In this case, I think prettiness is a liability rather than an asset."

"He won't hurt you, you know. He's not that sort of man. But I can't vouch for his temper if you taunt him with your connections. I suggest you watch your words. It'll go better for both you and the women if you do."

He seemed so sincere, she couldn't help but be affected. Here was a man who cared. Perhaps that could be used to their advantage. "You're English, aren't you? You know that what Captain Horn is doing is barbarous. Please, convince him to let us go, to bring us back to Santiago and abandon his purpose."

All signs of concern for her welfare vanished as his eyes hardened to shards of black coal. "I long ago lost any loyalty I might feel for the English, milady. Besides, I'd be the last person to convince the captain to release all of you."

"Why?"

"Because it was my idea to take the convict ship in the first place."

Her mouth dropped open. Then she shut it with a snap. She should have known. A pirate wasn't to be trusted, no matter what his nationality. He would never help them. They were entirely without hope.

"Take me to the captain," she said dully. There was no point in delaying any further; she might as well discover her fate now.

They walked in silence beneath the rigging to the quarterdeck that loomed before them. She caught a glimpse of the captain standing with his back to them at the helm above, and for a moment a chill raced down her spine. The stiffness of his stance, the boldly splayed legs, the broad, forbidding back . . . never had she seen such a frightening form of a man. Mr. Kent needn't worry. She had no desire to taunt Captain Horn. No desire at all.

Then Mr. Kent was taking her through the doors beneath the quarterdeck and into a wide room like the saloon on the *Chastity*. No one was there right now, thank goodness, for they were all too busy maneuvering the ship away from the *Chastity*. But soon the room would be filled with pirates, drinking and gambling and . . .

She shuddered to think of what else they might do. At least she and the women had a short respite. And maybe if she spoke reasonably to the captain, she could convince him to change his mind.

That thought foundered as Mr. Kent opened the door to the captain's cabin in the ship's stern and ushered her inside. She looked around, feeling a sharp lurch of despair at the sight of the cabin's lush interior and well-stocked gun cabinet. This wasn't the cabin of a honest man, who would take pity on a shipload of convict women. This was the cabin of a licentious murderer. And there would be no mercy for them, none at all.

"The captain will be with you in a moment," Mr. Kent murmured before leaving and closing the door behind him.

She scarcely heard him. She was too busy scanning her surroundings. She'd only been in one captain's cabin, and that was the one belonging to Captain Rogers. Its spartan, lean lines and minimal comforts made it look like a cabin boy's berth compared to this.

Every piece of furniture was made of the best mahogany, from the desk cluttered with instruments and papers to the cabinet that held guns and knives of every description behind its cut crystal doors. The royal blue curtains were shot through with gold threads, and a Persian carpet lay on the floor, an obvious extravagance where water was a constant threat.

But the most alarming thing was the large mahogany bed presiding over one corner of the spacious cabin, its posts carved with the same satyr motif that graced the ship's figurehead. A coverlet of insolent red silk was draped over the plush mattress, with a heap of jet-black pillows at one end. She walked to the bed in a trance, wondering aloud what debaucheries and horrors had been committed there.

Involuntarily, she reached out to touch the patterned scarlet silk as a sudden vivid image of the dark-haired pirate captain rose up in her mind. He must have had many women in this bed. A strange heat spread through her body to think of him bending over a woman, touching her body with those large hands, kissing her with that firm, mocking mouth—

"Looking for signs of thievery, pillage, and rape, Lady Sara?" came a voice behind her.

She whirled away from the bed, her cheeks stained crimson. Good heavens, it was him, the pirate captain himself. How utterly mortifying! Now she had something new to add to her list of humiliating experiences.

He closed the door, a smile playing over his lips as she stood there speechless. "The coverlet belonged to an obnoxious viscount on his way to America to marry an heiress," he said as he removed the saber from his belt and hung it on a hook by the door. Then he strode to his desk and cast her a brazen look. "I enjoyed removing it from the bed he was sharing with his mistress."

She winced, remembering what Mr. Kent had said about the captain's hatred of the nobility. Perhaps she should tell him the truth about her own dubious connections. That might make him more inclined to listen to her pleas. "Captain Horn, I think I should . . . er . . . set you straight on one matter. I am not . . . that is to say . . . you shouldn't call me Lady Sara."

In the muted light of the cabin, his sudden scowl made him look even more like a creature out of mythology, a dangerous, fearful creature liable to snap her up in his massive jaws at any minute. "Oh? And why not?"

"Because I'm not actually a lady—not in the sense you mean it, anyway."

Although she dropped her gaze from him, she could feel the force of his disapproval as he approached her. "You're not the Earl of Blackmore's sister?"

"Well, yes, I am. Sort of." She swallowed hard. "His father, the late Earl of Blackmore, adopted me after marrying my widowed mother. So I'm not really Lady Sara, you see, but Miss Willis."

When he was silent she ventured to look at him again,

surprised to find that he looked thoughtful rather than angry.

"Do you mean to tell me," he said, "that despite being adopted by an earl and made part of his family in every legal sense, you can't bear the complimentary title that any one of his other children is allowed to bear?"

She'd never heard it put quite that way. "Well, no, I can't."

He snorted. "That's the most ludicrous thing I've ever heard." Running one hand through his rumpled wavy hair, he shot her a forbidding look. "I swear, I'll never understand you English. You have more rules designed to cause enmity among families than I've ever seen. Younger sons can't inherit, daughters can't inherit, fathers are pitted against their heirs. It's a confounded mess."

His commentary on the social makeup of British society startled her. Pirates weren't supposed to have opinions on such things. Or express them so eloquently. "You must admit it's worked well for hundreds of years," she said in faint defense of her countrymen.

He quirked one eyebrow upward. "Has it?"

In those two words he managed to convey all his contempt for English ways. What could possibly have roused such feelings in him? Americans were testy about being a former British colony, to be sure, but this was rather extreme. And though she was dying to know why he hated the English, she didn't ask. She doubted that this proud pirate would answer her. Or approve of her asking the question.

He studied her, as if he wished to open up her mind and peer inside. She'd endured the ardent glances of lords and the lascivious looks of many a prisoner at Newgate, and all those sailors, of course. But never had a man looked at her with such concentration.

It was unsettling, to say the least. She dropped her eyes from his, searching for something to say that would shift that intensity away from her. "In any case, I'm sure that's not what you brought me here to discuss."

That shook him out of his silence. "Certainly not."
Moving behind his desk, he sat down in the armchair,
then gestured to a chair near her. "Sit down, Lady
Sara."

Though she did as he said, she protested, "I told you.
You can't call me—"

"It's my ship and my rules. I'll call you whatever I
damned well please." His gaze skimmed her body before snapping back to her face. "And it'll serve to remind me that you have a stepbrother lurking out there,
waiting to pounce on me at any moment."

His sarcasm brought her up short. Why, he wasn't
afraid of Jordan, not one jot. No doubt her revelation
had made him assume that Jordan was no longer a
threat to him. And that wasn't what she'd wished to
accomplish at all.

She straightened in her chair, folding her hands
primly in her lap. "The fact that Jordan is my stepbrother and not my brother doesn't change anything,
Captain Horn. He still won't forget about me. I assure
you he'll be after you just as soon as he learns what
happened. There'll be warships hunting you everywhere. You won't be able to sail for fear of my stepbrother."

Her words didn't have the effect she'd intended. A
smile spread across his handsome face. "Then I suppose
it's just as well we're not sailing anywhere else once we
reach our destination."

"What do you mean?"

He shrugged. "We're retiring from piracy, my men
and I. That's why we need wives."

That stunned her into temporary silence. She glanced
around the cabin at the gold fittings and extravagant
comforts. "*Retiring?*" she choked out.

"Yes. Retiring. As you may know, piracy's a very
dangerous profession lately. Most governments seek to
ferret out our kind and destroy us. And my men and I

have more than enough spoils to make us comfortable. We don't wish to end our illustrious career by kicking the clouds, if you know what I mean."

She nodded mechanically. She'd done enough work at Newgate to recognize the cant for hanging. But retiring? Pirates retiring?

Settling back in his chair, he laced his fingers together over his stomach and surveyed her with his disconcerting gaze. It seemed to touch her mouth, her cheeks, even her well-covered bosom. If another man had looked at her like that, she would have been appalled. So why was it that when he did it, her pulse quickened?

"The trouble is," he went on, his tone lower, huskier, "we have no country to retire in."

"What about America?"

"Not even there. Let's just say America holds little appeal for most of us. And I doubt any American towns would welcome a pirate band with open arms."

"I should hope not," she grumbled, then could've bit off her tongue at the look of scalding anger that passed over his face.

But he seemed to check it quickly, and when he spoke again, his voice betrayed nothing but bland indifference. "I see you understand our situation. Fortunately, my men and I have found an island inhabited only by wild pigs. It has a freshwater stream and lush vegetation, and it's large enough to support a substantial population. So we've decided to settle there, to build our own country."

His gaze grew dark, almost mesmerizing. "There's only one problem, you see. We have no women. And a colony without women . . . well, you can understand our dilemma."

The smile he gave her then was so unexpectedly charming, she had to force herself not to respond to it. She didn't want to be charmed by this . . . this wicked scoundrel. She didn't want that at all.

"But why these women? Why not pick wives in the Cape Verdes or—"

"Why do you think we were in Santiago?" He glanced away, his mood seeming to shift to a graver one. "Unfortunately, few women wish to travel to an unknown island where they'll be cut off forever from their families and expected to do their part in making it livable. Even the . . . er . . . ladybirds find that a less than tempting proposition."

Ladybirds indeed. A blush rose to her cheeks despite her attempts to stop it. She shifted uncomfortably in her seat. "Can you blame them?"

His gaze was on her again, and he smiled as if he took great delight in her embarrassment. "I suppose not. They have reasons to stay on Santiago. But the situation is entirely different for the women of the *Chastity*. They're doomed to a life of near slavery in a foreign land. We chose them precisely because we thought they'd prefer freedom with us to enforced servitude with cruel former convicts in New South Wales."

"I'm not sure I understand the distinction between former convicts and pirates," she snapped. "They're both criminals, aren't they?"

A muscle ticked in his jaw, making him look even more forbidding. "Believe me, there's a profound difference between my men and those cutthroats."

"You expect me to take your word for it?"

"You don't have any choice, now, do you?" At her disgruntled expression, he seemed to rein in his temper. "Besides, our island has more to offer than New South Wales, where the weather is pitiless and the government more so. We have perfect weather, easy living, plenty of food, and no government but our own. There are no jailers, no magistrates oppressing the poor and catering to rich nobility . . . 'tis a paradise. Or it will be when your ladies join us."

His eyes fixed on her, a burning zeal in their depths. He'd painted a pretty picture of his island, but Sara wasn't fooled. New South Wales might have proven un-savory in the long run, but at least the women would have had some choice there. They wouldn't have had to marry against their will. Though the inhabitants of the country might have regarded the convict women as prostitutes, there would always have been opportunities for the women to work hard and attain respectability. Some transported convicts even managed to make their way back to England and their families, though only a very few.

On Captain Horn's island, however, there'd be no such possibility. They'd be at the mercy of him and his pirates. "A paradise?" She rose from her chair in a sweep of dimity skirts. "You mean a paradise for you and your men. You've said naught that makes it a paradise for the women. They're to be forced to be your wives and forced to labor for a 'country' they didn't choose."

He rose, too, rounding the desk to stand scant inches from her, his brow lowered in a frown. "Do you think they'd have any choices on New South Wales? I've been there. I've seen how convict women are treated. They're parceled out to colonists as servant labor, though every man there intends that the only labor they'll do is on their backs."

At his crudeness, a hot flush again stained her cheeks. He lowered his voice to a harsh murmur. "Those who aren't chosen as servants are confined in crowded factories where conditions are worse than in England's gaols. And that's the fate you wish for your charges, Lady Sara? I offer them freedom and you offer them *that*."

His unfair accusations stung. "Freedom? That's what you call forced marriage? You say your colony will be better, but you've given me no evidence of it. You're going to parcel those women out to your men just as the Australian authorities do. You're offering them mar-riage, but it's still enforced servitude, isn't it?"

He stood there as rigidly as his ship's figurehead. His eyes narrowed. "Suppose they were allowed a chance to choose." His words were clipped, as if he already regretted them.

Surprise and then hope rose in her. "To choose what? Whether or not to go with you to your island?"

He scowled. "No. I mean, to choose their husbands. They can spend a week getting to know the men and seeing what's in store for them on our island. After that, however, they must accept the proposal of the man they most prefer."

"Oh." She considered that a minute. It was better than his heartless earlier offer, but certainly not as good as giving the women a choice between returning to the *Chastity* or going with the pirates. Though she wasn't sure they'd want to go back anyway. A tiny part of her knew that he might be right about what lay in store for the convicts if they continued on their journey.

If only she could be sure that his men truly did intend to retire. If only she had some inkling of their characters. She sighed. They were pirates. What more was there to know?

Still, he was offering something the women might not have gotten in New South Wales—the chance to choose the one who would enslave them.

She sought some way to make the choice easier. "One week is a short time," she began. "Why, we might not even reach your island until—"

"We'll reach Atlantis in two days," he interrupted.

"Atlantis?" she echoed. "Like the Greeks' Atlantis?"

For a moment, he lost his stern look. "Some say Atlantis was utopia, Lady Sara. And that's what we hope to create. Utopia."

"A utopia where men have all the choices and women have none."

"I'm offering them a choice."

"Could we have two weeks, perhaps?"

His expression hardened. "One week. Take it or leave

it. Either way, your women *will* take husbands. I'm giving up a great deal by letting the women make the choice instead of the men. The men will grumble about it."

"And what if a woman chooses not to marry?"

"That's not a choice." He tucked his thumbs under his wide leather belt with its strange-looking buckle. "At the end of one week, if a woman hasn't chosen a husband, one will be chosen for her."

"Thank goodness we're not bargaining over anything *important*," she snapped. "I'll have to speak to the women first, of course. I can't make such a decision for them."

"Of course." Moving to the desk, he settled his hips against it and crossed his legs at the ankles. "I hope this means an end to the ladies' caterwauling."

The words were a command. She shrugged. "*If* they agree to your terms, I suppose it does." Smoothing her skirts down with a clammy hand, she said, "May I go now, Captain Horn, and present your offer to them?"

"Certainly. I'll give you an hour. Then I'll send Barnaby for your answer."

She turned to the door, relieved to finally escape his disturbing presence.

But as she opened it, he said, "One more thing, Lady Sara."

She twisted her head to look at him. "Yes?"

"In case you thought otherwise, this offer refers to *all* the women on this ship. That includes you. You have one week to choose a husband from among my men." He paused, a wicked grin crossing his face as he swept his gaze down over her lips, her throat . . . her waist and hips. "Or I'll take great delight in choosing one for you."

Chapter 6

Oh, I command a sturdy band
Of pirates bold and free.
No laws I own, my ship's my throne,
My kingdom is the sea.

—R. B. DAWSON
"THE PIRATE OF THE ISLE"

Captain Horn's words rang in Sara's ears as she hurried through the saloon and out onto the deck. *That includes you.* What a beast! She'd avoided marriage for five years because she couldn't find the right man, and now he thought he could hand her over to any old scoundrel he picked for her!

Squinting in the brilliant sunshine, she hastened across the deck to the hatch that led down to the hold. He could just forget it! She would never let him shackle her to some foul pirate simply because he ordained it!

She bent to open the hatch, and a young pirate with cropped hair rushed to her side. "Let me help you, miss," he said as he unlatched it, then opened it for her.

The courtly action took her completely aback. When she stared at him in astonishment, he added, "I hope the ladies are comfortable below. If they need anything, anything at all, you tell me and I'll see that they get it."

Although it was hard to stay irate in the face of such

cordiality, she was still smarting from her encounter with Captain Horn. Such appearances of concern didn't fool her. "The only thing the ladies need right now is to be set free. Will you do that for us?" When he colored and mumbled that only the captain could do that, she snapped, "Then you're of no help to us at all," and descended the stairs, leaving him to close the hatch above her.

The air of the hold was thick with the sounds and smells of frightened women and children. Although the pirate ship was smaller than the *Chastity*, the hold was bigger and there were no constraining bars. Still, without berths stacked up along the walls, the women were forced to share the bedrolls that had apparently been laid on the floor for the "cargo" the pirates had expected to accumulate in the Cape Verde Islands. At least there was more light in the hold of the *Satyr* than there had been in the *Chastity*, thanks to the lanterns lining the walls and filling the ship's belly with the acrid smell of burning oil.

As soon as the women spotted her, they leapt off their bedrolls and rushed to the stairs.

"What're they goin' to do with us?" Queenie demanded.

"How long do we have to stay down here?" asked another woman, while one of the children clamored to be fed and another cried about being thirsty.

"I don't know when they're going to let us above decks," she answered as she reached the bottom of the stairs. "But I do know what they're planning to do with us. That's what the captain wants me to speak to all of you about."

Amid the shuffling of feet and the complaints of the children, she described the bargain she'd made with the captain, explaining about Atlantis Island and what the pirates wanted. By the time she finished, the women had fallen completely silent. Clearly they didn't know what to make of the captain's offer. *She* certainly didn't.

After a few moments, Louisa pushed her way through the crowd. Her blond hair hung in a tangled mass and her face was white as bleached ivory. "Do you mean to say that those men plan to force us to marry and then keep us captive on some remote island for the rest of our lives?" There was a note of panic in her voice. "We can never return to England?"

"Who gives a bloody farthing about returning to England?" Queenie retorted before Sara could answer. "Ain't nothin' for any of us back there. Besides, if we'd made it to New South Wales, we'd have been stranded there, too. You got to pay yer own passage back to England once yer sentence is up, and that ain't likely to happen, seein' as how it costs a bloody fortune to get back."

"But I have family in England, Queenie," one of the younger women cried. "I've got my ma to worry about. She's all alone—"

Sara clapped her hands for silence. "I know this sounds as dreadful to you as it does to me. But Captain Horn is quite determined to keep us, I'm afraid. He's already made his only concession by allowing us to pick the men we agree to marry."

"*Us?*" Louisa clipped out. A disbelieving expression crossed her face. "He says you must marry as well, and you a lady?"

"I'm not a lady. The Earl of Blackmore is only my stepbrother. But yes, he says I must marry, too." Catching onto the stairs as the ship dipped, Sara added, "We're all in this together. At the end of one week, either we choose husbands from among the pirates, or Captain Horn will choose husbands for us. We can make Atlantis our home or let it be our prison. It's up to us. He will give us no other alternative."

"It don't sound so awful," Ann piped up. "We'll have a man to care for and maybe children—"

"Not all of us crave a man and children to care for,

Annie," Louisa snapped. "Some of us would just as soon do without."

"What about those of us who don't attract a husband?" a voice called out from behind the rest. Sara looked to where Jillian, a woman of about sixty, sat resting on a sealed barrel of drinking water. "We ain't all young, y'know," she added. "There's some of us as won't be much of an attraction for them pirates."

"That's true." Sara frowned. She hadn't thought of that. There were three women among them who were well beyond child-bearing age. Somehow she didn't think the pirates, most of whom seemed no older than forty, would want to take a grandmother for a wife.

"And what if we ain't so pretty?" asked a young woman whose face had been scarred by smallpox. "What if no man wants us?"

Sara's frown deepened. Curse Captain Horn and his blithe assumptions. His beastly plan had a number of large holes in it. He'd said that the men would court the women, but if she knew anything about men, they would compete for the affections of the prettiest ones and ignore the others. Then what? After the pretty ones had chosen husbands, would he force the rest of the men to marry women they didn't want? And what about the women with two or three children? Did he expect his pirates to take whole families on? What if they refused? What would become of the children?

"I think Captain Horn hasn't considered all the possibilities," she told them. He might rail against England's class system, but he obviously knew nothing about planning a society himself. "It appears I must have another discussion with our good captain about all these things. Perhaps when he understands the complexity of the situation, he'll realize he can't expect us to agree to his plan."

Everyone nodded their assent, though some muttered that they'd just as soon have a pirate for a husband as a colonist. It was clear the women were divided on the subject of choosing husbands.

"For my own part," Queenie said, "I don't want to be tied down to just one man when there's an island full for the takin'."

When the others burst into laughter, Sara bit back a smile. It would be interesting to see how Captain Horn would handle incorrigible "soiled doves" like Queenie. An island full of convicts and pirates wasn't likely to be the utopia he envisioned. And maybe once the scoundrel realized that matters could hardly work out to his satisfaction, he'd be reasonable.

But somehow she doubted it.

Gideon sat at his desk with a whetstone, sharpening his saber. His hand slipped and he nicked a finger. Cursing, he wiped the blood on his leather vest. It was dangerous to have a blade in his hand when Sara Willis was on his mind.

Laying the saber in his lap, he stared blankly at the door. He couldn't believe he'd let her rattle him so badly. Confound the woman! She was an albatross about his neck. If it weren't for her, his conscience would be easy about taking the convict women from the *Chastity*. The women would be happy, he and his men would be happy, and everything would be just fine.

If it weren't for Miss Willis. Barnaby was right: they should have left the blasted woman on the *Chastity*. Then her brother—no, her stepbrother—could have dealt with her as he saw fit.

With a curse, Gideon tossed the whetstone onto his desk. What kind of brother was the man, anyway, to let a woman like her go to sea with a lot of convict women? The Earl of Blackmore ought to be horsewhipped. Gideon would never have let any sister of his—or even a stepsister, for that matter—do such a fool thing, and certainly not one who was gently bred.

He groaned. Now she had him thinking like a blasted

Englishman. It didn't matter that she was gently bred. She was no better than any of those convict women, and she deserved no better treatment than the rest.

Besides, it wasn't as if she were defenseless, not with that sharp tongue of hers. But he'd make her toe the line, even if he had to stop up her mouth with a gag to quiet her.

Her mouth. God help him, he could think of better ways to stop up that one's mouth . . . more pleasurable ways. For just a second, he let himself imagine what it would be like to kiss those impudent lips, to feel them part beneath his and—

There was a knock at the door, and he started, dragging his thoughts away from the delectable Miss Willis with a groan. "Come in," he growled as he took up the whetstone once more.

Barnaby entered with another of Gideon's men, and between them they dragged a mouse of a seaman whom he didn't recognize. "We found this one hiding in the longboat, captain." Barnaby thrust the man forward none too gently. "We think he came from the *Chastity*."

Gideon cast the man a stern glance. Without saying anything, he began once more to sharpen his saber, watching as the man paled. He stroked the saber's already razor-sharp blade with the whetstone, letting the snick of stone against steel echo in the cabin several times before he spoke. "Pray tell me," he said calmly, "who are you, and what are you doing aboard my ship?"

Although the man's hands shook, his gaze didn't waver from Gideon's. "My name's Peter Hargraves, sir. I sneaked aboard while you were havin' the women moved to the *Satyr*. I . . . I want to be a pirate sir."

Another seeker for riches. "And why would you want that? It's not an easy life, you know. You have to work hard for the gold, and do some unsavory things."

Hargraves looked a little ill, but he stood straighter. "Well, sir . . . um . . . the truth is, I got little choice. I'd been plannin' to go to New South Wales to make my fortune, but you put a stop to that. I can't return to England, so I stowed away."

At least he was forthright. Gideon continued to sharpen his blade. "And why can't you return to England?"

The tips of Hargraves's prominent ears reddened. "I ran away to sea to escape the hangman, sir. I killed a man. I can't go back there now."

I can't go back there now. There was a ring of truth to those words. But the rest of it . . . could the man be lying? Although his story seemed likely enough, there was something in Hargraves's manner that made Gideon think he wasn't telling the whole truth.

Then again, most of Gideon's men had secrets. That was why they'd taken their chances with piracy. And no seaman would stow away aboard a pirate ship unless he were desperate.

Gideon paused in sharpening his blade to survey the man with a critical eye. So he wanted to join the pirates, did he? He was small, but looked sturdy enough. He'd probably be good at climbing the rigging. But that skill wouldn't help Gideon, not anymore. "Tell me, Peter Hargraves, what do you know about farming?"

Hargraves stared at Gideon as if he'd gone mad. "Farmin', sir?"

"Yes, farming," Gideon retorted impatiently. "Or carpentry, or brickmaking. What do you know of those things?"

Hargraves glanced at Barnaby, who merely said, "Answer the captain, man."

"I . . . I don't know nothin' about them. I'm a sailor, sir, and a good one, too." When Gideon scowled, he hastened to add, "And I'm a right fierce fighter. I don't look it, I know, but I can put a man down who's twice my size."

Gideon's scowl only deepened. "I won't need good fighters or sailors once we reach our destination, so you're of no use to me. Barnaby, put him in chains until—"

"I know how to butcher and dress an animal!" Hargraves burst out.

Gideon set down the saber and the whetstone and cast the sailor a skeptical look. "Do you? Could you skin a pig and preserve it?"

"Aye." Hargraves was breathing heavily now. "My father was a butcher. Taught me everythin' he knew. I went to sea after he lost his shop."

A butcher. They could use a butcher on Atlantis. *If* the man was telling the truth. Still, it was worth the gamble to have a competent butcher in their midst. "I tell you what, Englishman. You may join my crew for as long as it takes us to sail to our destination." When Hargraves started to thank him, he held up a hand. "But you'll have to prove you're worth keeping beyond that. I'll tolerate no laziness. If you've got some fool idea that pirates are sluggards, you're wrong. If we don't get a good day's work out of you, we'll maroon you."

He ignored Barnaby's raised eyebrow. They'd never marooned anybody before, even the English nobles they hated, but Gideon meant to put the fear of God into the man. Maybe Hargraves would think twice the next time he thought to stow away aboard a pirate ship.

"Put him to sanding the deck," Gideon ordered, then picked up his saber once more.

But his first mate didn't move. "Captain?"

"Yes?" Gideon retorted without looking up.

"It's nearing mealtime. What are we to do about feeding the women?"

The women. They'd been so quiet for the past hour, Gideon had almost forgotten about them. "We brought on enough food to feed them. Have Silas prepare a meal for them and the children, of course."

"But shall we let them up on deck to eat?" Barnaby asked.

When Gideon glanced up, he noticed that Hargraves

was listening intently to their conversation. Perhaps the man hadn't been quite honest about his reasons for stowing away. Perhaps he had a sweetheart among the women. Well, that was an innocuous enough reason for his coming aboard, and Gideon couldn't blame him for it.

"No, not just yet. I have some things to discuss with the men before the women are allowed on deck."

"What sort of things?" Barnaby asked.

Gideon glared at his first mate. "You'll find out soon enough." He drew out his pocket watch and looked at it. An hour had passed since he'd last spoken to Miss Willis. It was time to hear whether the women had accepted his offer or not. "But bring Miss Willis back here. She and I have to finish our discussion."

Though Barnaby cast him a questioning look, he ignored it. He hadn't yet told the others about the offer he'd made the women. He didn't want to endure his men's groans and complaints until he was sure the women were agreeable.

Barnaby and his fellow pirate left, taking Hargraves with them, but still Gideon sat staring into space. He hadn't considered how difficult it would be to tell the men that he was giving the women a choice. What demon had come over him to let him suggest such a thing? It wasn't as if these women expected such privileges. In New South Wales, they'd have had no choices at all, or very little.

Opening a desk drawer, he dug around in the bottom until he found a little-used flask of rum he kept there for when he had the ague. He seldom drank hard liquor for any reason, but today it was warranted. He took a sip, coughed, then took another. A few more sips and his anger evened out a fraction.

So what if he'd given the women a choice? He wanted them to be happy. If they were happy, they'd do as they were told and add their skills to those of his men. Women were needed on Atlantis, not just to provide an outlet for the men's sexual urges, but to perform other tasks as well—cooking and weaving and gardening, things his men knew nothing about. And if giving the women a little freedom of choice made them more amenable to their situation, he'd do it. The men would understand once he explained it to them that way. Certainly he'd prefer that his own wife, whomever he chose, married him of her own free will.

A brief knock sounded at the door. Thrusting the rum flask into the drawer, he settled back in his seat and called out, "Come in."

Miss Willis entered. When she'd left his cabin before, she'd been full of fire and fury, but now she seemed more subdued, even afraid. Strangely enough, he didn't like that demeanor on her, and that made him speak more sharply than he should. "Well? What did the women decide?"

She seemed not to hear his question. "As I was coming in, I saw that you'd taken prisoner one of the crewmen from the *Chastity*. What do you intend to do with him?"

For some reason, her concern for a lowly English sailor irked him. "Make him walk the plank, of course." When her horrified expression showed that she believed him, he added, "He's joining my crew. That's all." Relief flooded her face, prompting him to ask, "Why do you care?"

She dropped her gaze from his. "I wouldn't like to see anyone from the *Chastity* harmed."

"How kind of you." For a moment, he toyed with the idea that Miss Willis was the one Hargraves had sneaked aboard for. Then he dismissed it as an absurdity. British sailors knew better than to fall in love with women above their station. And a pretty woman like Miss Willis would certainly never be romantically interested in a scrawny thing like Peter Hargraves.

In any case, that wasn't why he'd called her here. "Have the women decided to accept my offer?"

A change came over her as she tilted her head up to meet his gaze. The fear vanished, leaving behind a fierce determination that showed itself in the stubborn set of her mouth and the glint in her pretty brown eyes. "Not exactly."

"Not exactly?" He rose from behind the desk, rounding it to stand in front of her. "Remember, if they don't want to take the week to choose, I'm simply going to let my men pick whom they want—"

"No!" When he raised one eyebrow, she hastened to add, "I mean, they want to have the week, of course. It's better than the alternative. But they have some questions. *We* have some questions. About how this will work."

He settled one hip on his desk, watching her intently. She looked flustered, and that was just how he wanted her to feel. The more flustered she was, the quicker they could settle all this, and he could get her out of his cabin.

Why he wanted to get her out of his cabin, he preferred not to examine too closely. "Ask your questions, but be quick about it. I've got a ship to run."

As relief spread over her face, she tucked a tendril of hair up under her frilly cap and squared her shoulders. "Some of the women have children. Will the men who marry them take on the responsibility for their children as well?"

"Of course. We're not monsters, you know."

That brought a tiny frown to her face. Clearly she disagreed.

"And what about the older women? We have several women past child-bearing age. If none of the men wish to marry them, would you choose them a husband who might not want them?"

Confound her, he hadn't considered that. But that could easily be corrected. "I'll make an exception for the older women who can no longer bear children. If they

find no man who will marry them, they are free to remain unmarried."

Her breath came out in a sudden whoosh. "So if a
woman can find no man to marry her, she doesn't have
to marry."

"I didn't say that." The little witch was putting words
in his mouth now. "The women of child-bearing age
must still choose a husband, or one *will* be chosen for
them."

With a sniff, she crossed her arms over her chest. He
wondered if she had any idea how she looked standing
in the center of his cabin. With that ridiculous cap and
her demure dimity gown torn and dirty from the hurried transfer of the women to the *Satyr*, she reminded
him of an urchin begging favors of a lord. Except he
wasn't a lord, and she was certainly no urchin.

She proved that when she lifted her chin in a lofty
expression of defiance. "Suppose a woman is too plain
to attract a husband. Will you force some man to marry
her just because you want to pair them all up?"

Her words sparked his temper, as much because of
her logic as because of her contempt for his plans. He
stalked toward her, finding a grim satisfaction in the
sudden wariness that leapt into her face. "My men have
spent the last eight years at sea with only an occasional
night in port to satisfy their need for female companionship. Your women could be horse-faced and snaggle-
toothed, and my men would *still* want them, I assure
you!"

It wasn't entirely true, but he'd had enough of her
quibbling. She would follow his rules, if he had to lock
her up to do it!

She backed away from him, her cheeks pinkening. But
even when she came up against the door to his cabin
and saw she was trapped, she continued to plague him.
"I hardly believe that your men would want a wife
who's—"

"Enough!" He planted his hands against the oak door

on either side of her shoulders, pinning her between them. "Your women have a week to choose husbands. When that week is over, I'll do as I see fit with whoever's left unwed, and nothing you say will change that!"

"But you're not thinking this through," she protested earnestly, turning her pretty chin up another notch. "If you force people—"

"Why are you being so stubborn? Are you worried you won't find a husband? Is that it? Are you afraid that nobody'll choose you?"

The color drained from her face. "Why, you obnoxious, despicable—"

"Because you needn't worry about that. Plenty of men on this ship will find you attractive."

Before she could stop him, he tugged her mobcap loose, casting it aside on the floor. As she stared at him with wide eyes, her breath coming in quick, jerky gasps, he felt desire bolt through him, as sudden as a summer squall. Auburn strands of hair clung loosely to the bun she'd tortured them into, and her eyes were nearly the same color, a dark reddish-brown fringed with the longest, most delicate lashes he'd ever seen.

By God, she was beautiful. Peach-tinged lips . . . a wide, white brow . . . and satiny skin with just enough freckles to hint at a mischievous nature. He hadn't been this close to her before, hadn't had a good look at that delectable face.

He and his men had come across many Englishwomen during their days of pirating. And though he'd kissed one or two to irk their stuffy husbands, he'd never wanted any of them. Not the way he suddenly wanted this one.

That thought frightened the bejesus out of him. She wasn't for him. Let one of his men take the little witch into his bed and suffer her temper and her lofty expectations.

Yet that didn't appeal to him either.

He should push away from her now, but he couldn't. Not until he'd seen a little more. In a trance, he removed her hairpins until her hair tumbled down in a twisted rope about her shoulders. He raked his fingers through the thick mass until the strands scattered over his fingers like threads of silk. Soft, so soft. How long had it been since he'd touched a woman's hair like this? How long since he'd even been this close to a woman?

He twirled one coppery lock around his finger, and that seemed to rouse her from her stunned silence.

"Stop that," she whispered, a troubled expression crossing her face.

"Why?" He smoothed her hair down over one shoulder, thinking that she had the creamiest skin he'd ever seen, skin that was just begging to be touched.

She gasped when he stroked one finger up along the curved contours of her neck. "It's not . . . proper," she said.

That made him smile. "Proper? We crossed the line from proper to improper right after you left the *Chastity*. You're on a pirate ship, remember? You're alone in a cabin with a notorious pirate captain . . . you've lost your proper little cap . . . and I'm about to kiss you."

As soon as he'd said the words, he knew they were a mistake—and not because of the outrage that filled her face. It would be dangerous to kiss her. She wasn't the woman for him.

But he had to taste her once. Just a little taste.

So before a protest could even leave her lips, he brought his mouth down on hers.

Chapter 7

*Then shun, oh! shun that wretched state
And all the fawning flatterers hate:
Value yourselves, and men despise
You must be proud if you'll be wise.*

—MARY, LADY CHUDLEIGH
ENGLISH POET, "TO THE LADIES"

S ara was stunned into immobility. His lips, far too soft for a pirate's, moved over hers with gentle persuasion. His breath mingled with hers, surprisingly sweet. Then he ran his tongue over the seam of her lips, and she jerked back from him in shock. He'd kissed her! The . . . the scoundrel had actually had the audacity to kiss her!

"What's wrong, Lady Sara?" His voice was husky, his eyes dark and knowing. Lifting his hand to cup her cheek, he touched the pad of his thumb to her lower lip. "Haven't you ever been kissed before?"

A traitorous shiver rippled through her as he stroked her lip with his thumb. She tried to concentrate on being appalled by his actions, but it was hard to think when he was touching her. "Of course I . . . I've been kissed before."

He raised one eyebrow as if he didn't believe her.

88

"Whoever he was, he failed to convince you of your desirability." His callused thumb traced the smaller curves of her upper lip. "Who was it? Some knock-kneed suitor barely out of the schoolroom? A foppish lordling?"

He was laughing at her, the wretch! She shot him a withering glance. "It was an English cavalry officer, if you must know, and no fop at all." She brought her hand up between them to shove him away.

But he caught it and carried it to the back of his neck, holding it there as he looked down at her with gleaming eyes. "No fop perhaps, but not man enough to keep you in England. And not very adept at kissing, unless I miss my guess. Though perhaps you need more of a basis for comparison."

Before she could stop him, his mouth came down on hers once more, forceful, possessive, unyielding. This time there was no trace of gentleness in the lips that ravaged hers. He took her mouth as if it was his right, the way a pirate should. She grasped his hair, meaning to pull his head away from her, but at that moment the ship rolled, throwing him hard against her, plastering his taut thighs and lean belly against her so intimately she gasped.

In that instant when her lips were parted, he thrust his tongue into her mouth. And to her immense horror, she found it . . . rather thrilling. Shockingly thrilling. She froze, letting him explore her mouth, and when he drove his tongue in and out in a strangely compelling rhythm, she forgot where she was . . . who she was. Instead of pulling his hair, she curled her fingers into the springy strands to clutch his head closer. Her eyelids drifted shut as he slanted his mouth over hers more firmly, taking possession of it the way he'd taken possession of the *Chastity*.

Colonel Taylor's kisses had been cautious, hesitant, as if he didn't want to frighten his prey. Heaven help her, but she liked Captain Horn's boldness. The heated strokes of his tongue . . . his fingers splayed in the small of her back, drawing her closer . . . closer . . .

The kiss went on forever, growing more rough and more demanding the longer it continued. Then his hands began to roam down her hips and up her ribs in widening strokes until his thumb brushed the underside of her breast.

Wrenching her mouth from his, she cried, "You mustn't touch me like that! You mustn't!"

His breath came in ragged gasps as he stared down at her. "Why mustn't I?"

"Because it isn't . . . it isn't proper!"

Amusement glinted in his eyes. He shoved back a lock of hair that had fallen over his forehead during their tumultuous kiss. "Don't you ever do anything improper, Lady Sara?"

Lady Sara. That was why he was doing this, wasn't it? He wanted to humiliate her with kisses because her brother was an earl. It was as much a maneuvering tactic as Colonel Taylor's kisses had been, and that realization sobered her. "I am *not* Lady Sara. There is no such creature." She turned her face from his. "I'm Miss Willis, that's all."

"No, not Miss Willis." Clasping her chin, he forced her to look at him. "Miss Willis is too prudish a name for a woman with your passions."

"I don't have passions!" she protested. "I don't like—"

The rest of her words were cut off when he kissed her again, hard and deep, with the force of a man too long at sea. His thumb stroked her throat, then came to rest against the pulse that quickened with each new foray of his tongue.

She tried to fight him. Truly she did. Fisting her hands against his chest, she tried to thrust him away, but so feeble was her attempt that it had no effect at all. Grasping her wrists, he forced her hands down to his waist and pressed them there until her fingers opened and her hands flattened against him. Then he released her wrists, but only to pull her closer, melding his body to hers.

All thought of moving . . . speaking . . . even breathing left her. There was only this man with his rough hands on her, making her feel like a woman instead of a reformer or an earl's stepsister. He smelled of the sea and tasted of rum, a not unpleasant combination. His breathing, rapid and uneven, joined hers as he kissed her hungrily. This was something so beyond her experience that she let herself be swept up in it for the sheer enjoyment.

Then he gripped her hips and forced her against his loins, so close she could feel the hard bulge beneath his breeches. Sara stiffened. Her mother had been forthright in telling her how men and women made love, so she knew that the hard bulge was evidence of his arousal. Good heavens, she mustn't let him do this!

With a strangled cry, she pushed him away, managing to squeeze from between him and the door before he could stop her. Her lips burned from the force of his kisses and her heart thundered, but she ignored both as she rushed to the other end of the room, safely behind his desk.

Her cheeks glowed crimson as she watched him turn slowly to face her, his eyes glittering like twin shards of blue glass. She couldn't believe she'd let that beast put his hands on her. It wouldn't happen again. She wouldn't let it!

With a scowl, he stalked to the desk and leaned forward to plant his fists on it. A fearsome desire still glinted in his eyes, and his breath came heavy and hard. "You see, Sara, you *do* have passions. You can cling to your propriety all you want, but you and I both know you're not so proper as you pretend."

"I'm more proper than you could ever be!"

"Thank God for that," he muttered.

That he'd turned her insult into a compliment infuriated her. "Yes, you enjoy being a bully, don't you? You enjoy lording it over women and children! You're as bad as those English nobles you hate, who oppress their tenants and treat their women as chattel!"

The minute the words were out of her mouth, she regretted them, for his eyes darkened to an icy slate as he cast her a look of utter disgust. "You know nothing about me! Nothing! When was the last time *you* experienced oppression, Lady Sara? When was the last time *you* had to scrabble and scrape for a piece of bread or endure the fists of a—"

He broke off, thrusting himself away from the desk with his jaw clenched so tightly that the scar across his cheek whitened. He took a couple of deep breaths before he spoke again, his voice even but firm. "Your women and my men belong together. They understand each other. It's only you who don't understand, who can't see that I'm offering those convicts more than they'd get anywhere else—a home and the chance to have a husband and a family. And yes, a choice—"

"A choice? To be shackled now or later? What kind of choice is that?"

"Enough of this quibbling! Do you accept my offer as it stands, one week for the women to choose husbands? Or must I do this the way I'd originally intended, by letting the men take whom they will to marry?"

"What about—"

"Yes or no, Sara. That's how it is to be. If problems arise, *I* will take care of them with no help from you. Is that understood?"

"Perfectly." It was easier for her to deal with him when he was angry than when he was kissing the life out of her. Angry men she could understand. "You're a petty tyrant, and what you say goes." She sniffed. "Fine. We'll take the week you offer. But don't blame me if everything doesn't go as well as you planned."

His eyes blazed. "Everything will go *exactly* as I planned, I assure you."

The devilish self-confidence in his voice was so . . . so irritating! He simply refused to accept that there might be holes in his plan. Well, let him sort it out at the end of the week. He'd soon see he couldn't just pair people up as if they were cattle to be bred. And when everything fell apart, she would laugh—yes, laugh at him! Just see if she wouldn't.

Straightening her shoulders, she fixed him with a haughty glance. "May I go now, Captain Horn?"

"Gideon. You'll call me Gideon."

She couldn't ignore the intimacy his statement suggested. "I won't do any such thing. Just because you . . . you kissed me doesn't mean that—"

"That kiss was a mistake. It won't happen again." His eyes flashed, cold and impersonal as sapphires. "But we bloodthirsty pirates don't stand on ceremony, so call me Gideon anyway." He strode to the door, laying his hand on the doorknob. "*Now* you may go."

She didn't know whether to be insulted or relieved that he obviously despised kissing her. *Of course I'm relieved*, she told herself. *I don't want that scoundrel's hands on me again.*

"Well?" He opened the door as if to prod her out of it.

Gathering all her dignity about her, she rounded the desk and started toward the door. Her cap lay on the floor a few feet away and she stopped to pick it up.

"Leave it there," he ordered in harsh tones. "You look better with your hair down. Don't put it up again." When she gaped at him, wondering at his sudden interest in her hair after he'd seemed to want to be rid of her as quickly as possible, he added, "You'll have a better chance at catching a good husband with your hair down, Sara."

Her female vanity was stung by his implication that no man would look at her twice otherwise. Snatching the cap up, she began to hunt for the hairpins scattered across the floor, but he left the door and advanced on her with a muttered curse.

"If you put it up, I'll just take it down again." His voice lowered to a throaty hum. "And you know what happens when I take your hair down."

When he stepped nearer, she rose, deciding it might be more prudent to abandon her hair pins.

Before she could react, his hand snaked out to tear her cap from her fingers. Then he balled it up and stuffed it in his trouser pocket. "You may leave now. Silas is feeding the women; go have your dinner. But I expect you on deck in half an hour—and the other women with you."

"What for?"

"We should tell the rest of the ship about the conditions of our bargain, don't you think?"

The rest of the ship? The other pirates? Good heavens, until this moment, she hadn't thought about the fact that they'd have to be informed. She certainly had no desire to be around when they were.

He stood very close to her now, and when she lifted her face to his, his eyes challenged her to refuse. A trick of the light made her fancy she saw horns buried in the raven-black whorls of his hair. She shook her head to clear it. He wasn't a mythical creature, no matter how much he resembled one. He was human and could be bested. She just hadn't yet figured out how.

"What's wrong?" he bit out. "Afraid to face my men when I tell them that their happiness has been delayed, thanks to you?"

She sniffed. "I'm not afraid of anything."

His expression softened. Slowly he lifted a hand to stroke the hair away from her cheek. She withstood his touch, determined to show him that he didn't frighten her. Although God knew he did.

"I can well believe you fear nothing, Miss Sara Willis," he said, dropping his hand from her cheek. "I suspect you would take on the entire English realm—or the

American nation—if you had to." He lowered his voice. "But be warned—I'm no fancy English lord to be governed by a slip of a woman, no matter how sweetly she kisses. And if you stir up rebellion among those women again, you'll have good cause to fear me. I promise you that."

Then he swept his hand mockingly toward the door.

Head held high, she lifted her skirts and passed over the threshold, then hurried out onto the deck as he closed the door to his cabin. To her chagrin, several of the pirates looked up as she came on deck. When they exchanged knowing glances, she halted, a blush spreading over her cheeks.

Good heavens, how she must look with her cap gone, her hair down, and her lips reddened! What must they think of her!

What they thought was clear from their grins. She stiffened her spine, ignoring their laughter as she swept between them toward the hatch. The wretched scoundrels! They were probably used to seeing women leave their captain's cabin looking as if they'd just been seduced. No doubt they thought she'd already succumbed to the Pirate Lord's despicable overtures.

She crossed the deck purposefully. She *had* succumbed a little. But just a kiss. Well, two. Or was it three?

Good heavens, it didn't matter how many; that was the end of it. He'd said so, and she certainly intended to hold him to it. There would be no more kisses between them unless that blackhearted pirate forced them on her!

No indeed. Not a single one!

Petey joined the pirates on deck and perched on a nearby barrel, uneasiness in the center of his chest as he waited for their captain to speak. God save him, how was he to get the little miss out of this mess? When he'd sneaked aboard the *Satyr*, he'd had no plans in mind.

He'd only known that he dared not go back to England without Miss Willis. It was less a sense of duty and more a fear of what the earl might do to him and his family if he returned empty-handed.

Oh, sure, the blighter had seemed reasonable enough, but a reasonable man didn't send a spy after his sister and offer an ungodly sum for it. No, Petey dared not risk the earl's wrath. Tom needed that job in the earl's household, especially now that Father had lost the butcher shop. But Petey felt as if he'd jumped from the frying pan into the fire. The earl was a man to fear indeed, but the Pirate Lord—

Petey groaned. He'd nearly lost his bloomin' breakfast when the pirate captain had spoken of marooning him. It was a common practice among pirates, to be sure, and the thought of it terrified Petey. Thank the good Lord he'd thought to mention Father. Of course, Petey had exaggerated his own ability. He didn't know as much as he'd let on. And what did a pirate want with a butcher, anyway?

Slanting his hand over his eyes to block out the light of the dying sun, Petey looked up to where the Pirate Lord paced the quarterdeck, his large hands clenched together behind his back and his face drawn in anger. He'd been in a foul mood ever since he'd called for the men to assemble on deck and had sent for the women.

Petey wondered if the little miss had something to do with it. She had a tongue on her, it was true, and he wouldn't be surprised if she'd used it to chastise the captain. For her sake, he hoped not. Anybody could see that the Pirate Lord wasn't to be trifled with.

Suddenly the women emerged from the hatch behind Petey, led by Miss Willis. He caught her eye as she passed with them in tow, but she could only give him a helpless look before she went on.

"What's this all about?" he heard a man mutter beside him. It was the one who'd passed out the food a few hours ago, a man named Silas.

The first mate answered. "I don't know. But that Lady Sara has something to do with it. You can be sure of that."

Petey swallowed. Pray God she hadn't condemned all the women to some horrible fate with her troublemaking, though he had to admit the women had been treated well thus far. He scanned the crowd, looking for little Ann, but she was so short he couldn't catch a glimpse of her.

As soon as the women had gathered on deck, the Pirate Lord beckoned to Miss Willis to join him on the quarterdeck, and she went, though her face wore a wary expression that made Petey anxious. Once she stood at the captain's side, nearly dwarfed by the fearsome man's great height, the captain began to speak.

At first Petey could hardly believe the man's words. A colony? The pirates were starting a colony? And they wanted the women to join them as wives? When the Pirate Lord had taken the ship and said they wanted wives, Petey had thought it some wicked joke. But apparently the bastard meant it.

Pirates settling down? Who'd have thought it? Pirates generally loved their gold too much to settle anywhere. But the other pirates behaved as if this was no news to them. Indeed, Petey could see them looking the women over already, trying to decide which ones they wanted.

A shiver passed through him. His little Ann would be taken by one of them. Nay, that couldn't be! If Petey was one of the pirates now, he'd be allowed a wife as well, wouldn't he? And he would fight any man for Ann.

After that, Petey only listened with half a mind to the conditions that the captain had placed upon the courtship—that the elderly women would be exempt and the children would go with their mothers. All Petey could think of was Ann . . . how sweet it would be to have her to wife . . . how grateful she'd be to him for saving her from these pirates . . . how much he wanted to kiss her.

His pleasant musings were abruptly shattered when the first mate called out, "And what of the earl's sister, captain? Must she choose a husband as well? Or are we to assume she's already taken?"

Amidst the chuckles of the pirates, Miss Willis stared ahead in stony silence, her cheeks red as a dawn sky. Petey held his breath, waiting for the pirate captain's answer.

Captain Gideon cast his first mate a quelling glance. "You may not assume anything, Mr. Kent. And yes, she'll choose a husband like the rest."

A shiver of horror snaked through Petey. The bloomin' blighter! Force Miss Willis to marry one of these pirates? But that was unthinkable! Not a lady like her!

All his dreams of marrying Ann vanished. If Miss Willis was included in the women to be courted, Petey had only one choice: he must do his duty by her. He'd have to marry her—or at least pretend to marry her—to protect her from those other bounders until he could restore her to her brother safely.

Oh, but Ann—

Petey sternly scolded himself. Ann was a pretty little thing, to be sure, but his duty must come first. He couldn't let his family down by ignoring Miss Willis's welfare.

Captain Gideon was scowling now, as if the topic of Miss Willis's future husband didn't sit well with him either. But he continued speaking, his voice even and cold. "Now that you know the situation, boys, I expect you to behave with discretion. We want to start a colony, not a bawdy house. You'll treat the women with respect or you'll answer to me for it."

Miss Willis glanced at him, surprise on her face, but he ignored her. "Barring any bad weather, we should reach the island in two days. Until then, your duties will remain the same as usual, but you may visit with the women during your free time. See that you don't neglect your duties to do your courting."

His gaze fell on the mass of uniformed women that split the crowd of pirates in half, like a pretty ribbon tied to a black post. "The women will be allowed freedom of the ship as long as they don't interfere with the running of it. But at night they'll be locked in the hold and a guard posted in case any of you think to have the wedding night before the wedding."

Some of the men grumbled, but that quickly subsided when their captain frowned at them. Then he looked over the crowd, his gaze stopping on the man beside Petey. "Silas, I'm charging you with finding out what skills the women have. And make a list of what tools they'll need for sewing and such. Although we'd best steer clear of Santiago for a while, once we've reached Atlantis, I may send a few men back to one of the other Cape Verde islands for additional supplies."

"The women already have the necessary tools for sewing," Miss Willis broke in. She'd been quiet all this while, so the sound of her firm but gentle voice after the captain's harsh, commanding one came as quite a shock. "They were given implements and some cloth aboard the *Chastity*, and I believe most of them brought them aboard the *Satyr*."

The captain turned to her as if he'd noticed her standing there for the first time. There was no mistaking his dislike at having his speech interrupted. "Thank you for your informative report, Miss Willis," he said dryly. "Is there anything else you'd like to add?"

Under the force of his gaze, she colored, but stood her ground. "Well, yes, there is. If you don't object, Captain, I'd like to continue with the reading and writing lessons I've been giving the women." When Captain Horn raised an eyebrow, she hurriedly added, "Any of the men who'd like to join us may do so."

That brought a loud chorus of laughter from the pirates, and for a moment, Petey thought he saw the captain himself smile. But when the Pirate Lord turned back to his men, it was gone. "You heard what Miss Willis said, boys. You may join the ladies for schooling, if you like. But only when you're not on watch." He cast a long, hard glance over the crew, then added, "You're dismissed. Behave yourselves."

As the crew dispersed, Petey waited on his perch, since he couldn't get back to sanding the deck until it was cleared. While he waited, he watched the captain, whose eyes were on Miss Willis. She seemed oblivious to the fact that the captain followed her every move. But others noticed.

"No matter what the cap'n says, he wants that girl for himself," Silas said a few feet away from Petey.

Petey stole a glance at Barnaby, who looked skeptical.

"I'm not so sure of that," Barnaby said. "She's an English noblewoman, and you know how he feels about them."

"I don't care if she's a damned Hottentot from the South Seas. Didn't you see the way the man looked at her? Like he hadn't had a good meal in two weeks and she was a prime bit of beef." Silas tapped the tip of his pipe against his teeth. "Aye, he wants her all right. The trick will be gettin' her to choose him."

"That should be no problem. Any woman Gideon wants, he gets. If indeed he wants her, he'll have her begging him to marry her before the week is out, mark my words."

Petey turned to gape at the two men in horror. It was one thing to try to protect Miss Willis from one of the other pirates by marrying her. But to go against the Pirate Lord? God help him, that would be like putting his mouth in the maw of a shark!

Suddenly Barnaby seemed to feel Petey's eyes on him. He fixed Petey with a stern gaze. "What are you looking at, mate? Go on with you! Get to your duties!"

"Aye, aye, sir," Petey mumbled. He walked toward where he'd left the deck bucket and picked up the stone the sailors called a "prayer book," a palm-sized soft stone used for sanding the hard-to-reach spots of the deck. But as he dropped to his knees and began scrubbing the teak boards with wet sand, he couldn't stop thinking about Miss Willis. He had to find a way to speak to her. He had to warn her to tread carefully around the captain.

Because if she weren't very careful, Petey might find himself having to do something drastic to protect her from the Pirate Lord. And he didn't relish having a set-to with that monster of an American sea captain. Not one little bit.

Chapter 8

A sea-man is a cock o' the game,
young maidens find it true,
We never are so much to blame
to let them want their due.

—JOHN PLAYFORD
"THE JOVIAL MARRINER"

The sun edged down onto the horizon like a god's golden pendant lowering into the shimmering sea. Sara leaned on the rail and stared at its rippled image in the water, wishing she could just walk along that fiery path until she reached England and the safety of home. She hated to admit it, but Jordan had been right. This trip had been ill-fated from the beginning.

And that wretched captain only made matters worse. Oh, how he must have laughed after she'd left his cabin, after she'd succumbed to his kisses! How he must have reveled over her weakness! Instead of arguing on the women's behalf, she'd let him take all sorts of scandalous liberties with her. He'd distracted her quite effectively, no doubt for his own nefarious purposes.

It certainly wasn't because of any real attraction. He'd made that quite clear, both in his cabin and later, when he'd publicly spurned her before all his men, acting as if she were some . . . some piece of pirate booty to be doled out as he saw fit! Her cheeks grew hot just remembering it. He'd made her melt, then offered to hand her off to the first man who asked. The wretch! The scoundrel! She hated him!

"Miss Willis," said a voice behind her. She turned to find Louisa threading her way through the women who were seated everywhere on deck, eating their supper. With a plate of stewed beef and ship's biscuits balanced in one hand and a cup of water flavored with whisky in the other, Louisa approached her.

"You really must eat," Louisa said in the governess tone she was wont to use. She held out the plate. "You must keep up your strength."

"For what?" Sara sighed, though she took the cup. "It does no good to fight them, you know. They'll do what they want with us, regardless of what we say."

"That's not true." Setting the plate on a nearby box, Louisa picked up a biscuit and closed the fingers of Sara's free hand around it. "You've already convinced them to give us a choice. That's more than we had before."

"Some choice." In a burst of defiance, she crumbled the biscuit into the sea. She had no appetite, not after her encounter with that dreadful pirate captain. When she spoke again, her tone was edged with pique. "We can marry an old pirate or a young one, a daring one or a dull one, but still we must marry pirates and live out our days on some remote island where we may never again see our families . . ." Her voice broke at the thought of being separated from Jordan for the rest of her life.

No matter what she'd said to Gideon, she knew Jordan would never find her. How could he? He'd search in all the wrong places, never dreaming that the pirates were on an island. A tear slipped from her eye, and she brushed it away. She never cried. She was too practical for that. But tonight she felt very unpractical . . . and very weepy.

With a little murmur of understanding, Louisa

squeezed her arm. "There, there, now. Don't fret yourself over it. It'll be all right. You'll see."

A new, gruffer voice sounded beside Louisa. "If the lady ain't gonna eat her dinner, then she should give it to one o' the others and not waste it by throwin' it in the sea."

Sara and Louisa turned to find the peg-legged cook scowling at them. In one hand he held a pitcher of water and in the other the knobbed and worn stick he used as a cane. But the mottled brown and gray beard covering half his face gave him a fierce appearance that negated any hint of weakness one might take from the presence of a cane.

Another pirate to plague them. Sara was sorely weary of them, and she was certainly not in the mood to fight anymore tonight.

Apparently Louisa's mood was quite different, however, for she drew herself up and waggled her finger at him. "How dare you give the poor woman trouble over those nasty biscuits! If you made biscuits worth eating, sir, perhaps she wouldn't throw them to the fish!"

He blinked his eyes in astonishment. "Biscuits worth eating?" His voice rose. "Biscuits worth eating? I'll have you know, madam, that I bake the best biscuit on the high seas!"

"That's not saying much, considering that ship's biscuits are notoriously awful."

"It's all right, Louisa, you needn't defend me—" Sara began.

Louisa just ignored her. "Those biscuits were so hard, I could scarcely choke them down. As for that stew—"

"Look here, you disrespectful harpy," the cook said, punctuating his words with loud taps of his cane, "there ain't nothin' wrong with Silas Drummond's stew, and I defy any man—or woman—to make a better one!"

"As you wish. I suppose it *would* be better if I took over the cooking." Louisa lifted the hem of the flimsy apron assigned to the women as part of their convict costume. "Of course, I'll need a better apron and a decent cap, but I'm sure we can drum one up somewhere . . . oh, and if you'd be so good as to show me where the stores are kept—"

"I will not!" Silas's expression was an amusing mix of fury and astonishment.

To Sara's surprise, Louisa paid no attention to his anger. "Then how can I prepare tomorrow's dinner?"

"You ain't preparin' tomorrow's dinner!" he roared. "My kitchen ain't for the likes of an uppish female who probably don't even know how to leech the salt out o' beef!"

Sara rested her elbow on the rail, watching the interchange in silent amusement now that she was sure Louisa could take care of herself.

"How hard can it be to cook a decent meal? I've seen some of the best cooks in the world prepare dinner." In an aside to Sara, she added, "I was employed by the Duke of Dorchester for a time, you know. He had *two* French chefs in his employ. I should think I learned a thing or two from them."

"French chefs? English dukes?" Silas sputtered. "You ain't gettin' within a yardarm's length of my kitchen, you . . . you . . ."

"My name is Louisa Yarrow, but you may call me Miss Yarrow," Louisa said primly.

He looked so surprised by this condescending statement that Sara had to disguise her urge to laugh with a fit of coughing.

"It don't matter what I call you or what you call yerself," he growled, as he stepped near enough to Louisa to glower down at her. A sudden trough made the ship lurch forward, but while Sara and Louisa had to grab for the rail to keep their balance, he somehow managed to stay perfectly upright as if his feet had been welded to the deck. "You ain't gettin' near my kitchen, woman. I got enough to worry about, havin' to feed all these women. I don't need a troublemaker underfoot."

"Perhaps Louisa could help you just a little," Sara interjected. She had to admit that the stew didn't look or smell very palatable, and a quick glance around the deck showed that the women weren't eating their meals with any great enthusiasm, despite their hunger.

"That's a capital idea," said a new voice. Sara turned to find the English first mate standing at her elbow, smoking a cheroot. "Why not let the women help with the meals? God knows we could use a decent one for a change."

Silas scowled at the first mate. "You're takin' the side o' that woman? Well, I had enough o' your complaints. And hers." He turned and stomped away. "See if either o' you gets any more o' what I cook. I'll let this harpy serve you a thinnish French broth and see how you like it. You'll be beggin' for more of me cookin' in a week. Damned English fools. I swear . . ."

He continued to mutter under his breath as he picked his way between the women seated on the deck. But when Louisa started to go after him, Barnaby stayed her with one hand.

"Don't worry about him. He's an old curmudgeon who hates women. I've heard tell it's because he can't satisfy one in bed, if you know what I mean. Some sort of old war injury." Barnaby cast Louisa an ingratiating smile that showed fine white teeth. "If it's a husband you're looking for, you'd be better off with me. All my parts are in fine working order."

A chilly smile touched Louisa's lips as she snatched her arm away. "Are they, indeed? Then I suggest you find a wife who'd be happy to oil and pamper them and keep them in good working order. I'm afraid I'd be more likely to smash them to bits." With that, she lifted her skirts and hurried after Silas, leaving Barnaby to gape after her as he instinctively jerked his legs together.

"She's a cold fish, isn't she?" he commented as he turned back to Sara.

"Not exactly. She just doesn't like men very much."

"Ah," Barnaby said as if he understood.

But his frown showed that he didn't. How could he? He'd never been at the mercy of a man, never had his life utterly destroyed by the opposite sex. No man who hadn't also been tormented simply because of his sex could understand Louisa's hatred.

"And what about you?" he asked. "Do you hate men, too?"

Unfortunately, no, she thought, remembering the mortifying way she'd responded to Gideon's kiss. "Only those men who try to take away my freedom."

The sun had finally set, and the gray dusk heightened the dark intensity of Barnaby's black eyes as he scrutinized her. "You mean men like our captain?"

The trace of irony in his tone made her color. Everyone had just assumed she would swoon at their illustrious captain's feet. And if they knew even half the truth—that she'd practically done so—they would laugh at her. Dropping her gaze, she skimmed her fingers over the smooth sheen of the brass rail in front of her. "Yes, him. Certainly. He had no right to take us against our will."

Barnaby leaned back as he drew languidly on his cheroot. "Look around you, Miss Willis. Does it appear to you as if your convict women object to being freed from that ship?"

Turning around, she scanned the crowd of women. Someone had already lit the lanterns, illuminating little patches of women and men who were laughing and talking. The women were assessing the men, some covertly, others with more boldness. Under the protective overhang of some rigging, a youthful pirate slid his arm around a sweet-faced convict, who not only allowed it, but gazed up at him with a shy smile. Even the older woman who'd spoken up this afternoon about her limited chances of finding a husband was being courted by a hoary-headed sailor, one of the few older men on Captain Horn's ship.

Everywhere men hovered over the women like bees around a honey hive. Though they didn't seem to be overly aggressive or rude, there was a definite arrogance in the way they pursued the women, as if sure of being accepted. And many of the women weren't exactly discouraging them.

She sighed. "I suppose the women aren't entirely angry over the situation."

"Aren't entirely angry?" He chuckled. "I'd say they're quite content."

Suddenly there was a loud crack from across the deck and a shrill, high-pitched voice said, "Don't touch me, you filthy pirate! I don't have to suffer your grabbing hands just yet!"

Sara and Barnaby turned to see a man holding his reddened cheek as a comely young woman flounced off in a huff.

"Not all of them are content, sir." The wind blew a lock of hair into Sara's eyes, and she thrust it aside. "Some of them are merely resigned to their fate. They know they have no choice. Since they're used to accepting whatever hand life has dealt them, they'll make the best of it. But I'd truly hoped life would deal them a better one."

With that she walked away, unable to bear any more such discussions. Barnaby was no different from his master. He couldn't see the grim realities of the situation. No matter what she said, both men would continue to think that they had bestowed a great favor on the women by taking them captive.

Feeling even more morose than before, she rounded the end of the forward house headed for the fore hatch, only to be accosted by a sailor who stepped out of the shadows. Her instant spurt of fear turned to relief when she saw it was Petey.

"Come, miss, we got to talk," he muttered, pulling her toward the fore hatch.

"We certainly do." She followed him below decks,

casting a wary glance about her to make sure no one saw them. She waited until they'd climbed down into the 'tween decks to ask the question that had bothered her ever since she'd seen him coming out of the captain's cabin. "I suppose you sneaked aboard when they brought us on, but why haven't they killed you?"

"Cap'n decided he had a use for me." He lit the lantern in the 'tween decks, and as he turned back to her, the dull gold light reflected the grim look on his face. "They've made me one of the crew, but that don't mean I can do what I want. There's plenty of eyes watchin' me all the time. So we gotta make this fast."

"I guess you heard what Captain Horn said. That we must choose husbands."

He nodded, his hazel eyes darkening. "I heard. And I got a plan for that. When the time comes for you and the women to choose, you'd best choose me."

The idea took her by surprise. Marry Petey? Though she knew his suggestion was designed to protect her, she wasn't sure she liked it. A lifetime on a remote island would be bad enough, but a lifetime with a man she barely knew . . .

Of course, she didn't know any of these men, did she? But one of them might want her for herself instead of marrying her out of some sense of duty. "I don't know, Petey—"

"Hear me out. If you marry me, we won't have to be truly married, if you know what I mean." His reddening ears told her exactly what he meant. "That'll make things easier for you once we return to England. His lordship won't have no trouble gettin' the marriage annulled after we're back as long as we don't . . . er . . . you know."

"Yes, I know." Her eyes narrowed. "But surely you don't think we'll ever be able to—" Two of the pirates passed so close that she could hear them laughing overhead. She froze until they moved away from the open hatch, then leaned her head closer to Petey's. "Surely you don't think we'll get the chance to escape."

"We might. I know a bit about navigation and such. If this island lies close to any other islands, I can row us to one that's inhabited."

With a sigh, she twisted the chain of her locket around her finger. "Forgive me, Petey, but that doesn't sound very promising."

"I suppose not. But remember, the cap'n also said something about returning to the Cape Verde Islands for supplies. 'Tis possible we could stow away on that trip and take passage to England from there. Don't you worry, I'll think of some way to get us out of here and back home." His voice grew firm. "In the meantime, you'd best stay clear of the Pirate Lord."

"Stop calling him that. It gives him importance beyond his worth."

He grabbed her arm. "Listen to me, Miss Willis. Don't be fooled because the cap'n is lettin' the women make a choice. That one's trouble. And he's got his eye on you. That's why you need somebody else to court you, somebody safe, to keep him from gettin' his hooks in you."

A strange tremor passed through her at Petey's words. She told herself it was fear. After all, only a witless fool would be flattered by the attentions of a merciless pirate. And besides, Petey was wrong. "He doesn't have his eye on me. Didn't you hear what he said this afternoon before all the pirates?"

Petey scowled. "I know what he said, but I heard the men talkin' and they're all layin' odds that he'll have you in his bed before the week is out."

She colored. "Nonsense. You have nothing to worry about. I'd die before I let that monster put his hands on me again."

"Again?" Petey's fingers tightened on her arm. "What did he do to you while you were in his cabin? He didn't hurt you, did he?"

Cursing her slip of tongue, she said, "Of course not.

We had some words, that's all. But I don't think he likes me very much, and I despise him. So you needn't worry. He'll never succeed in marrying me *or* seducing me."

At least she hoped he didn't. She wasn't entirely sure she could resist him if he did. That thought gave her pause. "Perhaps you're right, Petey. Perhaps I should choose you as husband."

"It's for the best, miss, you'll see. But don't you worry, one way or the other, I'll get you out of this mess."

"I hope so," she whispered. "I truly hope so."

Chapter 9

I hope, while Women *have any spirit left, they will exert it all in showing how worthy they are of better usage, by not submitting tamely to such misplaced arrogance [from men].*

—''Sophia'' (believed to be Lady Mary Wortley Montagu) *Woman not Inferior to Man*

Night had just fallen when Gideon emerged from his cabin and sauntered out on deck. It was a clear, balmy night, with the sky dripping diamond stars over the ship like a king's jewel-studded cloak. He filled his lungs with the tangy salt air. He would miss this: the quiet nights aboard the *Satyr*, the creak of timbers, the slap of waves against the seasoned oak hull. Although in the future he and his men might occasionally sail to the Cape Verde Islands for supplies, they would no longer spend long weeks at sea under the brilliant sky.

He made a quick survey of the sailors on watch, then shoved his hands into his pockets and strolled the deck. A vague dissatisfaction nipped at him, destroying the pleasure he usually took in these nights at sea.

But then, he'd felt that dissatisfaction often lately.

That's why he'd formed his drastic plan for Atlantis, why he'd decided to give up piracy.

The sea chases, the thrill of taking gold from the noblemen he detested . . . none of it was enough anymore, and certainly not when he knew what would happen if he continued it. Piracy always brought its followers to an early death. There was no such thing as an old pirate.

Maybe some men didn't care about dying young, maybe some men wanted to leave this world in a blaze of excitement, but he wasn't one of them. He intended to live a long, full life and not end it on the gallows. Or on a ship, for that matter.

He'd given enough of his life to the sea, twenty-one years in all. He'd been only twelve when his cursed father had finally drunk himself to death, leaving his only child penniless, friendless, and alone. So when, after a year of fighting off hunger and looking for work, he'd been noticed by a sea captain who'd taken pity on him and offered him a position as cabin boy, he'd jumped at the chance.

Later, when the American government had commissioned privateers to harass the English, he'd eagerly sunk all the money he'd saved into purchasing a sloop. It had seemed as good a way as any to survive. Before long, he'd done well enough to exchange the sloop for a pinnace, and the pinnace for the *Satyr*.

Throughout those years, he'd looked for only two traits in his crewmen: that they have no wives or families, so their courage would be the fiercer because they had nothing to lose; and that they hate the British as much as he did.

His careful hiring had proved advantageous, for they'd served him well. When the war had ended, and the same American officials who'd prompted them to steal from the English now expected him and his crew to throw down their arms and make peace with them, he and his men had chosen a third path—piracy.

They'd had a good run of it, to be sure. But they'd

begun to tire of a sailor's uncertain and lonely life, and he more than any of them. To his surprise, the gold and jewels he'd stolen from his enemy didn't satisfy him. Even tormenting the lordlings had lost its appeal. He wanted more—a real future, not just a series of voyages and captures. He wanted to build something that was his, something good and solid. He could do that on Atlantis. They could all do that on Atlantis.

He scanned the milling crowd, noting that the men who weren't on watch were well on their way to gaining the women's affections. Soon he'd have to call Barnaby to bring the women below and lock them in, but just now he wanted to savor this moment. He'd accomplished his goal. He'd found women for his men. And they would all soon be working together for a common good.

So why did he feel so restless, so dissatisfied, when he should be rejoicing in his success? Why did he have this nagging fear that he'd handled the acquisition of the convict women badly?

Because of that blasted Englishwoman. Sara had planted these foolish doubts in his mind. Sara, with the caramel-tinted eyes and the soft, yielding body . . . Sara, who could make a man lust with only a toss of her copper hair. His loins tightened, and he groaned. No woman had ever affected him quite this way before. Like any sailor, he'd had his dalliances, yet no sloe-eyed island beauty had ever sent his blood racing like this at just the thought of her.

But it didn't matter what Sara did to his blood . . . or anything else, he told himself with a grimace. There was more to marriage than passion. His parents had proved that.

The last thing he wanted was to let his cock lead him to take up with some pampered daughter of an earl— even an adopted one. Her kind of woman was never satisfied with what a man could give her. Her kind of woman never gave a man a moment's peace.

Moving to the rail, he leaned against it with his back to the sea. No, Sara Willis wasn't for him. He'd have to look elsewhere among this crowd for a wife. With a curious distraction, he watched the dance of courtship playing itself out before him, wondering if he could indeed throw himself into it with the enthusiasm of his men. He ought to. That was what he needed—another woman, a different woman to pursue, one who more closely fitted his idea of a wife.

He shoved his hands in his pockets, then winced when his fingers touched a wadded up cloth. Sara's cap. The one he'd taken from her. The one that had covered her glorious mass of fine, silky hair.

With an oath, he jerked it out of his pocket and tossed it into the sea. He never should have taken down her hair. He certainly shouldn't have kissed her. His attraction to her was about as unwise as sailing directly into the wind, and kissing her had only sharpened his desire. Confound it, she was a witch to occupy his thoughts so constantly even when she wasn't in sight!

Wasn't in sight? He scanned the crowd uneasily. Indeed, she wasn't in sight. Not anywhere. Where was she? At the other end of the ship? Below decks with one of his men? That brought a scowl to his face.

While he was still looking for Sara, another woman approached him, a buxom blond whose eyes skimmed his flanks like a dock official inspecting a ship. She took his hand and put it on her waist with a coy glance from heavy-lidded eyes. "Well, well, if it isn't our good captain, the man who saved us from that wretched prison ship. You're lookin' for yer own woman to mate with, aren't you? And Queenie's just the woman for that." Tugging his hand up to rest on one of her ample breasts, she leaned into his palm with a pouting smile. "I've got everythin' a man like you could want, and more besides."

A frown of distaste crossed his brow as he jerked his hand from her breast. "Sorry, Queenie, I've got other things on my mind tonight." It was clear what this woman had been imprisoned for, and he was in no mood to put up with such solicitations. Sara mightn't be the woman for him, but neither was Queenie.

Unfortunately, Queenie didn't seem to realize that. Quick as lightning, she slid her hand to cover the bulge in his breeches created by his thoughts of Sara. "Ooh, guv'nor," she cooed, her accent thickening to a more cockney one as she rubbed him with practiced fingers, "y're lyin' through yer teeth. Y're horn-mad, you are, and I know just how to soothe that sort of madness."

He didn't even crack a smile at what was probably an unintentional pun on his name. Instead, he shoved her hand away from his groin. "Every man on this ship is horn-mad tonight, Queenie. Go find one of them to entice. I told you, I'm not interested."

She looked insulted. "You savin' it for somebody else, then?" When he lifted one eyebrow, a mulish expression crossed her face. "You savin' it for 'milady'? 'Cause if you are, y're wastin' yer time. She thinks herself too good for the likes of me and you. She'll not satisfy that burnin' in your breeches, I warrant you that."

The fact that she was probably right didn't make her words sit any easier. He paused a moment to fix her with his most blistering look, the one that sent his men scurrying for cover. The blood drained from her face.

"Thank you for the warning about Miss Willis," he said, his words dripping with sarcasm. "But I don't take advice from whores."

That was enough to send her flouncing off in a huff. But not enough to gain him solitude, for another woman appeared to take her place. *This could get tedious*, he thought. When he'd given the women a choice, he hadn't thought they'd be running after him with such enthusiasm. He started to walk away, but the woman called out to him.

"Cap'n Horn, sir! I brought you your supper!" When he halted and turned toward her, she thrust a plate loaded with food at him. "Mr. Drummond told me to bring you this."

She wouldn't look at him, and he suddenly realized this wasn't a task she'd wanted to perform. He should've known that not all the women were of Queenie's insolent stamp, but he was unused to having a woman do things for him, so he'd overreacted.

Relaxing, he took the plate from her. "Thanks. I must admit I'm hungry." She seemed at a loss for words, and now that she was standing nearer, he could see the fear on her face. "What's your name?"

"Ann Morris, sir." Her eyes flitted from him to the other women. Clearly she wanted to be anywhere but here talking to him, and for some reason that made him determined to allay her fears.

"Morris. That's a Welsh name, isn't it?"

Her eyes went wide. Then she nodded. "From Carmarthenshire, sir."

He smiled. "You needn't keep calling me 'sir,' you know. I'm no better than you or any of the other women."

"Yes, sir. I-I mean, yes."

He speared some meat on his fork and brought it to his mouth. It was tough and tasteless as usual, but he was hungry, and it was all Silas was capable of. As Ann fidgeted and shifted her stance as if preparing to dart off, he asked, "Have you eaten?"

Her head bobbed furiously up and down, making her curls jiggle. He flashed her a smile. That seemed to ease her fears some, for she stopped fidgeting. Between bites of biscuit and stew, he looked her over. She was a little thing, with fetching eyes of a color indeterminable in the lantern light and dark, curly hair cropped short about the ears, probably by the prison authorities. If it hadn't been for her womanly figure, he might have thought her only a child.

This was the sort of woman he ought to consider as a wife. She was pretty and personable. She probably knew how to provide those feminine comforts he'd never had in his life. Once she got past her fear of him, she'd be a sweet and pleasing companion.

A pity the only feeling she brought out in him was paternal. He sighed. "Are you and the women comfortable? Is everything below decks to your satisfaction?"

Her face brightened, making her look even more angelic. "Oh, yes, it's all very nice. Much nicer than on the *Chastity.*"

He sopped up some gravy with his biscuit. "If you don't mind my asking, how did you come to be on the *Chastity?*"

A sorrowful look crossed her face. She perched her small frame on a nearby box with a sigh. "I was sent to prison for stealing."

He suppressed his urge to laugh. "Stealing? You?" Somehow he couldn't imagine this timid little creature stealing anything.

But she nodded. "My ma was ailin', you see, and I needed medicines for her, but I couldn't afford to buy them. The little blunt I got from workin' at the millinery shop weren't even enough to keep me and Ma fed. So one day when I was passin' the open door to a cottage and nobody was about, I went in and . . . and saw a silver pot and took it."

Her eyes clouded over. "It was dreadful wrong, I know. I just thought if I could sell it, I could buy the cures for ma." She shook her head. "But the shopkeeper I tried to sell it to . . . he'd seen the pot before. He knowed then that I'd took it, and he . . . he gave me over to the magistrate."

Sympathy for the poor Welsh girl swelled within him. He couldn't keep the anger out of his voice. "And the English had you transported for that? For one silver pot?"

"Yes, sir. My ma—" Her voice broke. "My ma was so ashamed of me. She wouldn't own me, even to the day she died, because I'd ended in the gaol. And she was right. It was wrong what I done. It was very wrong." She turned her face away so that her profile was to him, and the lantern light flickered off her dampening cheeks.

She was crying. Poor little thing, she was crying. He laid his hand on her shoulder. "You did what you had to, Ann, and you weren't treated fairly. You weren't wrong. Your country was wrong. There's something badly lacking in a country where an old woman can't get medicine, and no one will help."

"I think so, too." She took a few shuddering breaths. "That's why I don't mind so much that you're takin' us off to an island. Things can be better there, if it's done right."

If it's done right. A twinge of guilt hit him. Sara didn't think he was doing it right. Not at all. She thought he was being officious and uncaring. She thought he was taking advantage of young innocents like Ann.

Disturbed by that thought and the confusing emotions it stirred in him, he took his hand from her shoulder and stared out at the ocean. "So you don't mind having to marry one of my men?"

She rubbed her tears away with one small fist. "Not now that Petey's here."

"Petey?"

He couldn't tell for certain in the lantern light, but he thought she blushed. "Peter Hargraves. You know, the sailor you took from the *Chastity*."

Not bothering to correct her false impression, he said, "Ah, yes."

She scanned the deck, then pointed toward the forward house. "There he is now, with Miss Willis."

His gaze swung instantly toward where she pointed. It was indeed the crewman from the *Chastity*, and Sara was at his side.

Gideon's eyes narrowed. So that's where she'd been, off talking to Hargraves. What was the man to her? And what was she plotting with him? He had no doubt she was plotting something; Sara seemed to spend all her time thinking of ways to thwart him.

He looked down at Ann and noticed she was watching Hargraves as closely as he'd watched Sara. Gesturing toward the couple, Gideon said, "Tell me something, Ann, what do you know about Petey?"

A shy smile touched her lips. "Oh, he's a fine man, he is. He kept watch over us on the *Chastity*."

Gideon ate more of his meal and watched the mysterious Petey head toward the foc'sle, leaving Sara to pick her way aft. "What do you mean?"

"He stood watch outside the cells every night. The cap'n ordered it. Petey kept an eye out for all of us." She ducked her head, but not before Gideon caught a glimpse of the hero worship in her eyes. "Especially me."

So Ann was infatuated with the little Englishman, was she? That's why she didn't mind marrying, and why she would never consider Gideon as a husband.

He didn't bother to examine the feeling of relief that swept him. He merely continued to eat. And watch Sara. "Why do you think he was talking to Miss Willis?"

Ann kicked her short legs back and forth against the box. "I don't know. Maybe because she looks out for us, too. Maybe they're talkin' about what to do once we reach the island."

Maybe, he thought. It wouldn't surprise him to find Sara enlisting the help of someone who'd already proved sympathetic toward the women. *Not that you gave her any other choice*, he thought. *Who else was she supposed to turn to for help?*

He scowled. Confound her. That woman had him doubting all his plans. And now she'd have Hargraves helping her.

"Did Miss Willis have anything to do with Hargraves's becoming the women's protector?" he asked.

Ann looked confused. "I don't think so. She didn't seem to know him any better than the rest of us."

"So she has no connection with Hargraves?"

"None that I know of."

He relaxed. At least he need not worry about that.

She cocked her head and stared up at him. "Why?"

"No reason." He'd finished his food now, and it was long past time for the women to be sent below. His men were getting rowdy, and soon some of them would make fools of themselves, or worse yet, accost the women more forcefully than they should, which wouldn't smooth relations any.

Handing Ann his empty plate, he said, "Forgive me, but I have some matters to attend to. Thank you for keeping me company."

She cast him a smile so brilliant that for a second, he almost envied scrawny Hargraves, the man who obviously had her affections. But the feeling didn't last. Although he wanted a sweet, quiet wife, Ann was just a bit too sweet and quiet for him.

Gideon crossed the deck to where Barnaby flirted with a bony-armed doxy and pulled him aside. "It's time to get the women below. Have Miss Willis help you." He scanned the deck for her, scowling when he saw her talking animatedly amid a large group of women. First Peter Hargraves, and now the women. Sara never stopped scheming, did she?

Barnaby had already started to walk away, but Gideon halted him. "Wait, I've changed my mind. Leave Miss Willis out of it. I'll take care of her."

"Oh?"

"I'm putting her in your cabin. You can bunk with Silas for the next couple of days."

"She won't like that."

Gideon flashed him a grim smile. "I don't care what she likes. If she spends her nights with the women, she'll cook up another rebellion. I want her where I can keep an eye on her."

A sly grin twisted Barnaby's lips. "That's the only reason for putting her in my cabin? The cabin right across from yours?''

"That's the only reason," Gideon snapped. Confound the English bastard. He was a buck of the first head, so he expected every man to be one. "I'm going to tell her now. Wait until I've got her inside, then send the women below."

"If you carry her off without a word of explanation, the women will want to know why. They look to her for help."

That was exactly the problem. "Tell them whatever you want about it, as long as it doesn't make them angry. But she's staying in your cabin regardless of what they think." With that, he strode away from his first mate.

For the hundredth time he cursed himself for succumbing to the whim that had made him take Sara aboard the *Satyr*. She'd been nothing but trouble from the moment she'd set foot on his ship.

The women scattered as he approached her, and he took that to be a bad sign. A bad sign indeed. "What are you plotting now?"

"Plotting?" she asked, her expression as innocent as a nun's.

But he knew better than to trust that expression. "Yes, with the women. You must've been plotting something, or they wouldn't have run off when I approached."

She tossed her head back, and the wind tugged a few feathery locks away from her face, putting her stubborn features in high relief. "We were merely discussing what time to meet for classes in the morning. They ran off because they're all terrified of you."

He could hardly argue with that, since he'd just witnessed Ann Morris's reaction to him. The thought that half the women feared him didn't lighten his mood. Hooking his thumbs in his belt, he cast Sara a cool glance. "Aren't you?"

Her eyes glittered in the lantern light, though he

couldn't help notice that her chin trembled. "I told you before. I don't fear anything, least of all you."

Stepping closer, he lowered his voice. "Really? Then you won't mind sleeping in the cabin across from mine."

Fear flashed in her face a second before she mastered it. "Wh-what do you mean?"

Pleased that he'd succeeded in ruffling her feathers, he took her arm and began leading her toward the quarterdeck. "You'll be spending your nights in Barnaby's cabin until we reach Atlantis Island." When she looked at him in horror, he added, "Don't worry, Barnaby will bunk with Silas. You'll have the cabin to yourself."

"But why?" She tried jerking her arm out of his grasp, and when he continued to propel her forward, she hissed, "I want to stay below with the rest of the women!"

"I know. You want to incite them to escape or rebel or engage in some other futile activity." He thrust her through the entrance to the cabin area under the quarterdeck, then released her. "Well, I won't have it. I run an orderly ship, and I won't have you wreaking havoc aboard. The men and women are getting along fine, and I'd rather keep it that way."

She whirled on him, mutiny showing in the set of her jaw and her fisted hands. "What do you intend to do? Imprison me in that cabin for the entire journey?"

"No. I just want you where I can see you, that's all." When her eyes flashed, he softened his tone. "You're free to go wherever you want during the day, to have your classes and such, but I don't want you closeted with the other women at night. Just call it a precautionary measure, and a mild one at that."

His words seemed to mollify her, for she relaxed her stance.

He took a few steps forward, then stopped in front of Barnaby's cabin. "Besides, you'll be far more comfortable in this cabin than you would below decks." He opened the door and gestured for her to enter. "See for yourself."

Keeping a wary eye on him, she slipped past him and into the cabin. He followed her inside, turning up the lamp so she could see better. Surprise, then pleasure suffused her face with color.

Barnaby's cabin was less comfortable than his, but not by much. Piracy had rewarded all of them well, evidenced by the wide bunk with its feather mattress, the full-length mirror that was testament to Barnaby's vanity, and the carved ebony wardrobe Barnaby had acquired in Africa.

Of course, Sara had few clothes to put in that wardrobe. He regretted that he'd never given her a chance to pack her trunks before he'd taken her aboard the *Satyr*. Doing something about the women's meager clothing would have to be the first order of business when they reached Atlantis.

"Will it do?" he asked as he folded his arms over his chest.

She turned to him. Her eyes grew shuttered and any signs of pleasure vanished from her face. "I suppose I can endure it."

As if he couldn't tell she liked it. He suppressed a smile. What a proud thing she was—it must be that noble blood running through her pure little veins. "Good. Then I'll leave you to your rest. I must make sure the other women are settled." He started to walk out.

"Gideon?"

At the sound of his Christian name on her lips, he froze. It felt so intimate, so sensual. He wanted to hear her use it again. He wanted to hear her murmur it in that low, throaty voice that—

Confound it, there he went again, thinking of her as a woman. A desirable, accessible woman. "Yes?" he said, more harshly than he'd intended.

"When we reach the island, what will the . . . um . . . sleeping arrangements be?" Though it clearly embarrassed her to ask, she didn't flinch when he fixed her with a narrowed gaze. Not even having considered the question until now, he didn't answer her immediately.

She lifted her chin just high enough to torment him with a tantalizing flash of long white throat. "Well?"

You'll sleep with me. The thought came instantly into his mind, and just as instantly he cursed himself for it. She wouldn't be sleeping anywhere near him on Atlantis if he had anything to say about it.

"The men will sleep on the ship and the women in our huts until the weddings." The men would grumble loudly about that, but it was the only solution he could think of at the moment.

She took a steadying breath. "And will I be allowed to . . . lodge with the other women?"

Casting her a long, meaningful look, he lowered his voice. "Only if you behave yourself."

A hint of her earlier willfulness glinted in her brown eyes. "You mean, only if I sit back and let you do as you wish with those women."

"Exactly."

She tipped her nose up high in the air. "In that case, I fear I shall never be able to behave myself."

"Then I'll have to respond accordingly, won't I? Even if it means keeping you in the cabin across from mine until the day of the weddings."

He waited until he saw the blush spread over her porcelain skin. Then, satisfied that he'd outraged her sufficiently to make her think twice the next time she wanted to cross him, he walked back to his cabin whistling.

Chapter 10

I'd a Bible in my hand,
By my father's great command,
And I sunk it in the sand
When I sail'd . . .

—ANONYMOUS
"BALLAD OF CAPTAIN KIDD"

Before the sun had fully risen the next morning, Sara was up. She took a few moments to perform her ablutions and throw her gown on over the shift she'd slept in, but there wasn't much she could do for herself with neither a brush nor fresh clothes. She did what she could, finger-combing her hair and scrubbing her face with sea water from the bucket left outside her door by some conscientious pirate. Then she hurried out of her cabin and onto the deck.

She needed to have a word with Petey. She wanted to tell him that if he found a chance to escape, he should do so even if he couldn't take her. But she had to find him first.

Just before they'd parted yesterday, he'd said he'd be on the early morning watch today. Maybe she could catch him alone before the rest of the ship awakened. She surveyed the deck, relieved to see that most of the pirates did seem to be still in their beds, and the few

126

who were on watch paid her little heed. But where was
Petey?

Perhaps they'd sent him up in the rigging as Captain
Rogers had often done. Shading her eyes against the
rising sun, she lifted her head and scanned the masts.

"Looking for someone?" a deep voice beside her said.

She jumped and whirled to face the intruder. Bother
it all, it was Gideon. Why wasn't he still in bed like the
rest of them?

Apparently he'd just performed his own morning ablutions, for his hair was wet and slicked back from his
forehead, with only the ends curling dry. His insolent
gold hoop earring winked in the early morning sun, as
if shouting his contempt for civilization. But far more
shocking was the absence of his shirt. Today he was
dressed like many of his men, with only a leather vest
to cover his upper torso.

She sucked in a breath. There was something so ap-
pallingly intimate about a man's nearly bare chest. His
was unfortunately quite broad and muscled, with just a
sprinkling of black hair that formed a ragged line beneath the loose leather ties of his vest and trailed down
to his golden belt buckle with its onyx inset. Clearly he
seldom wore a shirt, for his arms were tanned right up
to his shoulders, the skin so dark it almost blended in
with his nut-brown vest.

She realized she'd been staring only when he said, his
voice lower and huskier, "Who are you looking for?"

His words snapped her out of her terrible trance. "I
. . . I . . ." She thought furiously and said the only thing
that came to mind. "For you. I was looking for you."

Suspicion flashed in his sea-blue eyes. "In the rigging?"

"Yes. Why not?"

"Either you're very ignorant about what a captain's
duties are, or you're lying. Which is it?"

Ignoring the plummeting sensation in her stomach,
she forced a smile to her face. "Really, Gideon, you are

so suspicious. Last night you accused me of plotting behind your back, and this morning you accuse me of lying. Who else would I be looking for but you?"

Though his eyes bore into hers as if trying to ferret out the truth, she gave him her most innocent look.

He tucked his thumbs in his belt, his gaze still skeptical. "And why would you be looking for me?"

Good heavens, how was she to answer that? "Because . . . because I want to go below." Yes, that was a logical excuse. "I want to look in on the women and see about beginning our classes. I assume I need your permission for that, since you've posted a guard—"

"Don't you think it's a little early in the morning for school? Most of the women are probably still asleep."

It was clear from his raised eyebrows that he didn't believe her. Her heart sank. She wasn't proficient at lying, as Jordan had so loved to point out. Then again, she'd never before had such a desperate reason for it.

She turned away from him before her face revealed everything. "I hadn't thought of that. It *is* early. Perhaps I'll just take a turn around the deck." In the process, she could look for Petey and shake off Gideon.

"That's an excellent idea," he said, almost as if he'd read her mind. "It's a lovely morning, and not yet hot. You don't mind if I walk with you, do you?"

Bother it all. The suspicious lout was determined not to let her out of his sight. She forced herself to meet his gaze. "Do I have a choice?"

"You always have a choice, Sara." His rumbling voice sent little frissons of alarm up and down her spine. For the first time that morning, he gave her a dazzling smile. It threw her completely out of kilter, reminding her of the way he'd held her yesterday in his cabin and kissed her with heart-stopping passion.

The wretch was far too handsome for words. Why did God have to give such good looks to the most abominable men? First Colonel Taylor, and now this pirate. It was damned unfair.

She groaned. The scoundrel even had her cursing. Where would it end?

He offered her his arm in a courtly gesture utterly at odds with his scandalous attire. She hesitated to take it. He had a tendency to bring the worst out in her, and right now she wanted to keep her wits about her.

On the other hand, she shouldn't provoke him when she had no reason other than her weakness to his charm; it would be better to pick her battles. There were bound to be plenty of them to pick.

Tucking her hand in the crook of his bare elbow, she let him lead her into a stroll along the deck. Her bare fingers touched the skin of his naked arm in an intimacy she wasn't used to. In London, whenever she'd taken a man's arm he'd worn layers of clothing and she'd worn gloves.

This was nothing like that. No indeed. She felt it every time he flexed a muscle, and his skin radiated a heat that warmed her fingers, then sneaked up her arm to warm the rest of her body. Oh, how she wished she hadn't left her gloves behind on the *Chastity*. At the moment, she would give a king's ransom for even the slightest protection that flimsy kid leather could provide.

They walked in silence a while. They passed a pirate polishing the brass fittings on the capstan, but just as Sara tried to get a peek at the man's face to see if it was Petey, Gideon tucked her hand more firmly into the crook of his elbow.

"Tell me something, Sara. What made a lady like you agree to sail with the *Chastity*? Why risk such a harsh and dangerous journey?"

"It wasn't dangerous until you and your greedy pirates came along," she grumbled.

"It would've gotten plenty dangerous, I assure you, if you'd stayed on the *Chastity* much longer. Many a ship has foundered in the rough waters of the Cape, including a convict ship or two. Which makes it even more curious that a woman of your class would endanger herself for a lot of poor unfortunates." His tone hardened. "Surely if you needed entertainment, there were plenty of balls and parties to occupy an earl's daughter."

Why, the very idea! How dared he make such assumptions when he knew nothing about her!

Releasing his arm, she stalked away to stand by the brass rail. She could feel him behind her, a large, disturbing presence. "I've been a reformer all my life, and so was my mother before me. Her motto was 'It only takes one caring soul to make things right,' and I've lived by that motto as best I could."

She curled her fingers about her locket. Her earliest memories were of taking baskets of food to the prisoners and learning to sew by making patchwork quilts for the poor.

"And your father?" Gideon asked.

"My real father died in debtor's prison when I was two years old."

There was a long, shocked silence behind her. When Gideon spoke, his voice was laced with genuine compassion. "I'm sorry."

She sucked in an uneven breath. "I never knew him, but my mother loved him very much. His death changed her. After that, all she wanted was to find some way to better the lives of those who suffered. Despite having little money and even less possibility for a future, she interceded for prisoners with the authorities and appealed to the House of Lords to change the unfair laws. That's how she met and married my stepfather, Lord Blackmore."

He came up to stand beside her, leaning on the rail with folded arms. "I'm sure he put a stop to all her good works."

She glanced at him, but he was staring across the sparkling waters of the ocean with eyes that were bitter, unforgiving.

"Actually, he didn't," she said softly. "He supported her reform efforts until the day she died." She ran her fingers idly over the shiny rail. "She took me everywhere she went and instilled in me a belief that people could rid the world of injustice if they made the effort. And I guess I just . . . followed in her footsteps." She ventured a smile. "Now that she and my stepfather have passed away, I feel a responsibility to carry on the family business, so to speak."

"The family business? Sending a young woman of quality off with a lot of thieves and murderers?"

Angling her body toward him, she met his dark gaze steadily. "You called them 'poor unfortunates' before."

For a moment he said nothing. Then a small smile touched his lips, muting the harsh planes of his face. "Aye, I did, didn't I? Still, I can't believe your stepbrother approved of such a dangerous project, even if it was for a worthy purpose."

"No, he didn't." Clouds scudded by, passing over the sun and casting a fleeting shadow along the length of the ship. "He tried to stop me from going. But it was futile, of course. I'm old enough to go where I want, with or without his permission, and he finally had to accept that I would do as I pleased."

Gideon's smile vanished as quickly as the sun had vanished behind the clouds. "You make a habit of that, don't you?" He propped one elbow on the rail and set his other hand on his hip as he faced her. "But let me warn you, Sara Willis. Your family might indulge your willfulness and your schemes, but I won't. Your whims won't be tolerated on my ship. Or my island."

"*Your* island? I thought it was a classless utopia that didn't belong to anyone."

A cold scowl darkened his features. "It is. But someone has to make the rules and enforce them, and my men have elected me to do it. That means we follow *my* rules on *my* island." He paused. "I know that's hard for your kind to accept. You're used to getting what you want as the Earl of Blackmore's daughter. But you'll adjust to it eventually, or learn the hard way what it means to flout authority."

She ignored his threat, but the way he'd said "the Earl of Blackmore's daughter" with such contempt roused her curiosity. He seemed to have an unreasonable hatred of nobility, and she suspected it didn't stem simply from his being an American.

"I wonder," she said, her tone even, "who taught *you* 'what it means to flout authority.' I wonder what terrible English nobleman taught you to hate 'my kind' so bitterly."

For a moment she thought she'd gone too far. His eyes blazed as he pushed away from the rail. Every muscle in his lean torso was tensed, like that of a beast preparing to pounce, and she stepped back from him instinctively, her hand going to her throat.

"Trust me," he finally said, in a low voice edged with anger, "you don't want to know."

Turning on his heel, he stalked off toward the foc'sle, leaving her to stand there shaking.

With a cursory glance at the compass, Gideon turned the wheel a quarter-turn. The rays of the afternoon sun slanted across the ship's stern, warming his head and back. Unfortunately, he was already too warm, thanks to Sara Willis.

He'd avoided her the whole day by giving Barnaby charge of her, but it hadn't stopped him from thinking about her. That business about her mother had taken him by surprise. A reforming woman married to an earl. Amazing.

Of course, it probably hadn't been as dramatic as Sara had implied. Her mother's reform efforts, and Sara's, too, must have been limited to protected situations. Gideon had held enough English earls at swordpoint to know that they were a cautious, haughty lot who didn't allow their female relatives to travel about getting their hands dirty with the concerns of the poor.

Still, Sara *had* taken passage aboard the *Chastity*. She *had* argued for the convict women without concern for herself. Now that he thought about it, the only reason she'd told him that her stepbrother was the earl was to try to convince him not to take the *Chastity*. That wasn't the act of a timid or fastidious woman.

A smile touched his lips. Sara was about as timid as a warship. A very pretty warship, with sleek lines from stem to stern, but still a warship, intended for battle. When it came to the women and their well-being, she fought like any well-gunned brig. Her courage was daunting . . . and sobering. In his more frustrated moments, she even had him questioning his decision to take the convict ship.

Then again, that confounded soldier in skirts would make any man question his actions. God help the man who married her. She'd hound him night and day and never give him a moment's peace.

Except when he was making love to her. He groaned. Why was it every time he thought of Sara he imagined her in bed, her slender arms outstretched, her eyes shrouded in mystery as she beckoned to him like a siren calling a sailor?

No, not to him. Some other man must wreck himself on that shore, because it wasn't going to be him.

But then some other man would have the delightful experience of kissing her, of touching her silken hair, of stroking her naked body— He let out a low oath as his body instantly responded. If he didn't stop thinking about her, he'd go insane. Or have to spend the rest of his life taking cold baths.

"Gideon, you'd best go below and hear what that woman's teaching in her school," said a voice behind him.

Gideon turned to find Barnaby standing at the top of the ladder to the quarterdeck, an amused look on his face. There was no need to ask who "that woman" was.

"Nothing she says or does would surprise me." Gideon faced the helm once more, putting his back to Barnaby. He wasn't about to go anywhere near Sara again, not the way he was feeling now. Let Barnaby deal with her today.

"Maybe not, but that doesn't mean it's nothing to worry about. You've got more schooling than I have, but isn't *Lysistrata* the play where the women refuse to have relations with their husbands until the men agree to stop going to war?"

With a groan, Gideon clenched the wheel. *Lysistrata* was among the many works of literature that his father had forced down his throat once he was old enough to read. "Yes. But don't try to tell me she's teaching them that. It's Greek, for God's sake. They wouldn't understand a word, even if she knew it well enough to recite it."

"She knows it well enough to give them a free translation, I assure you. When I left her she was telling them the story with great enthusiasm."

Barnaby reached for the helm as Gideon swung away from it with an oath. "I should never have taken her aboard," he grumbled as he strode for the ladder. "I should have sent her back to England gagged and bound!"

He ignored Barnaby's answering laugh and climbed down the ladder, then headed for the hatch to the hold. He'd put a stop to this now, before she incited the women to mutiny.

As he descended into the darkness, he heard Sara's animated voice speaking in slow, measured words. He halted on the steps. She was recounting the scene where the herald of Sparta tells the magistrate of Athens how desperate the men are to put an end to the women's coldness. He couldn't help but smile. She was reciting the passage without any reference to the many phallic puns in the original. Only Sara could transform *Lysistrata*, the bawdiest of Greek plays, into a chaste tale.

Wiping the smile from his face, he finished descending the steps and turned to find Sara standing at the far end of the hold, her back to him. A group of about thirty women and children surrounded her, their faces rapt as they listened intently to every word. Despite the cloying tropical heat in the windowless hold, only the children fidgeted, and their mothers hushed them whenever they ventured to do more than whisper their complaints.

He scowled. He'd had it right from the beginning—the blasted woman was nothing but trouble. How was it that she held an audience of hot, tired women in the palm of her hand with only a few words? These weren't the sort of women who were easily led. They'd all seen the nastiest side of the world.

Yet Sara told a tale in that rich, captivating voice of hers and they believed every word, ready to follow her into all kinds of trouble. Well, he wouldn't let that happen. Not again. Matters were progressing well, and she wouldn't spoil it with her continual attempts to foment unrest.

He strode forward, heedless of the murmuring that began among the women when they saw him. Then Sara turned, and her gaze met his. Instantly a guilty blush spread over her cheeks that told him all he needed to know about her intent.

"Good afternoon, ladies," he said in steely tones. "Class is over for today. Why don't you all go up on deck and get a little fresh air?"

When the women looked at Sara, she folded her hands primly in front of her and stared at him. "You have no right to dismiss my class, Captain Horn. Besides, we aren't yet finished. I was telling them a story—"

"I know. You were recounting *Lysistrata*."

Surprise flickered briefly in her eyes, but then she turned smug and looked down her aristocratic little nose at him. "Yes, *Lysistrata*," she said in a sweet voice that didn't fool him for one minute. "Surely you have no objection to my educating the women on the great works of literature, Captain Horn."

"None at all." He set his hands on his hips. "But I question your choice of material. Don't you think Aristophanes is a bit beyond the abilities of your pupils?"

He took great pleasure in the shock that passed over Sara's face before she caught herself. Ignoring the rustle of whispers among the women, she stood a little straighter. "As if you know anything at all about Aristophanes."

"I don't have to be an English lordling to know literature, Sara. I know all the blasted writers you English make so much of. Any one of them would have been a better choice for your charges than Aristophanes."

As she continued to glower at him unconvinced, he scoured his memory, searching through the hundreds of verse passages his English father had literally pounded into him. "You might have chosen Shakespeare's *The Taming of the Shrew*, for example—'Fie, fie! Unknit that threatening unkind brow. / And dart not scornful glances from those eyes / To wound thy lord, thy king, thy governor.'"

It had been a long time since he'd recited his father's favorite passage of Shakespeare, but the words were as fresh as if he'd learned them only yesterday. And if anyone knew how to use literature as a weapon, he did. His father had delighted in tormenting him with quotes about unrepentant children.

Sara gaped at him as the other women looked from him to her in confusion. "How . . . I mean . . . where could you possibly—"

"Never mind that. The point is, you're telling them the tale of *Lysistrata* when what you should be telling them is, 'Thy husband is thy lord, thy life, thy keeper. / Thy head, thy sovereign; one that cares for thee / And for thy maintenance commits his body / To painful labour both by sea and land.'"

Her surprise at his knowledge of Shakespeare seemed

to vanish as she recognized the passage he was quoting—the scene where Katherine accepts Petruchio as her lord and master before all her father's guests.

Sara's eyes glittered as she stepped from among the women and came nearer to him. "We are not your wives yet. And Shakespeare also said, 'Sigh no more, ladies, sigh no more / Men were deceivers ever / One foot on sea and one on shore / To one thing constant never.'"

"Ah, yes, *Much Ado About Nothing*. But even Beatrice changes her tune in the end, doesn't she? I believe it's Beatrice who says, 'Contempt, farewell! and maiden pride, adieu! / No glory lives behind the back of such. / And, Benedick, love on; I will requite thee, / Taming my wild heart to thy loving hand.'"

"She was tricked into saying that! She was forced to acknowledge him just as surely as you are forcing us!"

"Forcing you?" he shouted. "You don't know the meaning of force! I swear, if you—"

He broke off when he realized that the women were staring at him with eyes round and fearful. Sara was twisting his words to make him look like a monster. And succeeding, too, confound her.

"Out!" he roared at the women. "All of you! Get out now! I wish to speak to Miss Willis alone!"

He didn't have to say it twice. The women were tired, hot, and scared, and all they needed was his command to make them flee the hold in a whisper of skirts. Sara stared in woeful despair as the hold emptied. "Come back! He can't make you leave! He has no right—"

"Sorry, miss," the last of the women murmured, an anxious look on her face. Then she ducked her head and shooed her children toward the ladder.

When they were gone, she whirled on him, eyes flashing. "How dare you! You have no right to walk in here and just dismiss my pupils, you . . . you bully!"

The fact that her accusation had a ring of truth to it didn't make it any easier for him to stomach. In a few stiff strides he was beside her. "I'm tired of you calling me a bully, Sara. True, we took your ship, but since then, have you been mistreated? Have you been raped? Beaten? Locked in your cabin?"

"No, but I'm sure it's only a matter of time! And you *did* force yourself on me yesterday!"

Sara regretted her words the moment she said them. Yesterday's kiss was supposed to have been forgotten by both of them. She, of all people, shouldn't have mentioned it—especially in such an inflammatory manner.

His body tensed, the scar on his cheek standing out in vivid contrast to his tanned skin. Taking two quick steps forward, he caught her about the waist before she could get away. "Is that what happened yesterday? I forced myself on you, and you suffered my kisses? Strange, but I don't remember it like that." His voice lowered to a rough murmur. "I remember your mouth opening beneath mine. I remember you burying your hands in my hair and clinging to my neck. That's not how most women respond to force."

Furious at having her own weakness thrown in her face, she balled her hands into fists against his chest, but he jerked her against him, plastering her body against his taut thighs and lean waist. "You have no idea what force is, Sara, no idea at all. Maybe it's time someone showed you what real force is like."

"No-o-o . . ." she whispered as he bent his head to hers, but his mouth cut off any further protest.

His kiss was hard and relentless, his hold on her tight and unyielding. She squirmed and shoved at him, trying to free herself. With eyes glittering, he responded by setting her on top of the high trunk. Then he grabbed her wrists and twisted them behind her back, holding them with one large hand while he used the other to catch her jaw and hold her head still so he could kiss her again.

His was a punishing kiss, designed to make her hate him. And she did. At that moment, she truly did. He tried to force his tongue between her teeth, but she held them tightly clenched, determined not to let him win this battle. When she realized there was no way to escape his grip, she fought him the only way she could think of: she bit his lower lip. He drew his head back with a curse, but he didn't release her, even though she'd drawn blood.

"That, my dear Sara, is 'force,' " he ground out. "And you don't like it one bit, do you?"

She could have sworn she saw guilt in his eyes, but dismissed the notion at once. This . . . this brute was incapable of guilt!

Then his gaze softened in the lantern light of the windowless hold, and his tone altered subtly to a more soothing cadence. "Not that I blame you. I don't like it either. I don't want you fighting me."

His eyes seemed to drink in every line, every shade of her face. He softened his grip on her chin, then bracketed her throat lightly with his fingers. As she held her breath, he stroked his thumb and fingers down both sides of her neck. "No," he said, his voice growing husky. "I prefer to have you as you were yesterday . . . soft . . . lovely . . . yielding . . ."

The words themselves were a caress, and the way he looked at her mouth, as if it were a particularly juicy morsel, made shivers dance down her spine. She fought the traitorous sensations. "You can't have me at all."

"Can't I?" A knowing smile touched his lips. He lowered his head and she braced herself for another brutal kiss. Instead, he pressed his lips to the pulse on the side of her neck.

His lips were warm and buttery soft, nothing like they'd been a few moments ago. She tried to sit still, to pretend he wasn't heating up her blood and making her tremble like a needle on a compass. Whole surges of feeling were taking over her body. She couldn't seem to stop them. His mouth moved higher to tease her ear, then scattered kisses along a path to her cheek, his rough whiskers scraping her skin.

Ignoring the desire that trickled through her defenses, she dragged in a shaky breath and kept as aloof as any woman could when a man was treating her body to a thousand delicate caresses. But when he began bestowing kisses on every part of her face except her lips, she found herself actually wanting his mouth on hers, craving his kiss there.

And like the scoundrel he was, he seemed to know exactly what she wanted. He drew back for a moment, his gaze fastening on her trembling lips. Then he covered them with his.

It was soft. Stealthy. Devilishly exquisite. He traced the curve of her lips with his tongue, then boldly drove it into her mouth. She told herself to fight him like the proper earl's daughter she was. He had no business doing this to her.

But the fight had gone out of her. He felt so strong, so male. The ship's hold was his domain, dark and secretive and full of temptations. Even the rocking of the ship seemed to conspire with him, forcing her to lean into him to keep her balance on the trunk. He thrust his tongue into her trembling mouth with possessive strokes, and every one made her weak in the knees . . . and the belly and the loins. Good heavens, no one had ever made her feel this . . . this treacherous restlessness, this urge to respond to every kiss with an equally fervent one of her own.

By the time his hand trailed down her neck, then her breastbone to rest on one of her breasts, there was no resistance left in her. She did nothing. Nothing at all, except to arch into his kiss like a shameless wanton.

Gideon felt the change in her at once, especially when he released her hands, because instead of pushing him away, she slid them beneath his vest to grip his waist. Confound her, she was amazing. Why didn't she despise him for the cruel way he'd kissed her at first? He despised himself for it, so much that he'd kissed her again just to show her he wasn't the monster she believe him to be.

Now all he could think of was touching and fondling her. His body was thinking for him, and he couldn't seem to stop it.

Her response to him was so innocent, so untutored . . . so alluring. It made him want to tear off her clothes, lay her down on one of the bedrolls, and bury himself inside her. He groaned as her arms tightened about his waist. He had to control himself. He had to act with restraint, to finish his demonstration of how dramatically force differed from mutual satisfaction. Then he could put her away from him.

But later. Much later. After he'd touched her all over, explored the body that had kept him awake hour after hour last night.

The layers of cloth between his palm and her breast frustrated him. Without stopping to think, he tugged loose the lace modesty piece demurely filling out the neckline of her muslin gown. She tore her mouth from his, her eyes wide, uncertain. As the scrap of lace drifted to the floor, he caressed the upper swells of her breasts and waited for her maidenly resolve to kick in.

When it didn't, when she just sat there staring at him like a startled doe, he slid his hand inside her bodice to cup the soft weight of one breast. He had to touch her. He'd go mad if he didn't.

That brought a response. "You shouldn't . . . touch me . . . like that," she breathed, though her nipple tightened into a sweet little pebble beneath his hand.

"No, I shouldn't." He flattened his palm against her breast and kneaded it with slow, deft strokes. "But you want me to, don't you? You want me to." He'd make her admit she wanted him if it was the last thing he did. Never again would she accuse him of forcing her.

She turned her face away, but didn't stop him. "I don't . . . I mean, I . . . I don't want . . . I . . . I . . ."

He took her mouth again, silencing her as he buried his tongue in the sweet, hot warmth of her mouth the way he wanted to bury himself in another part of her. When he had her clinging to him, he reached behind to unhook her bodice enough so he could inch the sleeves of it off her shoulders. Impatiently he tugged loose the ties of her chemise, then drew the muslin down to bare her breasts.

Although she moaned low in her throat and jerked beneath his kiss, she didn't pull away. By God, she was sweet, the sweetest woman he'd ever tasted. As he stabbed his tongue restlessly between her luscious lips, he filled his hands with her breasts, his blood beating a fierce tattoo through his veins.

Her woman's flesh was soft, so very soft and yielding. And he was hard as iron. When had a woman ever made him this hard?

As she clung to him, he dragged his lips from hers, but only to kiss his way down to one satin-skinned breast. Her eyes widened in shock when he took it in his mouth and sucked hard on the nipple. But she didn't fight him. No, she arched into him, her fingers digging into the bare skin of his shoulders. Her fingernails would leave marks there later, but he didn't care. He wanted her. Here. Now.

Warning bells sounded in his head. He ignored them. The scent of her, the salty taste of her skin, drove him to distraction. He could have resisted her if she'd been the cold English lady he'd expected. But she was a fiery warrior queen who recited *Lysistrata* to rouse her troops. A woman like that he couldn't resist. He wanted her. She wanted him. What else mattered?

"Gideon! Oh, good heavens!" she breathed as he lavished attention on first one breast, then the other, wanting to devour them.

"Aye, it's heaven," he muttered against her breast. "You're heaven, sweetheart." She was an angel, this Englishwoman, whom he craved with every beat of his lecherous American heart. He would have her. He ought to have her. She belonged with him. And she wanted him. No matter what she said, her body belied her. She wanted him.

He made these excuses to himself as he kissed her again, this time with a hunger that even the pleasures of her mouth couldn't assuage. He wanted more. He had to have more. In a fever of need, he bunched her skirt up in his hands, drawing it up along her slender calves and past her bent knees.

Sweeping his hands beneath the muslin and over her pale, smooth skin, he fit himself into the vee of her parted thighs. She would belong to him and no one else. No one should have her but him.

He would show her how much she wanted him. He would bring her to realize it, so she could never thrust him away again. And with that jumbled thought, he slid his hand between her legs.

Chapter 11

*We are no more free agents than the queen of clubs
when she victoriously takes prisoner the knave of hearts.*

—LADY MARY WORTLEY MONTAGU
LETTER, 13 JANUARY 1759

The feel of Gideon's fingers on her most private
place jolted Sara out of her half-dream. "No," she
whispered as she jerked her mouth from his. "No, you
mustn't!"

His hand cupped her, giving instant relief to the sweet
tension he'd built in her body. "Ah, but I must," he
whispered. His gaze was dark, knowing, as if he realized exactly what she was feeling. "You want me to. Let
me touch you, Sara. Let me show you how it could be
between us." He rubbed her in a most interesting way,
making her feel fluid and hot, like the sun-warmed tropical sea.

"Yes," she breathed, despite her reservations. She
closed her eyes to shut out the knowledge shining in his
face, the knowledge of her weakness. An almost irresistible urge to give in to his deft hands possessed her,
coupled with a strange urge to touch him, to run her
hands over his body and do to him what he was doing
to her.

As he continued to rotate his palm with unerring accuracy over the place that ached for his touch, she splayed her fingers over his muscle-bound ribs and further in, over his chest, matting down the crisp, tight hairs with her questing hands. His skin, like rumpled velvet, seemed to jump beneath her fingers. Dragging in a harsh breath, he moved one of her hands lower, past his wide belt to cup the hard ridge in his breeches.

Her eyes flew open. His expression no longer looked knowing, but stark, raw, and needy as only a man could look needy. He made a guttural sound in his throat as he thrust his hips against her hand. At the same time he flattened the heel of his palm against her, and a wave of pleasure hit her at once, so intense she nearly jumped off the trunk.

"Oh, my Lord," she whispered. Every part of her shook and quivered. Every part of her craved more. Not conscious of what she did, she undulated against his hand, seeking a repeat of the pleasure.

His eyes glittered. "That's it, sweetheart. Let yourself enjoy it." He parted her curls with his fingers, then slid one inside a passage that had somehow grown wet and slick, allowing him easy access. "Sweet Jesus, you feel good, so good." With an almost animal growl, he crushed her mouth under his once more.

Faintly, Sara heard a noise from somewhere above them, the grating of wood against wood, but she thrust the sound from her mind. Then a voice called down from above, "Cap'n? Cap'n, you down there?"

Gideon tore his mouth from hers and jerked his hand back, a curse rumbling from his lips. "Yes, Silas, I'm here. I'll be with you presently."

Shame washed over Sara in buckets as she came out of her sensual fog. Good heavens, her hand was on his breeches! And he'd been touching her with an intimacy only allowed a husband!

As she snatched her hand away, the sound of descending footsteps echoed down to them. "I've got to talk to you," Silas said, his words punctuated by the clumping sound of his wooden leg on the steps. "It's about that woman Louisa—"

"If you come any nearer, Silas," Gideon barked, "I'll have you keelhauled, I swear I will!"

The clumping noises halted abruptly. Sara frantically dragged down her skirts, but when she tried to scoot off the trunk, Gideon wouldn't let her. With firm hands he held her thighs still.

His gaze locked with hers as he called back up to Silas, "Go to my cabin. I'll meet you there shortly. I've got something else to attend to first."

Her heart pounded in time to the sounds of Silas clumping back up the steps. She was the "something else," and if she let herself be "attended to," she could count on his casting her aside with easy nonchalance once he was done with her.

Well, she wouldn't let that happen. Not with this man, this unscrupulous pirate. The hatch door slammed closed above and Gideon bent to kiss her again, but this time she was prepared. Bracing her hands against his chest, she turned her face away. "No," she whispered. "No more."

His breath came hot and heavy against her ear as his arm crept back around her waist. "Why not?"

For a moment her mind was blank. What reason could she give that would make any sense to him? If she protested that they weren't married, he would simply put an end to that objection by marrying her, and that would be disastrous.

Then she remembered Petey's plan. "Because I've already promised myself to another."

His body went still against hers. An oppressive silence fell over them both, punctuated only by the distant clanging of the watch bell. But he didn't move away, and at first she feared he hadn't heard her.

"I said—" she began.

"I heard you." He drew back, his face taut with suspicion. "What do you mean, 'another'? Someone in England?"

She considered inventing a fiancé in London. But that would have no weight with him, would it? "No. Another sailor. I . . . I've agreed to marry one of your crew."

His expression hardened until it looked chiseled from the same oak that formed his formidable ship. "You're joking."

She shook her head furiously. "Peter Hargraves asked me to . . . to be his wife last night. And I agreed."

A stunned expression spread over his face before anger replaced it. Planting his hands on either side of her hips, he bent his head until his face was inches from hers. "He's not one of my crew. Is that why you accepted his proposal—because he's not one of my men? Or do you claim to have some feeling for him?"

He sneered the last words, and shame spread through her. It would be hard to claim she had feelings for Petey when she'd just been on the verge of giving herself to Gideon. But that was the only answer that would put him off. Her hands trembled against his immovable chest. "I . . . I like him, yes."

"The way you 'like' me?" When she glanced away, uncertain what to say to that, he caught her chin and forced her to look at him. Despite the dim light, she could tell that desire still held him. And when he spoke again, his voice was edged with the tension of his need. "I don't care what you agreed to last night. Everything has changed. You can't possibly still want to marry him after the way you just responded to my touch."

"That was a mistake," she whispered, steeling herself to ignore the flare of anger in his eyes. "Petey and I are well suited. I knew him from before, from the *Chastity*. I know he's an honorable man, which is why I still intend to marry him."

A muscle ticked in Gideon's jaw. "He's not a bully, you mean. He's not a wicked pirate like me, out to 'rape and pillage.' " He pushed away from the trunk with an oath, then spun toward the steps. "Well, he's not for you, Sara, no matter what you may think. And I'm going to put a stop to his courtship of you right now!"

Terror struck her at once. He could do anything to Petey, anything! "No!" she shouted as she leapt off the trunk and ran after him. "No, Gideon! Stop!"

But he was already halfway up the steps. As she raced after him, her dress came down around her shoulders. She stopped to hook herself up, watching helplessly as he vanished through the hatch above.

Bother it all! she thought as she struggled with the hooks. If she didn't get up there quickly, Gideon would no doubt have Petey thrown overboard or worse. And she couldn't let him get away with that. Petey was her only hope of escape, and not even that wretch of a pirate was going to hurt him!

Having just come off the port watch, Petey lay in his hammock carving an image of a ship into a bit of old ivory. The crew's quarters were deserted, for everyone else was either courting the women or serving on watch duty. If he had his druthers, he'd be with them. He'd be seeking Ann out.

That was impossible, however, and knowing that some foul pirate was even now probably trying to gain her affections put him in a savage mood. He'd taken the only path possible, but it didn't sit well with him to think that sweet Ann Morris was forbidden to him.

Suddenly, the door to the crew's quarters shot open, crashing against the wall with such force that Petey nearly fell off his hammock in surprise. In strode the Pirate Lord himself, looking every inch the devil's spawn, with eyes like night fires and fury on his scarred face. His gaze fell on Petey at once, so virulent that it struck terror into Petey's breast.

Petey slid warily off his hammock, then backed

around it as Captain Horn stalked toward him. "Good even, Cap'n. Is everythin' all right?"

The captain caught him by his shirt front and lifted him a few inches off the ground until Petey's face was level with his. "You can't have her, do you hear? Not now, not ever!"

Shocks of fear crept up along Petey's spine. It was all he could do to keep from quaking. "Wh-who do you mean, cap'n?"

"You *know* who I mean, Englishman." The pirate's eyes narrowed. "Unless she lied to me about choosing you as husband."

Ah, so that was who he was talking about. The little miss. Petey swallowed hard. What a bloomin' nightmare. "Miss Willis didn't lie, cap'n. I . . . I asked her to be my wife, and she accepted."

As the captain moved one hand from his shirt front to clutch him by the throat, Petey tightened his fist on his carving knife. If any other man had taken him by the throat, Petey would have had him on the floor with the knife in his gut. But this was the pirate captain. With such a madman he must tread carefully.

"Let him down!" came a voice behind the captain. It was Miss Willis herself, her hair all atumble about her shoulders and her face blanched white as the ivory scrimshaw in Petey's other hand. "Let him go, I say!"

"Stay out of this, Sara!" the captain ordered, his fingers tightening around Petey's throat. Despite the fact that the pirate still held him up by the shirt, Petey's breath was half cut off by the pirate's hold on his neck. He sucked hard, trying to force air through the thin passage.

Miss Willis ignored the captain's words. Coming up behind him, she clutched at his bent arm. "You're hurting him! Let him down!"

"I'm teaching him a lesson," Captain Horn ground out. "He needs to be reminded of his station, which on this ship is somewhere beneath cabin boy!"

"And for that you would strangle him to death?"

"For that, yes. And for presuming to court you." The captain glared at Petey, whose struggle to breathe was becoming more acute. "He doesn't have the same rights as my men. I should have made that clear before."

"But I chose him!" She latched onto the captain's arm like a barnacle. "You said we could choose our own husbands! And I did! I chose who I wanted!"

The sudden silence in the cabin was deafening, punctuated only by the creak of hammocks swaying with the ship's motion. Slackening his hold on Petey's neck only slightly, Captain Horn turned his head to fix Miss Willis with a penetrating glance. "Are you telling me that you truly wish to have a low sailor for a husband?"

"If my only other choice is a pirate, yes!" It was an emotional outburst, but as the captain continued to stare at her, she added more firmly, "Of course I wish it. And if you tell him he can't marry me, then you take away the choice you claimed to give me." She took a deep breath. "If I can only choose a man you approve of, I have no choice at all, do I?"

The captain scowled at her. Then he threw Petey to the floor with a coarse oath, knocking the scrimshaw and the carving knife from Petey's hands. Petey gasped for breath as Captain Horn hovered over him, wearing the look of a man who'd just been struck in the noggin by a yardarm and was itching to tear apart the one who'd done it.

When the captain flexed his fingers, then curled them into hard fists at his side, Petey scrambled to his feet and took a fighting stance. He didn't want to fight the captain, for his policy had been to stay as unnoticed among the pirates as possible. But fight him he would, if that's what it took to keep himself and the little miss safe.

"Stop this!" Miss Willis cried. "Stop it now, both of you!"

Captain Horn ignored her. Regarding Petey with a

mixture of contempt and amusement, he beckoned him on with one hand. "Take your shot, Hargraves. Go ahead, take it!"

Incensed by the pirate's condescension, Petey kicked out in a movement designed to knock an opponent off his feet. Next thing he knew, he was flat on his back on the floor with the captain standing over him.

A grim smile crossed the captain's face as he planted his foot on Petey's chest. "Very good, Hargraves. A smooth maneuver. But whoever taught you to fight that way should also have taught you to ignore your opponent's taunts. Fighting like an Asian requires thinking like an Asian, which means not letting your emotions get the better of you."

Petey stared up at him in awe. He'd never met another sailor who knew of such things. But he should've realized that if anyone knew them, it would be the Pirate Lord.

To Petey's surprise, the captain suddenly removed his foot, then held his hand out to him. Petey hesitated a moment before accepting the man's help in rising to his feet.

Miss Willis pushed around the captain and hurried to Petey's side, her face distraught as she ran her hands lightly over his arms and chest. "Are you hurt? He didn't hurt you, did he?"

"No, miss, just my pride." He cast her a rueful smile. "Don't fret yourself over it. I'm fine."

It was only when he caught Captain Horn's assessing glance that he realized he was behaving more like a servant than a fiancé. As he slid his hand around Miss Willis's waist, ignoring her startled expression, he noticed that the pirate watched them with interest.

"Such a touching scene." Captain Horn's face wore a look of suspicion and muted anger. "And to think I never guessed until now the grand passion going on beneath my very nose."

"Like Miss Willis said, she chose me." Peter thrust out

his chest, affecting a protective stance . . . a little too late, unfortunately. "She probably told you that she and I became friendly on the *Chastity*." It was the story both he and Miss Willis had agreed upon last night, though they'd known some would find it less than convincing.

Apparently the captain was one of them. "She did claim something like that."

Claim. Clearly the man didn't believe either of them.

Then the scourge of the seas cast a slow, lascivious glance over Miss Willis, making her tremble beneath Petey's arm. "She and I have also become quite 'friendly' in the past two days. Haven't we, Sara?"

Petey turned to her, surprised to find her blushing furiously. She cast him a guilty look, then lowered her gaze to her hands. "I-I don't know what you're t-talking about."

"Of course not," the captain ground out. "I should've expected a two-faced English *lady* like you to deny the truth about our 'friendship.' Well, you may deny it to me, and you may even deny it to this sailor of yours." He lowered his voice to a threatening hum. "But you'll have a hell of a hard time denying it to yourself."

With that strange remark, the captain turned on his heel and stalked out of the foc's'le, slamming the door behind him and leaving Petey feeling all at sea. There was something between the captain and Miss Willis, that much was obvious.

Miss Willis spun away from Petey. "The wretch! The abominable wretch!"

For the first time since she'd entered the crew's quarters, Petey noticed how disheveled she looked. The modesty piece she always wore was gone, and one of the ties from her chemise dangled outside her bodice. His blood ran cold. "What did he mean, 'friendly'? What's that bloody pirate been doin' to you?"

For a moment she said nary a word. "Nothing I didn't allow him to do," she murmured finally.

He groaned. If he ever got Miss Willis out of this

mess, her stepbrother was going to murder him. "So he touched you? Did he ... I mean, was he ..." Petey broke off. The saints be cursed. How did a low sailor like him ask an earl's stepsister such an indelicate and insulting question?

But he didn't have to ask. He could tell from the way she colored that she understood his question. Steadying her shoulders, she fixed him with a too bright gaze. "He didn't ... deflower me, if that's what you're asking. And he won't. Not ever." When his only response was to raise an eyebrow, she added, "You needn't worry about me. I can take care of myself."

"I can see that. That's why y've got the cap'n sniffin' after you like a tomcat on the prowl."

She cast him a look that could've cut glass, it was that sharp. "I can handle Captain Horn, Petey. You just concentrate on getting us away from these wretched pirates."

Then she hurried from the cabin, leaving him to wonder just how he was supposed to manage her escape when he couldn't even keep her safe from the Pirate Lord—or herself.

Chapter 12

"What do you think?" Sara asked Louisa, as they stood on deck peering at the horizon shortly after breakfast the next morning. It had been almost half an hour since the lookout had shouted "Land ho!" and they could still make out only a speck of mottled brown past the glassy sea.

"Hard to say. It's still too far away to tell much."

A crowd of women surrounded them, pushing against the rails in their eagerness to glimpse their new home. Ann Morris shoved her way through to stand at Sara's elbow, her dark curls framing an eager, rosy face. "Is that it?" Ann shifted a stack of dirty plates from one hand to the other. "Is that Atlantis Island?"

"We're not sure," Sara said, "but we think so. We seem to be making for it. And the captain did tell me it would take only two days' sail."

Ann squinted at the speck. "P'raps we should ask Pe-

154

tey to let us get a look at it through the spyglass. He'd find a way to get one for us, I'll wager."

"Oh, I'm sure if Miss Willis asked, he'd be only too happy to oblige," Louisa remarked absently. "Now that she's going to marry him, he—"

A sudden crash made both Sara and Louisa whirl toward Ann. The little woman stood staring down at a pile of broken crockery, her fist pressed to her mouth.

"Ann?" Sara asked as the Welshwoman bent and began to gather the broken pieces up, placing them quickly in her apron. "Ann, are you all right?" She knelt beside Ann, who was crying now, big, fat tears rolling down her apple cheeks. "Good heavens, what's wrong?"

"Nothin'," Ann protested, keeping her gaze averted from Sara. "It-it's nothin'. I just lost my grip on them, is all."

"But you're crying—"

Louisa's hand on Sara's shoulder cut her off. Louisa bent to murmur in her ear, "Leave her be. I shouldn't have said that in front of her, but I thought she'd already heard the news."

"Heard what news?" Sara lifted her head to ask.

"That you and Petey are engaged, of course."

It was true that Sara had told as many of the women as possible once she'd left the crew's quarters last night, but she hadn't thought it would disturb any of them. Sara stared blankly at Louisa, then glanced at Ann, who'd gathered up all the crockery and had now risen to hurry away through the crowd.

That's when the truth hit Sara. Oh, how could she have been so stupid? She'd paid no attention to Ann's worshipful comments about Petey, to the way she'd always fussed over him on the *Chastity*.

Ann was in love with Petey—and Sara's engagement to him must be killing her. She must've had her heart set on marrying Petey herself. Guilt hit Sara full force. She'd blithely agreed to Petey's plan without stopping to think whom else it might hurt. Poor Ann.

It didn't help to tell herself that Petey probably didn't even share the Welshwoman's affections, and that he'd be gone as soon as he could find a way off the island. No, it didn't help one jot. Ann had never had much in her life, and now the only hope she'd clung to was being ripped away from her. By Sara, who'd never wanted anything but to make the women happy.

She watched as Ann beat a hasty retreat into the galley. Then she rose and turned to Louisa. "Did you know she had her eye on Petey?"

Louisa nodded. "But don't worry. I understand why you and Petey joined together, even if Ann doesn't. You're the only two in this unholy crowd who aren't criminals of one sort or another. I can't really blame him for not wanting to marry a convict, and I certainly can't blame you for not wanting to marry a pirate." She shrugged. "People generally stick to their kind. It's something I learned . . . a long time ago."

The wistfulness in Louisa's voice made a lump form in Sara's throat. Louisa had never spoken much about her past, but Sara had made some conjectures. The man she'd stabbed had been the eldest son of a duke. It would've been easy to fall in love with such a man, but as a governess, Louisa could never have hoped to marry the heir to a title. Still, if she'd been in love with him, what could the man have done to make her angry enough to stab him? A simple refusal to marry her didn't seem like enough provocation for a woman of Louisa's breeding and intelligence. There must have been more to the story, much more.

But Louisa wasn't the type to talk about her crime as some of the others were wont to do, so Sara wasn't likely to find out the truth. It was a pity. She would like to help Louisa.

Help Louisa. The way she'd helped Ann. Louisa could do without such help.

"I don't see any trees," Louisa commented, obviously

determined to turn the subject away from herself.

Still swamped with guilt, Sara returned her gaze to the horizon. Now the speck had grown to a shapeless blob, still brown and unlikely looking. "That's what Gideon calls a 'paradise'?" she speculated aloud.

Louisa slanted a curious look at her. "Gideon? You're on a first-name basis with our good captain?"

Hot color stained Sara's cheeks. "No, of course not. I-I meant to say, Captain Horn." That was something else she had to feel guilty about—her disastrous encounter with him yesterday. He'd avoided her ever since, and with good reason. She should never have allowed him such blatant liberties. It gave him the wrong idea entirely.

"I wouldn't get too close to Captain Horn, if I were you," Louisa remarked in a low voice, her face carefully blank.

"I'm not friendly with him."

Louisa arched one eyebrow. "Good. Then you won't mind that he sent Barnaby down to the hold late last night to fetch Queenie to his bed."

Her gaze flew to Louisa's. "He did *what*?"

"You said you weren't close to him."

Jerking her gaze back to the horizon, Sara fought for some semblance of nonchalance. "I'm not. I'm just . . . appalled that he would do such a thing after he told the men to behave as gentlemen until the marriage vows were said." *And after he spent the afternoon trying to seduce me.*

A hot surge of jealousy swept through her despite all her attempts to quell it. Glancing up to where Gideon was manning the helm and shouting orders to his sailors, she grimaced. In his scandalous leather vest and form-fitting breeches, he looked exactly like what he truly was—a randy satyr who would seduce anything in skirts. She'd been right not to trust him. For all his soft words, his overtures to her had been meaningless. He'd never intended anything but a quick seduction.

And to think she'd almost given in to him! What a dreadful mistake that would have been!

Louisa shrugged. "He's the captain. Surely you didn't expect him to follow the same rules he set for his men."

"That's exactly what I did expect." Sara sniffed. "He talks about starting a colony and making it a paradise, but what he really wants is a harem for him and his men. He wants to make us all into Queenies."

"Shh," Louisa whispered. "Here she comes now."

Sara told herself not to pay any attention to the woman. But she couldn't resist peeking to see if Queenie indeed looked as if she'd spent the night with the captain.

There was no doubt about it. Queenie had definitely spent the night with *someone*. She wore a cat-in-the-cream smile as she swaggered across the deck toward the other women, and her face literally glowed with good health.

"Good mornin', all," she chirped. Stretching her shapely arms high over her head, she gave an exaggerated yawn. "Afraid I'm a little late gettin' around this mornin'. Had a long night, you know." With a languid grace Sara hardly knew the woman possessed, she let her arms slide back down like wilting flower petals, then struck a seductive pose. "I tell you, ladies, you mustn't worry about the kind of husbands these pirates make. Judging from last night, I'd say they'll do nicely . . . quite nicely indeed."

Most of the women chuckled. Sara couldn't. Turning her flaming face back to the horizon, she fought down the bitter words rising in her throat. What did it matter if Gideon *had* bedded Queenie? What did it matter if the wretched tart *had* enjoyed it? They deserved each other. Queenie represented the worst of the convict women and Gideon the worst of the pirates; they'd be perfect together.

Then Sara felt, rather than saw, Queenie press through the crowd to stand next to her. Clamping her lips shut, Sara continued to stare at the island, which now loomed much closer and larger than before.

"Is that it?" Queenie asked, bracing her crossed arms against the rail. "That's Atlantis?"

"We think so," Louisa thankfully answered. Sara couldn't have answered civilly at that moment if her life depended on it.

"Don't look like much," Queenie grumbled. "There's no green. And where's the water?"

Sara's eyes narrowed. Queenie was right. There was no evidence of a spring or any sort of vegetation. Surely this couldn't be what Gideon had meant by "paradise." If so, he had a strange idea about what paradise required.

A somber silence fell on all the women as the ship neared the island. *After everything these women have endured*, Sara thought, *at least Gideon could have had the decency not to deceive them about what lay ahead at Atlantis.*

As they watched, however, the ship started to veer to the right. It was still making for the island, but now it seemed to be making for the furthest end of it.

"Maybe this ain't the island after all," one of the women standing behind Sara remarked. "Maybe we just got to get around it."

"I don't think so," Sara mused aloud, now very curious. "If they'd wanted to avoid it, they could have passed it from a greater distance."

The women surged forward against the railing as each sought to get a better look at the huge expanse of dead grass and half-submerged boulders that was now so close they could make out the forms of white seagulls flitting in and out of the jumble of rock.

The ship turned fully to the right and was sailing parallel to the island. It took several minutes to round the rocky outcropping on the end, for Atlantis was wider than they'd expected. But as the ship passed the point, putting them in view of a new side of the island, the women collectively gasped.

This side was as green and lush as the other side had been brown and dry. Feathery coconut palms lined the sandy curve of shore, and beyond them a veritable jungle of exotic trees, twisting vines, and matted undergrowth stretched upward toward the top of the island, a peak that appeared to be several miles inland.

Thatched huts of various designs were nestled into the forest banking the beach, and at one end of the natural lagoon a dock that looked substantial enough to accommodate the *Satyr* stretched out into the water as if waiting to claim them. Another vessel was moored to it on the side away from them, a sloop about half the size of the *Satyr*, but obviously quite seaworthy and probably still capable of carrying a large cargo.

As the ship slowed, Sara glimpsed a silvery sliver of a stream bisecting the shore. Beside it lay a couple of rough wooden carts, obviously used for hauling containers of water. There was even a rude track along the beach where the cart had obviously been dragged.

Paradise. She had to admit it. Clear blue waters filled with tropical fish, colorful fruits dripping from the trees, and a light, warm climate. Heaven itself.

The sound of wood scraping against wood jolted her from her thoughts, signaling that they'd reached the dock. As men scurried to weigh anchor and secure the ship against the newly cut posts, the women began to point out sights and to chatter excitedly about their home.

"So what do you think, ladies?" came a voice behind them. "Does it meet your expectations?"

As a chorus of women exclaimed over the island, Sara tightened her lips. Gideon. Apparently, with the ship docked he now had time to come boast about his precious island. Bother it all. She had half a mind to tell him exactly what he could do with his paradise.

From his standpoint behind Sara, Gideon surveyed her stiff back and rigid stance, wondering what she was so angry about now. He'd expected her to be pleasantly surprised by the delights of Atlantis Island, not furious.

Why in blazes do I care? he thought sourly when she refused to look at him or say anything. *She made her bed with that blasted Hargraves. Let her lie in it.*

The trouble was, he couldn't stand to let Hargraves have her. God knew she was a troublesome wench, with a tongue that could strip the barnacles off a ship's hull. But he couldn't help remembering how it had felt to hold her and kiss her, how, for just a few moments, she'd been an eager, melting softness in his arms. Confound her, thoughts like that had kept him up half the night, making him call for Queenie and just as quickly turn her over to Barnaby when he realized she wasn't what he wanted.

As if she'd heard his thoughts, Queenie sidled up to him and slipped her hand in the crook of his arm. "Good mornin', guv'nor. Hope you're feelin' as good this mornin' as I am."

He stared at Queenie incredulously. The last time he'd seen her, she'd been railing at him for not bedding her. It had taken both him and Barnaby to convince her to vacate his cabin after he'd made the disastrous mistake of calling for her. What was her game now? He knew she'd spent the night with Barnaby, and judging from the first mate's smile and her pleasant expression, it had been a good one. What did she want with him?

Then Queenie slanted a glance at Sara's unyielding back, and Gideon instantly understood. Obviously, Sara had heard about his calling for Queenie. And Queenie must've let Sara believe that she'd spent the night with him.

So that was why Sara refused to look at him or speak to him! She was angry about Queenie. The thought gave him immense satisfaction. Despite all Sara's protestations that she didn't want him, she was jealous over some tart she thought he'd made love to.

Then a sobering thought hit him. She might merely be pretending to a moral disgust over his supposed lechery. It would be just like Sara to look down her nose at him for seeking relief for the very fires she'd roused in him . . . and refused to quench herself.

As Queenie plastered herself to his right side, he glared at Sara's back. The little witch. She had no right to be angry. He'd done nothing to be ashamed of, and even if he had, it was all her fault for making him ache for her.

He started to thrust Queenie away, then stopped himself. Why should he? If Sara was jealous, let her have a taste of what he'd suffered yesterday when he'd seen her fussing over Hargraves like a frigging mother hen. Maybe then she'd admit that she didn't want that ugly sailor.

And if it wasn't jealousy that had roused her temper, at least he'd have the pleasure of rubbing her nose in his "lechery."

The other women had disappeared, helped off the ship by his men so they could explore the island. Only Sara remained at the rail. He grinned. Draping his arm casually about Queenie's shoulders, he said smoothly, "Good morning, Miss Willis. And what do *you* think of our island?"

She faced him, paling when she saw him with Queenie. But she quickly recovered herself. "It's lovely." Her voice lowered in acid condescension. "It's the perfect place for you and your lecherous companions to sport with your unwilling concubines."

A slow smile touched his lips. "You mean, 'sport with our prospective *wives*,' don't you? And I assure you, not all of them are unwilling." He cast a glance down at Queenie's ample bosom. "Some of them are more than happy to be here."

The look on Sara's face was priceless. He would wager his ship that she was jealous, though she'd never admit it, even to herself.

Then she tilted up that stubborn chin of hers and said in a lofty voice, "Some of them have no self-respect. I'm not talking about them. They have their own consciences to deal with."

Queenie bristled. "Why, you haughty little bi—"

"That's enough, Queenie." He dropped his arm from around her shoulder. "Why don't you join the other women? I have some things to say to Miss Willis."

For a second he thought Queenie would refuse, but apparently she decided it wasn't a battle worth fighting, because she shrugged and released her hold on his waist. "If you say so, guv'nor. I'd like to see if the beds are as comfy on land as they are on sea." And with a last come-hither look in his direction, she strolled off down the deck, her hips swaying provocatively.

Gideon returned his gaze to Sara only to find her watching Queenie's retreat with a murderous look. He chuckled. "You don't like her, do you?"

Smoothing her hair back with one hand, she turned to walk away. "I have no feelings about her whatsoever. Now, if you'll excuse me, Captain Horn . . ."

Her words died off as he caught her arm. Easily matching her stride, he goaded, "Aren't you just a bit curious, Sara? Haven't you the least interest in hearing how I found Queenie's performance last night?"

"Absolutely not!" A flood of crimson spread over her cheeks. "Let me go!"

He slid one arm about her waist and bent to whisper, "Don't you want to know what we did together? Whether I kissed her as I did you? Whether I fondled her breasts and the secret place between her legs—"

"Stop it." Her body trembled against his. "Stop saying these things!"

There was such misery on her face he couldn't bear to torture her anymore. "I didn't touch her, you know." The admission left his lips before he could prevent it. "I sent her to Barnaby without so much as a kiss."

She went very still. "I . . . I don't care what you did with her. It's nothing to me." But he could tell from the relief in her voice that she was lying.

"It was you I wanted," he went on. "And it's you I'm going to have, no matter what I must do to get you."

It was true. Last night had taught him one thing: he couldn't stomach another woman in his bed when he wanted only Sara. He had to make love to her at least once, if just to get her out of his thoughts.

"You can't . . . have me," she said haltingly. "I'm promised to another."

"It doesn't matter." During the long hours of aching for her last night, that was one thing he'd decided—that somehow he'd seduce her away from Hargraves. "You're meant for me, not him. And one day soon, I'll make you admit it. You can be sure of that."

Chapter 13

O! how short a time does it take to put an end to a woman's liberty!

—FANNY BURNEY, ENGLISH NOVELIST
EARLY JOURNEYS AND LETTERS OF FANNY BURNEY

It took Sara only two hours of wandering the beaches of Atlantis Island to admit, albeit grudgingly, that Gideon's love of the place was justified. With every step she took, her slippers sank into sands white and fine as marble dust. The air smelled fragrant and rich, like the air in that London greenhouse she'd once entered during a dinner party.

And the colors! Vivid pinks and brilliant yellows dotted the forest of willows and aging oaks. Barnaby had explained to her that although the island was located in the tropics, the south trade winds and cold currents of the North Atlantic kept the temperature moderate, thus enabling orange and lemon groves to thrive alongside date palms and bamboo. According to Barnaby, winters were nearly nonexistent and the summers mild.

That explained the lush flora, but what about the varied fauna? So far, she'd seen wild goats and rabbits roaming the higher promontories. Huge sea turtles waddled along the shores, and wherever she walked, she startled grouse and pheasants out of the brush and into the air. Were they all native to the island, she wondered, or brought here long ago by some other hopeful colonists who'd since given up the ghost? What had made this small bit of the world a paradise from end to end?

Well, not quite end to end. There was the other part of the island—the dry, brown expanse they'd seen when they'd first approached. When she'd asked Barnaby about it, he'd explained that it was the result of a strange weather phenomenon. The same trade winds that made the island mild in climate also dried out the side of the island they blew constantly over. Since the unattractive side faced the trade route, it wasn't surprising no one had bothered to settle there. When ships had been blown off course far enough to find Atlantis, they'd eyed it as an unlikely source of provisions and had sailed on by.

It was like some ancient Garden of Eden hidden away where no one could find it. No one but Gideon, that is. Trust him to be the one to stumble across it.

She glanced furtively down the beach to where he stood, wearing only his buff trousers and his belt with the saber slung from it. Stretching his arms up, he caught hold of a rounded cluster of yellow fruit hanging from what appeared to be an odd sort of palm tree with flat, waxy green leaves. A banana tree, they called it. She watched as he drew out his saber, then used it to sever the cluster from the tree in one lethal swipe.

As he twisted at the waist to lay the cut fruit in a cart already heaped high with the strange yellow crescents, his muscles flexed and worked, a fine sheen of sweat glistening off the black hair of his chest. At just that moment, he glanced her way and his gaze caught hers. For a moment his eyes were rich and unfathomable, and she felt the force of his gaze like a sensuous whisper, across her brow . . . her cheeks . . . her lips. A sudden, all too painfully familiar heat flashed over her, flaming into a blush. Mortified to be caught staring, she pivoted away from him, but not before catching a glimpse of the slow, knowing grin that curved his mouth.

Good heavens, the man was a danger to all woman-kind! She, of all people, should be immune to him, having known her share of criminals in the course of her reform work. Yet she was far from immune. Of all the people on God's green earth, why must it be a no-torious pirate captain who made her blush and feel weak at the knees like some starry-eyed young girl at her coming out? She'd always been too sensible for such infatuations, with the exception of Colonel Taylor, and even with him she hadn't lost all common sense the way she had with Gideon.

Although she hurried down the beach away from him, she couldn't ignore the warmth spreading from the most intimate parts of her body. Oh, yes, Gideon be-longed in this Garden of Eden. He was as temptingly made as the first Adam must have been. God hadn't shirked his duties when creating Gideon Horn. No, in-deed. In fact, she wondered if God hadn't put just a jot too much effort into it. He should have given the man something more useful than good looks and a treach-erous charm. Humility, for example.

She tried to imagine a humble Gideon, but it was im-possible. Such a creature would be beyond even the Al-mighty's powers of imagination.

Spotting Louisa, who sat on a fallen log a few feet from where the beach ended and the brush began, Sara hurried to her side.

"What are you smiling about?" Louisa grumbled. "Don't tell me, you're already being seduced into liking this island."

"Seduced" was a good word for it, Sara thought. "You must admit it's not what you expected."

"It's exactly what I expected. Have you seen those huts yet? They're the crudest buildings imaginable! No window shutters . . . plank floors . . . roofs of thatch. The only thing in their favor is the featherbeds, which do look comfortable, I'll admit. But what else can you expect of pirates? Of course they would pay attention to their beds. That's all they care about. Men! I swear, the communal kitchen that Silas has been using is as primitive as—"

"Silas? You seem to be on awfully familiar terms with Mr. Drummond all of a sudden."

With a snort, Louisa ducked her head. "Not at all. Silas . . . I mean . . . Mr. Drummond and I have just learned to . . . tolerate each other's company. He finally realized he needed my help, that's all."

Her help? Louisa's "help" had consisted of taking over the poor man's kitchen and ignoring every attempt he made to regain power. If he'd learned to tolerate that, he was a better man than she'd thought. "Well, I must admit the meals have been quite edible since you offered your 'help.' And I'm sure that with a little work we can make the huts presentable."

"That's the only reason they brought us here, you know. To clean and cook and sew for them."

"Oh, no, they want much more than that," Sara said acidly, remembering Gideon's knowing, seductive look.

Louisa stiffened. "You're right, of course. They want our bodies, too. And I'll be damned if I let any of them have mine. They'll have to tie me down first."

"Don't say that too loudly. You might give them ideas." Sara glanced around at some of the women who'd already chosen mates. "Unfortunately, you and I may be outnumbered in our desire to remain unmarried."

Louisa shot her a long, curious glance. "You and I? You've chosen a husband, too, remember?"

With a groan, Sara cursed her slip of the tongue.

"Or have you changed your mind and decided to leave Petey to Ann, after all?"

A surge of guilt hit Sara all at once. Poor Ann. "Where is she, anyway?" Sara asked, ignoring Louisa's question as she scanned the clusters of men and women around them. She'd meant to look for the young woman earlier, to see if she couldn't patch things up between them, but in exploring the island she'd forgotten about her good intentions.

Louisa jerked her head toward the stream not far from them. "I saw her wander up there a little while ago. I think she wanted to be alone."

"Oh, of course." Sara cast a concerned glance up along the sides of the stream and felt a little shiver of worry when she didn't see the Welshwoman. "Perhaps I'll just go look for her. She shouldn't wander so far away from everyone when the island is still unfamiliar to us. She might get hurt."

"Do as you wish. But if you don't mind, I'm returning to the dirty little hovel they call a kitchen. We'll be eating dinner soon. The pirates have killed the fatted calf in our honor—actually, a fatted wild pig—and if I leave the final cooking of it to Silas, he'll torture it into the toughest, most inedible dish imaginable."

With that, the young woman strolled back in the direction they'd just come, leaving Sara to climb the slippery banks of the stream alone. The moment she began her ascent, she realized that her half-boots, adequate for treading the well-polished decks of the *Satyr*, were not at all useful for scrambling over the slick rocks bordering the stream. It took some work to keep her balance while holding her skirts above her ankles, and she was so intent upon not falling that she didn't hear the soft voices of a young couple talking in the woods until she was nearly upon them.

Then she halted, straining to hear more. In moments she picked out Ann's dulcet voice, answered by a deeper male one. Good heavens, was one of those dreadful men even now taking advantage of Ann's wounded heart? Sara wouldn't stand for that. Ann had been through enough already.

Pushing determinedly through the thick growth along the edge of the stream, she stumbled suddenly into a clearing. The couple before her, locked in a passionate embrace, sprang apart at once. And to her surprise, Petey was the "dreadful man" holding Ann.

Her mouth gaped open. "Oh . . . I'm . . . I'm so sorry. . . . I thought . . . I was worried—" She turned, her face several shades of red. "Never mind. I'll just go back to the beach—"

"Wait!" Peter called out as she started off. She heard his boots crunching through the brush after her. "Please, Miss Willis—I can explain."

Sara shook her head as she pushed doggedly on. "You don't need to explain anything." But by that time he'd reached her side and caught her by the arm, forcing her to halt.

"Listen, please." When Sara lifted her eyes to him, he added, "I told Ann everythin'—about why I'm marryin' you and who you are. I told her I work for your brother. I had to."

"Please don't blame him," Ann burst out. When Sara looked at the young woman, she was pained to see how red Ann's eyes and nose were.

She went on haltingly. "I-I came up here to be alone . . . because . . . well. . . ."

"She was cryin'," Petey interjected. "I seen her come up here alone, and I was worried she might hurt herself, so I followed her and found her sittin' all by herself on that tree there and sobbin'." He cast Ann a tender look. "She thought you and me was in love. I couldn't let her go on thinkin' it, not when it hurts her so." His voice lowered. "Especially since it ain't true."

The look that passed between Ann and Petey then was so sweet that a lump swelled in Sara's throat. Suddenly she wished it was she and Gideon sharing that look.

As soon as she thought it, she groaned. Gideon, indeed! The man knew nothing of affection or sweetness. All he wanted was to own her body, and he wanted that only because she wouldn't give it to him. He was like a little boy coveting his playmate's toys.

Ann's gaze was on Sara now. "Since Petey's explained it all to me, Miss Willis, I understand what he has to do. Truly I do." It sounded as if she were trying to convince herself more than Sara. Dropping her gaze, Ann smoothed her skirts with her plump, soft hands. "There's no other way out of it. Petey must marry you to keep you safe from the pirates. I see that now."

To keep you safe from the pirates. Ann said not a word about her own sacrifice, about being kept safe from the pirates herself. She just accepted the notion that Sara was somehow more important, that Sara deserved more protection than she did.

Never had Sara felt so loathsome—or been so aware of the unfairness of England's class system. Here was a woman whose every chance for happiness had been snatched from her, a woman whose only crime had been in stealing to buy medicine for her mother. She'd lost her freedom and her mother before she'd even been old enough to find a husband or have children. At last she'd found a man she cared for, one who obviously cared for her. And he too was to be snatched from her for the most frivolous of reasons—so Sara wouldn't face a scandal if by some slim chance she were rescued from Gideon and his men.

It wasn't right. Despite her talk of fairness and equality, Sara had tacitly accepted Petey's sacrifice as if it were her due, without even stopping to ask if it was what he truly wanted.

Well, not anymore. "Peter isn't going to marry me." Sara's voice was firm. "If I'd guessed how you two felt about each other, I wouldn't have agreed to this arrangement. Now that I know, I certainly can't go through with it."

"But miss—" Petey began.

"That's my final word, Petey. We don't know what the future will hold, and I won't let you marry me when you love another." When he opened his mouth to protest again, she cut him off. "We might be here for years. You never know. It's foolish to behave as if this might end any day."

A hopeful look passed over Ann's face, but Petey crossed his arms stubbornly over his chest. "And what about the Pirate Lord? He's got his eye on you, y'know. If he thinks y're free—"

"I'll deal with that in my own way," Sara said, hoping she sounded more brave than she felt.

"I don't like it," Petey grumbled, then noticed how the hope faded from Ann's face. He moved swiftly to her side and slid his arm around her waist. "It's not that I don't want to marry you, love. It's just that I got a duty to Miss Willis."

Sara sighed. Petey would never relent as long as he thought she needed protecting. And certainly from the way Gideon had spoken to her that morning, he intended to pursue her no matter what.

She went very still. Actually, that could work in her favor. "I know what we can do. We can use Gideon's stubbornness against him. After all, he said he would do whatever he must to have me."

"When did he—" Petey began.

"Never mind that," she said quickly. "The point is, as long as I insist on choosing you, he can't force me to choose him." Her words came out more quickly as her idea took shape. "Indeed, the more I resist, the more likely he is to put off making the women choose until I'm free to choose him. And since that day will never come, we can stall him endlessly."

"Endlessly?" Petey's voice held extreme skepticism. "Beggin' your pardon, miss, but I can't see the Pirate Lord waitin' on your leisure forever. He's bloomin' stubborn."

Truer words were never spoken, she thought. "Still, all we need is time to think of a plan, a way to get us all freed." She cast the couple a fond glance. "In any case, it's better than forcing the two of you into a miserable situation." She faced Ann. "What do you think? Can you two pretend to be strangers when you're around the others?"

Ann bobbed her head. Clearly she'd do anything to hold on to Petey.

"Good. That's what we'll do then."

Petey tightened his grip on Ann. "And if the pirate surprises us? If he grows tired of workin' on you and turns to some other lass? If he abides by his promise to make the women choose husbands in a week? What then?"

"Then the two of you will marry, and I'll fend for myself as best I can." When he scowled, she added in solemn tones, "You know that's the only thing to do, Petey. Do you really want to see Ann given to some man without her consent? Because that's what Gideon will do if she doesn't choose anyone."

That apparently decided him. In a gruff voice that held a hint of relief, he agreed to her plan.

"Good. Now, why don't you two go on back before someone realizes you're both missing? And you'd better separate before you reach the beach."

"Aren't you comin' with us?" Petey asked.

"In a minute. I want to explore the area a little."

Petey looked as if he might protest, but when she cast him a mutinous glance, he shrugged and led Ann off toward the stream.

The truth was, she wasn't ready to face Gideon again. Those pirate's eyes of his seemed to see right through her civilized veneer, to show it for the thin protection it was. She was still reeling from his admission this morning—that he'd turned down a night with Queenie because he wanted her. She needed a few moments alone to prepare herself, to marshal her wits for the battles he forced her to fight. A few moments, little enough to ask.

She should've known Gideon would never allow her that.

"They make a pretty couple, don't they?" came a

husky male voice behind her, startling her nearly out of her skin.

"What?" Whirling, she found the pesky object of her thoughts ducking beneath the low-hanging branch of a gnarled oak to enter the clearing.

Instantly her heartbeat accelerated to a panicky rhythm. How long had he been there? How much had he heard? Did he know what she and Petey were planning?

"Wh-who makes a pretty couple?" she stammered, stalling for time as she searched his face for some hint of what he'd heard.

As usual, he excelled at hiding his thoughts. "Ann Morris and Petey, of course." He leaned back against the oak, looking irritatingly sure of himself. "I just saw them headed down the stream."

The faintest sprinkling of sunlight through the branches limned his dark hair with golden highlights, and his trousers hung low on his hips, exposing far too much of his muscle-taut belly. If not for those trousers, he would certainly look the part of the first Adam, all well-wrought sinew and tanned skin. An image of him in a fig leaf sprang into her mind before she squelched it.

Jerking her gaze from the tempting picture he made, she focused on the break in the trees through which Ann and Petey had disappeared. Oh, how heartily she wished she'd gone with them. Then she wouldn't be trying to lie about them to a half-naked man who stirred the most unladylike thoughts in her. "Yes, well . . . Ann and Petey are good friends, you know. He thinks of her as a little sister. He looks after her."

Gideon pushed away from the oak. "The same way he looks after you?"

"Yes, of course," she babbled, then corrected herself. "No, I mean, not the same exactly. His affection for her is more . . . more brotherly."

"Brotherly?" He stepped closer, his booted feet barely

making a sound on the patchwork quilt of dead leaves and live brush on the forest floor. Skepticism laced his tone. "It's a pity she feels so differently . . . less, shall we say, sisterly."

Sara's gaze shot to his. Bother it all, how did he know that?

At her look of surprise, he shrugged. "Ann practically worships Hargraves. Told me so herself a couple of nights ago. I even got the impression that she hoped to have him for herself." His eyes narrowed, scanning her face. "It must be breaking her heart to see him with you."

Sometimes Gideon was far too perceptive for his own good. She gave a dismissive shrug, though her blood pounded in her ears. She mustn't let him guess the truth! "You obviously misunderstood Ann. Really, Gideon, she thinks of Petey as a brother. I'm sure of it."

"Then why was it *her* he escorted down to the beach, and not you?"

She swallowed. This was becoming more and more thorny. "I . . . told them I wanted to be alone." That, at least, was true. "After days cooped up on a ship with hundreds of other people, I needed some space to breathe. Surely you can understand that. With all the women demanding so much and the children always asking questions, I just couldn't take it anymore. I mean, days and days of . . . ." She trailed off. Good heavens, she was babbling, and whenever she started babbling, he suspected her of lying.

She shot him a quick glance, but he no longer seemed to be paying any attention to her. His gaze had shifted to a spot above her right shoulder.

"What is it?" she asked, starting to turn.

"Don't move!" Though he gave the command in a low voice, he spoke so forcefully she obeyed at once. When his expression grew grim and he still kept his gaze fixed beyond her shoulder, a little shiver of fear skittered down her spine.

She kept her voice as low as his. "Tell me what's going on, Gideon."

"Listen carefully, and don't panic." With his eyes still on that wretched spot behind her, he slid his right hand slowly to the hilt of his saber.

"What am I not supposed to be panicking about?" she snapped. He was scaring her to death, the wretch, and probably for nothing!

His gaze shifted to her face for the briefest instant before returning to the object of his intense perusal. "There's a black mamba in the tree behind you." She opened her mouth, but before she could even ask the question, he added, "It's a snake. A poisonous one."

She paled as a horrible chill seized her. A poisonous snake? Behind her? "H-how close?"

"Close enough." His face was expressionless, as if he didn't wish to scare her. That in itself terrified her. Moving in infinitesimal increments, he lifted his left hand toward her. "Take my hand." When she started to move her hand toward his, he ground out, "Slowly, Sara, slowly. Not too fast."

Sweat beaded along her upper lip as she inched her hand upward. The wind rustled the leaves of the trees overhead, and she froze, her heart leaping into her throat.

"You're doing fine," Gideon said reassuringly. "Right now, he doesn't seem too interested in us. Let's keep it that way."

He drew out his saber with his right hand, using the same measured movements she was using.

Her body trembled violently. "Wh-what are you going to do?"

"Chop his head off."

Trickles of sweat dripped down the side of her face. "What if you miss?"

"You damned well better pray I don't."

Praying was easy; a thousand prayers were already springing to her lips. *Please, God, don't let Gideon miss.*

Please, God, don't let the snake get me. Oh, please, dear God, don't let me die on this wretched island without ever seeing home.

Suddenly Gideon's hand met hers, and he clasped it in a tight grip.

After that, everything happened at once. With his left hand, Gideon jerked her to him, while with the right, he swung his saber in a wide arc toward the tree. As she pivoted against him, she caught a glimpse of an inky raised head seeming to come right out of the tree. There was a swish of blade against air, a flash of steel, and a horrible hiss.

Next thing she knew, the blade of the saber had severed the snake's head cleanly from its body, and both had dropped to the ground.

With a cry, she buried her face in Gideon's hairy chest, but not before she saw the snake's body writhing wildly on the ground only a foot away. "Oh, my God," she cried as she clutched at Gideon. She felt rather than saw him stab his saber into the ground. Then both of his arms enveloped her in a hug so tight she could barely breathe.

"It's all right, sweetheart, it's all right," Gideon said over and over as he cradled her in his arms. "The snake's dead. It can't hurt you now."

"B-but it could have," she stammered. "It was so close . . . it was just there!" It wasn't like her to panic, but she'd never even seen a poisonous snake, much less been menaced by one. Coming on top of everything else, it was just too much. "If it . . . if it had gotten me—"

"But it *didn't*." Cupping her face firmly, he lifted it until she was staring at him. "It's all right, I promise. I wouldn't have let it hurt you."

She couldn't seem to get enough breath. She sucked in air in great gasps, and still the panic closed her throat. "What . . . if you . . . hadn't . . . been here," she choked out. "What . . . if . . ."

"But I *was* here." Her panic now seemed mirrored in

his eyes. He clutched her close, stroking her back with soothing hands. "I'll always be here. I'll never let anything hurt you. I promise."

"Are . . . are you sure it's dead?" She knew it was a stupid question, yet she had to ask.

"It's dead." He moved aside a little and gestured to the ground. "See? It's not moving."

She peered over his shoulder to where the scaly black rope lay limp across a blanket of leaves. A shudder rocked her body. "Is it . . . is it very poisonous?"

"It doesn't matter now."

"Curse you, Gideon, tell me the truth! Could it have killed me?"

A muscle ticked in his jaw. "Let's just say I've never heard of anybody surviving the bite of a black mamba."

The irony of it hit her all at once. "I should have known there'd be snakes here," she said woefully as she clung to him. "What would the Garden of Eden be without the serpent?"

He ventured a smile. "I don't know. Boring?"

Boring? She stared at him incredulously. Had he just said . . . after what had nearly happened . . . but then, this was Gideon.

She beat her fists against his chest, taking him by surprise. "This is all a game to you, isn't it? You don't even care that you've dragged us from our homes to this wretched place where there are deadly snakes and . . . and God knows what other monstrous beasts! You wanted something, so you took it, and you don't care what it does to us . . . to me!"

She collapsed into sobs, her brush with death still too fresh. Everything that had happened over the past few days hit her with a sudden fierceness. Since he'd taken the ship, she'd scarcely had time to mourn the fact that she'd never see England or Jordan again.

But now reality struck her with a vengeance as she stood in the strange clearing with its unfamiliar plants and its dead snake. Suddenly the tears wouldn't stop.

They bubbled out of her like an overflowing soup pot. She couldn't contain them, and at the moment didn't even want to try.

Looking worried, Gideon held her close. At first she fought him, her anger warring with the need to be comforted, but he wouldn't release her. He just kept muttering, "I'm sorry, sweetheart. I'm so sorry."

Finally she went limp in his embrace, letting the tears come out of her in great gasping sobs. After the first storm passed, she even leaned into him, craving his strength. There was no one else to give her comfort. Although he was her adversary, he was also strong, and she needed his strength just now. She needed it very badly.

She didn't know exactly when his comforting became something else. Maybe it was after her sobs had died off into the occasional hiccup. Or maybe it was when she saw how shaken he looked, and felt compelled to reassure him, "I-I'm all right now, truly I am," as she brushed tears from her eyes.

But suddenly his mouth was on hers, gentle, soft, as if begging forgiveness. To her shame, she kissed him back, seeking the reassurance only he could provide. Their kisses were tender, full of mutual comfort.

He shifted her closer, his hand curving into the small of her back to flatten her against his lean, hard body as he showered soft, repentant kisses over her lips and cheeks, her closed eyelids, her tangled hair.

"I should've left you on the *Chastity*," he whispered against her mouth. "Atlantis is all right for the others, but not for you."

"That's not true. It's not right—" *For any of us*, she would have said, if his mouth hadn't covered hers again.

Only this time his kiss offered more than comfort. It offered pure, hot passion, a hungry desire that quickly swept her up until she found herself responding with an eagerness that matched his own.

She couldn't help it. Despite everything, she needed him to get her through this, to make her forget the snake. As if he understood exactly what she wanted, he shifted her in his embrace so he could touch her, caress her, stroke her. His hand covered her breast, kneading it with a restless energy that sparked fires in her loins. Her breast ached for his touch, had ached for it ever since yesterday. And that fact sparked fresh tears.

He kissed them away with slow tenderness, his breath hot on her cheeks. "Don't cry anymore, Sara, my Sara. Please don't cry. I don't want to hurt you." He backed her to a nearby tree, then pressed her against it, leaving his hands free to roam her waist and her hips. The next thing she knew, he was inching her skirt up her legs. "I only want to give you pleasure. That's all."

Try as she might, she couldn't deny him. She didn't want to. It felt right to have his hands touch her, his fingers bare her thighs, questing upward to find the part of her that craved him so intensely it frightened her. The forest itself seemed to hold its breath as he kissed her again and again with fierce need, thrusting his tongue more deeply into her mouth with each stroke. His fingers found the aching place between her legs, and his thumb rubbed the little nub nestled in her silky folds of skin, making her respond instinctively by arching against his hand with a little mew of pleasure.

"That's it, sweetheart," he whispered against her mouth. "Let me give you pleasure. Only pleasure."

Some part of her sensed that this was his way of making up for the snake, of making amends for all he'd done. And though her rational mind wanted to scream that it wasn't what she wanted, her body said otherwise.

It craved this sweet losing of herself to him. It craved his touch, his body against hers. To her shame, the more he stroked her between the legs, the more wantonly she yearned for it . . . yearned for him.

"Yes, sweetheart," he breathed against her cheek, "take it. It's there for you. Let yourself take it."

She didn't have to wonder what he meant. An unfamiliar tension built inside her, like the eager anticipation she'd felt as the *Chastity* had left the Thames and slid into open sea. Ahead was danger . . . and excitement. She could feel it just beyond her grasp . . . beckoning, drawing her.

Every whisper of the leaves, every sliver of light dusting Gideon's hair, every luscious tropical scent conspired to draw her on. He no longer kissed her, too intent on caressing her. His face grew strained, his eyes burned with an unholy light, yet he kept stroking and fondling her, building the tension until with unexpected quickness it exploded inside her and rocked her with wave after wave of pleasure.

A hoarse cry escaped her lips as she clutched Gideon close, quivering and shaking against him. Oh, sweet God. Sweet, sweet God. Was this what it was like between a man and a woman? This . . . this piercing excitement . . . this shattering closeness? She'd never dreamed . . . she'd never imagined . . . no one had ever told her such things could happen.

Now that she knew it could, she understood why Gideon had offered it as an appeasement, why he thought he could tempt her into his bed.

And that understanding brought the bitter tears rolling forth once more.

Chapter 14

For up and down in sea-port town they court
   both old and young;
They will deceive; do not believe the sailor's
   flattering tongue.

—ANONYMOUS, "ADVICE TO YOUNG MAIDENS
            IN CHUSING OF HUSBANDS"

Gideon didn't know why he pulled away from her. He knew he'd given her pleasure. He'd felt her convulse around his finger, felt her shudder and tremble with the shocks of her climax. It would take very little to lift her legs and thrust into her, to bury himself in her softness as he'd ached to do ever since the day he'd first seen her.

Yet he didn't. This fresh onslaught of tears . . . this he couldn't bear. She cried like a woman who'd lost all hope, who'd looked shame in the face and seen her own likeness there. Each sob wrenched him as no woman's sobs had ever done before. It made no sense, none at all.

Angry at himself for his reaction, he drew down her skirt and released her, muttering a soft curse as he turned and walked swiftly back to where the dead mamba lay. He stood there staring at the snake, its body frozen in an S curve on the dried leaves, but he couldn't shut out the sounds behind him. The little gasps she made with each sob, the hiccuping breaths, beat a tattoo in his brain, wiping it clean of lustful thoughts. Only moments ago he'd been hard as iron, wanting her so badly he could feel the ache of it in the very root of his loins.

Well, he certainly wasn't hard now. How could he be, with those sobs of hers? Sweet Jesus, he couldn't stand them. She hadn't cried when he'd taken her from the *Chastity*, and she hadn't cried when they'd argued. To hear her cry now when she'd been so strong before just reminded him how he'd torn her from her home and family. She hated him for it. He could hear how much.

But she'd wanted him, too. She cried now over her loss, but a few minutes ago she'd wanted him.

Now her sobs were quieting, and he could hear her shifting her position, probably straightening her clothes to cover up all evidence of what they'd done. But what else could he expect from her? Miss Prim-and-Proper Reformer thought she was too good to be caught in the arms of a pirate. Damn her for that.

With another savage oath, he jerked his saber out of the ground and wiped it on some leaves. "You'd better go back to the beach. I should check the area to make sure there's not another snake around. They sometimes travel in pairs." Though it was true, it was really just an excuse. But he couldn't face her right now, not when she was so upset and he felt this ridiculous guilt.

"Travel in pairs?" She sounded horrified.

Digging his fingernails into his palms, he resisted the urge to return to her side and reassure her. "Don't worry. If you stay beside the stream, you'll be all right. Go on. I'll be along in a few minutes."

A short silence followed. "Gideon, I suppose I . . . that is . . ." She paused. "Thank you for saving my life."

"You've got nothing to thank me for," he bit out, unable to forget those heart-wrenching sobs.

"But—"

"Go back to the beach, Sara." He didn't know which was worse—her tears or her thanks.

Almost at once he heard a telltale crunching of leaves behind him, moving quickly away from the clearing. Obviously she wasn't staying around to repeat her thanks. And that irritated him almost as much as the thanks had.

Everything she did irritated him. He groaned. No, not everything. Not the way she responded to his lovemaking, her sweet little mouth clinging to his . . . warm, generous, inviting.

His unruly body grew hard again, making him scowl. She wasn't going to do this to him, confound her! He had too much else to handle on the island without worrying about one infuriating lady of the realm.

Letting loose a number of foul curses, he thrashed about in the surrounding brush with his saber, relieved not to scare up any more mambas. Unfortunately, he hadn't been quite truthful with Sara about snakes on the island. He and his men had tangled with quite a few since they'd been here.

Returning to the snake, he gave the blasted thing a good kick. If not for it, Sara wouldn't be so set against Atlantis. He sighed as he sheathed his saber. No, that wasn't entirely true. She'd been set against it from the beginning. The snake had only sealed her hatred.

He stared across the little clearing at the glossy, sun-washed leaves of a banana tree and the fruit that hung heavy from its middle like a jeweled chain about the belly of a sheik. Wild jasmine scented the air, the warm, pleasing air that lacked the damp chill of his native Yorktown. By God, how he loved it. If only he could make her see it as he did.

He snorted. Of course—make a rich English gentlewoman with a titled family appreciate the unspoiled beauty of Atlantis. It would never happen. Ladies of the realm did not sport on wild beaches with great abandon. They looked down their noses at dirty pirates.

They did whatever they could to get themselves back to their cold, bloodless England. If anybody knew that, he did. Wellborn English were never what they seemed.

Glancing down at his belt, he stared at his mother's brooch. How he hated all those blasted nobles! They thought they deserved the privileges they enjoyed. They thought they owned the world. Thanks to them, he'd been left to the mercy of a cruel man who had no sense of how to treat a child. Or anyone, for that matter.

That's why years later, when the War of 1812 had begun, Gideon had been more than eager to do his part for his country. He'd seen how English navy ships would take American sailors right off American ships, claiming they were English deserters. He'd nearly been taken once himself. And he knew all too well what cruel people the English were.

But he'd shown them all. He'd put all of them in their places.

Until Sara. He raked his hand through his hair. What had she done to him? She'd almost made him forget who she was and what she represented. She was passionate, not at all what he'd expected of an English lady.

But he mustn't let her passionate nature fool him. Once her passions cooled and her prim English upbringing resurfaced, she'd turn on him. That's what always happened.

He mustn't give her the chance. Whirling on his heel, he started toward the beach. No, he definitely wouldn't give her the chance. Oh, he'd make love to her, all right. He'd have her in his bed. But that was as far as he'd let it go. He wouldn't let her ruin his life, the way his mother had ruined his father's.

Who's ruining whose life? a little voice inside him said. *Sara had an earl for a stepbrother and a position in society until you took it away from her.*

Gritting his teeth, he came up along the stream and began to navigate his way down to the beach. All right, so he'd taken that from her. He hadn't had a choice.

What should he have done, left her on that ship to lead her brother after them?

That's just an excuse, that long-buried little voice repeated. *You didn't have to take her, and you know it.*

He stopped short, staring blindly ahead of him. His conscience hadn't bothered him in a long time. The day his father had died cursing his mother, Gideon had decided that a conscience was a luxury he couldn't afford. Obviously his mother had never listened to hers. And his father hadn't heeded his when he was strapping the tar out of a seven-year-old child. Gideon had figured he was better off without a conscience, too.

Why did the confounded thing have to pester him now? And over a woman, no less, an English noblewoman.

It was Sara's tears that had done it to him, he thought sourly as he continued down the stream. That's what it was. And women used tears to get what they wanted. His mother had probably done the same thing, and he'd be better off if he reminded himself of that once in a while.

"Cap'n!" came a call from the beach below, jolting him out of his uncomfortable thoughts. He looked down to see Barnaby and Silas waiting for him. Barnaby furiously smoked a cheroot, and Silas mumbled to himself as he clumped back and forth, drawing little furrows in the sand with his peg leg.

Hurrying his steps, Gideon was beside them at once. "What is it? What's wrong?"

"The men are grumbling," Barnaby said. "You know how you told them they were to sleep on board the ship until the weddings? Well, now that they're back on the island, they don't want to sleep shipboard. They want to take up residence in their homes again."

Gideon shrugged. "Then we'll keep the women on the ship. I don't see the problem."

Barnaby and Silas exchanged glances. Then Silas scratched his beard. "That won't work neither. The women don't want to stay aboard ship any more than the men."

"I don't care what they want," Gideon growled. "It's either stay on the ship or choose their husbands. Since they're not ready to choose, they'll have to stay on board until their week is up." And he certainly didn't want to rush the choice of husbands, or he'd be pushing Sara right into the arms of that blasted English sailor.

Not that he wanted to marry her himself, mind you. But he didn't want her marrying anybody else just yet, either.

Silas scowled, looking as if he didn't like Gideon's answer. "But them women, well, they've been on board a ship for weeks. It ain't healthy for them. Anybody can see that." He paused to look off over the sea. "Now, you take that little Molly, the one that's gonna have a baby. She don't need to be sleepin' on no bedroll when there's comfy beds here. It's like Louisa says, the women deserve a little . . ." He trailed off when he caught both Gideon and Barnaby gawking at him. "What're you two lubbers starin' at?"

"When in the bloody hell did you ever care about making a pregnant woman comfortable?" Barnaby asked, taking the words right out of Gideon's mouth. "And when did you stop calling Louisa 'that woman'? Don't tell me Miss Yarrow has softened your shriveled heart."

Red color crept up Silas's neck until his bearded face looked a mottled crimson and brown. "She ain't done no such thing. Just because she's got a little sense in her oncet in a while—" He broke off when Gideon and Barnaby burst into laughter. Turning away from them, he began to stride purposefully down the beach. "Aw, to hell with you both. It ain't none of your business what a man chooses to think of a woman. And it ain't like I . . ."

He passed out of hearing, his mumbling drowned out by the surf.

"I don't believe it," Gideon said. "Silas Drummond, captivated by a woman?"

"I wouldn't say captivated. I think it's more like flummoxed. No woman has ever stood up to him before. They're usually terrified of him . . . or disgusted by his wooden leg and his inability to give them satisfaction in bed. But ever since Louisa started fighting with him, he's been a different man. This morning, I even caught him dabbing bay rum behind his ears."

"How the mighty have fallen." Gideon knew one thing. He would never act like such a fool over Sara. Never. He glanced at Barnaby. "You're not in danger of losing your head, too, are you?"

"You should know better. I like women, to be sure, but they've got their place." He grinned. "Preferably, in my bed."

Gideon would once have shared Barnaby's opinion. Now he found it slightly unsavory, and that disturbed him. "Well, I see you won't be bothering me about a wife for some time. Not as long as Queenie is giving you what you want for free."

"True, true. But I assure you the other men are going to make your life hell until they get their wives, especially if you insist that they sleep on board the ship."

"That doesn't leave me much choice, does it? I've got to figure out a way to convince the women to stay on the *Satyr*—for a while, anyway." Sara, at least, would be more than glad to sleep in her cabin, especially after her encounter with that confounded snake.

The snake.

A sudden grin broke over his face. "Look, Barnaby, call the men and women together in front of my hut. I think I can convince our prospective wives that they don't want to sleep alone in our island dwellings." Turning back to the stream, he began to retrace his steps.

"Where are you going?"

"You'll see. Just gather everybody together. I won't be long."

Half an hour later, Gideon stood on the beach before the entire company with the noon sun beating down, a canvas bag in his fist. They all looked disgruntled, both with him and with each other. The women and men were divided, the men standing near the brush line and the women clumped together by the ocean. His men wouldn't look at him, but their faces were set mutinously.

The women, however, looked at him with challenge in their eyes, no doubt put there by the little troublemaker standing in their midst with head held high like Joan of Arc. How she'd gone from heartfelt tears to bold crusader as quick as lightning, he didn't know. But no matter. She'd soon learn who she was dealing with.

He held up his hand for quiet and got it for the most part, although some of the women continued to mutter in loud whispers. That ended, too, when he shot them a dark glance.

Pitching his voice above the sounds of gently rolling surf, he addressed them all. "Barnaby tells me that the lot of you are unhappy with the current sleeping arrangements." Both groups broke into explanations at once, but he silenced them with a shouted "Quiet!"

When he had their attention, he went on. "I understand that none of you wish to stay aboard the ship. And since the women still have four days to choose their husbands—"

"Five days, Captain Horn," a feminine voice interrupted. When he scowled at Sara, she added quietly, "We have five days left."

It was the first time their eyes had met since their stolen kisses in the woods, and it pleased him to see a blush spring to her cheeks when he prolonged the glance. "If you say so. I won't argue with you." He broadened his gaze to include the other women. "And none of you need worry that I'll go back on my word concerning the choosing of husbands."

As the men groaned and the women relaxed, he shot his men a quelling look. "We'll give the women the time they ask, won't we, lads?" It was more a command than a question.

"But Cap'n," one brave seaman called out, "do we have to be thrown out of our comfy houses just because these women are too uppish to share our beds without a courtship?" Choruses of "Yes" and "Why must we?" told Gideon that the other men shared the sailor's opinion.

Gideon waited until their voices died down before he went on. "That's the matter we're here to discuss. And I think when the women hear what I have to say, they'll see that it's wisest they sleep aboard ship."

"Look here," Queenie called out belligerently, "your men have been shipbound for less than a week, but we been sailin' for near to a month already. You told Miss Willis we'd be sleepin' on land, and that's what we want to do!"

The women murmured their assent. Gritting his teeth, Gideon glanced at Sara. She tilted her chin up stubbornly. Just as he'd suspected, she was behind this little mutiny. But if he couldn't handle a mob of women, he wasn't much of a pirate captain, was he?

"I understand how you feel, ladies." He gentled his voice, although he felt anything but gentle. "The problem is, this island is no place for women to stay alone at night. There are wild animals and other dangers." When the women exchanged looks, he added, "Miss Willis can tell you about those dangers herself. Only an hour ago, she was nearly killed." Reaching inside the canvas bag, he pulled the mamba out and held it up to show its full length, letting its tail trail along the ground. "By this."

There was a collective gasp from the women. "Snakes?" one woman shrieked as she caught sight of the ghastly headless reptile. "Oh, Lud, there are snakes here?" The others turned anxiously to Sara, whose gaze was fixed balefully on him.

Cocking an eyebrow at her, he smiled, then went on. "Fortunately, I was close by to kill it, but if I hadn't been . . ." He trailed off dramatically, letting them come to their own conclusions. "Of course, when all of you are married, your husbands can watch out for things like this, but in the meantime, you'd be much safer remaining on the ship than sleeping alone in our huts."

"Some paradise this is." Queenie kicked petulantly at the sand. "You're mad, guv'nor, if you think we're gonna sleep in a place where there's snakes roamin'."

"Yes," Louisa added. "You promised us a new land, and instead you brought us here to be eaten alive. I'm not setting foot on this island again until you rid it of snakes." She scowled. "And while you're at it, why don't you see that those huts are properly furnished? They're barely fit for one person to inhabit, much less two."

Fueled by Louisa, the women began to grumble about all the things they'd found wrong with the island. Sara just crossed her arms over her chest and smiled sweetly at him.

"There's nothing to worry about once you're married, ladies," he repeated, feeling as if someone had suddenly tugged the rug out from under him. The women were supposed to be throwing themselves into his sailors' arms to gain their protection, not threatening to mutiny. "My men know how to handle the snakes. As for the conditions in the huts—"

"Yes, Captain Horn," Sara interrupted in a honeyed voice, "do tell us about what improvements you intend to make. I'm sure you'll agree they're inadequately fitted out for us. As far as I can gather, there are no bedrooms to accommodate the women with children. Surely you don't expect them to share their husbands' beds in front of small children."

"Sara—" he began in a warning tone.

She went on blithely, the women crowding behind her as if she were their standard bearer. "Then there's the lack of secure doors and windows to keep all of your 'wild animals' and snakes out. Even your fearless pirates have to sleep sometimes, don't they? How will we be protected from snakes then? Not to mention the woefully inadequate cooking facilities and the lack of—"

"Silence!" he roared, making even her jump back a step. Blast the woman, he would find a way to muzzle that mouth if it was the last thing he did! He wiped sweat out of his eyes, speaking through gritted teeth. "I suspect that the kitchen facilities in the ladies' previous London dwelling were far more inadequate."

Thankfully, his reference to London's prisons shut most of their mouths. Even Sara couldn't seem to find an answer to that.

But his earlier encounter with her had taught him a few things about how not to unduly anger the woman. "Nonetheless, Miss Willis, we don't want you and the others to think we aren't willing to make concessions. You'll have your kitchen and your doors and windows. I had intended all along to send some of my men to Sao Nicolau for supplies once we determined what the women might want or need. If you'll give me a list of what's required, I'll make sure that a handful of my men go in the sloop as soon after the weddings as—"

"After the weddings?" Sara interrupted. "What are we to do in the meantime?"

"Sleep on board the ship. I know it's not the best accommodations, but with all the dangers to the women and your obvious concerns, it's the best I can offer."

If he thought he'd won this battle, Sara's too sweet smile gave him pause. "Under the circumstances, you leave us no choice." She paused, her expression growing smug. "In fact, your proposal has such merit that I think we shall stay aboard the *Satyr* indefinitely . . . at least until your men have made the dwellings habitable. We'll be happy to do that for as long as it takes, won't we, ladies?''

As the women chorused their agreement, a new swell of protests rose from his men. Gideon gritted his teeth. This was *not* turning out as planned. Although his men had gained their huts, Sara had made sure it was a hollow victory. He could force the women to live in the huts with their husbands after the weddings, but he was beginning to see that the women would refuse to cooperate as long as Sara kept helping them find reasons for not making this work.

His only choice was to send some men back to the islands as soon as possible and delay the weddings until they returned. Perhaps if the women saw that he and his men truly intended to make the island comfortable for them, they might relent.

At least delaying the weddings would give him more time to separate Sara and that blasted Hargraves. If only he could send that particular sailor off the island with the other men . . .

His eyes lit up. Why not? Hargraves hadn't been that pleased about living on the island. He'd seemed much more interested in the riches to be gained by piracy. Perhaps if he had some incentive, the man might choose never to come back.

Gideon hid his elation beneath a fierce scowl as he faced the women, bracing his hands on his hips. ''I tell you what, ladies. You decide what you need, and I'll send some men to Sao Nicolau in the sloop tomorrow for supplies. When they return in a few days, we'll get right to work on improving your homes. We can have them quite comfortable for you in a short time. That ought to satisfy you, don't you think?''

And I'll be rid of Peter Hargraves at last, he thought smugly as Sara turned to discuss what he'd said with

the women. *You haven't won this battle yet, sweetheart, no
matter what you think. You may have gotten your way on
the matter of sleeping arrangements. But you've just lost your
English fiancé.*

Chapter 15

In spite of all romantic poets sing,
This gold, my dearest, is an useful thing.

—MARY LEAPOR,
ENGLISH POET AND COOK-MAID
"MIRA TO OCTAVIA"

Crushing his hat in his hands, Petey hesitated outside the open entrance to Captain Horn's hut just after dusk. The place looked empty. It was dark as pitch, especially with only stars hereabouts to light the night.

Should he knock? But on what? There wasn't any door. Even though the captain's hut was the best of them all, it still had no window shutters, nor a proper door with a latch. Was it any wonder the women didn't want to be living in these wee cottages?

The rest of the island wasn't so bad, however. He'd taken a stroll about today, looking it over. It was a right nice little bit of land. Something could be made of such a place, if somebody cared enough to do it.

But that wasn't his concern. Right now, what mattered most was why the captain had sent for him. It was a mite alarming, to say the least. Petey steered a wide path around the man as a general rule. The pirates had made it clear that Captain Horn was fair and not given to unreasonable punishments, yet there was no telling

195

what the man would do now that he had his eye on
Miss Willis.

Miss Willis. Petey groaned. The little miss had surely
set the captain back on his heels today. Petey ought to
be grateful to her for trying so hard to delay the weddings. After all, she did it to help him and Ann.

But she'd pushed the Pirate Lord to anger, and that
didn't sit too well with Petey. A trickle of sweat rolled
down his nose, and he wiped it away with his thumb
as he peered cautiously into the ominous black hole of
the hut. The captain was obviously asleep or gone. No
point in staying here to risk angering the man even
more.

He turned away, but just then a deep voice rumbled
out of the hut's dark interior. "Don't just stand there,
man. Come in."

Petey jumped, then gulped down his fear. Here he'd
stood, hesitating like an ass, while the man had been
watching him the whole time. That pirate captain was
plain unnerving, that's what he was.

"I didn't see you there," Petey muttered as he entered
the dark room.

No response. There was a scratching sound, a tiny
spark, and then an oil lamp's low flame, which grew
larger as the captain turned the wick up. Now Petey
could see that the pirate stood beside a table. At least
the man's saber appeared to be out of sight, which was
exactly where Petey liked it.

"Take a seat, Hargraves." Captain Horn gestured to
a chair, then picked up a bottle of what looked in the
lamplight like rum. "Would you like to wet your whistle?"

Petey managed a nod. He needed something to get
him through this. He didn't sit down, though. He didn't
like to sit in the presence of his enemy, especially when
that enemy was offering him strong drink.

As soon as the pirate poured a goblet of the golden
liquor and handed it to him, he took a great, burning

swallow, then wiped his mouth on the sleeve of his shirt. Unable to withstand the suspense any longer, he took another swig for bravery, then spoke. "You wished to see me, Cap'n?"

Casting Petey a cool glance, Captain Horn set the rum bottle on the table and corked it. "Relax, Hargraves. I'm not going to have you keelhauled. I merely wish to show you something I think you'll find interesting."

That put Petey on his guard at once. There was nothing Captain Horn could show him, unless it was the sharp end of a saber, and that was of no interest to Petey. Was that what this was all about? Did the captain think to fill him up with rum, then take his head once his guard was down?

Petey braced himself as the captain went to a trunk in the corner and opened it. When the man picked up a long object and turned, Petey nearly fainted, expecting to see the pirate's famous saber.

The man held a scepter instead.

Torn between relief and shock, Petey gawked at the golden, jewel-encrusted rod that winked and sparkled.

As if he knew exactly what Petey had been fearing, Captain Horn smiled and twisted the scepter in the air almost as he would a sword. "Have you ever seen something so beautiful, Hargraves?"

Unable to do more than shake his head, Petey continued to stare at the scepter. Surely it was merely the lamplight that made it shine like a handful of fallen stars. Petey knew such things existed, but he'd never thought to see one with his own eyes.

Without warning, the pirate tossed the scepter in the air toward him. As it twirled, the hundreds of tiny facets reflecting the glow of the lamp, Petey sprang to snatch it from the air, barely saving it from hitting the rough plank floor. It was cold and heavy in his hands, and the metal gleamed so brightly, he knew it must be solid gold. He rubbed his fingers over it in wonder. A diamond the size of his thumbnail marked one end of the rod. Then a seemingly endless string of perfectly rounded pearls spiraled up the long rod to the ball, which was embedded with rubies and emeralds the size of walnuts. He was so enraptured that it took him a second to realize that Captain Horn was speaking again.

"I acquired it during my days as a privateer." The pirate sipped his rum, his eyes intent on Petey. "One of your English ambassadors was carrying it to the Prince Regent. It was a gift from an Indian rajah, I believe. No doubt the rajah thought to appease the English thirst for land with such a gift, but we both know it would take more wealth than that to satisfy your lust." The captain gave a smile as wide as it was wicked. "And since rumor had it that George would soon have a scepter of his own, I decided he didn't need another."

Only with an effort did Petey swallow his outrage at such blatant disrespect for His Majesty. The pirate was baiting him, and Petey dared not rise to it. Fingering the facets of a pigeon-blood ruby, he asked, "Why are you showing this to me?"

"It's yours." Petey snapped his head up only to find that the pirate was no longer smiling. "I mean it. It's yours. I have no use for it. What good is a scepter in paradise?"

Setting the scepter down carefully on the table, Petey eyed the pirate with suspicion. "And why would you be wantin' to give it to me?"

"Can't you guess? I want you to give up your claim to Miss Willis."

Stunned, Petey shook his head to clear it. The man would give a solid gold scepter to have one trouble-making Englishwoman in his bed? Either he was mad . . . or he was already wealthy enough to buy ten scepters. Or even more likely, this was some sort of game in which Petey would be the loser regardless.

"And what am I to do with it? As you say, what good's a scepter in paradise?"

"Ah, but you won't be in paradise. You're leaving.

Tomorrow. When my men sail out for Sao Nicolau, you'll be traveling with them."

Hope leapt in Petey's chest, but he fought it down. "You'd truly let me leave?"

The pirate shrugged. "Why not? If you abandon your claim to Miss Willis, such as it is, you can leave the island and go wherever you wish. I know you told me you couldn't return to England, but there are plenty of other places where you can live quite comfortably once you sell that scepter."

God help him, the man meant it. For a brief moment, Petey actually considered taking the blooming thing and heading out for parts unknown.

But his sense of responsibility wouldn't let him. What good was all that gold if it meant betraying his family and Miss Willis's trust in him? He had to live with himself, after all.

A shame that he couldn't use the pirate's offer to get Miss Willis off the island, but Captain Horn obviously wouldn't allow that. So he was stuck here. He couldn't leave her to the mercies of the Pirate Lord when the man was clearly determined to have her.

Petey started to hand the scepter back, then hesitated. Did he dare pass up this chance for escape? The longer he and Miss Willis stayed here, the more likely the pirate captain would get his hands on her anyway. She might pretend to be immune to the man, but Petey could tell she was more than a little enamored of him. The balmy air, the intimate living circumstances, the isolation . . . all of it would soon lead her to succumb, with or without Petey around. And if the pirate was willing to offer a golden scepter just to get Petey away from her, the man would never allow her to marry Petey.

Indeed, with that being the case . . . "Why are you givin' me the chance to leave? Why not just kill me? It's not as if anybody would stop you." When the pirate cast him a sinister glance, Petey added hastily, " 'Tisn't a suggestion, mind you, but a question. It seems to me that pirates being what they are—"

"Cruel, bloodthirsty killers, you mean." The captain propped one boot on a chair, his eyes glittering. "There are all sorts of pirates roaming the sea, just as there are all sorts of sailors. I don't know what you've heard of me, Hargraves, but I don't murder men in cold blood, and certainly not for a woman. I've killed in the heat of battle, 'tis true, but even that was before I became a pirate, when I served my country as a privateer."

"But the things I've heard, the things they say—"

"What else would you expect a baronet to say after he's been shown to be a coward? He says the pirates drank blood and ravaged innocents and that's why he didn't lift a finger to stop them when the ship was taken." There was an unmistakable thread of bitterness in his tone. "The truth is, my reputation for taking prizes against high odds during the war made it easy to be a pirate afterward. When merchant ships saw my flag hoisted, they didn't put up much of a fight. They knew they were outgunned and outmanned, and they didn't intend to risk their lives for a few caskets of silk. If you recall, that's exactly what happened with the *Chastity*."

His eyes narrowed to menacing slits. "But that doesn't mean that if you refuse my offer and stay, I'll stand by and let you have her. I won't. In the end you'll lose, and you won't even have the consolation of my gold." He took his foot off the chair and leaned forward, planting his hands on the table as he eyed Petey with suspicion. "Why all the questions, Hargraves? You'd give up any hope of riches and adventure just to marry Miss Willis?"

"No, of course not," Petey said hastily, before the pirate's suspicions could be truly roused. "You can be sure I'd prefer this scepter and the chance to be off this island to Miss Willis any day." He paused, weighing his words. "I just don't understand why you don't feel the same."

Captain Horn drew himself up with the bearing of one of those nobles he so disdained. "That's none of your concern. Do you want the thing or not? Because if you don't—" He broke off as he reached for the scepter.

Petey jerked it back. "I want it." He wasn't sure if he was playing this right, but it didn't look as if he had any choice. "I want it. I'll be off your island tomorrow."

For a moment, Petey could've sworn he saw relief in the captain's face. Then the man's expression hardened. "One more thing—you're not to speak to her of any of this, you understand? You must promise to leave tomorrow without a word to her."

"But she deserves—"

"That's the bargain. Take it or leave it."

"All right. I'll not say anything to her."

But that was one promise Petey didn't intend to keep.

London was never like this, Sara thought as she looked out over the lagoon from the porthole in Barnaby's cabin. A quiet that was so thick your thoughts were like shouts in the night . . . smells that tempted the senses instead of offending them . . . the sky a heavenly blanket of stars unsoiled by the black fog of a thousand households' smoke.

Best of all, mankind's influence was scarcely to be seen. How long had it been since she'd seen such a place? Even the countryside of England bore the marks of civilization. There were plenty of wild, unspoiled pockets in the British isles, to be sure, but she never got to see them. Any trip to such a spot would have taken her away from her work, and her work had inevitably carried her to the filthiest, most cramped corners of London. Until she'd sailed with the *Chastity*, she'd forgotten what it was like to breathe without having nauseous smoke or the fumes of horse leavings assault her lungs.

Taking in a deep, satisfying breath, she glanced across

the prow. There she spotted the stalwart pirate who stood guard, and all her enjoyment of the island dimmed at once. The guard was one of several. Gideon hadn't been foolish enough to let the women stay alone on the ship. Though she doubted she and the others could have sailed the *Satyr*, they might have tried if given the chance, and Gideon had apparently guessed that.

With a sigh, she turned from the window to stare at the luxurious cabin that was now her prison. At least for the moment. There was no telling what would happen after Gideon made them choose husbands. She refused to choose Petey now that she knew about Ann. But if she didn't . . .

One will be chosen for you. She swallowed hard. What would Gideon do? Assign himself to her as husband? Or was that more of a tie to her than he wished? Sometimes she thought all he wanted was to bed her and be rid of her once it was over. At other times she thought he felt something more, like today, when he was comforting her about the snake . . .

A shudder skittered through her body. That awful snake. And Gideon had faced it so bravely for her.

Now, Sara, she chastised herself, *you're thinking of him as some errant knight who wishes to rescue you. He's not a knight. He's a very wicked pirate with designs on you, and you must remember that.*

A pity that all she could remember was the gentle way he'd cradled her as she'd cried, the warmth of his mouth on hers, the sweet, hot slide of his hand over her breasts . . .

Stop that! she told herself with a groan. *You must put that . . . that arrogant beast from your mind!*

Only she couldn't. To her sorrow, she just couldn't.

Suddenly she heard a noise. It was soft, almost like a knock. Surely she hadn't heard right. The women were all below, and none of the men would be knocking gently at her cabin. Except Gideon, of course.

She smiled at the absurdity of that notion. If Gideon were to come to her cabin, he'd be pounding on the door.

The sound came again, and this time she was almost certain it was a knock. Curious now, she went to the door and opened it only to find Petey standing outside, glancing furtively around the now dark saloon that her cabin opened onto.

Unfortunately, across from her cabin was Gideon's. Jerking Petey inside, she eased the door shut. "Are you mad, Petey? If Gideon finds you here—"

"He's not on the ship . . . he's in his hut. But I share your worry, miss, believe me. Especially now."

"Especially now? What do you mean?"

Petey looked grim. "The pirate is payin' me to leave Atlantis tomorrow with his men. He says I may go where I wish from there, long as I don't return here." At her stunned look, he added, "I agreed to go, of course. 'Tis the only way to bring your brother back."

It took her a moment to assimilate what he was saying, but when she did, hope leapt in her breast. "That's wonderful! You're leaving! You can bring Jordan to rescue us all!" Then a sudden doubt assailed her. "Do you really think you can find your way back? This island has been isolated for centuries."

"That's only because it's off the main trade route." A fleeting grin touched his lips. "But I been watchin' the compass and takin' reckonings of our course ever since we left the Cape Verde Islands. I think I can find it again well enough. I'm sure he don't expect that a low sailor like me would've paid attention, since I told him from the first that I jumped off the *Chastity* because I didn't want to go back to England. I know that's why he's lettin' me go."

Was it? She chewed on her lower lip worriedly. It didn't seem right that Gideon would let Petey go so easily. "But Petey, this could be some awful trick. What if he has his men take you out somewhere and maroon you?" Her voice dropped to a whisper. "Or . . . or even murder you?"

Cocking his head, Petey stared at her with the solemn intensity characteristic of him. "D'ye truly think he would? D'ye think he's that sort of man?"

The question took her off guard. Was Gideon a killer? Of course he was. He was a pirate, wasn't he?

Still, her heart couldn't believe it, not after today. "No, I guess not." When Petey nodded, she clutched his arms. "But I could be wrong. And if I am—"

"He won't kill me. He told me he wouldn't. And I don't know why, but I believe him." He scowled. "But that don't mean he won't do other things. Soon as I'm gone, he'll try to take you for his woman, Miss Willis, depend on it. 'Tis the only thing that worries me about leavin' you."

It was the only thing that worried Sara as well, but this was no time to think of it. If Petey didn't go for help, they would all be forced into marriage, and she refused to see that happen. "You mustn't worry about me. I can hold my own against Captain Horn, never fear. We still have a few days before we choose our husbands, and I may have bought us a few more days today. After all, it will take the pirates time to improve their homes, and perhaps if we continue to balk, Gideon will . . . will . . ."

She hesitated. She could tell from Petey's expression that he didn't believe a word of it. "It doesn't matter anyway. You must go. It's our only chance."

Raking his hands through his hair, Petey nodded wearily. "I know. But I feel like I'm failin' you somehow." His voice softened. "You and Ann."

Sara chewed on her lower lip. Ann was another matter entirely. "You know she'll wait for you."

"They won't give her that choice." His expression grew so woeful that Sara laid her hand around his bony shoulders to comfort him. "I'd take her with me if I could, but the cap'n would never allow it. Besides, it'd alert him that I been lyin' about you and me. In any case, she's told me she can't go. She's a criminal now. If I go back to England, like I have to, she'll be in danger of being caught again and somethin' worse happenin' to her. So I got to leave her here for the moment."

"Don't worry," Sara said, wishing she could sound more hopeful. "I'll do what I can to make sure none of the other pirates has her to wife."

"I can't bear to think of her bein' forced into it—"

"I know. It'll be all right; you'll see. You concentrate on getting away from here and bringing back help, and I'll take care of Ann."

To her surprise, Petey suddenly threw his arms around her and clutched her in a bone-crushing hug. "Oh, Miss Willis, you're too good. I've failed you every step of the way, and here y'are, lookin' out for me and the one I love."

"Stop saying you've failed me. You haven't. You've done everything humanly possible and then—"

Whatever she might have said was drowned out when the door to her cabin swung open and slammed against the wall. She and Petey sprang apart at once, but it was too late. Gideon was staring at them with thunder on his face.

"You and I had a bargain, Hargraves. And it appears you aren't keeping your end of it."

Though the blood drained from Petey's face, he pulled himself up straight. "It wouldn't have been right to leave without sayin' good-bye. An honorable man wouldn't have done it."

"An honorable man wouldn't have sold her out for gold, either. Did you tell her that? Did you tell her you were more than happy to take wealth over her?"

When Petey merely shrugged, the look of fury on Gideon's face made Sara's heart skip more than one beat. The man was truly terrifying when he was angry, though she wasn't quite sure why he was so angry about this. It wasn't as if he hadn't seen her and Petey together before.

"Get out," Gideon added in a low, threatening voice. "Get out of this cabin and off my ship. You'll get your gold, though I ought to toss you to the sharks. Be on that sloop tomorrow, or I swear I'll do just that."

Casting her a quick, apologetic glance, Petey sidled between her and Gideon, then fled out the door. For a moment, she felt paralyzed by terror, but she recovered her composure quickly. It wouldn't do to let him know she was afraid of him. He'd take advantage of that.

She took a deep, steadying breath as she crossed her arms over her chest to cover her trembling. "I suppose you think you've won now. You've gotten rid of Petey, so you assume I'll just fall into your arms."

With an inscrutable look, he stepped further into the cabin and closed the door behind him. "I know better than to assume anything where you're concerned. You never concede defeat easily. But at least I've eliminated your best ammunition." His eyes roamed her with a familiarity that brought flame to her cheeks. "And I promise, sweetheart, I can handle anything else you throw at me."

He took a step toward her, then stopped. A grim purpose showed in his face as the lamp lit him in an unholy light. Stretching out his hand, he stroked the line of her jaw, leaving fire behind wherever he touched. Just this morning, he'd touched her like that, making her blood sing, dragging cries of pleasure out of her.

But he was different now. She couldn't put her finger on how. He was just different. In his steely eyes shone the same cold calculation she'd seen the first day of the capture. This wasn't the Gideon who'd held her while she cried. This was a Gideon who wanted only her body, who would take her without a jot of caring.

Though she found this Gideon as seductive as the other, this one terrified her as the other hadn't. And this one had the power to destroy her.

Carefully backing away from his outstretched hand, she whispered, "What happens after the battle is over, Gideon? You marry me? Is that what you want? For me to choose you as husband?"

At once his expression grew shuttered. Tucking his thumbs in his belt, he stared at her, a sneer forming on his lips. "Are you saying you *would* marry me? A disgusting, blood-hungry American pirate?"

"That's not the question, is it?" She thrust the heavy weight of her hair back over her shoulder, and his eyes followed her movements hungrily, making her regret the gesture. Tucking her hands beneath her arms, she hastened to add, "You haven't said that *you'd* marry *me*, an English noblewoman."

"Why don't we skip discussion of our impending nuptials until we see if we suit each other?" With a sudden lunge that took her by surprise, he grabbed her around the waist, pulling her into his embrace. "Unlike Hargraves, I like to sample the goods before I pay the price . . . *milady*."

He spoke the last word with such sarcasm that her heart sank. He only called her "milady" when he wanted to remind himself of how much he hated "her kind." And the rest of his crude words, meant to demean her, were more of the same.

"You won't be sampling anything of mine!" She shoved against his chest. "Release me at once, you . . . you . . ."

"Despoiler of women? Wicked ravisher? Come now, Sara, say what you like, but we both know you want me to make love to you. This morning—"

"This morning you were different," she blurted out. When his gaze burned into her, she added quickly, "You cared about me. And yes, I wanted you to make love to me. I admit it. But not now, not when you're like this. Not when you detest me so."

"Do I act like I detest you?" He ground his hips

against her until she felt his arousal. "Do I *feel* like a man who detests you?"

She shoved her hands against his chest, now almost frantic to get away from him. "I'm not talking about what you think of my body, Gideon. I'm talking about what you think of *me*. I've heard the contempt in your voice when you speak of my class and my position in society. I've seen how you look at me sometimes, with anger and resentment, as if you hate me for being English and . . . and privileged."

"That's neither here nor there." He caught her chin in his hand, trying to force her head up so he could kiss her. "Your body wants my body, and God knows mine wants yours. So let's satisfy both our needs and be done with it."

"No!" she cried, wrenching her head from his hand. "I'm not a plump hen for you to gobble up simply because you're hungry! Nor will I bear the brunt of your hatred for my 'kind'!"

This time when she shoved at him, he released her, though his breath came hard and fast as he trained his frigid gaze on her. "What do you want from me? Undying love? A vow of constancy? A proposal of marriage? What's your game?"

"That's just it, Gideon. I have no game. And since you can't seem to believe that, I . . . I want no part of you. Leave me alone. If you can't see me as plain Sara Willis, then stay away and let me find someone who can."

"You mean Hargraves."

"I mean, a man who doesn't hate what I am." Sadness laced her tone. "And I don't think you can be that man."

A sudden coldness seemed to freeze his body, for he went rigid and pale. "You're right. I can't." He started to leave, then hesitated. "But I doubt you'll find anyone else here to fit your lofty expectations, now that your friend Hargraves is leaving. My men hate your kind as much as I do. Your tastes are much too refined for any of them anyway."

His voice lowered a notch. "And we both know *I'm* the only one who can satisfy your other needs, the needs you keep pretending you don't have. So who will be your choice of husband, Sara? Who?"

That question echoed in her ears as he bent his head to clear the doorway and then was gone. A thousand curses upon the man for knowing her so well! Yes, who could she choose if not him? Who?

Chapter 16

She fell in love with the Sailor strait,
And on him she could ever wait,
She loved him so tenderly,
A sailor's wife she fain would be.

—ANONYMOUS
"THE LADY'S LOVE FOR A SAILOR"

Taking a furtive glance around and seeing no one,
Louisa ushered Ann into Silas Drummond's tiny
hut, which lay a few yards from the entrance to the communal kitchen.

"I thought Silas said we wasn't to come in here," Ann
whispered.

"I don't care what he said. The man clearly needs
help." Louisa waved her hand to take in the entire
room. "This place is a pigsty."

Soiled clothing lay in discarded piles on the scarred
wooden planks of the floor. Dirty dishes were strewn
about the room. Obviously Silas didn't believe in washing or putting away anything, despite the cupboard that
sat in one corner and the wardrobe and trunk in another. The room looked like the cave dwelling of an
ogre.

Well, Silas might act like an ogre, but that was only
a pretense. Louisa wasn't about to let him live in this

filth any longer. While he was off hunting grouse with Barnaby, she and Ann would set the place to rights. Although he'd complain about it later, he'd like it once he got used to it. What man wouldn't?

Besides, she could endure his grumbling as long as he never did more than that. In the five days since the capture, he'd mumbled and cursed and shouted, but he'd never once lifted a hand to her in anger. There'd even been moments when he'd shown her great kindness—like when she'd burnt her hand on that cursed galley stove. He'd found her an ointment to soothe it. And when she'd complained about the hardness of her bedroll on the ship, she'd gone back one night to find a feather mattress in its place. At the time she'd guessed he might have put it there, but now she knew for sure, because she could see her bedroll lying on his bed.

But that was Silas, all bark and no bite. So the least she could do for him was set his house to rights. "Well, let's go to it, Ann," she said as she rolled up her sleeves. "We've got quite a bit of work to do before the men return."

With a nod, Ann stepped toward the crude table and swept some biscuit crumbs into her apron. "I wonder if Petey's made it to Sao Nicolau yet. It's been three days this mornin' since they left. They ought to be there by now, don't you think?"

Louisa cast the Welshwoman a sidelong glance, but all she saw in Ann's face was a wistful regret, which was better than the horribly sad expression the woman had worn for the first two days of Petey's absence. "Most likely the men have been there and gone. They'll be sailing into Atlantis in a day or two."

"But not Petey."

"No," Louisa said in a soothing voice, "not Petey." It still surprised her that Petey had been so willing to abandon them. She'd always thought herself a good judge of character, and he hadn't seemed the type to run off.

"Now that Petey's gone," Ann said, "who do you think Miss Willis will choose for her husband?"

"I don't know. Sara dislikes all the pirates enormously."

"Not all of 'em. She's fond of the captain. I expect he'd be the only one she'd consider choosin'."

Louisa had bent to sweep some rotting banana peels into a dustpan, but now she straightened and stared at Ann. "Captain Horn? And Sara? Have you gone mad? Sara *despises* the captain."

Ann shook her head. "I don't think so, Louisa. She fights with him, but I think she pines for him, too. And it's clear as day he's got his eye on her."

With a snort, Louisa swept more refuse into the dustpan. "Oh, of course. That's why he called for Queenie that night we arrived—"

"But he didn't do nothin' with her. I heard her tell one of the other girls all about it. He sent her to Mr. Kent instead. And I'll wager it was on account of Miss Willis."

Louisa stopped short on her way to Silas's bed to pull off the dirty linens. Sara? And Captain Horn? What a dreadful thought! It could never work, those two together. If Sara believed she could handle that pirate captain, she was much mistaken. He was the sort of man to break a woman's heart, especially one that hadn't been toughened like Louisa's. "If you're right, they've certainly been discreet about it. He seems to avoid her, and she does the same."

"Aye, but they watch each other when they think the other's not lookin'. One day she was laughin' at somethin' Mr. Kent said, and Captain Horn scowled so fiercely at 'em both I thought for sure they'd go up in flames. Right after that was when he put Mr. Kent to helpin' the men bring lumber from the far side of the island. He's got an eye for her, and I think she's got one for him, too."

"Oh, I hope you're wrong. He's not the right man for her."

"I dunno." Ann bent to pick up a pewter cup lying under the table. "He's not so bad as you might think. He was right nice to me when we talked once. Asked me about Ma and all. He's not so bad once you get to know him."

"Getting to know him is precisely what I intend to avoid," Louisa muttered as she snatched the sheets off the bedroll that lay in the midst of a spartan wooden frame. Captain Horn terrified the wits out of her. He was too much like Harry, her former employer's son, for her tastes. Although she'd never seen Captain Horn hurt anyone, she couldn't help believe his bite would be far worse than his bark, which was fierce enough. In any case, she had no desire to find out for certain.

Nor could she bear to think of sweet Sara in that hard man's arms. She didn't care what Ann said, the thought was just dreadful. The next chance she had to be alone with Sara, she'd talk some sense into the woman.

Suddenly, Ann let out a low whistle from across the room. "Dear me, what's this?" Setting aside the pewter cup she still held in her hand, she picked up a large carved wooden object half-hidden behind a balled-up pair of rank-smelling woolens.

Louisa glanced at what Ann was holding and shrugged. "It looks like a carving of a woman."

"Yes, but with such big— I mean, have you ever seen a woman with . . . with . . ."

"Bosoms," she said dryly. "You can say the word, you know."

Taking the carving from Ann, she turned it in her hands. The woman did indeed have disproportionate breasts for her body. They were large as pumpkins. They matched a set of buttocks that were truly spectacular in size, but then, a woman would need those buttocks to keep the weight of those breasts from making her keel over. Louisa examined the small head and feet, recognizing the style from things she'd seen in books. "I suspect this comes from one of those African places where they worship fertility goddesses."

Ann looked puzzled. "Fertility goddesses?"

"I read about them in a travel journal a long time ago." *Back when I spent my evenings reading, when I had a life ahead of me. Back before Harry started fondling my "bosoms"* . . .

"But what's a fertility goddess?" Ann persisted, jerking Louisa from her unpleasant thoughts. "And why are her . . . bosoms so big?"

"Because she represents the fertility of women." When Ann looked blank, Louisa added, "Women feed children from their breasts, so the craftsman made them big to show women's nurturing qualities."

Clearly Ann was completely unfamiliar with the concept of symbolism. The young woman took the carving back from Louisa. "Do you think Silas worships it?"

"I doubt it," she said dryly. "Judging from what Barnaby told us, Silas can't . . . er . . . father children. No, I suspect his interest in it is more prurient."

"Aye, and probably nasty, too."

"Yes, probably so," Louisa said, biting back a smile.

Ann was now scrutinizing the carving. " 'Tis a funny-shaped thing, if you ask me. All teats and buttocks and nothing else. I wonder, do the women in Africa look like this?"

"I doubt it. If they did, we'd already have seen a mass exodus of the English male populace to Africa."

Ann giggled. "Aye, but they'd be disappointed. A woman like that couldn't even lie down, could she? Her breasts are so big, they'd hang off the sides of her, and she'd have to balance atop that enormous rear end. She'd never get any sleep and that would keep her husband awake at night."

"I don't think her lack of sleep would be what kept her husband awake at night," Louisa mumbled.

Ann looked at her with a complete lack of comprehension, and this time Louisa couldn't contain her smile. Really, sometimes Ann was like a child. Despite everything she'd gone through, she still looked at the world with fresh eyes. Louisa had never been that innocent. She'd never been allowed to be.

"You know, Silas shouldn't have something indecent like this laying about," Ann said. "One of the children might see it." She brightened. "I know! We should put clothes on it! That would make it all right, don't you think?"

"Oh, by all means. Do clothe the woman," Louisa said, laughter bubbling up from the back of her throat.

Ann flitted about the room looking for something appropriate. "Ah, this'll be fine," she said, her back to Louisa. She fooled with the thing a bit, then turned and held it up for Louisa's approval.

It took Louisa a second to recognize what Ann had chosen to clothe the poor beleaguered fertility goddess in, but as soon as she did, she burst into laughter.

Silas's drawers. Ann had clothed the carving in Silas's dirty drawers.

After that, Louisa couldn't stop laughing. Ann had tied the legs around the carving's neck so that the back side of the unlaced drawers covered her front. It was truly a sight to behold. And when Ann looked at her in all innocence, obviously unaware that the lady's clothing was as indecent as the lady herself, Louisa laughed so hard her sides hurt.

"Louisa, are you all right?" Ann asked as she went to her friend's side. "I swear, you're behavin' strange today. Really strange."

Louisa couldn't even speak. All she could do was laugh and point at the carving.

"This?" Ann asked as she held the carving up. "What's wrong? Don't you like her fine woolen dress?"

Louisa erupted in more peals of laughter. Unfortunately, it was just at that moment, when Louisa was laughing herself to death and Ann was waving the carving about in the air, that Silas chose to make his untimely entrance.

"What are you females doing in here?" his raspy male voice roared from the doorway, making them both jump.

Ann dropped the carving at once, watching with horrified eyes as it rolled across the wooden floor, losing its exotic gown in the process. Louisa managed to rein in her laughter, though a few chuckles still bubbled out of her.

"We wasn't doing nothin', truly," Ann began to babble. "Louisa said . . . I mean . . . we thought . . ."

"It's all right, Ann." Louisa faced Silas, laughter still in her eyes. But when she saw his livid expression and reddened face, she sobered at once. "I'm sure Silas knows better than to blame you."

"We was just tryin' to help." Bending to pick up the carving, Ann held it out to Silas. "Honestly, Mr. Drumm—"

Silas made a choking sound as he saw what Ann held in her hands. "Get out." Snatching the carving from her, he tossed it across the room. "I said get out of here! Now!"

Ann hurried to the door, and Louisa followed quickly behind, but just as she approached Silas, he grabbed her arm. "Not you, Louisa . . . just her. I got a word or two to say to you."

Her heart sank, and for the first time since she'd met Silas, Louisa felt fear. This wasn't the man who'd given her salve for her burn. This was a different Silas. She'd never seen him look quite so furious. His eyebrows were drawn into a tight frown, and even his beard seemed to bristle up. She must have been daft to think he would overlook her coming into his hut while he was away. Daft indeed.

Well, it didn't matter. She'd dealt with plenty of angry men before, and the best way to fend them off was not to let them take advantage of you. She'd learned that lesson the hard way.

Wrenching her arm from Silas's grasp, she faced him, her posture stiff. "It'll do you no good to scold me, Silas. I didn't do anything wrong. Someone had to clean up this . . . this pigsty you call a house, and since you obviously weren't going to ask anyone—"

"You aimed to do it behind my back."

There was a wealth of resentment in his tone that suddenly made her realize how he might see this. "Not exactly. I just . . . I thought you would appreciate it more once it was done."

"Oh, you did, did you? You thought I'd appreciate havin' my things tossed about and made fun of?"

She colored. "That wasn't what it seemed. We were just—" She broke off when she realized she couldn't possibly explain that to his satisfaction. "We weren't trying to cause trouble. We just wanted to help . . . to . . . to pay you back for being so kind to us."

His eyebrow shot up. "To *us*?"

Her blush deepened. "To me."

That seemed to give him pause. He stared at her a long moment. Then, to her surprise, he turned away and headed across the room. Taking his pipe off a shelf, he filled it with tobacco, then lit it and took a couple of puffs before cradling it in his right hand. The pungent smell of tobacco smoke filled the room. When he faced her, his anger seemed to have faded.

Instead, he watched her with eyes half-hooded by his bushy eyebrows. "You're a meddling woman, Louisa Yarrow, do you know that? A meddling woman if ever I saw one." He paused to draw hard on his pipe, his brown eyes watching her the whole time. "What puzzles me is why you meddle in *my* life when there's plenty of other men on this island for you to pester. That's all I want to know."

"I didn't think of it as pestering you."

He ignored her caustic comment. "Why me, Louisa? Why am I the only one?"

She grew uncomfortable under his intent stare. Turning away from him, she began to snatch up his soiled clothing. "You're the cook, that's all, and I wanted to make sure we got some decent food for a change. You must admit you're not the best cook, Silas."

He didn't protest the insult hotly, as he usually did with everyone else. To her shock, he said, "Aye, 'tis true. I served Gideon well as a sailor before I lost me leg, and that's why Gideon puts up with me cookin'."

She hadn't known that. It made her revise her opinion of Captain Horn a little.

"But that don't answer my question," Silas continued. "You don't know much more about cookin' than I do. I heard you were a governess back in England, not a cook."

"I was. But in the years I worked for the Duke of Dorchester, I . . . became interested in cooking. I used to spend a lot of time in the kitchen." Yes, quite a bit of time. It had been the one place Harry could never catch her alone, the one place she was safe from his groping hands. That she'd learned a bit about meal preparation had just been a side benefit.

"I still say you ain't tellin' me everythin'. I've scolded you and grumbled at you, and it don't seem to bother you. Why ain't you scared of me the way the others are?"

"Because I know you won't hurt me!" she blurted out, then wished she hadn't. Why must he ask all these uncomfortable questions?

"Ah. I thought that might have somethin' to do with it." When Louisa looked at him in surprise, he added, "Who was it who hurt you? What man hurt you so bad inside that you only feel safe with a man you think can't bed you?"

Her face turned crimson. "I don't know what you're talking about."

He set his pipe down with a scowl. "Aye, you do. I been thinkin' on it. The only reason a woman like you would turn away Barnaby for me is if she didn't want a man to touch her."

She'd never said it to herself. She'd never even thought it. But deep inside, she knew that was indeed why she'd latched onto Silas. He was good and kind . . . and impotent. She'd never have to fear that he'd come up behind her and force himself upon—

She bit her lip hard, trying to contain the raw feelings that always brought her close to tears.

He came toward her, his face intent. "I ain't blind, Louisa. I've seen how you flinch when a man touches you. I've seen how terror leaps up in your eye before you fight it back and sharpen your tongue to make 'em keep their distance." He stopped a few feet from her. "You think if you make yourself useful to me, I'll marry you, even though supposedly I can't bed you."

"That's not true," she protested feebly before the word "supposedly" sank in. "What do you mean, 'supposedly'?" Then, realizing how awful a question that was, she stammered, "That is . . . well . . ."

"Don't trouble yourself over it. I know what that fool Barnaby probably told you. Said I couldn't make love to a woman, didn't he?"

She debated whether to admit it, but finally decided she owed him that much honesty. "Yes."

"He told you I didn't like women 'cause I couldn't bed 'em. That's what he said, ain't it?"

Averting her face from him, she nodded.

"Well, it ain't true."

Her gaze shot around to meet his. "Wh-What do you mean?"

"I mean, my parts are in as good a working order as that damned Englishman's."

"But why—"

"It's a long story." His lips thinned into a tight line beneath his mustache. When she looked at him expectantly, he sighed and rubbed his beard. "At the time I lost me leg, I had a common-law wife on one o' the islands in the West Indies. A Creole, she was. Gideon brought me home to her for healin', and she took care o' me. But me lack of a leg bothered her. She tried not to let me see how much, but one day I found her rollin' about in the bed with a merchant. 'Twas then I knew she'd never love me again . . . if she ever had."

When he turned away and went to the table, dropping heavily into a chair and picking up his pipe again, Louisa wanted to follow after him and give him comfort. Poor Silas. It wasn't right; he was a good man. How could any woman stop loving her husband for something so trivial, so unimportant?

"We parted ways then," he went on. "She went to her merchant, and I went back to sea as the *Satyr*'s cook. But the men all thought the problem between us must've been in the bedroom. They thought I'd injured somethin' else when I injured me leg." He stared down at his pipe. "I . . . sorta led 'em to think it. It bothered me less to have 'em thinkin' my wife left me because I couldn't give her what any woman has a right to than to admit she just didn't . . . like me. The men . . . they thought it was tragic and all, and I let 'em think it. Gideon knew the truth, but nobody else. And he always kept my secret."

He drew hard on his pipe, then exhaled, the smoke swirling up about him like incense. "Truth be told, after that I weren't interested in women anyway. She'd trampled on my heart, and I didn't think to find nobody else to care for me again. So I . . . went without a woman, 'cept when I could get away in secret to find a whore in some port."

With a sinking feeling she wiped her clammy hands on her skirt. She knew where this was leading. And she didn't know what to do about it.

He lifted his face to hers, his eyes as clear as the sky outside. "Then you came along, a spitfire like I never seen. You were the tonic a man takes to brace himself for livin'. And I knew I had to tell you the truth."

"Don't say any more. Please, Silas—"

"I got to say it, Louisa. I just got to. You cozied up to me because you thought I weren't a real man, because some bastard made you afraid o' real men. I'd like to flatter meself that there was more to it than that—"

"There was!" She couldn't let him think that she just chose to be around him because she thought he was safe. When he stared at her over his pipe, disbelief in his expression, she added softly, "Truly, there was more. You're kind and gentle and—"

"I ain't kind and gentle, lass!" he roared as he jumped to his feet. "That's what I been tryin' to tell you. When I see you in the mornin', lookin' like the freshest rose that ever bloomed on these shores, the blood pounds in me ears. I want you so bad, I want to haul you into me arms and kiss the life out o' you. What I feel for you . . . it ain't gentle." He tossed his pipe down, his eyes now alight. "And you want gentle. You want a man who'll treat you like a piece of delicate glass, and—"

"No, that's not what I want."

"It ain't that I don't think you deserve it," he went on as if he hadn't heard her. "I *know* you deserve it. You deserve a whole man—"

"Stop it!" She flew to his side. "Don't say such nonsense! You *are* a whole man! You happen to be missing a leg, but that doesn't mean anything." When he looked at her, startled by the passion in her voice, she added, "Not to me. It doesn't mean anything to me."

His eyes narrowed as he stroked his beard. "What're you saying, lass? You got to speak plain with me, because I ain't good at guessin' what a woman's thinkin'. That's one thing I learned from me wife."

Louisa paused a moment. What was she saying? That it didn't matter if he touched her and held her? That she might even like it?

Oh, she was so confused. She'd sworn after the last

time Harry had forced himself on her that she would never let a man touch her again. She'd driven that kitchen knife through his leg, hoping to hit something else, and for her pains, she'd gotten fourteen years' transportation.

But Silas was so different from Harry. Although both men were arrogant, Harry's arrogance had stemmed from a belief that everybody was put on this earth to serve him. He would never have said she deserved someone gentle. He'd always thought she should be proud that he saw fit to rape her once a week.

Silas's arrogance, on the other hand, was a defense much like hers. It was a way to keep the men from laughing at him for his wife's cuckolding him. She knew what it was like to use pride and scorn as a defense. Pride and scorn had seen her through her trial. They'd seen her through this capture. No one seemed to understand that the way Silas apparently did.

But was his understanding enough? If he did "haul her into his arms," would she feel as if she wanted to die, the way she'd felt when Harry had jerked up her skirts and thrust himself into her?

There was only one way to find out. "I think I'm saying . . ." She halted, not sure how to put it. "I mean, I *know* I'm saying . . . that if I have to choose a husband, I would rather it be you than anyone else."

"Even after what I told you? Because you got to understand, Louisa, I can't live in the same house with you and not touch you." His voice grew rumbling and deep, striking her with both fear and excitement. "I want to make love to you, lass. I don't want none of them other women, so if it ain't you, then I'll just go on as before. But if I marry you, I can't promise not to touch you—"

"Then don't promise it," she said, surprising even herself. Stepping up to him, she laid her hands on his arms. They were strong arms, strong enough to break her in two, to take her by force . . . to hurt her badly. Yet she could feel them tremble beneath her fingers, and that eased her fears. Surely a man who could tremble at her touch wouldn't hurt her . . . would he?

She lifted her face to his, her courage nearly failing her when she saw the blatant desire in his eyes. The only thing that kept her from racing out of that cottage was the fact that he hadn't grabbed at her . . . not yet, anyway.

"I want to try, Silas. With you. No matter what you say, I trust you not to hurt me. You won't, will you?"

"Never." His hands crept up to rest lightly on her waist. "But if you stand this near me for a minute longer, I swear I'm gonna kiss you."

Her breath quickened despite all her fears. "All right."

He looked at her as if he hadn't heard her correctly. "What did you say?"

"Kiss me, Silas."

She didn't have to ask again. He wasted no time in getting right to it. And as his mouth met hers, she forgot all about Harry, the heir to the Dorchester dukedom. She forgot about prison and her trial and the capture. All she could think was that Silas the grumbler kissed like something from the great beyond. And she'd been long overdue for a taste of such heaven.

The kiss grew long and deep and hard, yet she found herself clinging to his vest and pressing her body against his. It was only when she felt his erection that she jerked back, the old fear welling up in her again.

But he was smiling now, an unusual thing indeed for Silas. "Don't fret it, love. I don't expect you to throw yourself into me arms with grand abandon so soon. But now that I know you can tolerate me kissin', I know the rest will come."

"Are you sure?" Why was her breath suddenly stuck way down in her lungs? And why did she already want him to kiss her again? "I-I thrust a kitchen knife in the leg of the last man who . . . lay with me."

Silas's smile faded. "Did he deserve it?"

"In my opinion, he did," she said emphatically. She couldn't even look at him. "He . . . he took me against my will many times."

His fingers tightened on her waist. "Aye, he deserved it then. He deserved that and more." His eyes were solemn as he tipped up her chin until she was looking at him. "And if ever I deserve it, you thrust a knife in my leg, too. I'll even let you ruin me good leg, if that's what it takes to have you as me wife."

His words were so sweet, so dear, that tears welled in her eyes. "Oh, Silas," she said, throwing her arms about his neck, "I don't deserve you."

"Aye, you do." He tugged her close, resting his chin on top of her head. "The man who made you think so poorly of yerself was a bastard, but one day you'll tell me all about him so I can make you forget his treachery once and for all. Then we'll go on. Together. We'll make babies, and we'll be happy, and the devil take anybody who tries to stop us."

Yes, my love, she thought as he raised her head for another heated kiss. *Yes, oh, yes.*

Chapter 17

A little alarm now and then keeps life from stagnation.

—Fanny Burney, *Camilla*

Sara stood in the hold of the *Satyr*, taking stock of what clothing the women had managed to carry away from the *Chastity*. The other pirates were expected back tonight or tomorrow, and she wanted to be ready to portion out the clothing they were bringing. It was only when she rubbed her eyes that she realized how the light was waning in the hold. It had been early afternoon when she'd come down here, the time most of the women avoided the hold because of the heat. But now it must be almost dusk. Soon she would have to light a lamp.

Suddenly, she heard the hatch to the hold being opened and footsteps descending the stairs. She went still. It was probably one of the women, but she found herself half-hoping, half-fearing it was Gideon.

He'd avoided her ever since that night in her cabin, treating her as if she were a nasty contagion. Whenever she ventured to speak to him about some matter concerning the women, he gave her a dismissive answer and went on about his business.

Though his behavior wounded her, she told herself it was for the best. If Petey succeeded in his escape, she would soon be leaving this place, and she ought to leave it as unencumbered as she'd come. That is, if she could find a way to stop Gideon from forcing the women to choose husbands. Tomorrow they were to choose, and she still had no clue how to prevent it, to buy enough time for Petey to return with Jordan.

Then the legs of the person descending the stairs came into view between the open steps. It wasn't Gideon, that was for certain. Gideon didn't wear skirts. No, it was Ann Morris, and as she rounded the staircase, Sara was alarmed to see she was crying.

As soon as Ann caught sight of her, she ran toward her, fresh tears rolling down her cheeks. "Oh, Miss Willis, what am I to do? How am I to endure it?"

Sara enveloped the small woman in her arms. "There, there, dear, what's wrong? Are you missing Petey again?"

It took several moments to get the story out of Ann, but when she did, Sara's alarm increased. One of the pirates was courting her, and when tomorrow came, Ann feared that she'd be forced to marry the man.

"He's nice enough, I-I suppose," she stammered through her crying, "but . . . but . . ." Here she burst into violent sobs.

"But he's not Petey," Sara whispered.

Ann nodded, wailing all the louder.

"I won't let you marry a stranger," Sara vowed as she held the small woman more tightly. She stared ahead unseeing. "This ridiculous plan of Gideon's to populate his island has gone far enough. I refuse to let it continue any longer."

Rubbing tears from her eyes with small fists, Ann asked, "What are you going to do?"

"You'll see." Sara hurried toward the stairs. It was time she and Gideon had another conversation about this foolishness. He must be made to understand that he couldn't simply hand wives out to his men as if they were so much stolen goods. She wouldn't stand for it!

When she and Ann left the ship, they didn't have to go far to find Gideon. He was discussing something with Barnaby and Silas in front of his hut. But as soon as she strode into the middle of them, their conversation died off.

"What do you want?" Gideon ground out, impatience clear in every line of his face.

Straightening her shoulders, Sara met his forbidding scowl with a scowl of her own. "I want you to put an end to this madness of forcing the women to choose husbands. Isn't it bad enough that you and your men carried us here against our will? Must you also insist on tormenting the women by making them marry men they scarcely know?"

"They have a choice."

She snorted. "Oh, yes, their famous choice. They can choose a husband or have you choose one for them. But they can't choose to remain unmarried, can they?"

"Do any of them really want that choice, Sara?"

Turning to Ann, who stood nervously behind her, Sara pulled the young woman forward. "Some of them do. Ann, for one. She . . . er . . . left behind a sweetheart in England. She isn't ready to transfer her affections to just any man."

"Left behind a sweetheart in England?" Gideon repeated caustically. "Truly? Or did she just lose one when he sailed away and left her three days ago?"

When Ann burst into tears and fled the scene, Sara faced Gideon with an accusing expression. "*Now* look what you've done!"

To her surprise, Silas cast Gideon a look of disgust, then took a deep puff on his pipe. "You shouldn't have said that, Cap'n. That girl's a delicate one, she is."

Barnaby rolled his eyes. "Louisa has softened Silas so much, I scarcely recognize him."

"Now see here, you blasted Brit—" Silas began to protest.

"That's enough, both of you," Gideon ordered, before

returning his attention to Sara. "I'm not changing my mind about this, Sara. I'm sorry Ann is unhappy, but don't you think she'd be better off with a husband and children than pining for some 'sweetheart' who's probably forgotten all about her by now?"

"Oh, that's just the sort of thing a man would say!" Crossing her arms over her chest, Sara glared at him. "Besides, Ann's not the only one, Gideon. Some of the other women are also reluctant to marry men they scarcely know. Why can't you give them more time?"

"Time for what? For you to tell them how they'd be happier as servants in that godforsaken New South Wales?"

"To prepare themselves to be good wives. Unhappy women don't make good wives, whether you realize it or not." A sudden inspiration came to her. He was always talking of how they would make Atlantis into a real community, a place they could all be proud of. Well, they needed the women for that, didn't they? "Of course, perhaps you don't care if they're good wives. As long as they're good bed companions, I don't suppose it matters if they do their share of the work on Atlantis or not."

A thunderous scowl crossed Gideon's face as her meaning registered. "You know quite well it matters."

She gave a calculated shrug. "Not to them. Why should they put their backs into making a place better when they haven't even been allowed any liberties? They're being forced to take husbands from men who've spent their lives as criminals, who suddenly claim to desire an honest life. Yet those same men show no concern for what they think or feel. They care only about having their own needs met."

Even Silas bristled at that one, and Gideon's eyes blazed as he said in an undertone, "You go too far, Sara."

She opened her mouth to answer him, to protest that

she hadn't gone far enough, when a voice cut through the tension.

"Fire!" a man shouted. They turned to see one of the pirates running up the beach, kicking up sand as he went. "Fire in the kitchen!"

Sara and Gideon both swung around. Sara saw it first, a plume of smoke, thin and gray against the dusk light. "Good heavens, it *is* a fire!" She grabbed at Gideon's arm and pointed.

"Confound it all!" Whirling toward Barnaby, Gideon ordered the first mate to gather the men. "Go aboard the *Satyr* and get as many buckets as you can find. And hurry! If the other roofs catch fire, there'll be no stopping it!"

As Barnaby scurried to do his bidding, Gideon shouted to the other men. Several pirates and women were already coming up the beach, and Sara, Gideon, and Silas led them to the fire at a run.

Beside her, Sara heard Silas mutter, "Please, God, don't let Louisa be in the kitchen. Anywhere else, but not in the kitchen." He was scanning the beach as he ran, his expression lined with worry.

They reached the kitchen to find it completely ablaze.

"Louisa!" Silas shouted.

He started for the kitchen door, but Gideon held him back. "You can't go in there, man! It's a blasted furnace!"

Suddenly, Louisa appeared beside them and threw herself into Silas's arms. "I'm all right, Silas, I promise," she said, her voice muffled against his chest as he clutched her tightly, thanking God loudly for saving her. "I wasn't in the kitchen when it started."

"We've got to put it out before it catches the other huts," Gideon said.

"Too late for that." Silas gestured to an adjoining hut, his face grim. A spark from the flaming kitchen had already caught its roof afire. "The weather's been so dry this week that they'll all go up like kindlin'."

"Where are those confounded lads with the buckets?" Gideon swore as he scanned the beach.

Sara followed his gaze, then caught sight of the linens she and the women had hung out to dry earlier that day. Many of the women were already milling around in front of the kitchen, wringing their hands. "Ladies! Go get those linens, soak them in water, and bring them here! And hurry!"

Gideon cast Sara a quick approving glance. "Good idea. We can use them to beat out the fire." As he took off his shirt and headed for the ocean, he told the remaining men, "Help the women! We've got to stop this before it spreads!"

Ann came up beside Sara from out of the crowd, her face etched with concern. "What about the children, miss? What should we do with them?"

"Take them back to the ship, and keep them there till this is over."

Ann hurried off, gathering children before her like a hen corralling her chicks. After that there was no more chance for conversation. They were all too busy filling whatever vessels they could lay their hands on with sea water and tossing it on the fire, or soaking linens and using them to beat at the flaming roofs. Unfortunately, the thatched roofs were very dry and much too high to reach easily. The women could get to the lower edges with their linens, but they couldn't reach the higher parts. And though the men were taller, even they couldn't throw the water as high as was necessary to soak the roofs enough to halt the fire. There weren't nearly enough men to throw the water, either, since at least a third of the pirate company was still away at Sao Nicolau.

After hours of dragging buckets up from the ocean and soaking linens to use in beating at the flames, there were ten huts afire and the kitchen had already burned to the ground. Weary in every muscle, Sara picked up a pile of sheets and started back toward the water's edge.

Gideon grabbed her by the arm. "No. There's no use."

She stared at him. The unnatural firelight flickered over his soot-blackened face. The complete desolation in his expression made her ache. He watched the fire with a grim gaze that tugged painfully at her heart.

"Perhaps if we—" she began.

"No. It's too late."

"What about the rest of the island? There will be nothing left!"

Pain spasmed over his features before he masked it. "I don't think the forest will catch fire. The huts are a good distance from the trees. Besides, the woods are green and won't burn well. But the huts are gone. We might as well accept that. Now we've got to get aboard the ship and cast off before it catches fire, too."

His bleak acquiescence tore at her. "You can't just leave it all to burn!" Sara cried as the other women gathered around her.

"He's right, lass," Silas interjected. He came up beside Gideon. His brown beard was gray with streaks of ash, and sweat poured from his red forehead. "We can't stop it. We'll have to let it run its course and pray it doesn't sweep the rest of the island."

"Maybe if we wet down the other huts—" Sara began.

"As if any of you cares what happens to our houses," Barnaby exploded beside her. He'd fought the fire valiantly, and now his fancy clothes were water-stained and streaked with soot. "One of you women left the fire going, and I think we ought to know who it is. Louisa?"

"Leave her alone," Silas barked, tugging Louisa into the curve of his arm protectively. "The lass ain't done nothin'."

"Maybe it was Ann," Barnaby spat. "I haven't seen her. Have any of you? She was angry about having to choose a husband. Maybe she decided to wreak a little havoc on her enemies."

The men nearby began to grumble, their eyes hostile.

"Don't be absurd." Sara swept her matted hair back with a weary hand. "Ann couldn't do such a thing."

Undeterred, Barnaby fixed his gaze on Sara. "All the same, one of your blasted convict women did it. We've never had a fire on this island before. One of your women set fire to our kitchen, and you probably put them up to it."

"Shut up, Barnaby!" Gideon growled. "It doesn't matter who started it. We've got more important things to worry about—"

"Cap'n?" interrupted a small voice from among the men. The crowd parted to let a young boy pass through: Gideon's cabin boy. His face was pale and streaked with tears. "It's my fault, sir. Mr. Kent called me outside to help with gathering wood, and I f-forgot to put the fire in the stove out. I was cooking b-bacon in the pan, y'see, and I thought I put it aside—"

"It doesn't matter, lad," Gideon said gently, ruffling the boy's hair. "But you were brave to come forward." He looked sternly at Barnaby and the other men. "And no purpose will be served by throwing accusations about. We'll be better off spending our time emptying the huts of anything valuable and saving the *Satyr*."

The men went pale. Clearly none of them had thought about the ship, but now they cast it worried glances. Sara did, too. Even she knew that canvas sails burned all too easily.

"Go tell the men to clear out the rest of the huts, Silas," Gideon ordered, "then get them aboard ship." He turned to Sara. "Gather the women and make sure they all get aboard. And find Ann."

"She's already aboard. I sent her to the ship with the children when this started."

"Thank God. I didn't even think about the children." He raked his fingers wearily through his hair. "It's time the rest of us joined them. We don't know how long or far it will rage before it plays itself out."

"But Gideon, we can't just let it burn!"

"Do as I say, Sara!" he snapped. When he saw her recoil, he added more softly, "Sometimes you have to recognize when you've lost. It seems Mother Nature has taken the matter out of our hands. Now all that's left is to pray she doesn't take the entire island away from us."

Chapter 18

*"I'll sit beside you your grief to lighten
And put my arm round your waist, asthore,"
And in a while she began to brighten
With hugs, and kisses, and the divil knows more.*

—JAMES N. HEALY
"MY SUNDAY MORNING MAIDEN"

I t was several hours later when Sara finally ventured out on the deck of the *Satyr*. She and the others had fallen into their beds exhausted just before midnight, when Gideon had told them there was no point in staying up any longer. The fire had mostly died out by then, but no one had possessed the strength to see it through to the bitter end.

Bracing herself, she looked toward the beach that lay a few hundred yards away, then let out a horrified gasp. Though nothing had changed since her last view of the island, it seemed even more shocking after a few hours sleep.

Every building had been destroyed—every single building, down to the wood floors. The impassive moon shone down on what remained—wide black squares on the sandy ground, like so many patches on a creamy quilt. Smoke drifted up from those to poison the clear night air and lend an unreal cast to the entire scene.

At least Gideon had been right about the forest not catching fire, she thought. Though some of the dried palm fronds had burned, the fire hadn't been strong enough to devour the green wood and damp, rich vegetation. The wind had been in their favor as well, for it had swept the fire toward the stream, which had acted to protect the forest beyond it, although some of the trees on this side of the stream had caught fire.

She moved further out on deck to get a better look, and that's when she saw Gideon. He stood with his back to her, his hands clenching the railing as he stared at the beach a few hundred yards away. He'd obviously not bothered to put on more clothing after the ocean baths they'd all taken earlier in an attempt to get off some of the soot and ashes. He still wore only the trousers and belt he'd worn then. No shirt, no vest, no boots.

He'd never looked wilder. Or more alone. A sudden pang tore at her heart. This was his island, his paradise, his dream. A moment's carelessness had reduced it all to ashes in the space of a few hours, and he had no one to turn to, no one to lean on. His men had been asleep for hours, as had the women. In any case he'd never lean on any of them.

There was only her, and though she knew he wouldn't appreciate her concern, she couldn't bear to abandon him, too. She came up behind him, laying her hand on his bare back. "Gideon?"

His muscles went rigid beneath her hand. "Go away, Sara."

Startled by the fierceness in his voice, she began to do as he'd asked. Then she thought better of it. He didn't need to be alone right now, no matter what he said. Sliding her hand in the crook of his bent elbow, she stepped up next to him. "I can't. I just . . . feel like I ought to do something."

"There's nothing for you to do. Go back to bed and leave me alone."

Looking up at his profile, she saw that it too was stiff

and cold, aloof. But there was nothing aloof about his eyes. Naked pain shone there, a pain as deep as the vastness of the ocean that rocked the ship to and fro. She couldn't bear to leave him when he was hurting like this.

"Atlantis means a great deal to you, doesn't it?" she whispered.

"Sara—" he began in a warning tone.

"But it doesn't have to be the end, you know."

A choked cry escaped his lips as he whirled to face her, wrenching his arm out of her hand. "It *is* the end! Confound it, woman, don't you have eyes? It's gone, all of it!" One sweeping arc of his hand took in the entire shore beyond them. "There's nothing left, not so much as a plank!"

"But we can rebuild, can't we? Make new, better homes?"

"Rebuild?" He scoffed at her, planting his hands on his low-slung hips. "Do you know how long it took us to build those crude dwellings, to saw down the trees and fashion planks and find enough thatch for the roofs? Months!"

"This time it wouldn't take so long. You'd have help. We could help you."

A muscle worked in his jaw. "Ah, yes, *you* would help us. You, who hate us. Right before the fire started, you threatened to abdicate all responsibility for the colony if you didn't get your way. As it turns out, your threats didn't matter. We were brought down anyway. You're probably all chuckling in your beds to see it."

The words hit her with the force of a slap. He certainly had good reason to think them, but still . . . "That's not true. You know we did what we could to help put out the fire."

"Perhaps." When she cast him an outraged look, he grudgingly amended, "All right, yes. You and the women did help. But that doesn't mean you'd help us rebuild. Why should you? You've nothing to gain from it but criminals for husbands."

She winced at his sarcastic echo of her earlier words. She wasn't ashamed of what she'd said, not at all. But she didn't like hearing it repeated under these circumstances, when he and the men had just lost everything.

"Things have changed," she murmured. "I wouldn't want . . . *we* wouldn't want to see you without homes. I'm sure we could put our differences aside long enough to . . . to help you set the island to rights."

He leaned back against the railing, his expression a mix of anger and frustration. "Really? How very generous of you."

Her temper flared, but she caught herself before she could retort. That was what he wanted, to drive her away so he could sink into desperation. But that was not what he needed.

"Yes, really. I want to help, Gideon. I want to help you restore Atlantis." Summoning up her courage, she added, "That is, if you're willing to fight for it instead of letting it die."

His eyes blazed. "You are the most sanctimonious, annoying female I've ever met!" Shoving away from the railing, he caught her shoulders, gripping them almost painfully. "Don't you *ever* give up?"

"No." Despite the fury she'd purposely roused in him, she kept her gaze steady. "It's that reformer blood in me, I'm afraid. I have to keep going until I reform everything." She added, almost defiantly, "And everybody."

He cast her a cold look. "You'd best not try it with me. I don't take well to reforming."

Suddenly his anger seemed to shift, transforming into something else, something dark and frightening and most certainly wicked. He flexed his hands on her shoulders, then edged them further in until his hands clasped her neck, his thumbs resting on each of the veins where her pulse beat madly. He lowered his voice to a rumble as he added, "Perhaps it's time I made you realize that."

He cradled the back of her head with one hand, and panic rose in her throat as she lifted her hands to press against his chest. "What are you doing?"

"You keep trying to reform me." His eyes glittered in the moonlight. "Well, there's only one way to fight that. By corrupting you."

There was no mistaking his meaning. He brought his other hand down to clasp her waist and tugged her closer. Alarm, and just a tiny thrill of anticipation, sprang full-blown in her chest. "Wh-what makes you think I can be corrupted?"

He drew her head close until his lips were an inch away from hers, his breath fanning across her trembling mouth. "Everybody can be corrupted, Sara. Even you."

Then his mouth was on hers, hard, purposeful . . . and yes, corrupt. His whiskers scraped her skin as he took her mouth wholly, thoroughly, the way a man bent on corruption ought to. She tried to gather her scattered wits, to marshal them to fight him, but it was hopeless. His mouth seduced hers to open, then his tongue swept inside with slow strokes that blanked out every thought in her head.

It was a wicked kiss, the kind calculated to make her respond wickedly. And she did. She slid her arms about his neck and returned his kiss with shameful eagerness, barely conscious of straining against his half-naked body as she rushed madly toward her own damnation.

Soon his hands were roaming her body, skimming lightly over her thinly clad ribs until they came to rest just beneath her breasts. His tongue drove inside her mouth over and over, playing with her tongue as he brought his thumbs up to caress her nipples through her dimity gown.

With a groan she tightened her arms about his neck. At once, his kiss shifted, growing fierce and needy. He dropped his hand to cup her derriere and urge her body nearer.

A noise came from one of the hatches, and they sprang apart, panting like two race horses in the final stretch. She glanced around, the color rising immediately in her cheeks. Thankfully, there was no one there.

When she looked at him, he was staring at her as a wolf stares at a rabbit. "Come to my cabin, Sara. Now. Stay with me the rest of the night."

She stared at him, at first uncomprehending, her mind so befuddled by his kisses that she scarcely knew where she was. As his words sank in, however, she opened her mouth to protest. Then she saw the look on his face. It betrayed a need beyond mere lust. It belied all his insistence that he was immune to reforming. He wanted her, yes, but he needed her, too, though he didn't know it yet.

At her hesitation, he went still, his lips tightening into a thin line. "No, I don't suppose the proper Lady Sara would do that."

There was so much wounded pride, so much anger in his voice that when he released her and started to turn away, she blurted out, "You're wrong."

He faced her once more, his eyes searching her face.

Under his scrutiny, she thought better of her words. "I-I mean—"

"I won't let you take the words back. Not tonight."

After that, he gave her no chance to protest or complain or even answer. He swept her up in his arms, the moonlight catching the hard, intent slant to his mouth, the hungry look in his eyes. While she was still gaping at him, her heart beating wildly in her chest, he carried her across the deck and through the doorway beneath the quarterdeck.

Seconds later, when she saw the half-open door to his cabin loom up before them, she blushed furiously. Good heavens, what was she doing? Had she completely lost her wits? She was letting a pirate carry her to his bed!

Oh, yes, a pirate . . . who kissed like a god, who made her feel things she'd never felt in her life. She wasn't mad; she was just tired of fighting, tired of craving his hands on her and having to resist her desires.

He kicked the door open and carried her inside, then kicked the door shut behind them. The latch fell into place with an ominous clunk. Shyly she glanced around the cabin she'd entered only twice before. The flame burning in the lamp by his bed flickered briefly, then glowed strong, swinging back and forth with the ship's motion to sweep golden light across the scarlet coverlet and inky pillows . . . the same scarlet coverlet that hundreds of women had probably graced.

Her heart pounded faster. She shouldn't be here, not with him. She couldn't be one of those women.

Or could she? She glanced up at his face, searching for some indication that this meant more to him than yet another conquest. But once his eyes locked with hers, even that possibility ceased to matter. She was lost in his need, a need that mirrored her own.

Keeping his heated gaze on her, he lowered her to stand before him, so close to his bed that she grazed it with her knee when she steadied her balance on the shifting floor. "Turn around," he said thickly.

She didn't know why, but she obeyed his command. When his hands unfastened her bodice, a shudder swept her . . . a shudder of anticipation. He undressed her like a man who knew exactly what he was doing. Her white, virginal gown dropped to the floor, leaving her in her cambric shift.

It was only when he drew her shift off her shoulders and down to bare her breasts that she knew a moment's panic. Though he'd bared her breasts before, he'd never done it quite so blatantly. And certainly never in such compromising surroundings. It made their union seem somehow inevitable.

When he began to slide her shift past her hips, she caught his wrists with both her hands. "Gideon, please

". . . I mean, I've never . . . that is, I'm . . . I'm—"

"—A virgin." He turned her around to face him, his expression so earnest that her heart began to trip faster. "Don't you think I know that? No woman has ever fought so hard to preserve her virtue. But there's no need to fight now."

He skimmed a hand up her body to mold her naked breast, teasing the nipple until she sighed. "You're as ready for this as I am, sweetheart. And if you don't believe me now, you'll believe me shortly. I promise you'll never regret the loss of your virtue."

Though she suspected he was right, she colored a deep scarlet when he slid her shift the rest of the way off, leaving her as naked as the day she was born.

Drawing slightly back from her, he cast her a long, seductive look, lingering on her breasts, her belly . . . the thatch of hair between her legs. She couldn't believe she was suffering his gaze, even welcoming it. But then, if anybody had told her a month ago she'd be standing next to a pirate captain's bed, craving his touch like a dockside tart, she'd have mocked them.

A woman of character would hide herself—but she was sorely tired of being a woman of character. No man had ever looked at her like this before, and though it embarrassed her thoroughly, she took a certain feminine pride in his admiring gaze.

Under that look, her breathing grew as labored as his. That is, until he stroked one finger from the underside of her breast down her belly to her thighs. Then she stopped breathing completely.

"You have a body made for corrupting," he said in a harsh whisper. "And I intend to corrupt it thoroughly tonight."

A tiny thrill went through her at his words, a thrill that only sharpened when he sat down on the bed, then caught her about the waist, drawing her close to stand between his legs. His mouth fastened on one of her breasts, sucking hard on the nipple until she gasped.

Oh, why did he have to make it so exquisite? Why couldn't he be clumsy or awkward or even cruel? Then she could fight him.

But he was the perfect master of seduction. While his mouth caressed one breast, his fingers kneaded the other until the tip was a tight knot, aching for his touch, for his hot mouth and clever fingers. She clutched his head closer, and he groaned.

"You taste so good," he murmured against her breast. "And I've wanted you for so long . . . so damned long . . ."

Then he was drawing hard on her breast again, distracting her as his hands stroked her rib cage, her waist, her thighs. He caught her unawares when he slid his legs between hers, then tugged her forward until she straddled his lap, her knees bent and resting on the bed on either side of his hips. The move opened her blatantly to him, so blatantly she hid her crimson face against his shoulder.

But he wouldn't let her hide from him. Tipping her chin up, he stared at her face, a devilish smile playing over his lips. "Remember what I did to you in the forest? Would you like me to do that again?"

She could only stare at him in mute embarrassment, unable to utter even a word. He dropped his hand to her thigh, then glided it up the soft inner skin. A shiver of desire whispered over her, and to her mortification, her lower body undulated toward him just a fraction. With a knowing look, he inched his hand up until it brushed her dewy curls. But he stopped there.

His eyes locked with hers, gleaming with purpose. "I want to hear you say it, Sara. Tell me what you want. Tell me you want me inside you."

Her cheeks flamed even more. Oh, he was too cruel. He was paying her back for all the things she'd said to him, all the times she'd refused him.

"I know you do," he said with the most infuriating confidence. "But I want you to say it. I won't have you telling the women tomorrow that I ravished you against your will." His thumb parted her damp hair to rub against the tiny nub there, making her jerk and press herself shamefully against him. But his thumb danced away after that brief caress.

"Say you want me, Sara," he growled. "Say it!"

Now his hand was stroking the inside of her thigh again, making her ache to feel those sensuous strokes higher up. She squirmed, trying to get nearer that terrible hand and its tempting offer of pleasure, but he took his hands off her when she did so.

"Please, Gideon . . . please . . . touch me . . ." The words were out before she could stop them. Her voice didn't even sound like hers, so breathy and sensual. Another woman possessed her body, making her act like this wanton, and she couldn't seem to stop it. "Please . . ."

He scowled. "That's all I'm going to get from you, isn't it? Very well. It's enough. For now."

Then he slipped one finger deep inside her in a velvet stroke that wrung a sigh from her lips. He began a slow motion . . . enter . . . retreat . . . enter . . . retreat. She rocked against his hand, and when his glittering gaze on her became too much, she hid her face again in his shoulder.

His hair brushed her cheek, smelling of smoke and cinders. Although he'd bathed since they'd fought the fire, he still bore the scent of the Prince of Corruption— of flames and ashes and brimstone.

It didn't matter. He stood at the gates of hell beckoning her in, and she rushed toward them without a thought. God forgive her, but she did want him. She wanted him more than anything she'd ever wanted. She'd been headed for damnation ever since that day in the forest, and tonight had only sealed her fate.

He nuzzled her cheek, then his mouth sought hers, taking it with a savage eagerness that increased her need. His tongue mimicked the movements of his fingers, driving in and out. She could feel his arousal press between her legs but could pay it little heed when he caressed her with such deep, erotic strokes. He broke off their kiss, his breathing harsh, guttural. Her hair fell into her face as strange new sounds erupted from her lips. The press of his hair-roughened chest against her now sensitized breasts only heightened the delicious sensations.

He brought her to the brink of the same pleasure he'd given her before, then abruptly withdrew his hand. A whimper of protest escaped her lips before she could stop herself, and her eyes shot open.

He wore a decidedly wicked expression. "Not this time, sweetheart. This time we'll reach it together."

As she stared at him, uncertain what he meant, he lifted her off his lap and laid her back on the bed, then stood up beside it. Tugging at his belt buckle, he yanked off his belt and flung it aside. She heard it clatter to the floor halfway across the cabin as he tore loose the buttons of his trousers, then dragged them off.

Her mouth formed a silent "O" to see him completely naked. So this was what men looked like. She doubted anybody could have prepared her for the sight of Gideon with his clothes off. His lean, scarred belly . . . his navel ringed with dark hair . . . his thick, corded thighs that attested to many hours spent balancing on a moving ship's deck—all of it tantalized and shocked her at the same time.

But what stunned her most was what lay between his thighs. Fully aroused, he was man enough to stun any woman. He was going to put *that* inside her? He would kill her!

"I . . . I can't . . ." She lifted her gaze to his face, desperate to make him understand. "I can't do this!"

She sat up and reached for a pillow to cover herself, but he was too fast for her. He climbed onto the bed, kneeling next to her, and she waited for him to mock her for her fears. Instead, he lifted her clenched hand to his mouth and kissed her fingers till they relaxed and opened.

Before she knew what he was doing, he'd taken her hand and placed it on his hard shaft. She tried to draw her hand back, but he closed his fingers around hers. "You see," he murmured in a strained voice, "it's not so bad, is it? It's only flesh. Flesh that aches for you, that belongs inside you."

He moved her hand on him, letting her feel the tight, smooth skin encasing his hardness. His fingers dropped away from her, and she continued the motion until he swore and pushed her hand away. "I'll go insane if you keep that up, sweetheart. I'm too ready for you." He flashed her a smile. "And you're ready for me."

When she opened her mouth to protest that she could never be ready, he kissed her, his arms clutching her so closely she could scarcely breathe. Before she knew it, he was shifting her body to lie beneath his and spreading her legs apart with his knees.

Then he was sliding inside her. She gasped at the intrusion and wrenched her mouth from his in shock.

"It's all right," he whispered in soothing tones. "Relax, sweetheart. Just relax."

"How am I supposed to do that?" she snapped in fear. She was all too aware of him inside her, over her, around her. She'd never felt so totally helpless, so conquered.

A lock of black hair fell over his forehead, making him look devilish, though his next words were anything but. "I don't know," he muttered with a shade of uncertainty. "I've never taken a virgin before."

He moved further inside her, and she stiffened. "How wonderful," she said sarcastically, as the sense of intrusion only increased. "You're a novice at this."

His lips twitched, as if he were suppressing a grin. Or a groan. "I'm only a novice at taking virgins. But I'm about to remedy that situation."

He inched further inside her, then stopped abruptly,

his eyes growing solemn as he stared down into her face. "You know it'll hurt some when I break your maidenhead, don't you?"

She nodded wordlessly.

"Do you trust me not to hurt you more than necessary?"

Every muscle in his face seemed taut from the effort of entering her slowly, and his eyes glittered with need. Yet he held off, waiting for her answer. That reassured her as nothing else could have. He might be a pirate, but he would not deliberately harm her.

Though she feared he had the power to hurt her deeply.

"I trust you," she whispered.

"Good." He sheathed himself fully inside her.

It was only a quick little burst of pain, but enough to make her cry out. He caught her cry with his mouth, kissing her until she relaxed. Then he began to move, sliding into her with long, slow strokes. At first it felt tight and unfamiliar. Then the slick friction of him inside her began to warm her, to rouse intriguing new sensations inside her. She felt herself open and loosen for him, like a sail unfurling to accept the mighty thrust of wind against it, inside it.

He held himself over her, his eyes the blue of the sky and the stormy sea. He thrust deeper, harder, making her ache for more.

It was sweet heaven and the torments of hell in one. Having him, but not enough . . . wanting him, but too much. Only half-conscious of what she did, she clutched at his arms to anchor him against her. He groaned, desire flaring higher in his face as he increased his tempo. He drove into her now as if he feared losing her, and she dug her fingernails into his arms to ride out the storm.

She felt as if he reached to the very heart of her. The ship rocked him and he rocked her, thrusting deeper and deeper, building the tension inside her until she cried out with needing him.

"My God," he muttered as he drove wildly inside her, like a mythical sea beast riding the waves. "My God, Sara . . . my Sara . . . yes, my Sara . . ."

Her head tossed against the pillows as the pressure built inside her, making her cry out and strain harder and harder to fuse her body with his.

"Yes . . . oh, yes—Sara!" he half-shouted, half-groaned, as he drove himself in her to the hilt. Jerky shudders wracked his body as he spilled himself inside her. She broke over the edge and felt herself careening through space.

As she cried out her pleasure beneath him, she fleetingly thought that he'd finally done exactly as he'd promised. He'd corrupted her. And to her endless shame, she'd reveled in it. She was wicked, truly wicked indeed.

Oh, how glorious it was to be wicked.

Chapter 19

One has no sooner left off one's bib and apron, than people cry—"Miss will soon be married!" . . . Mighty ridiculous! they want to deprive us of all the pleasures of life, just when one begins to have a relish for them.

—ELIZA HAYWOOD
ENGLISH ACTRESS AND PLAYWRIGHT
THE HISTORY OF MISS BETTY THOUGHTLESS

Sara was dreaming. Gideon stood with her at an altar, looking civilized and very English. His black hair was cropped close to his ears beneath a tall felt hat, and his saber was missing. He wore a fashionable frock coat of deep blue superfine, and she wore a gown of shimmering white silk, with a ruched bonnet rounded with ribbon and sprigs of orange blossoms.

But when she looked about her, the church was filled with convict women and pirates who were gambling and drinking and profaning the sacred place. Through the open doors she could see Petey and Jordan, but they didn't enter. Instead, they cast her scornful, disparaging looks before turning their backs on her.

She strained toward them, but Gideon clasped her arm, ordering her to be still. Suddenly his frock coat vanished, revealing the leather vest and saber beneath them, making her realize they'd been there all along.

"This is where you belong now." His expression was distant and rigid, and his fingers dug cruelly into her arm. "You belong with us. You're one of us."

"But I must speak with my brother . . . I must see Jordan . . . please let me see my brother . . ."

She awakened to the sound of her own voice whispering Jordan's name.

It took her a few moments to realize she'd been dreaming, and another few moments to remember where she was. Shaking her head to clear it, she sat up in the empty bed and glanced around Gideon's cabin, a quick surge of shame pinkening her cheeks. Good heavens, she was naked in his bed.

A flood of memories from the night before washed over her: Gideon forcing her to admit she wanted him . . . the second time they'd made love, when he'd coaxed her atop him and let her set the pace . . . feeling sated and drowsy, drifting off to sleep as he held her close in his arms.

At least she hadn't awakened in his arms. She couldn't have borne that. Last night, it had seemed perfectly right to give herself to him. Their argument earlier, the fire—all of it had conspired to throw them into each other's arms.

But now, in the harsh morning light, she knew it had been a mistake. A monumental mistake. Petey would be coming back with Jordan. How could she face them, knowing she'd dishonored herself and her family?

Of course, she couldn't tell Gideon that. No, she wouldn't be able to explain anything to him—why she'd been so weak last night . . . why she couldn't continue to be weak. He wouldn't understand why they couldn't continue as lovers.

That is, if he wanted them to. He might not. He still hadn't even said he wished to marry her.

She frowned. Not that she wanted to marry *him*. No indeed. As her dream had proved, marrying him would only compound her error.

Quickly she slid from between the sheets that still bore the crimson stain signaling her loss of innocence. She paused a moment to look at it. Gone, all gone. She would never be a maid again.

But she had no time to fret over that now. She must dress and leave before he returned, before he made her forget her good intentions. All too conscious of the soreness between her legs, she scanned the floor for her shift, but there was no sign of it anywhere. She searched around frantically. None of her clothes were here.

"Looking for this?" came a voice from the doorway to the cabin.

She whirled around, her heart leaping into her throat. Gideon lounged in the doorway with her shift hanging from one finger. He was dressed in gray trousers and a snowy shirt unbuttoned nearly to his waist. In the light of morning, he looked handsome and charming and so utterly male he took her breath away.

A curse on the man! Why must he be so appealing?

"I thought you might try to run off while I was away, so I took the liberty of removing your clothes from the cabin." His gaze slid with telling slowness down the length of her naked body. "I see that was a stroke of genius."

She blushed furiously. It was one thing to stand in front of him undressed in the middle of the night when she was drunk with passion. It was quite another to do it in broad daylight. She cast a furtive glance through the open doorway. What if one of his men were to enter the saloon? How mortifying that would be!

She held out her hand. "Please, Gideon, give it to me."

He sauntered into the room and closed the door behind him. With a smile, he hung her shift on a hook by the door, then came toward her. "Not yet. I like looking at you in the morning. There's plenty of time for dressing later."

"But . . . but . . ."

His hand snaked around her waist to pull her close. That familiar light was in his eyes again, the one she'd seen every time he'd looked at her last night. And to her complete shame, she felt herself growing soft and liquid under the fire of it.

"Good morning," he murmured as he bent his head toward her.

"Please, Gideon—"

"That's it, sweetheart. Say 'Please, Gideon . . . more, Gideon . . . I want you, Gideon'—"

"Why, you arrogant—"

He muffled her words with a kiss, a long, hungry one that reduced her to pudding. When at last he pulled away, she was speechless and he was grinning. "Much better. I see I've been following the wrong approach with you. I should've kissed you every time you opened your mouth."

She puffed up like an angry cobra. "Now, see here, Captain Horn—"

This time when he cut her off, he wasn't content with just a kiss. This time he lifted her and carried her to the bed, his mouth making love to her every step of the way. And when he followed her down onto the bed, shedding his clothes quickly before parting her thighs with his knees, she could only open to him, rising to meet him as he entered her with a fierceness that left her aching.

This time their lovemaking was quick and wild, with the urgency of two people who fear they'll never have another chance to mate. To her consternation, she was as eager as he. She wanted him inside her, around her, driving out her fears. She wanted him to be hers, even though she knew he never could be.

Afterward, she lay cradled in his arms spoon-fashion. Despite the sounds of footsteps tramping on the deck just on the other side of the wall and Barnaby ordering the sailors about, she felt peaceful and content just being in Gideon's arms.

How had she come to this pass? What perverse demon made her forget all her good intentions the second
he touched her? No doubt about it, Gideon truly was a
satyr, a very talented, very clever satyr who could seduce her whenever he wished. Worst of all, he knew it.

He pressed a kiss to her ear, his breath fanning her
hot cheeks. Then he splayed his fingers over her naked
belly provocatively. "What is it the Song of Solomon
says? 'Thy belly is like a heap of wheat set about with
lilies.' "

Good heavens, now the cursed man was quoting Bib-
lical poetry in the most outrageous context. He truly
was wicked.

"And thy breasts—" he began.

"Gideon!" she protested, twisting to glare at him as
her face flamed. "Really, that passage is quite indecent.
It's not meant to be . . . repeated aloud."

He smiled down at her, his expression unrepentant.
"I'm a pirate. I'm supposed to say indecent things."
Eyes twinkling, he tugged loose two locks of her hair,
then arranged them over her shoulders and her breasts.
"But if you insist on being prudish, I'll speak of something less . . . indecent. Like your hair." He stroked it
with a delicacy she wouldn't have expected of him. His
voice was soft and almost wistful. "I love your hair. It's
like copper coins and raw silk and Miss Mulligan's curtains."

"Miss Mulligan?" She scowled up at him. "Who, may
I ask, is Miss Mulligan, and what were you doing with
her curtains?"

"Come now, Miss Willis, don't tell me you're jealous."

The wretch. Of course she was jealous. But she'd
never let him know that. Tipping up her chin, she tried
for a nonchalant tone. "Wouldn't I be a fool to be jealous
of a pirate who's probably bedded half the women in
Christendom?"

That wiped the grin off his face. With a clipped oath

he fell back against the pillows. "Not quite so many. Probably only a quarter of the women in Christendom, though I do try to bed a woman every half-hour or so. It keeps me young."

Ignoring his sarcasm, she snapped, "And Miss Mulligan was one of them, I suppose."

"Oh, of course. I bed seventy-two-year-old women whenever I get the chance."

All at once, she felt like a complete fool. "Oh."

"You *are* jealous, aren't you?" He propped himself up on one elbow. "And with no need whatsoever. Miss Mulligan was an elderly spinster who ran one of the many boarding houses my father and I stayed in."

Glancing up into his face, she saw that his eyes had a faraway look. "I wasn't quite seven years old when we lived there," he went on, "and we were only there for six months. That was longer than we stayed in most places." He played with her hair, letting the strands slip through his fingers to pool over her shoulders. "But I remember the curtains in her drawing room so vividly. They were made of some scarlet, silky material, and when the sun shone through them, they looked like fire. I thought they *were* fire."

A smile touched his lips. "They fascinated me. Whenever Father was drunk and took the strap to me for doing my lessons badly, I'd run and hide behind those curtains in the drawing room, hoping that the fire would protect me." His eyes met hers. "I guess, in a strange sort of way, it did. He never found me when I was behind those curtains. And whenever Miss Mulligan discovered me there, she gave me milk and cookies and let me curl up in the bed with her while Father slept off his drunk. For a boy of six, that was heaven. She was kind and motherly and smelled of rosewater. I used to love the smell of rosewater."

A lump formed in her throat. She could just imagine Gideon as a small boy, hiding fearfully behind the curtains of a drawing room, turning to an old woman for comfort. She touched her fingers to his cheek. "Did your father . . . take a strap to you often?"

His gaze met hers, startled, then aloof, like the look a sleepwalker gives a person who wakes him. Lying back on the bed and tucking one arm under his head, he stared up at the ceiling. "Often enough to make an impression on me, if that's what you mean." He cast her a quick, cool glance. "You probably think he should've done it a few more times, to flail some goodness into me. What's that the Bible says? 'Spare the rod and spoil the child'?"

"Oh, don't quote *that* wretched verse! It's awful how people use it to justify cruelty. Beating a child doesn't teach him anything but humiliation and fear."

He stared at her a long time as if trying to fathom her. "Yes," he finally said. "That's exactly what it teaches."

Her heart twisted in her chest. Poor Gideon. No wonder he sought to create his own paradise. The world he'd been raised in sounded as if it was far from paradise. More like hell even.

"Where was your mother while all this was going on?" she couldn't help but ask. "Did she approve of your father . . . beating you?"

His face grew shuttered. Abruptly he rose from the bed and drew on his trousers. "She wasn't around."

Sitting up in bed, Sara clutched the sheets to her breast. "What do you mean? Did she die?"

Folding his arms over his bare chest, he rested his hip on the edge of his desk. His features were as remote and cold as the figurehead on the prow of his ship. "Something like that. It doesn't really matter, does it? She wasn't there."

She sniffed. "If you don't want to talk about her—"

"I don't." When she cast him a wounded look, he added, "We've more important things to discuss, Sara. Like what's going to happen today."

The abrupt change of subject threw her off guard. "Today?"

"When the women choose their husbands. Or have you forgotten?"

Oh, yes. *That.* Actually, in the wake of the fire and their night together, she *had* forgotten.

He went on without waiting for an answer. "Obviously we can't wait until new lodgings are built. That'll take weeks. The men who went to Sao Nicolau returned this morning, so there's no reason to delay. I need to know—" He broke off, a vulnerable expression crossing his face. "That is, I want to know whom you intend to choose."

"Why? So you can approve him?" she snapped.

"What in blue blazes is that supposed to mean?"

It took all her effort to force some calmness into her tone. "The last time we discussed this, you made it quite clear you didn't wish to marry me yourself."

"That's not true. As I recall, I said I wanted to 'sample the goods first.' "

"Oh, yes, I remember." She hugged the sheet protectively to her chest, unable to hold back her bitter words. "Now that you've 'sampled the goods,' did I pass your test with flying colors? How many of the other women have you 'sampled' in your quest to find the perfect bedmate?"

"Confound it, Sara, you know I haven't touched another woman since I met you." He raked his hand through his hair, looking more uncomfortable than she'd ever seen him. "What we did together last night . . . that was *not* a test. But it did prove something to me. If I were doing the choosing, I'd choose to marry you and no one else. Unfortunately, by the terms of our agreement, I'm not doing the choosing. You are. And the question is, who will you choose?"

Confused and torn, she wrenched her gaze from his. Marry him? How could she? Though it would likely be more than a month before Petey and Jordan arrived here, they would come; she felt sure of that. And when they did, she intended to leave with them. On the other hand, the thought of staying with Gideon on this in-triguing island, helping him build a new world, was so enticing, she could almost say yes to anything he wanted.

But that was a foolish thought. She didn't belong here. And in any case, he was just looking for a convenient bedmate. For some reason he'd chosen her, but that didn't mean anything.

"It's not as if I really have a choice at all," she said evasively. "I'd prefer not to marry anyone, but you won't allow that. If I don't choose you, you've already said you would choose for me, so that means I either choose you for my husband or let you assign yourself as my husband. It's all the same, isn't it?"

Eyes blazing, he clenched his hands into fists at his sides. "You would choose not to marry at all rather than marry me? Even after what we shared last night, you think me not good enough to marry?"

"It's not that, Gideon!" But when he stared at her, clearly waiting for an explanation, she found herself at a loss for one. She certainly couldn't tell him the truth—that she expected to be rescued from the island soon. "It's . . . it's . . . I'm just not ready yet. Marriage is so very final. If given the choice, I wouldn't marry on so short an acquaintance."

"How forward-thinking of you," he bit out. "Giving your virginity to a man isn't final, but marrying him is." He stared at her another long moment, his eyes bleak and angry. Then he stiffened. "Very well. You won't have to 'marry on so short an acquaintance.' I certainly won't force you to."

Scooping up his shirt, he headed toward the door.

"Wait! What do you mean? What are you saying?"

Without a word, he stepped outside the door and picked up a bundle of clothes, then tossed them inside the cabin. "Here. These are clothes I had them bring you from Sao Nicolau. Get dressed. I expect to see you on deck in half an hour." And before she could ask him anything else, he was gone.

She stared at the closed door, a disturbing emptiness settling in her chest. What had she done? What was he up to now? She should never have given in to him last night. This was a disaster, a complete disaster! And how in the name of God was she to get herself out of it?

Gideon stood on top the quarterdeck a half hour later, his face grim as he scanned the crowd in search of Sara. Where was she? She had to be here for this.

If he was going to make this sacrifice, he wanted her to witness it. After all, he was only doing it for her and her precious women. God knows nobody else would be pleased by his pronouncement. His men would howl in outrage.

But he didn't care. He'd made his choice, and he fully intended to see it to the end, even if it meant angering his men. Besides, what he was doing would help their situation, no matter what they thought.

It would certainly help his. It might be the only thing that would.

He surveyed the crowd again. It looked very different from the last time he'd stood on the quarterdeck to address the men and women. True, the mood was just as somber as it had been then, thanks to last night's fire. But the fire had also drawn all of them closer. The women were more easy with the men, and the men more considerate. Some of the men and women had already paired off, and the sight of that pleased him. Sara might not approve, but at least his plan was working.

Suddenly the object of his thoughts emerged from beneath the quarterdeck, glancing up at him with an expression of dread. His pulse quickened at the sight of her, like that of a blasted cabin boy with his first woman. She was wearing the white embroidered native blouse and flowing plum skirt he'd had the men buy for her. She looked wonderful in it, her hair loose and free about her shoulders and the wind blowing the thin cotton to cling to her legs, leaving little to the imagination.

Bedding her should have put an end to this unreasonable desire for her. But it hadn't. It had only made it worse. He wanted her again, this very minute. The irony of it was enough to make him choke. After all those years of sneering at English noblewomen, to be craving one now was a real blow to his pride.

But he'd never been foolish enough to let his pride keep him from pursuing what he wanted, and he wanted Sara . . . in his house and in his bed. He'd chosen his wife. Now all he had to do was make her choose him.

Wrenching his gaze from her, he faced the group. It was time to take the first step in his plan for doing just that.

"Good morning. I'm glad to say that we all seemed to have survived the fire intact. No one was lost." He leaned forward to plant his hands on the rail. "We did lose all the dwellings last night, but I don't intend to let that stop us. Someone—" Here he broke off, his gaze flickering briefly to Sara before returning to the crowd. "Someone made me see that Atlantis is worth fighting for." There was a murmur of approval among his men, echoed to a smaller extent by the women.

"Now that the rest of the men have returned from Sao Nicolau," he went on, "we have most of the materials we require for rebuilding. What they haven't brought, we can probably get on the island."

He squared his shoulders. Now came the hard part. "Miss Willis has said that the women would be willing to help us rebuild. So I've decided to offer them a compensation of sorts for their help." He paused. "I'm giving them another month to choose their husbands."

First there was a startled silence. Then a low rumbling began among his men, and their faces grew dark and disapproving. Barnaby looked at him as if he were mad, though Silas seemed surprisingly calm.

Gideon held up his hand for silence. "I know some of the women have already found potential husbands, and if they wish to go ahead and marry, they may do so. But as for the rest of the women, we'll be busy rebuilding, and it's only fair that they not be forced to deal with the additional complications of married life while they're helping us."

At last he dared to look at Sara. Her mouth gaped open. Ann rushed to her side, her face wreathed in smiles, but Sara just stared at him. To his surprise, there was no hint of triumph on her face. Just a shock that slowly changed to gratefulness.

He tore his gaze from her. She had nothing to be grateful for, though she didn't know it. One way or the other, she would be his. He was probably mad to want to marry her, given his past. But it was the only way to have her. Already she felt guilty over what they'd done together. He'd seen it in her eyes this morning. The only way to get rid of that kind of guilt in a woman was to marry her.

"We'll all be sleeping aboard the ship now," he continued, "unless some of you want to pitch tents or spend your evenings lying on the beach under the stars. Otherwise everything is the same as before. The men will treat the women with respect and honor their wishes. Is this agreeable to all?"

He fell silent, waiting for the storm of protest to begin. But except for a few token complaints, the men seemed to have accepted his announcement. Perhaps they, too, had seen the wisdom of it. Some of them might even be having trouble with their own women. Perhaps they all needed more time to reach an agreement.

"Barnaby will be in charge of making assignments concerning the rebuilding, and Silas will oversee the unloading of the sloop. As for the women, I'll consult with Miss Willis on how they can help. That's all. You're dismissed."

As he climbed down the steps to the deck, he looked

for Sara, but she was surrounded by women asking her questions. Then he spotted Barnaby making for him, a scowl on his face. Gideon waited for his first mate to reach him.

"What in bloody hell is going on with you?" Barnaby said, with more than his usual impertinence. "First you agree to send half the men off for supplies, and now you postpone the weddings. I say we just marry the women and get the bloody thing over with, then think about building houses!"

"Yes, and we both know the extent of your experience with women," Gideon retorted. "You bed them and toss them aside. Well, you can treat mistresses that way, Barnaby, but you can't do that with wives."

"And since when do you know how to treat a wife? When was the last time you had even a mistress for more than a month?"

"It's true, I know." Gideon looked past Barnaby to where Sara stood, her hair shining in the morning sun like ribbons of fire. "But that's something I intend to remedy."

Barnaby followed his gaze with a scowl. "I knew it. It's that woman again. She's gotten to you." When Gideon didn't answer, Barnaby added, "Is that who you plan to marry? Do you truly think that stiff-necked prude will choose you?"

Gideon suppressed a smile at Barnaby's none-too-apt description of Sara. "Given time, she'll choose me. You can be certain of that."

"Ah, so that's what this is all about. You're giving yourself time to court 'milady.' I suppose that means the rest of us can forget about her."

He shot Barnaby an assessing glance. "Didn't you just dismiss her as a 'stiff-necked prude'?"

"Some men *like* prudes, you know."

Gideon saw red. "Not if I can help it. You let the men know that Sara Willis is mine. None of them are allowed to even kiss her cheek, understand?"

Barnaby held up his hands in surrender. "Of course, Captain, of course. Don't worry. Nobody is fool enough to try to steal your woman."

Your woman. He liked the sound of that. "Good. And now, if you'll excuse me, I wish to have a word with 'my woman.' "

With that, he left Barnaby's side and strolled over to where Sara stood speaking with Louisa.

"Louisa, would you leave us, please?" he said, when the two women turned to look at him. "I need to speak to Sara alone."

"Certainly," Louisa muttered, though he noticed that she kept her eyes on him as she moved just out of earshot.

He scowled at her until she hastened off down the deck. Then he turned his attention to Sara. "That woman never lets you out of her sight. What is she, your protector?"

"She just worries about me, that's all."

"Well, she needn't worry about you anymore. I'm looking out for you now."

A soft smile transformed Sara's face. "Yes, I can see that. Truly, Gideon, it was so kind of you to give us more time. You won't regret it. It will be better for everyone. You'll see."

He stared at her intently. "For you, too?"

She blushed. "Yes, of course." She glanced away, touching her fingers to the locket she always wore. "There's something I must discuss with you, Gideon. I . . . that is . . . what happened last night . . . I don't think it should be repeated."

"You mean, the fire?" he asked, deliberately being obtuse. He couldn't believe she was saying this to him, especially after his grand gesture!

Her gaze shot back to his. "You know quite well I'm not talking about the fire. I mean, us sharing a bed. It's not proper for—"

"It's a little late to be concerned about proprieties, don't you think?"

"Perhaps. But I . . . still think we shouldn't . . . repeat last night." When he cast her a look of complete incredulity, she hastened to add, "If we're to consider marrying, then we need to know each other better, and I don't mean in bed. I-I can't think straight when you're making love to me—"

"Good."

"It's *not* good. Marriage is a lifetime decision. I want to make it with a clear mind."

"I can clear your mind," he growled and reached for her.

But she shrank back from him. "No! That's exactly what I mean. You want to make me forget about everything but you. Then I'll find myself married to you and wondering how it happened. I don't want that; I want to know what I'm doing when I agree to marry you."

Confound the woman. Why must she always be *thinking* about everything? Why couldn't she be like other women, content to let a man sweep her off her feet?

He stopped short. That was exactly what his mother had done—and what a disaster that had been. No, Gideon didn't want history to repeat itself. He wanted Sara not to have any regrets once she agreed to marry him.

Still, he'd be damned if that meant not touching her or kissing her or having her in his bed. He'd give her plenty of time to think . . . but that didn't mean they couldn't enjoy each other occasionally in the meantime. He just had to make her realize that she wanted him as much as he wanted her. And there was only one way to do that.

"All right, Sara. We can get to know each other. We can rebuild Atlantis and talk and never once touch, if that's what you wish." At her startled look, he lowered his tone. "I don't think that's really what you wish. But I'm willing to let you find that out for yourself."

He paused, giving her time to think about what he'd

said. When he continued, his voice was the merest whisper. "Let me warn you, however. When you change your mind—and you will—it'll be your turn to come to me. Because the next time we make love, you'll have to be the one to ask."

Then summoning all the strength of will he possessed, he turned his back and walked away.

Chapter 20

With pretty, courteous, dainty knacks
we please the females well,
We know what longing women lacks,
most surely we can tell.

—JOHN PLAYFORD
"THE JOVIAL MARRINER"

Sara made it through the first week surprisingly well. During the day, there was so much work to do, and so many quarrels among the women over who was to do what, that she scarcely had time to breathe. Water had to be hauled and the men fed. Grass had to be cut and dried for thatch, and mattresses had to be sewn from the canvas cloth the men had brought from Sao Nicolau.

Still, she saw Gideon often enough to remind her of their one night together. He sought her out for her opinions on how the houses should be laid out. Whenever he needed something of the women, he came to her first, and they spent a great many hours debating the best way to allocate their meager resources.

She found excuses to seek him out as well. Much as she chastised herself for it, she liked watching him work, his muscles glistening with sweat under the warm sun. He took to eating his luncheon with her beneath the trees, offering her the bananas she'd come to like and hunks of pork freshly roasted on Silas's makeshift spits. Sometimes his fingers brushed hers accidentally when they were sharing the meal, but otherwise he kept his hands to himself.

That should have made things easier. It didn't. At night, she lay awake in her cabin, thinking about him in his huge bed just across the saloon from her. Sometimes she closed her eyes and imagined him running his fingers over her shoulders, her breasts, her hips. Sometimes she furthered the fantasy by touching herself, and that was the worst of all . . . to know he could make her behave so wickedly.

The second week was harder. By then, after much jostling and quarreling, everyone had fallen into a routine. Each had taken the jobs that best suited them, and were diligently working to put Atlantis back together. That meant less time for discussing things with Gideon and fewer excuses for seeking him out. What's more, he sometimes didn't stop for lunch, although he ate with her when he did.

Yet she was aware of him no matter where she was, even when he was laying out the buildings or supervising the cutting down of trees. She found excuses to see him, then made excuses to herself for the flimsiness of her excuses. She found herself touching him casually . . . his arm or his shoulder or his elbow. She didn't mean to, of course. It just happened. And whenever it did, he went very still, fixing her with a hungry gaze that always made her jerk her hand away.

He began bringing her gifts in the evening—a scented soap, some satin for a bonnet, a sculpted shard of bright orange coral that he'd found while he and the men were spearing fish. He never once gave her anything that she might think was stolen, and that warmed her, for he must have plenty of jewels he could offer.

Then he'd linger to walk the decks with her, speaking of his hopes for the island. Despite her determination not to let his words affect her, they did. How could she not be affected by his dreams for a society where men and women could work and live free of the cruelties of unfeeling governments? Where punishments fit the crimes, and people like Ann weren't deprived of what they needed most?

The worst part of the night came then—when he walked her to the door of her cabin. She always half-hoped he would kiss her and was disappointed when he didn't. Once in bed, her imagination would take over where reality left off. Long gone were her thoughts of his hands on her body. Now she dreamed of feeling his mouth on her. It would start with her reliving their kisses, but it always progressed to fantasies of his mouth kissing her breasts and belly and even her most private place.

It was dreadfully scandalous and made her so ashamed. Sometimes she even awakened to find herself touching her own body in wanton ways she'd never dreamed existed. She burned at night. She burned during the day. But Gideon, curse the man, seemed as determined not to touch her as ever.

By the end of the third week, however, that had changed. Gideon began to touch her when she least expected it. He would casually reach up to smooth back her hair from her eyes or take her arm to lead her down the gangplank in the morning. When they ate together, which was now almost every meal, he seemed to delight in "accidentally" brushing her breasts as he leaned over to reach something, or taking a seat so close beside her that their legs touched whenever they moved.

If she'd had any sense at all, she would have pointed out how he was cheating on his promise not to touch her. But she'd long ago lost all sense. She lived for those furtive touches. She took unreasonable pleasure in the gifts he brought her and the way he deferred to her judgment on certain matters.

Even worse, her nighttime imaginings had progressed to unabashed memories of his making love to her. She no longer tried to suppress her fantasies, but gave free rein to them. And her hands—her treacherous, wicked hands—had become truly uncontrollable.

Unfortunately, they didn't satisfy the clawing need growing in the pit of her belly, the need to have him kiss her and stroke her and yes, make love to her again.

It was those thoughts that engrossed her on the last morning of the third week. It was early, not even dawn yet, and she'd left everyone else sleeping on the ship. Needing a place to think, she wandered down the beach toward the stream.

A few rules had been established for the little colony, and one of them concerned bathing. Since the water in the stream was too cold for bathing in the early morning, the women were allotted the early afternoon hours for bathing and the men the late afternoon hours, after they'd finished their dirty work for the day. The system had allowed the women the privacy they craved, especially those women who hadn't yet decided on husbands.

So when Sara came upon the stream, she was surprised to find Gideon standing naked in the middle of it, bathing in the chilly water. Quickly she ducked behind a tree to keep him from seeing her.

She couldn't believe it. Did he come here every morning? And why, when the water was so much warmer later in the day?

She should leave him to bathe alone, she told herself sternly. But her erotic nighttime dreams were still too fresh. She couldn't bear to leave just yet. With a furtive glance down the sloping ground to the beach to make sure no one had seen her, she peeked back around the tree at Gideon.

The stream was so shallow that the water came only to his knees. He had his back to her as he scooped water up and sluiced it over his body. He looked magnificent . . . his dark hair dripping down over his broad back etched with scars, firm buttocks that flexed with his every movement, and hairy legs slightly parted to help him keep his balance on the pebbly stream bed.

Heat spread up from her loins to her breasts to her face as she watched him. What would he do if she simply stepped out from behind the tree and into his arms? No, she couldn't do that. She mustn't.

Suddenly he turned around, though he didn't see her. She quickly suppressed a gasp. Good heavens. He was fully aroused. He was mumbling something and scowling as he scrubbed his chest with a soapy rag.

Then, to her complete horror, he laid his hand on his member and began to stroke it. She told herself to leave at once, but her feet stayed rooted to the forest floor. She was utterly fascinated. So *that* was how he managed to keep himself aloof from her when she practically panted to have him in her bed.

But if that were the case, why was he scowling? Why were his movements almost violent, as if he couldn't stroke himself hard or fast enough? Perhaps it was the same for him as it was for her. Touching herself had been as futile as throwing water on those fiery huts had been. Not enough. Never enough.

Suddenly, he looked up and saw her. His eyes locked with hers, full of heat and need and hunger. For a moment, she stood there transfixed, her mouth open and her feet incapable of movement.

Then she panicked. With a cry of shame, she lifted her skirts and took off at a run, as hard and as far as her legs would carry her.

As she stumbled down the beach, she chastised herself furiously. She should never have gone to the stream. She should certainly never have watched him bathe or . . . or touch himself. The minute she'd seen what he was doing, she should have sneaked away. Now that he knew she'd been watching him, he was sure to guess her dreadful secret—that she wanted him as much as he wanted her.

With a choked cry she raced up the *Satyr*'s gangplank

and past the drowsy, curious gazes of the pirates who slept on the deck. Glancing behind her, she half-feared she would see him following her. But thankfully he was nowhere to be seen.

Nonetheless, it was only when she reached her cabin and latched the door closed, that she felt safe. And even then, it was several minutes before she could still her thundering heart and stop listening for the sound of his boots treading the planks outside her door.

The rest of the day, she avoided him. She couldn't face him after what she'd witnessed. It was unthinkable. She busied herself on the ship, helping the women drag the bedrolls up from the hold to the top deck for airing. But she couldn't stop her thoughts . . . and the erotic images that plagued her.

What was wrong with her? How was it that the man hardly ever touched her, yet she thought of him every waking moment? It wasn't fair.

By late afternoon, frustrated beyond endurance, she sought out Louisa, hoping that the woman's tart tongue would lash some sense into her. Louisa wasn't fond of Gideon. She would remind Sara of all his faults, and that was just what Sara needed.

When she went in search of Louisa in the ship's galley, however, she found Silas instead. As she walked in, he was lifting a huge mound of bread dough onto the floured surface of the table.

"Louisa—" he began, then broke off when he looked up and saw it was her. "Ah, Sara, you'll do, I suppose," he said in his usual gruff manner. "Come knead this bread. I have to make sure the meat don't burn."

"Where's Louisa?"

He shrugged. "Who knows where that woman's gone off to? She'll be back soon, I wager, but this dough must be kneaded now. Trust Louisa to disappear when I need her."

His grumbling didn't fool Sara. The man was utterly in love with Louisa. Indeed, the two of them had become completely inseparable in the last two weeks. They'd already asked Gideon, as a ship's captain, to perform their marriage ceremony and were as engrossed in each other as any newly married couple she'd ever seen. It made her almost envious.

"Come now, girl, help me with this bread," Silas repeated, waving her toward the table.

"I don't know how to knead bread." At home, the servants did such things. But on Atlantis, where there were no servants, she'd learned a great many skills she'd never had use for before.

Today, however, she wasn't in the mood to learn anything . . . except how to get Gideon out of her thoughts.

"Kneadin' bread is simple enough," Silas said, ignoring her protest. He pushed down on the ball of dough until it flattened, then folded it over and repeated the motion. "You see?"

"But I'll ruin it."

"Balderdash." Grabbing her by the arm with floury fingers, he drew her to the table. "You can't ruin it. The more you punch it, the better 'tis. The harder you handle it, the higher it'll rise. Take me word for it. It'll take anythin' you give it."

She eyed the dough skeptically, but did as she'd seen him do, timidly at first, then with more confidence. The dough was so resilient and springy, it did seem as if she couldn't hurt it. And he *had* said it would take anything she could give it.

As she continued the kneading motion, her thoughts wandered back to Gideon. What was she to do about him? How could she get past this frustration she felt every time she was near him? This wasn't supposed to happen to respectable ladies. Men lusted after women, of course, but only fallen women lusted after men in return. Or so she'd been taught. She was beginning to think that everything she'd been taught was suspect.

Otherwise, how could she have found such enjoyment

in the arms of a pirate? And she'd certainly done that; she couldn't deny it.

Now, what was she supposed to do about it? He'd said she would have to ask him to touch her. She couldn't imagine doing so. Why, he might not even care about her anymore. Maybe he'd decided a noblewoman wasn't worth his time. The very thought of that made her go cold with fear.

She stabbed the dough furiously with her fists. It didn't matter what he thought one way or the other. She'd be returning to London without him. It was inevitable.

Silas's voice interrupted her thoughts. "Hold up, lass. I know I said you couldn't hurt it by punchin' it, but I didn't say to kill it."

She realized she'd been punching the bread silly, and swallowed hard. "I'm sorry . . . I . . . my mind was wandering."

He took the bread from her, rolled it in some lard, then placed it in a bread pan. "Aye, wanderin' in troublesome places, I'll wager. What has you in such a dither?"

She cast him a wary glance. "Nothing . . . important."

He returned to ladling gravy over the meat. "It's our good captain, ain't it? He's been troublin' you again."

"Yes . . . well, no. Not the way you think." When he cast her a searching glance, she turned her back to him and fiddled with the latch to the pantry. "He . . . he's been the soul of courtesy."

"And that bothers you?"

"No, of course not. It's just that . . . I don't know what to make of it. Sometimes I think he dislikes me very much. Other times . . . he . . ."

Other times, he makes love to me with passion and caring. But she could hardly tell Silas that, could she?

"Depend on it, the man don't dislike you," Silas said in a calm voice. "Gideon just finds it hard to trust any woman. Especially one of your kind."

There was that horrible phrase again—*your kind*. She whirled around to face Silas. "Why does he hate 'my kind' so? Which one of 'my kind' ever hurt him?"

He set down the gravy ladle and stared at her a moment, stroking his beard thoughtfully. "If I tell you what I know, will you keep it to yourself?"

Her curiosity roused, she nodded vigorously.

He gestured to a chair. "Then you'd best sit down, lass. It's a hard tale, and a long one. But if anyone should hear it, it's you."

Taking a seat at the scarred table, she folded her hands in front of her and looked at him expectantly.

"His mother," he said. "That's who hurt him."

She looked at him blankly. "I don't understand."

"Gideon's mother was a duke's daughter. A very wealthy lady from a very powerful English family."

An awful feeling crept over her. Gideon was English? His mother had been a noblewoman? *Gideon's* mother?

"You look surprised." Taking up his pipe, Silas filled it with tobacco from a pouch in his vest pocket. "I s'pose that's to be expected. Pirates aren't known for their fine bloodlines."

"But how? Who?"

Silas stuck a straw in the stove fire, then used it to light his pipe. "I can tell you the how. The who ain't so clear, least of all to him." He tossed the straw in the fire and puffed hard on his pipe. "He told me most of the story when he was drunk one night. We'd seized a ship that day, with an old woman on it named Eustacia. Hearin' her say her name rattled him bad enough to send him to the bottle. Mebbe you noticed as how Gideon don't drink much. I think he fears endin' up like his father. Anyway, that night, he said his mother's name was Eustacia, or so his father'd said when *he* was drunk."

"Gideon told me a little about his father. The man sounded like an awful person."

"Aye, he was. Gideon hates him. But he hates his

mother more. He blames her for leavin' him to the care of his bastard father.''

"I don't understand. How does a duke's daughter meet a man like Gideon's father? Wasn't his father American?''

"Nay. His father was as English as you. Apparently, he was Eustacia's tutor. He must've been a charmer, seein' as how he got her to run off with him.'' Silas's expression grew grim. "But after she bore Gideon, she got tired of the poor life she led with Elias Horn. She asked her family to take her back, and they agreed.'' He stared at her from above his pipe. "But they made her leave her son behind.''

Sara gasped aloud. "They didn't!'' When he nodded, she said, "But why?''

He shrugged. "I dunno. Mebbe to hush up the scandal. Mebbe they hoped that if Elias and Gideon wasn't around, they could keep it all quiet more easy-like. Who knows how an English noble thinks?''

She flinched. She knew he didn't mean it as a criticism of her, but it demonstrated how suspiciously the entire crew of the *Satyr* regarded her countrymen. And her class. No doubt their hatred had been nurtured during the American Revolution, which had probably just ended around the time Gideon was born.

But for Gideon, there was more to it even than that. Remembering how bitterly Gideon had spoken of his mother, she felt heartsick. No wonder he hated her "kind.'' No wonder he'd been so reluctant to trust her.

Still, his distrust wasn't quite fair. She would never leave her own child behind, no matter what her family asked of her. She couldn't understand how Eustacia could have done it.

"Did he ever go looking for her, ever try to hear her side of the story?'' she asked.

"If he did, he never told me. Would've been near to impossible, anyhow. His father took him off to America when he was just a wee thing. Said he wanted a new life for them. But his wife still tormented his mind, and he drowned his sorrows in drink many a night. Gideon once told me they lived in fifteen different towns when he was growin' up. His father couldn't keep a position as a teacher on account of his drinkin'."

That explained why Gideon wanted Atlantis so badly. He'd never had a home, and he was determined to make Atlantis into one. He wanted a home and someone to care for him, though he would never admit it aloud.

"What made him run away to sea? His father's beatings?"

Silas shook his head. "He didn't have no choice. His father drank himself to death when Gideon wasn't even thirteen, so Gideon went to sea to keep from starvin'."

"At thirteen? He was only thirteen when he went to sea?" A crushing pain built in her chest. At thirteen, she'd been coddled by a doting mother and a kindly stepfather and given everything she wanted, while Gideon had been huddled in the cold rain on a ship's deck, running errands and shining a man's boots.

Her feelings must have shown in her face, for Silas's voice was gentle when he answered her. "It weren't so bad as all that, lass. Bein' a cabin boy made a man out o' him, and that was a good thing, don't you think?"

Tears sprang to her eyes unbidden, and she turned her face away to hide them. All the times she'd unfairly accused Gideon of cruelty came back to haunt her. If anyone had known cruelty, it was Gideon.

Yet he wasn't cruel. Far from it. Yes, he'd taken them against their will, and she still thought him wrong for that. But he'd done it thinking he was doing something good. He'd done it for the sake of his precious colony, a place where he could put an end to cruelty.

Indeed, she'd seen how well he governed. He always listened to both sides of a dispute and settled them fairly. He'd kept to his promise that the women would be treated with respect, enforcing that rule with an iron hand. When she'd wanted to begin teaching the women again, he'd shocked her by agreeing. He'd even taken to sleeping in his half-finished house, so his cabin and comfortable bed could be used by Molly, the pregnant woman whose time was nearly come, and her daughter Jane.

He wasn't at all the dreadful, wicked man she'd first taken him to be. And that made him far more dangerous to her than before.

"You care for the lad, don't you, Sara?" Silas said, breaking in to her thoughts.

Wiping her tears away, she slowly nodded. "But he hates me for being an English noblewoman like his mother."

"Nay." His voice was kindly. "Gideon may be bitter, but he ain't no fool. He knows a good woman when he gets his hands on one. I think he cares for you somethin' fierce."

"Then why didn't he tell me about her?" she blurted out. It wounded her to think he hadn't trusted her enough for that. "He told me about his father, but he refused to tell me about his mother, even after we—" She broke off with a blush. "It's because he thinks I'm ... I'm like her, isn't it? He thinks I only care about my family and the privileges I enjoyed in London. That's why he won't tell me things."

"That ain't true. Mebbe he thought you were like his mother at the first, but he don't think that now. I'm sure of it. He sees you for what you are."

"And what is that?"

"The kind of woman he needs ... someone who'll soften the hardness his mother put there."

I can't do that, she wanted to cry. *Even if he would let me, I won't be staying here long enough to be what he needs. I'm going to abandon him, just like his mother did. I'm going to leave when Jordan comes.*

But she didn't want to leave, didn't want to abandon him. For the first time since Petey had left, she recognized the truth. She didn't want to return to the grime and sorrow of London. She wanted to stay here to teach the women, to watch the colony grow, and yes, to be with Gideon. She wanted to soothe his hurts and heal his heart.

And she could tell Silas none of that.

"If he ain't talkin' to you 'bout things, you got to be talkin' to him," Silas said.

"Talk to him? And say what?"

"How you feel. What you want. It took a mighty lot of my courage to speak to Louisa about . . . well, about things. But thank the good Lord I did, else I wouldn't be havin' her for a wife now."

"I can't talk to Gideon." How could she tell him what she wanted when she wasn't even sure of it herself? And how could she tell him how she felt when she might be abandoning him any day?

Quickly she rose from her chair and headed toward the entrance. "I'm sorry, Silas, I have to go."

"Wait!" When she paused and turned toward him, he picked up a bucket and held it out to her. "If you don't mind doin' an errand for me, I need this taken to Gideon's new house. He was askin' for it this mornin', said he needed it to haul away wood shavings."

"I told you, Silas, I can't talk to Gideon now."

"Oh, it's all right. No need to talk to him. He ain't at his house. He's helpin' Barnaby catch fish at t'other end of the island." When she hesitated, eyeing him suspiciously, he pointed down to his wooden leg. "It's a far piece for me with me leg an' all, and Gideon'll be wantin' it later."

"Very well." She took the bucket. Anything to appease Silas, she thought, so she could get out of here. She had to get away before she poured all her heart out to him and told him the full extent of her dilemma.

Silas meant well, but he couldn't help her decide what to do about Gideon. She was the only one who could do that.

Chapter 21

I thank the goodness and the grace
Which on my birth have smiled,
And made me, in these Christian days,
A happy English child.

—ANN AND JANE TAYLOR
ENGLISH AUTHORS OF CHILDREN'S BOOKS
"CHILD'S HYMN OF PRAISE"

Gideon sat on a bench in his half-finished house, sanding the edges of a plank that he meant to use as a shelf in the small kitchen he was building for Sara. When he'd begun the kitchen, he'd thought she might like to have her own, instead of sharing the communal one.

He'd meant it to be a surprise, but now he was having doubts about it. Three weeks had gone by, and his goal of winning Sara was not as near as he'd hoped. It wasn't that she hadn't softened toward him. Sometimes she behaved almost like a wife. Two nights ago, he'd returned to the cottage to find all his clothes cleaned and repaired. He knew she'd done it, because Barnaby had seen her enter his cottage that morning.

If she saw him laboring in the hot sun, she brought him a bucket of cold water when she thought he wasn't looking, and Silas had revealed that she was always requesting that Louisa prepare Gideon's favorite foods. He'd never experienced the kind of feminine attentions that most lads got from their mothers and then their wives. It was a novel experience to have someone care that much about his welfare. He liked it. He liked it a lot.

The trouble was, she wouldn't talk about his intention to marry her, even when he pointedly raised the subject. Obviously, his fumbling attempts at courtship had left her unmoved. But what did he know of courting a woman? He'd never even had a sweetheart, just the occasional brief acquaintance with a ladybird or two that left him feeling unfulfilled and morose.

Still, he'd had hopes for him and Sara. This morning when she'd come upon him bathing, he'd been sure that he'd finally broken through her maidenly qualms. But no, she'd fled his presence and avoided him all day after that.

His right hand suddenly slipped, scraping the knuckles of his left hand with the holystone. Muttering a curse, he tossed the board and holystone aside. Confound the woman and all her hesitation. Cold baths were becoming standard with him. He went to bed hard and woke up harder.

It wasn't supposed to be this difficult. He'd spent months at sea without a woman and not felt as much frustration as he'd felt in the last three weeks. But it was one thing to be stuck at sea, and quite another to be constantly in the presence of the only woman he wanted without being allowed to touch her. It was all he could do to keep from grabbing her and kissing her senseless when he left her at the door to her cabin at night.

But he knew better than to try seduction. It hadn't worked before, so there was no reason to believe it would work now. No, he must stick to his plan and pray that she relented before the month was up.

He stood up and stretched, then turned to pick up the

board again. That's when he saw her standing in the doorway to his cabin, a startled look on her face and an empty bucket in her hand.

"What are you doing here?" she blurted out.

Her confusion brought a smile to his lips. "It's my house, remember?"

"Yes, but Silas said—" She broke off. Dropping her gaze to the bucket, she mumbled, "A curse on that meddling man!"

"What meddling man?"

"Silas, that wretched liar. He told me you needed this bucket. He begged me to come over here and give it to you, and said you were out catching fish with Barnaby. Obviously he was lying about it just to throw us together."

Thank you, Silas, he thought. He took a step toward her, pleased that she didn't break and run as she had this morning, and struggled to find something to say that would keep her there. "Why would Silas try to throw us together now? He hasn't tried it before."

That didn't get the reaction he'd expected. She colored to the roots of her hair. "Because he and I were . . . talking about you." Her head came up and her eyes locked with his. "He told me about your mother."

Gideon went still. All his pleasure at having her there abruptly vanished. His mother? Silas had told her about his mother? That blasted old fool. When Gideon got his hands on him, he'd yank his beard out. How dared Silas tell her? Whirling away, he picked up the holystone and the pitcher of sand and strode into the other room, his bedchamber. She'd never dared to enter it before, and he prayed she wouldn't now. The last thing he wanted to discuss with Sara was his treacherous mother.

But Sara followed him, apparently without any qualm. "He didn't lie about that, did he? Your mother really is an English noblewoman? A duke's daughter?"

"Yes." He stalked to the window, staring blindly out at nothing. "What of it?"

"Did she really abandon you and your father?"

A groan escaped his lips. Blast. He gripped the holystone until his knuckles whitened. He could feel her pity without even looking at her. That's why he hadn't told her in the first place. He hadn't wanted her to know his secret shame, to pity him when he wanted her to feel something else entirely.

"Did she?" Sara repeated.

The holystone thudded on the floor as he faced her. "Yes."

Just as he'd expected, she looked stricken. And her eyes most definitely showed pity. He flinched at the sight of it.

"Did you ever look for her?" she asked. "Perhaps she regretted it later. Perhaps—"

"Trust me, she didn't regret it."

"How do you know?"

"I just do."

She got a stubborn look on her face. "Oh, because she left you once, you decided to cut her off and never—"

"She sent a letter, all right?" The pain lashed him all over again. By now, he ought to be immune to it. Why did it still hurt so much? He went on, knowing Sara would plague him until he told her. "I asked about her at the British consulate when I was ten. I only had her first name, so they thought I was lying . . . or that my father had lied when he told me about her. They made it quite clear that no English *lady* would run off with her tutor."

He'd gotten a harsher beating than usual from his father for going to the consulate. The consul had apparently told Elias Horn about Gideon's secret visit, assuming Elias had put Gideon up to it for some nefarious purpose, and had warned the man to keep his "ragamuffin" son away from the consulate.

"A letter came for my father at the consulate a few months later," he went on coldly. "I don't know, maybe the consul actually took the trouble to hunt her down.

It was from my mother. She said she wanted nothing ... to do with me." He could hardly speak the words. "A few years after that, my father received word that ... that she was dead and the family wanted no further ties to either of us. And then my father proceeded to drink himself to death."

By then, Gideon had already buried his childish hopes of finding his mother and convincing her to take him back. He'd endured his father's drunken thrashings in silence, knowing that Elias only beat him because Gideon was *her* son, as he so often liked to say. That's when Gideon had begun swearing that one day he would pay the English back ... all of them ... for their superior airs and their lack of morals, for thinking they could do as they pleased with impunity.

And he'd kept his oath, hadn't he? He'd made fools of every nobleman he'd ever met, praying that one of them might be his mother's kin. He'd exulted every time he'd snatched the jewels from the neck of some haughty English bitch.

Until Sara. Sara had changed everything.

"But didn't she leave you anything?" Sara persisted. "A will? Some ... some sign that she regretted her actions?"

It irritated him that she refused to believe an Englishwoman capable of such abominable behavior. With jerky movements, he removed his belt, then tossed it at her feet. "That belt buckle is the only thing she left me, and I'm sure she didn't intend to leave that. It was her brooch before I had it made into a buckle."

Sara bent to pick it up. Slowly, she turned it over and over in her hands. He watched as she traced the ring of diamonds and the massive onyx center carved in the shape of a stallion's head.

"No doubt you've seen plenty of brooches as expensive as that in your life," he said, unable to keep the bitterness out of his voice even now. "You probably owned several."

"Yes, I did. I didn't ask for them, though. I didn't expect them. They just . . . came along with being an earl's stepdaughter." She lifted mournful eyes to his. "Why did you keep it if you hate her so much?"

He tried to shrug, but her questions were like a knife probing at an old sore, and it was hard to be nonchalant. "When I was five, I kept asking why I had no mother, so Father showed me that and told me the whole story. A few days later, I stole it from him and kept it with me. You see, I never wanted to believe that—" He broke off. He'd never wanted to believe that his mother had purposely left him behind. It had been too painful for a child of five to consider. "Years later, after I learned he was telling the truth, I kept it to remind me of what she'd done and what kind of woman she was."

"I don't understand. How could any woman abandon her son?" There was so much sadness in her voice that he could hardly stand it.

He spoke more harshly than he intended. "I don't know. I guess she missed having servants cater to her every whim. She missed expensive gowns and champagne and well-sprung carriages. She missed the jewels she wore dripping from her fingers at evening parties—"

He broke off before the bile could choke him. Turning away from her, he looked out at the island. His island. He took several deep breaths, letting Atlantis's sweet air calm him. Only Atlantis had the power to purge the pain of his mother's treachery from him.

When he went on, he was thankful he sounded calmer. "My father didn't have much to give her, I warrant you. He made a decent living, but nothing approaching the level she was used to. When she knew him, he wasn't a drunk, or so he told me. He only started drinking after she deserted him." Anger crept into his voice once more. "Apparently, he had trouble understanding why a husband and a son didn't compare to a huge house with fifty servants and diamond brooches the size of her delicate, noble-born fist."

She was quiet a long time. When at last she spoke, her voice was a ragged whisper. "I'm not like her, Gideon. I know you think I am, but—"

"Don't put words in my mouth, Sara!" He whirled on her, his fists clenched. "Confound it, I know you're not like her! You're nothing like her, *nothing!* Trust me, my mother would never have traveled with a crowd of convict women. She wouldn't have quoted Aristophanes to a pirate. She would've fainted at the sight of that snake, and she would certainly never have helped put out a fire!"

He dragged in a heavy breath as his gaze locked with hers. "But then, no other English noblewoman I've ever seen would have done those things, either. Most of the earl's wives and daughters who traveled on the ships I attacked showed little backbone and less intelligence."

"Can you blame them? They were probably all terrified."

She said the words a little defensively, bringing a half-smile to his lips. That was just like Sara, to take up for a group of women she didn't even know. "Perhaps. But *you* weren't. You shook your fist at me and spoke your mind. Face it, Sara, you're not the average English noblewoman."

"But if you don't . . . hate me for being what I am, why haven't you . . . I mean . . ." She broke off, her cheeks glowing crimson.

He stared at her. Surely she wasn't trying to say what he thought. "Why haven't I *what*, Sara?" he said in a carefully modulated voice.

"Nothing."

A keen disappointment lashed at him. "Why can't you admit it? Why do you pretend you don't want me, and put us both through this torture?"

"Because it's wrong for me to want you!" She cast him a look of sheer desperation. "I shouldn't want you! It's not right!"

"Why? Because you're an earl's daughter and I'm just some dirty pirate?" He felt as if she'd just reached in and dug out his insides with dainty fingers. Turning back to the window, he braced his hands on the sill. "Maybe I was wrong about you, after all. With the women, you can forget they're criminals and beneath your station. But with me—"

"That's not what I meant! It's just that . . ."

When she floundered, he ached worse than before. He felt her approach. She laid her hand on his arm, and he flinched. "Don't," he said in a harsh whisper. "If you can't come to my bed, then don't touch me."

"But Gideon—"

Grabbing her hand, he turned and twisted it behind her back, jerking her up against his body. "Do you remember what you saw this morning, Sara? What I was doing by the stream? That's what a man does when he's got a need so deep he can't satisfy it, when he wants a woman who doesn't want him."

"I *do* want you," she whispered earnestly, the color high in her cheeks. "Truly, I do. You're right. I want you so much I can hardly bear it."

"But you wish you didn't," he bit out.

"Yes. I can't deny it. I despise what you've done in your life, the ships you've taken by force and yes, the way you've kidnapped all of us. I can't help that. I was brought up to believe that such things are wrong."

He stared at her, unable to say anything. For the first time in his life he felt guilt over the life he'd led. He'd had reasons for leading such a life, true, and for most of his career his government had sanctioned his actions. But that didn't make them any less wrong in her eyes. And suddenly he wished very much he could wipe those years away, if only for her.

"But no matter how much I tell myself that it's wrong to want you," she went on softly, "I can't stop myself. It's as natural to me as . . . as . . ." A faint smile touched her lips. "As lecturing people about their sins. I want you, Gideon, more than anything. And I'm willing to forgive the rest because I do."

Though his heart leapt at the words, he dared not believe them. "You say that only because you pity me for what my mother did. You've made it quite clear you don't want a criminal in your bed, a man who had to kidnap women just to find a wife, a man who delights in stealing the jewels off—"

She cut off his bitter words with a kiss, pressing her sweet, lithe body against him as she caught him by the shoulders. He went still, his pulse thundering in his ears.

"Sara," he warned when she pulled back from him. "Don't do this. You don't know what you want."

"I do know what I want." She slid her fingers along the bare skin of his shoulders, her eyes a luminous, dusky brown in the fading afternoon light. "I want you to make love to me. You said I'd have to be the one to ask next time. Well, I'm asking." Her voice trembled. "Make love to me, Gideon. Please?"

That sweet little "please" nearly undid him. His blood raced hot, but he didn't move an inch. "That's not enough for me anymore. I want you for my wife, Sara. That's what *I* want. And if you can't be that—"

"I can." She seemed surprised by her answer, but only for a moment. Then a look of resolve crossed her face. "I will. I'll marry you and help you make Atlantis into the kind of colony it deserves to be."

He could scarcely believe what she was saying. How many times had he dreamed of this, hoped for this? Was his mind playing tricks on him now?

"Will you marry me, Gideon Horn, dreaded pirate captain and lord of the seas?" she asked with mock solemnity, a smile tugging at her mouth.

In that instant all his control broke. His answer was to drag her into his arms and take her mouth in a kiss that he knew was too hard, too fierce. But he couldn't help himself. She was his at last! Sara was *his*. And he was so hungry for her, he didn't know how in God's name he could keep from ravishing her where she stood.

But he didn't have to worry. Sara seemed perfectly eager to be ravished. She twined her arms about his neck, straining her slender body against him as her tongue met his stroke for stroke. Her mouth was hot and sweet, and he couldn't get enough of it. He nipped at her lower lip, then sucked at it to soothe it.

Her small, soft breasts were crushed against his chest, making him insane to touch them. Dragging down the neck of the native blouse she wore, the one he'd bought for her, he filled his hand with her breasts, shaping and caressing them until he heard her moan.

Then he tore his mouth from her lips and kissed a path downward, reveling in the salty taste of her skin, the smooth slope of breast ending in the puckery nipple. Sucking at it hard, he felt her arch against his mouth with a little cry.

"Gideon . . . oh, Gideon, yes," she whispered, firing him all the more.

Only with an effort did he keep his hands and lips off her long enough to growl, "We should go back to the ship, to your cabin—"

"No!" She dropped her hands to the buttons of his trousers, fumbling frantically to undo them. "No, let's make love here, in our house."

Our house. It wasn't a dream, after all. She was here with him—she'd promised to be his forever. He yanked loose the ties of her blouse, then shoved the flimsy thing down her arms to bare her breasts completely.

Between kisses and caresses and muttered endearments, they took much longer to undress than he wanted, but he didn't mind when she looked at him so radiantly and gave her body to him so willingly. By the time they were naked, they stood by the bedroll he'd taken from the hold.

But he paused beside it, tamping down on his lust fiercely.

"What is it?" she whispered as he held her from him.

"I don't want to take you like a rutting pig." Kneeling down on the thin mattress, he took her hand and tugged her close until she was standing a few inches from him. "I want you to remember this forever."

"What do you mean?" Her eyes went wide as his fingers parted the thick, damp curls between her legs. Trembling, she clutched at his shoulders and looked down at him warily. "What are you—" She broke off when he kissed her between the legs, right on the soft folds of skin he'd bared. A prolonged sigh slid from her lips. "Oh-h-h, Gideon . . . *Gideon* . . ."

He caressed her slowly and deeply at first, exploring every part of her with his tongue and lips and teeth. When he felt her fingers clasp his head, urging him against her, he pleasured her with everything he possessed until he thought he'd burst with the need to bury something other than his tongue inside her.

She was hot and wet, and the musky taste of her drove him wild. His hands gripped her thighs harder and harder. He wanted to be inside her very badly, but he wanted something else more . . . to bind her to him, to make her never regret choosing him. So he went on and on and on until he felt her jerk beneath his mouth and heard her utter a darling cry of release.

Only then did he tumble her down on the bed and enter her, his muscles straining as he drove himself deep inside her. He wanted to strike to the very soul of her so she could never, ever leave him. She would be his forever. He would see to that.

She arched against him, throwing her head back and grabbing at his arms to anchor him to her. God, she felt tight and warm, and so, so good, he thought as they fell into a wild, sensuous rhythm together. His blood pounded and he was near to exploding already, but he held back until she convulsed around him. Then he lost all sense of where he was, spilling himself inside her with a guttural moan of pure satisfaction.

He didn't know how long he lay there atop her, inside her. It must have been only a few seconds, but it felt like hours of drifting slowly to earth with her body locked to his, of hearing her quick, shallow breaths and feeling her sweat-slick skin undulate beneath his.

When he could manage it, he slid off to lie on his side facing her. She curled against him like a furling sail after the storm is spent, her arm folded against his chest and her legs intertwined with his. Tucking one hand under her head, she traced the whorls of hair around his flat nipples with the other.

His glance fell to the silver locket she always wore around her neck, and a sudden curiosity to know everything about her assailed him. He tapped it with his finger. "Such a pretty locket. Who gave it to you?"

"My mother." A shy smile touched her lips. "It contains a lock of her hair. I know it probably seems silly to carry such a thing, but—"

"Not at all. You and your mother must have been very close for you to wear it all the time as you do." He envied her that, though the ache of his own mother's betrayal seemed to have lessened suddenly.

"I miss her a great deal. I could always rely on Mama to listen to whatever I said and give me sound advice."

He stared past her at the rudimentary bedchamber they lay in, and suddenly wished it were somehow grander, better. "What would your mother have thought of this . . . of us?"

Sara dragged a finger down his chest. "Believe it or not, I think she'd have approved. Mama had a very open heart, and she was a good judge of men. When I was infatuated with Colonel Taylor, she told me from the beginning he wasn't right for me. But I think she'd like you."

Pleasure at her last words warred with a violent jealousy. Sara had been infatuated with someone? Somebody other than him? Tightening his arm possessively about her, he asked, "Who was Colonel Taylor?"

She ducked her head, looking suddenly uncomfortable. "A man I nearly ran away with. My family didn't approve of him."

"Because he wasn't a duke or something, I suppose."

"No. Because they could tell he was a fortune hunter. Jordan had done some research into his background and discovered he hadn't a penny to his name. After he told my stepfather about it, my stepfather threatened to cut my portion off entirely if I didn't break with the man."

Gideon stiffened, thinking of his own father. "Just because the man had no money doesn't mean he wasn't in love with you."

"That's what I thought, too," she surprised him by saying. "So I went to Colonel Taylor and offered to run away with him. I told him it didn't matter to me if I was disinherited." Her voice grew strained. "Apparently it mattered to him. He made it quite clear that he didn't have the funds to keep up a wife who could not, as he put it, 'bring anything but her fair face to the marriage.'"

Gideon heard the pain in her voice and wished with astonishing fervency that he could find Colonel Taylor and teach him a lesson or two with a cat o' nine tails. "The man was obviously an idiot to pass up the chance to have you. Thank God your stepbrother found out the man's true character before it was too late."

She went very still in his arms. "Yes, thank God." After a moment, she added in a small voice, "Gideon, what if . . . my brother should happen to come here? I told you before, he's not going to rest until he finds me."

An unreasoning alarm gripped him before he dismissed it, telling himself there was nothing to worry about. "He'll never find Atlantis, not without a guide. Even the Cape Verdeans don't know about this place."

"But if he did," she persisted. "What would you do?"

He stared into her solemn eyes. "I wouldn't let him

take you from me, if that's what you mean. I'd fight any man who tried to take you away." Some of his earlier distrust reared its ugly head, and despite himself, he added bitterly, "Or are you perhaps hoping for that, hoping that the earl will rescue you?"

"No, of course not!" Guilt flashed in her eyes briefly, but it was gone so fast, he wasn't sure if he'd imagined it. She cupped his cheek, caressing the skin with her light touch. "When I said I wanted to marry you, I meant it. But I do miss my brother. I-I would like to let him know I'm all right."

Those few words drove a stake into his heart. He released her, rolling away to lay on his back. "Yes, you English noblewomen do seem to have a great attachment for family."

"Stop that, Gideon." She moved over and laid her head on his chest. "Stop comparing me to your mother. I'm not going to leave you, not if I can help it. All I'm saying is that it wouldn't hurt for me to send a letter to my brother, putting his mind at ease and telling him I'm happily married to—"

"A pirate? That should make him very happy."

"A *former* pirate." The corners of her mouth twitched upward. "At least you're not a fortune hunter. You won't even let me go home, much less lay a claim to my portion."

Guilt struck him with a vengeance. "Don't even talk about going home. You know you can't; there'd be questions. They'd try to make you reveal where we are." When she looked insulted, he added hastily, "I'm not saying you would, but if you didn't, they might try to keep you there until you did. And if you couldn't get back here, I couldn't go after you. They'd hang me."

She paled. "I hadn't thought of that." Then she brightened. "Perhaps we could go to England together, in disguise or something. Haven't you ever wanted to see the country where you were born? To find your family—"

"Never. Not after what they did to me and my father."

"And that's another thing . . . aren't you just a bit curious to find out if your father gave you the whole truth? What if there's another side to the story? What if your mother left because he was beating her or something awful—"

"Leaving me behind to be beaten instead?" he growled. "That's worse than what he told me."

That seemed to unsettle her. "Well, yes, but it could've been something else—"

"No. I saw that letter from her." Grasping her chin, he tipped it up until she was looking at him. "Why all the questions about them? And why all this talk about going to England if you're so pleased to be marrying me?"

A forced smile touched her lips. "I'm sorry, Gideon. I just can't help worrying about my brother and what he must be suffering right now. It's not that I want to leave you. But I do want to reassure him."

He stared at her. A deep, hollow fear of losing her crept through him like a nasty poison. If he forbade her to communicate with her family, she'd grow to hate him for it. This wasn't a need that would go away.

On the other hand, if he let her send a letter, would that be enough for her?

"If I tell him I'm safe," she persisted, "perhaps he won't try to find me."

"I don't know about that. If I were your brother, I wouldn't rest until I found you and skewered the randy lad who took advantage of you."

She paled, pressing her fingers to his lips. "Don't say that. I won't let anyone skewer you, especially not my brother."

The sudden fear in her eyes eased his worries some. "All right. You can send a letter to your brother. I suppose that wouldn't hurt anything."

She threw her arms around him, snuggling close.

"Thank you, Gideon. Thank you so much."

Feeling generous, he smiled down at her head with its cloud of tousled red hair and stroked it fondly. "I suppose the other women may write letters to their families if they wish, too."

Her head shot up to reveal an expression of pure pleasure. "Oh, Gideon, that would mean so much to them! Most of them have no one, of course, but some would like to contact their families, I'm sure."

"I'll have one of the men mail the letters from Sao Nicolau when they go to fetch the minister this week."

"The minister?"

He dropped a kiss on her freckled nose. "Yes. I can't very well perform the wedding ceremony for myself, can I? There's an Anglican minister living on Sao Nicolau who might be willing to come here for a few days. And some of the other women might prefer to be married by a churchman as well."

"I don't know about that." She traced a finger along a scar on his chest. "I daresay half of them have never darkened the door of a church."

"Why, Miss Willis," he teased, "don't tell me you're actually admitting that not *all* of your precious, beleaguered convict women are lily-white maidens."

A stormy frown darkened her brow as she stabbed one finger at his chest. "You, sir, have no room to criticize anyone for not being lily-white. Plundering ships and kidnapping women and—"

He muffled her lecture with a kiss, tugging her over until she was sprawled gloriously across him. Only a few seconds passed before she answered his kiss, her mouth opening sweetly to the thrusts of his tongue.

Yes, he thought as he grew hard again and felt her legs parting eagerly. This was the way to handle Sara—kiss her until she forgot what she was angry about. Make love to her until she forgot about all those blasted convict women and England and her stepbrother.

Especially her stepbrother. Because he had a nagging fear that he hadn't put an end to talk of that blasted English earl.

Chapter 22

*The gold's no more than dross to me, alas! my heart is
   sunk full low,*
*The want of thy sweet company will surely prove
   my overthrow:*
*Therefore, dearest, do not leave me, here tormented on
   the shore;*
Let us not sever, love, for ever, lest I ne'er shall
   see thee more!

—ANONYMOUS, "THE UNDAUNTED SEAMAN"

"**A**nother story, tell us another story!" the children chanted as they sat around Sara on the beach.

Two days had passed since she'd agreed to marry Gideon—two glorious, blissful days. The children had noticed her mood, of course. How could they not, when she wore a silly grin all the time and wandered about as if in a dream? That was why they'd been able to convince her today to skip their lessons in favor of stories. And she didn't even care. At the moment she was so happy, she'd gladly give tea and crumpets to the devil if he asked her nicely for them.

Ann, however, was more practical-minded than she for once. She clucked her tongue at the children. "Now there, lads and lasses, she's already told you three stories. Surely that's enough for now."

"I don't mind—" Sara began.

A deep male voice interrupted her. "I'll tell the children a story, if they'd like."

Sara turned to find Gideon standing behind her, looking more content and carefree than she'd ever seen him. He strolled up to her, a mischievous smile on his tanned face. The wind ruffled his raven-black hair, blowing it around his cheeks and softening the usually hard lines of his jaw. When he winked at her, she couldn't help but smile. Why, sometimes the man seemed like a little boy himself.

"I'm sure they'd love to hear a story from you, Gideon," she said. "Wouldn't you, children?"

There was an awful silence behind her. She glanced back at the children who were regarding Gideon with a mixture of awe and fear. He had shown little interest in the children until now, probably because he was so busy supervising the rebuilding of the island. As a result, they knew little about him except that he and his men had captured them and their mothers.

If the children had been older, they might not have been so intimidated by him. But they were, after all, very young. The eldest boy was only six and the eldest girl merely nine.

Ann broke the uncomfortable silence with a sniff. "Don't be shy now. I *know* you little ones would enjoy a story from the captain. Surely you're tired of hearin' me and Miss Willis all the time, ain't you?"

Under Ann's stern gaze, the children began to nod one at a time, though with more fear than enthusiasm.

Gideon squatted down beside Sara, his manner easy as he flashed the children a smile. "Look here, all of you. I know you've heard some fearsome things about me. And I'll not lie to you. Some of them are true. I *have* stolen a jewel or two in my day, and I've fought many a battle, mostly in defense of my country."

The children stared at him wide-eyed. He went on, pitching his voice above the surf. "But a lot of what you think about me isn't true at all. The ship is named the *Satyr*, not the *Satan*." He gave them a wicked grin. "And while I may resemble him in some respect, I am *not* the devil." Tilting his head down, he parted his hair with both hands. "Look close. Do you see any horns hiding in this hair of mine?" He sat back on the sand and removed one of his boots, then held up a bare foot and wiggled his toes. "What about hooves? Do you see any hooves? I don't." He pulled his foot up as if to inspect it himself. Then he wrinkled his nose. "No hooves, but they sure do smell."

Molly's little girl, Jane, who was sitting in front, giggled, then covered her mouth with her hand.

Pressing his advantage, Gideon stuck his foot in front of Jane and wriggled his toes again. "Want to smell my foot?" When she shook her head with another giggle, he waved his foot in the air in front of her. "Maybe you'd like to check to see if I've hidden a hoof somewhere? Behind the toes maybe? Under the heel?"

A couple of the other children giggled.

"Go on then. See if you can find my hooves." Jane reached out a tentative hand to touch his toes. "Now, don't tickle me," he warned. "I'm very ticklish."

Sara suppressed a smile. There wasn't a ticklish bone in that man's body, and she should know, having explored every inch of him quite intimately.

Jane brushed his heel with her fingers, and he let out a fake laugh. "Stop, please stop!" he cried in mock fear. "I told you I'm ticklish!" That, of course, prompted bolder attempts to tickle him, and soon the other children were trying to make him laugh. Before long, they were swarming all over him, a mass of tickling, squealing, laughing children.

She watched, a lump forming in her throat. He would make such a good father. She could imagine him tumbling around in the sand with his own dark-headed boy or wide-eyed girl. How glad she was that she was marrying him!

Now if only she could be sure that Jordan wouldn't ruin everything.

She brightened. He might not come, of course. Thanks to Gideon's change of heart, she'd been able to send a letter to Jordan telling him not to. With any luck, it would reach him in enough time to convince him that she was fine and that he need not come after her. After all, only three weeks had passed since Petey'd left, and he probably hadn't even found a ship sailing from the Cape Verdes to England yet. Why, her letter might end up leaving on the same ship as Petey's.

And even if the letter reached England after Jordan left and even if Jordan did show up on the island, it would be too late anyway. The minister would be here in two days, and then she and Gideon would be well and truly married. *No* one could part them then. Even Jordan wouldn't expect her to leave behind her husband, the man she loved.

The man she loved. A pang gripped her chest. She did love Gideon, so much she could hardly bear it sometimes. She'd realized it the night he'd told her about his mother, the night he'd made love to her with such sweetness, it had nearly broken her heart. She'd wanted to tell him then, but her feelings were so fresh, so new, she didn't think she could stand it if he didn't say the words back. There was a part of him that still didn't quite trust her, no matter what he said, and he wouldn't feel completely sure of her until they married.

How had this happened? When had making a former pirate captain happy become the most important thing in her life? She didn't know; what's more, she didn't care. Her feelings weren't going to change.

That's why she'd agreed to marry him. There'd no longer been any point in pretending that she could just blithely sail away with Jordan if he came for her. She could no more leave Gideon than she could stop breathing.

Besides, she had no desire to exchange the serenity of

Atlantis for London. In London she'd always felt as if she were sticking her fingers in a leaky dike to keep the dirty flood of poverty and crime and death from inundating the city. She'd gotten little help from the people who were supposed to be her peers, and indeed, they'd scoffed at her for her efforts. No matter how hard she tried, there were always far more losses than gains.

On Atlantis, however, she could really help people. Thanks partly to her, the women had begun to rely on themselves. The men had begun to show a newfound respect for the women, to ask what they wanted, and to make little courtly gestures that endeared them to their sweethearts. They truly were nice men, most of them.

Together the men and women were building something lasting. It did her heart good to watch people who'd been discarded by their countries regain their self-respect and find a useful purpose in life. Every day she woke up eager for the new day to begin, eager to explore more of the island and find new enjoyments to share with Gideon.

There was only one thing she felt guilty about—that she hadn't pressed Gideon on the issue of the women. They'd both avoided the subject of the marriages, afraid to tear the fragile thread of happiness that joined them. But she'd have to bring the subject up soon. The month he'd given the women would end in two days, and though most of the women had chosen husbands, some still balked at marrying, particularly those who'd left behind devoted husbands or sweethearts in England.

Surely when she explained their reasons to Gideon he would make an exception for them. She'd come to realize in the past weeks that Gideon was a rational man, capable of great generosity. For all his cynicism, he hoped for something better and was willing to strive to find it. He would see her side of it once she showed him it was the best thing for the colony.

She watched him settle the laughing children about him and begin to tell them a story about One-Eyed Jack, the ship's parrot with a liking for salt beef. Trailing her hand idly in the sand, she watched him with her heart in her throat, lovingly memorizing his every feature. His scarred cheek, which she'd once thought looked ominous and now looked so dear . . . his blunt, capable fingers that had brought her to wild fulfillment several times in the past few days . . . his absurdly naked feet with the black hair sprinkled across his toes. . . .

Oh, yes, she loved him top to bottom. And though he hadn't yet said the words, she knew he would. He had to. She wouldn't let him not love her.

He finished his story and the children clamored for another, but he held up his hands as if in surrender. "I'm sorry, children, but I can't. Not just now. Silas and the others are waiting for me. We're going on a hunting expedition."

When there was a chorus of discontent, he said, "You all like roast pork, don't you?"

The children nodded.

"Well, then," he went on as he stood and brushed the sand from his breeches, "we must get some for you. But we'll be back before nightfall, and then I'll tell you another story, all right?"

"Yay!" the children shouted.

When he went to Sara's side, Ann stood, casting him and Sara an indulgent smile as she motioned to the children to gather around her. "Come, children, let's go down the beach a ways. I think I saw a turtle's nest not far from here."

Sara cast her friend a grateful smile as the children tripped off down the beach, leaving Gideon and her alone.

"You'll be gone all day?" she said as soon as the children were out of earshot, unable to keep the disappointment out of her voice.

He grinned as he came up and drew her into his arms. "You sound like a wife, and we're not even married yet."

"Do you mind?" she said archly.

"Not for one second." He kissed her soundly, his hands roaming to places they certainly shouldn't. Not on an open beach, at any rate.

When he drew back, she clung to him, feeling inexplicably reluctant to let him go. It wasn't as if they normally spent every waking moment together. But for some reason, today she couldn't bear to part from him. "I could go with you."

He laughed. "And do what? Load our rifles? Butcher the meat and dress it? Carry it back for us? You've got better things to do than trail through the brush with a group of smelly men on the hunt."

"You know that's not the reason you don't want me to go," she accused. "You and the others just want to be free to grunt and scratch yourselves and swig grog without having to worry about what we women will think of you."

"Now that you mention it—"

"Oh, go on with you," she said in a tone of mock disgust, pushing him away. "Just don't expect to come to bed tonight stinking of grog and pig's blood."

"Don't worry." He caught her to him. "After half a day of grunting and scratching myself and swigging grog, I'll be more than ready for a bath." He tugged the neckline of her blouse out with one finger and peeked inside it wickedly. "And a few other pleasures I can think of."

"Gideon!" she protested, a blush staining her cheeks. Would she ever get used to his bold behavior?

Probably not, she thought as his eyes darkened and his hand tightened on her waist. She was already trembling in anticipation of his kiss.

"Captain!" shouted a voice from inside the forest. "Are you comin' or no?"

With a groan, he released her. "Yes, confound it," he called. "I'll be there in a minute."

"Don't worry about me. I'll be fine." She reached up

to kiss his cheek. "Go enjoy yourself. And bring us back a good fat porker for the wedding feast."

"That's exactly my intention, my love," he said with a smile. Then he turned and strode up the beach toward the trees.

Her heart pounded as she watched him stop to wave, then disappear into the forest. *My love.* He'd called her *my love.* It probably meant nothing, but it gave her hope. Soon he would say more than that; she was sure of it. She could hardly wait until then, so she could say the words back.

Lifting her skirts with a sigh, she wandered along the beach. She was so absorbed in her dreamy thoughts of Gideon that she didn't notice how far she'd wandered from the others.

Until someone grabbed her from behind. Clapping a hand over her mouth, he dragged her back toward the trees. Terror struck her, and she began to struggle furiously in the man's arms.

"Let go of her, Petey!" hissed a voice as she and her captor entered the woods. "You're scaring her!"

"Don't scream, little miss, all right?" a familiar voice murmured in her ear. "I'm letting go of you now."

Her only answer was to jab him in the ribs with her elbow.

"Ow!" he cried as he released her. "What the bloomin' hell was *that* for?"

She whirled on him, eyes blazing. "For scaring the bejesus out of me, you dunce!"

"Bejesus?" said another familiar voice. Jordan moved from behind a tree, looking gaunt and pale and very out-of-place in his tailored frock coat and trousers. "Your vocabulary has changed somewhat since last I saw you, Sara."

"Jordan!" she cried, her heart leaping into her throat at the sight of her dear, dear stepbrother. She threw herself into his open arms and buried her face in his shoulder. "Oh, Jordan, you're here!"

"Yes, moppet, I'm here." His arms tightened painfully around her. "Are you all right? Have those devils hurt you?" He held her at arm's length as he scanned every inch of her. "You look all right, but I know that doesn't mean anything."

"I'm fine," she whispered. "Truly I am."

He brushed her hair from her cheek as his eyes searched her face. "You have no idea the tortures I've suffered, imagining what horrors—" He broke off, a grim expression on his face. "But it doesn't matter now. I've got you back at last. You're safe now."

Guilt struck her. Safe? How was she to tell him she'd been safe all along? Here she'd been enjoying herself, making a new life and falling in love, while Jordan had been suffering on her behalf.

It wasn't all her fault, though. Oh, if Gideon could only see her brother now, he'd understand just how unfairly he'd behaved by kidnapping them all.

Gideon! Good heavens, what was she to do about Gideon and Jordan?

She pulled away from her brother. As she groped for some way to tell him how matters had changed in the past month, she covered her confusion with questions. "How did you get here so quickly?"

"As soon as the *Chastity* returned to London, the captain came directly to me with his tale of the capture. I set off at once for the Cape Verdes, the last place where the ship had made port. As I worked my way through the islands, hoping for some information about where the pirates camped, I found Petey on Sao Nicolau, waiting for a berth on a ship back to England. He led me here."

She hadn't even considered that such a thing could happen—although if she'd been thinking, it would have occurred to her that Jordan would leave as soon as the *Chastity* docked in England. Now he was here. And she wasn't the least bit prepared for him. "Where's your ship?"

"Petey did a hasty survey of the island before he left here, so he brought us into a secluded harbor where my men could wait while he and I fetched you and his fiancée."

"Speakin' of which, guv'nor—" Petey began.

Jordan waved him off. "Yes, go on and find her. But make it quick, before the ship is discovered. Sara and I will wait here for you."

Good, she thought as Petey hurried off. She needed a few moments alone with Jordan without Petey's interference.

He turned back to her, his face grim. "I know you want the other women rescued, Sara, but I had to be sure you were safe first. Once Petey finds his fiancée, we can return to the *Defiant*."

She looked at him in surprise. The *Defiant* was the pride of his fleet. She could hardly believe he'd risked it for her.

"I would have brought the Navy right to this place," he went on, "but I knew if I did, your reputation would be sullied forever. I had already paid the captain of the *Chastity* to lie about what happened during the pirate attack, so I thought I'd best bring one of my own ships and not risk a scandal."

"But Jordan—"

"Don't worry," Jordan went on, as if she hadn't spoken. "I have enough armed men and cannons of my own to put an end to this nest of pirates. We can sink the *Satyr* before the bastards are even aware of what happened. Then we can—"

"No! You mustn't do that!"

He looked at her as if she were mad, then his face altered. "Oh, yes, I'd forgotten. Petey told me that the women were sleeping aboard the ship. Well, then, there's nothing for it but to take the *Satyr* safely out to sea before we attack. I have enough men—"

"Jordan, please! You can't do any of that!"

"Why not?"

She wrung her hands, searching for a way to tell him. "Because I won't let you. I can't let you hurt Gideon."

"Gideon?" he echoed, his eyes glinting hard as oak in the dim sunlight that filtered through the trees. "You aren't by any chance speaking of Captain Horn, are you? The Pirate Lord? A man who has plagued English seas for the past decade? A ruthless criminal with—"

"He's not ruthless! And he's not a criminal. Not anymore."

"You mean, because he claims to be settling on this island? Petey told me all about the man, whom he absurdly seems to admire. But I'm not blinded by romantic legends of piracy, Sara. I see the man for what he is."

"But he's not what you think! He's not this . . . this terrible creature they've made him out to be in the papers. He's intelligent and kind and—"

"And he kidnaps women for sport."

She swallowed. That one was hard to justify. "Not for sport. But yes, he did kidnap us. It was a foolish thing to do, and if you give me enough time with him, I can persuade him to release those women who wish to leave the island."

"Give you enough time?" He grabbed her by the shoulders. "Sara, this isn't one of those puling old men on the Navy Board whom you can sweet-talk into doing what you wish! This is a war-hardened criminal!"

"You don't know him!"

"And you do?" His eyes narrowed as he scanned her form, taking in her casual attire and bare feet. "Exactly how well do you know this pirate?"

Fighting down a blush, she averted her face. "Well enough. I love him, Jordan. He's asked me to marry him, and I've accepted. We're to be married day after tomorrow."

"Over my dead body!" he exploded. "If you think for one minute that I'll stand by and let you make a mistake like this—"

Her gaze snapped back to his. "It's not a mistake! I know perfectly well what I'm doing!"

"Yes, just as you knew what you were doing when you set your sights on that deuced Colonel Taylor!"

She jerked back from him. "Why you . . . you . . ." She broke off, dragging in great gulps of the air in an attempt to control her temper. "How dare you compare them! Colonel Taylor wanted my fortune! Gideon wants nothing from me but my affections!"

Jordan rubbed the back of his fisted hand, looking as if he wanted to plant it in someone's face. Probably Gideon's. "Listen to yourself, Sara. You're defending a man who's hated the English nobility from the day he first set sail. Do you have any idea how many Englishmen that pirate has stolen from? How many women he has ravished, how many—"

"He would never ravish a woman—not unless she begged it of him," she blurted out. Then furious color stained her cheeks, making her look away. Bother it all, she shouldn't have said that, not to Jordan, of all people. "I-I mean—"

"You mean he has seduced you," he said, his voice thunderous. He stuck his hand in his breast pocket and pulled out a pistol. "Now I'll have to kill him."

She threw herself at him, holding on to his rigid arm with all her might. "If you hurt one hair on his head, I'll never forgive you!"

"I can live with that," he growled as he tried to thrust her away. "Now where is the bastard—"

"Don't you dare! I'll . . . I'll betray you to the pirates before you can leave this island! I swear I will!" Gideon's men wouldn't harm Jordan without her say. They'd come to trust her, and perhaps even respect her.

Gideon, however, she wasn't so sure of. If Gideon thought for one minute that Jordan had come to take her back, Gideon would throw him in irons. She must do whatever she could to keep the two men apart.

Jordan stared at her with mouth agape. "Turn me over to the pirates? You would do that?"

"I can't let you hurt him, don't you see? I can't let you bring your men in here and destroy Atlantis! We've worked too hard to see it ruined. Can't you understand? This is a town now, a place where people live and work and have families. You can't just bring your . . . your cannons in here and level the place. I won't let you!"

"It means that much to you, does it?"

"This place means everything to me," she said quietly, and meant it.

His gaze dropped from hers as he replaced his pistol in his breast pocket. "Very well. I'll do as you wish."

She stared at him suspiciously. "What do you mean, 'as I wish'?"

"I won't bring my cannons in here. I'll sail away without ever letting the pirates know I was here." His gaze bore into hers. "But only on one condition."

"Condition?"

"That you leave with me."

Her heart dropped into the pit of her stomach. She should have anticipated this. Jordan had always been willing to do whatever it took to protect her, even if it meant this sort of wretched blackmail.

"Keep in mind," he added when he saw her expression, "that my men have orders to attack unless I return to the *Defiant* by noon. I'm not leaving until you leave with me, even if it means watching the destruction from here on the island."

A chill shook her. "Jordan, don't ask this of me. There are some women here who want to leave, and you should take them, to be sure, but as for me—"

"You're the only one I care about, Sara. I'm not leaving here without you."

"I don't *want* to leave! Haven't you heard a word I've said?"

"Yes. But I don't think you mean what you say." His voice turned placating. "Soldiers know of this phenomenon. It happens all the time to men in captivity. While they're cut off from society, they lose their perspective and begin to understand and trust their captors. After they're rescued, however, they realize they weren't in their right minds at the time."

Not in their right minds, indeed! "Oh, how can I make you see? I *am* in my right mind. I know what I'm doing!"

"Then prove it to me. Come with me to England, Sara. Leave these scoundrels to their colony." He planted his hands on his hips. "If after a few weeks, you feel the same way you do now, I'll bring you back."

"No, you won't. I know you, Jordan. Even when you've been proven wrong, you don't acknowledge it. You'll take me from here and then make excuses about why you can't bring me back." She fixed him with a pleading gaze. "If you force me to leave here with you, it'll destroy me, do you hear? I'll hate you for it. I promise you that."

Her words made him flinch, but only for a second. Then his face resumed its implacable expression. "Better you hate me now than live to regret staying here. If you don't come with me, I promise I'll take every one of those pirates prisoner and bring them back to England, and the women with them. I have enough men and arms to do it."

She shuddered at the thought of what havoc his men and arms might wreak on the island. How was she to stop him? How could she make him see that she truly knew what she was doing?

Suddenly, the sound of branches crunching underfoot made them both start. Petey approached them through the trees, tugging Ann along with him.

"There you are," Jordan growled. "It's about time. We have to leave."

Petey glanced at Ann, then squared his shoulders. "We're stayin' here, Ann and me. We're not goin' back to England with you, guv'nor."

Jordan clenched his fists. "Have you all gone mad? What did this pirate do, cast a spell over you?"

"I can't go back to England, milord," Ann whispered, looking a little in awe of Jordan. "They'll just send me off to New South Wales again. Or else I'll have to spend the rest of my days runnin' from the magistrate. And Petey don't want to risk it." She cast her love a shy smile. "He'd druther stay here with me than go off to England without me."

"Look here, Miss Morris," Jordan said, "I'm sure I can speak to a few people and ensure that you don't have to suffer transportation again."

"It ain't just that, my lord," Petey broke in. "It's . . . well, this is a right nice place. I was only here a day the last time, but it was long enough to see that it would make a pleasant home. I got nothin' waitin' back in England for me. Tommy don't need me. He's got his own family. It would take me years of sailin' to make enough blunt to buy even a little cottage, and I'd be separated from Ann a good bit of the time. But here, if I don't mind some hard work, I can have everythin' I want." He gazed adoringly down at Ann. "Everythin'."

"And what do you think that pirate captain will do when he discovers you here after we're gone?" Jordan bit out.

Petey's eyes went round. "Truly, my lord, I don't know. But he's a man of reason. Once I explain as how I had to do my duty by Miss Willis an' all, he'll understand."

Sara wasn't so sure of that, but had no desire to dampen Petey's enthusiasm. "You see what I mean?" she snapped at Jordan. "Even your servant doesn't want to leave Atlantis."

"Atlantis." Jordan snorted. "What a name for a pirate's den. The Greeks would turn over in their graves." He glared at Petey. "Stay here, then. I only hope you live past morning to enjoy it."

He turned to his stepsister. "But *you*, my dear, are

coming with me. Or I swear I'll hunt that deuced pirate captain down and sever his charming head from his treacherous body!"

She studied her stepbrother's face with a sinking heart. He really meant it. If she didn't get him away from here, he'd kill Gideon or take him prisoner, which would be as good as killing him. Not to mention what Jordan's men might do to the island and its inhabitants.

"If I go with you, will you swear to leave without harming anyone? And will you swear not to tell a soul about this place?" It wasn't ideal, but it was the best she could do under the circumstances. Bringing Petey here had been like opening Pandora's box, and she couldn't reverse the damage completely.

"I can't prevent my men from revealing the location of the island," he growled.

She glared at him. "If the Earl of Blackmore can't do it, then I don't know who can."

"Sara, you try my patience—"

"The men don't know who lives on this island, miss," Petey broke in, earning himself one of Jordan's darkest scowls. "His lordship didn't tell them what they were about before they reached the Cape Verde islands, because he wanted to keep 'em from spreadin' scandal about you later. And he kept quiet afterward to prevent any of 'em from jumpin' ship in Santiago out of fear of meetin' the Pirate Lord. Most sailors is terrified of Cap'n Horn."

"Good, let's keep it that way." A measure of relief swept through her. If Petey was right, perhaps she could at least keep other men from returning here to capture or kill the pirates later. She faced her brother, crossing her arms over her chest. "I'm not going with you unless you swear to leave the island unscathed and keep your silence about it, especially with your men."

Jordan cast her a searching glance. "If I do, you'll return to England? You'll forget this nonsense?"

"I'll return to England, but I won't forget a blessed

thing. I fully intend to take you up on your offer to bring me back here once I've convinced you that my feelings won't change."

"Devil take it, Sara—"

"That's my bargain, Jordan. Do you accept it?"

He glanced away, staring through the trees to the brilliant sunlit surf. Then he snapped his gaze back to her. "Yes. Anything to have you off this cursed island."

"I must have your word as a gentleman on it, do you hear? I won't have you dropping broad hints to your friends in the Navy about where they can find a certain pirate's den."

"You're a deuced stubborn woman, you know that?"

"I learned it from you."

He sighed, raking his hands through his auburn hair. "That's probably true. Well, then, I swear by my honor that I won't reveal the whereabouts of this island. *Now* can we leave?"

"What about the other women? The ones who don't wish to stay?"

"I thought everyone was happy in your paradise," he said sarcastically.

She dropped her gaze. "Some of the women . . . are not suited to this place. Can't we take them with us?"

"Not unless you want to alert the pirates to our presence. We were lucky to find you alone. All it takes is one woman to give the alarm. Then I'd be taken prisoner and my men would attack." He lowered his voice. "Of course, if you'd allow me to land my men, we could easily rescue the women—"

Her head snapped up. "Absolutely not."

"Then let's go. Let's leave this cursed place."

"In a moment." She turned to Ann. "Tell the women I'll be back for them. When I return, anyone who wishes to leave may do so." Removing her locket, she held it a moment, then kissed it and handed it to Ann. "And give this to Gideon. Say I'll be back for it. Make sure you tell him that, do you understand?"

"Sara," Jordan broke in, "that belonged to your mother."

"Exactly." A lump formed in her throat, but she ignored it. She would get her locket back one day soon. She would! "Gideon knows what it means to me, and he knows I'd never leave it behind. I can think of no other way to reassure him that I'll return."

How inadequate that would be in the wake of his mother's betrayal. Her leaving here so secretively would destroy him. He might never forgive her, and the possibility of that made her want to weep.

She faced Petey, intending to have him tell Gideon that she'd left under protest. Then she paused. No, if Gideon knew she'd been forced from here, nothing would stop him from following her to England. She couldn't have that. He must believe she'd left of her own free will.

"Tell Gideon that I'll return, no matter what, but don't say a word to him of my bargain with Jordan, do you hear? He'll follow me to England and get himself hanged, and anyone who goes with him. Swear you won't tell him the truth of why I left. Both of you, swear it."

After a moment's hesitation, Petey nodded. Then Ann followed suit.

Sara's heart ached at the sight. By making them swear this, she was ensuring that Gideon would suffer great pain. But she'd rather he suffered some pain than be taken prisoner the minute he entered English waters. In England, his fate would be short, cruel, and final. She couldn't even bear to think of it.

"Come on, Sara," Jordan said impatiently. "My men have orders to attack if I don't return to the *Defiant* by noon."

"All right." She hugged Ann, then Petey. "I *will* be back," she told both of them tearfully. "It may take months, but I'll return to Atlantis as soon as I can."

As she walked off with Jordan, he cast her an angry glance. "You act as if you're going off to your execution instead of returning to the arms of your family and your rightful home."

"The arms of my family? I used to think of you as family, Jordan." She stared stonily ahead, scarcely noticing where they walked. "But now? Now I regard you as my jailer. And I'm afraid I will regard you that way until the day you bring me back here."

For once, her brother had the wisdom not to retort.

Chapter 23

If all men are born free, how is it that all women are born slaves?

—MARY ASTELL, POET AND FEMINIST
PREFACE TO *SOME REFLECTIONS UPON MARRIAGE*

By the time the men who'd gone hunting reached the beach in the early evening, they were in high spirits. They were weighted down with several pig carcasses and had even bagged a few partridges. Amid much boasting and joking, they swaggered toward the communal bonfire and called for ale.

Gideon, however, had no interest in ale. He wanted Sara. He could hardly wait to tell her of the waterfall they'd stumbled upon at the edge of a grove of orange trees. Already he was making plans to return with her in the morning. They could bathe in the falls, then feed each other oranges, a fitting prelude to an afternoon of lovemaking in the solitude of the forest.

Shifting his small canvas bag from one hand to the other, he thought of the gifts he'd brought her—an odd piece of sparkling rock, several oranges, a piece of scrimshaw. He was especially proud of the scrimshaw. It was a perfect miniature of the beach at Atlantis, a bit of carved ivory no bigger than his thumb. He'd traded his best hunting knife to one of his men for that scrimshaw. If she didn't think it was the sweetest thing she'd ever seen, he'd be surprised.

But where was she? He'd thought for sure she'd be here waiting. He glanced up at the cottage and saw a light burning in the window. She must already have retired to their house. If that were the case, then the sooner he could get to her, the better. Catching sight of Louisa standing silently by the fire, he motioned to the men who were carrying the pigs on poles to come forward. With wide grins, they set the dead animals before her like lords bestowing jewels on a queen.

"We eat well tonight, Louisa." Gideon threw the other, larger canvas bag he'd been carrying at her feet. "Roast the partridges first. We'll eat them while we're waiting on the pork. And don't let that husband of yours spoil it by cooking it badly, do you hear? You've got a good hand with pork. Let's see what you can do with it."

"Aye," Silas said good-naturedly at Gideon's side. The man had drunk more than he should have, and was now well enough into his cups that he apparently didn't much care if his cooking was maligned. "The lass surely has a talent for cookin' pork, don't she?" He cast her a lascivious look. "And that ain't the only thing she's got a talent for, either. Take my word for it, lads."

The men nudged each other, exchanging winks and chuckles, then casting Louisa sidelong glances to witness her reaction. Usually a comment of that kind would have elicited a deep blush from her, followed by a sharp retort. Since her acid tongue was a source of amusement for the men, they always delighted in seeing how she'd take their ribaldry.

"That's enough of that, Silas," she said quietly.

The men looked at her, waiting for more of a reaction. When they got none, Silas said, "Is that all you've got to say then, lass?" He hung on Gideon's shoulder for support. "What d'ye think, lads? Have I tamed the little woman at last?"

"Silas, please hold your tongue," Louisa begged.

Something in the urgency of her voice, in the uncharacteristic lack of sharpness, caught Gideon's attention. When Silas started to mumble something else, Gideon ordered him to be silent. Then he faced Louisa. "What is it? What's wrong?"

Her anxious gaze flitted to the men behind him. "Perhaps we should speak more privately—"

"There's no need for that." A sudden chill shook him as a thousand fears sprang into his mind. And foremost was the one he could scarcely bear to voice. "Is it Sara? Has something happened to her?"

Louisa stared down at the sand. "Nothing's happened to her. That is . . . well . . ."

"Where is she?" He glanced back at the cottage, his heart leaping into his throat. If something had happened to her . . . he started off toward the cottage, but a familiar voice behind him stopped him.

"She's gone, Cap'n."

Slowly he turned to find Peter Hargraves standing in the jagged circle of light cast by the fire.

"What the hell are you doing here?" Gideon growled as Peter's words sank in. "And what do you mean, 'She's gone'? Gone where?"

Ann Morris moved up beside Petey, tucking her hand in the crook of his elbow as he twisted his hat round and round in his hands. "Well, Cap'n, you see . . . that is, I . . ."

"She's gone off to England with her brother," Queenie said as she flounced into view. "And Petey's the one that brought the bloke here to fetch her." A look of smug satisfaction crossed her dissipated face. "It's like I told you before, guv'nor. You wasted yer time settin' yer sights on that tight-arsed bluestocking."

"Queenie, hold your tongue," Louisa snapped as Gideon went pale.

Fixing Petey with a furious gaze, Gideon growled, "What is she talking about?"

Louisa stepped in, her face sympathetic. "Apparently, Petey was workin' for Miss Willis's brother, the Earl of Blackmore. It was Petey who brought the earl and his men back here this morning aboard his ship, the *Defiant*. After they got Miss Willis, they set sail for England."

Gideon's blood froze in his veins. Sara was gone? The earl had taken her? It must have been by force, for Sara would never have left him otherwise. Not after the things they'd said to each other, the way they'd made love and planned for the future and—

He groaned, remembering the conversation they'd had about her brother and how much she missed him. She'd said she wouldn't leave Atlantis. But she'd also said she wanted to return to England for a visit.

Clenching his fists, he thought back over everything she'd said, her concern for what might happen if her brother came. She'd been expecting Hargraves then, hadn't she? If Hargraves had been in the earl's employ, then Sara must have known all along that her brother would be coming to get her. While she'd been making love to him, she'd been counting the days until her rescuers arrived.

No, he couldn't believe it. Not his Sara.

"Did she know from the first that you were working for her brother?" he asked Hargraves, clinging to the tiny sliver of hope that she might not have been aware of why Hargraves was aboard the *Chastity*.

Hargraves looked bewildered by the question. "Aye, captain."

Betrayal sliced through him, cutting deeper even than his mother's betrayal. He'd been right from the beginning. English noblewomen didn't willingly consort with the likes of him. But they certainly did whatever they could to survive until they could be rescued, even if it meant letting a randy pirate captain make love to them.

The events of the last month and a half hit him with startling clarity. "That's why she agreed to marry you, isn't it?" He glanced out to sea, struggling to keep his composure in front of his men, although he felt as if a cat o' nine tails was shredding his heart into tiny pieces. "The two of you planned on keeping her safe from me until she was rescued. But when I gave you your chance to leave, you seized it. And she stayed behind to soften me up, to lull me into complacency while she plotted her escape."

He threw the bag of gifts into the surf with an oath. "To think I believed that she really liked it here, that she really wanted to make something of Atlantis. What a fool I was! What a stupid, besotted fool!"

"Now, Gideon," Silas said, worry in his tone, "you know quite well that girl weren't lyin' about wantin' to make somethin' of Atlantis. Anybody could see she loves the place almost as much as you."

He whirled on Silas. "Then why did she sail off with her brother the first chance she got?"

"You can't blame that on her!" Hargraves protested. "She didn't want to leave. He *made* her."

Gideon stared at Hargraves. "What do you mean, he *made* her? By God, if he took her from here by force, I'll follow him and make sure he never takes anything of mine again!"

Ann stepped between Gideon and Hargraves, her face pale. "Petey didn't mean that exactly, Captain Horn. Miss Willis left of her own free will, she did." When Gideon scowled darkly at her, she hastened to add, "But she weren't leavin' for good. She said to tell you she'd be back as soon as possible. Oh, and she asked me to give you this." Ann fumbled in her apron pocket before producing a small silver object. She held it out to him. "She said it was her assurance to you that she'd return."

He took the object, recognizing Sara's silver locket. For a moment, hope swelled in him. She'd always worn that locket. He knew how much it meant to her. Surely she wouldn't have left it behind if she hadn't intended to return.

Then again, his mother had left a valuable brooch behind when she'd abandoned him and his father.

Closing his fingers around the locket, he looked at Hargraves. "If that blasted earl didn't force her to leave, then why did she go at all? There was no reason to leave with him. We were to be married. She said she wanted to stay with me."

Hargraves and Ann exchanged glances. "I dunno, Cap'n," Hargraves answered nervously. "Um . . . maybe she had matters to take care of in England before she could settle here?"

But the hesitant look on Hargraves's face made it clear that even he didn't believe that. Suddenly, another interpretation of her leaving the locket behind occurred to him, an interpretation so painful he could hardly stand to think of it. "Or maybe," he said coldly, "she never intends to return at all. Maybe this locket is just a ruse to keep me from going after her and taking her brother's ship."

Alarm flickered in Ann's face. "Nay, you mustn't believe that, captain. Her brother brought plenty of men and arms with him. If he'd wanted to destroy you and your men, he could have. But he didn't. She wouldn't let him. She begged him not to fight with you, and he agreed."

"Aye, he agreed because he knew he and his merchant seamen would be no match for me! The coward! To creep onto Atlantis and steal away my intended wife without even attempting to take up arms against me! If I'd been in his place, I wouldn't have given in to Sara's pleas so easily! I'd have willingly fought any man who dared to—"

He broke off, remembering suddenly what he'd said to Sara only two nights ago. *I wouldn't let him take you from me, if that's what you mean. I'll fight any man who tries to take you away.* Obviously she'd remembered them as well. She'd taken them quite to heart and had made sure that Gideon never got the chance to hurt her brother.

Rage surged up in him, a rage as mighty as any tempest the sea could produce. That's all she'd cared about—protecting her brother, who was probably some fop with a lame sword hand and a fear of pistols!

No matter how Ann or Hargraves tried to defend her, the truth was, when given the choice between him and her family, Sara had chosen her family. She might talk of reforming the world and making Atlantis into a colony they could be proud of, but it was just talk. Otherwise, she would never have left him for her brother.

Clutching her locket tightly, he scanned the faces of the people standing around the fire. What about them? What about the other inhabitants of Atlantis, the ones she'd claimed to care about? She'd fought for the women and offered to teach the men. They'd all trusted her. But when her chance for freedom had come, she'd seized it without looking back, without even staying long enough to say good-bye.

She'd talked of giving the women a choice, but she hadn't taken any of them with her. Instead, she'd sneaked off the island with her coward of a brother, leaving the rest of them behind. A curse upon the woman! He'd been wrong about her from the very beginning!

These noblewomen were all of the same cloth—deceitful, weak, and determined to do whatever they must to return to the arms of their rich and powerful families. How could he have ever believed differently?

"Please, Captain Horn," Ann's gentle voice broke into his thoughts, "you must believe that she intends to return. You know Miss Willis would never promise such a thing if she didn't mean it."

He faced Ann with a grim expression. "You may believe that if it gives you comfort, but I know better. She left without a care for any of you, and certainly without a care for me. She won't be back. And Atlantis is better off without her."

"But it wasn't like that—" Hargraves began to protest.

Gideon silenced him with a dark scowl. "As for you, Mr. Hargraves, I don't want to hear another word out of you. I gave you more gold than you'd ever seen in your life to get you away from here, and you repaid me by bringing the wolves to my door." An awful possibility occurred to him. Striding up to Hargraves, he took hold of him by the shirt. "And now they all know where this island lies, don't they? I suppose the earl was just waiting until he got his sister safely off the island before he sent in His Majesty's Navy to rout all of us. We are as good as dead now, thanks to you!"

Hargraves shook his head furiously. "His lordship kept the Navy out of it to save Miss Willis's reputation. I swear it. He told his men naught about who lived on this island for fear they'd jump ship in Santiago at the sound of your name. And the little miss refused to leave unless he promised to continue keepin' his silence about Atlantis."

Gideon stared hard at the monkey of a man who'd nonetheless always managed to stand up to him. "And why should I believe you?"

"If I thought the island was to be taken by the Navy boys any minute, Cap'n, why would I have stayed? I could've left on the *Defiant* and taken my lady with me."

The man had a point. Gideon was still rational enough to realize that.

His gaze flitted from Hargraves to Ann, whose face showed every bit of the fear that Hargraves tried so bravely to mask. "Please, sir," she said, in a voice wrung tight as a spring. "Don't hurt Petey. He stayed here for my sake. He believes in Atlantis as much as I do. I couldn't bear it if . . . if somethin' happened to him."

"Don't you worry, Miss Ann," Silas put in. "The cap'n ain't gonna hurt Mr. Hargraves none. Not as long as your man intends to behave himself on the island."

"Stay out of this, Silas," Gideon warned. He stared at Hargraves another long moment and fleetingly thought of what pleasure it would give him to see the man flogged for having a hand in Sara's leaving.

But he'd never approved of flogging, and he certainly couldn't do it while sweet little Ann stood there, her heart in her hands, begging for mercy. Besides, Hargraves had only done what he saw as his duty. It was Sara who had betrayed them all, Sara who'd abandoned him.

With an oath, he thrust Hargraves away from him. "Fine. You and Ann do as you wish. But you'll stay out of my sight if you know what's good for you."

He'd turned toward his cottage, his bleak, empty cottage, when another voice stopped him.

"What about the weddings?" Queenie asked. "Do we still have to choose a husband in two days time?"

He leveled Queenie with a cold stare. He wanted so badly to tell her she'd have to choose a husband in two days. It would serve the impudent tart right to be forced to the yoke of one of his men.

But even before Sara had left, he'd seen the foolishness of trying to dictate who married whom, especially if he wanted the men and the women to have genuine affection for each other. That was one thing Sara had taught him. Not even desire could replace respect and affection in a marriage, and those could never exist when people were forced into the union. He'd forced her into being with him, and now he was paying dearly for it.

"There will be no weddings except for those of you who wish to marry."

As astonishment struck the women, Louisa stepped forward. "Thank you, Captain. That's good of you. And may I speak for the women in saying that we appreciate your kindness."

"Kindness? I don't do it out of kindness! I do it because it's what Atlantis needs. That's all I've ever cared about. That won't change just because Sara is gone. She may have left all of us, but this place will go on . . . *we* will go on."

They would make Atlantis a place to be envied, by

God, with or without Sara. Then one day he'd find her and throw it up in her face, show her what she had left behind. Because this time he wasn't a little boy who had no say in what happened after a woman abandoned him. This time he had all the say in the world.

Chapter 24

She said, "I'll never forsake my dear,
Although we're parted this many a year."

—ANONYMOUS
"THE SAILOR AND HIS LOVE"

Nearly a week had passed since Jordan and Sara had arrived in England, after a month at sea. It was evening, and Jordan stood at the bottom of the stairs in his London town house, pacing and glancing at the hall clock every five seconds. Sara was late. She'd agreed to attend the Merringtons' ball with him tonight, and now she was half an hour late at least.

He wasn't sure how he'd persuaded her to go. This morning she'd said a horrified no, acting as if he were asking her to run naked through the streets. Then this afternoon when he'd arrived home from a day at Parliament, she'd changed her mind.

Thank God. It was time she went out into society and put that deuced pirate out of her mind. A few dances with men of her own station, and she'd realize how foolish she'd been to fall for a pirate captain. Besides, people needed to see her so he could put an end to any breath of scandal that might remain. God knows he'd gone to enough trouble to protect her reputation.

He'd covered up her experiences with the pirates by

paying the owners of the *Chastity* a huge sum to claim she'd been sent back unscathed with the ship's crew after the pirate attack. He'd let it be widely known that she'd been recovering from the trauma of her experience in the weeks since then. So far, everyone seemed to believe the tale.

Thomas Hargraves entered and cleared his throat loudly just as Jordan made his fifteenth circuit of the hall. Though Jordan wasn't in the mood just now to be accosted by his butler, he hid his irritation. After all, Hargraves had lost his brother forever, thanks to Jordan, and some sort of amends for that had to be made.

"What is it, Hargraves?" He cast another glance up the staircase.

"It's about Miss Sara, my lord. You told me to report on her comings and goings while you're at Parliament during the day, and I thought I would do that before you leave for the evening."

Jordan looked at the hall clock, then sighed. "Why the devil not? I've got nothing better to do at the moment."

"Yes, my lord." Hargraves took out a sheet of paper and bent his head to read it, his balding pate shining under the light of the candles. "At 9:11 this morning, after breakfasting with you, Miss Sara took a bath, attended by Peggy. Peggy helped her to dress—in the pink cambric walking gown, I believe—and Miss Sara came downstairs at 10:05."

There was a slight rustling of paper before he continued. "Then she played the pianoforte in the drawing room. I believe the first tune was 'Down by the Banks of Claudy.' " He tapped his chin. "Or was it 'Down by the Sally Gar—' "

"I don't care what she wore or what she played, Hargraves!" he burst out impatiently. "I just want to know what she *did*."

"Yes, my lord," Hargraves said, sounding a bit miffed. "She played the pianoforte until 10:32, at which time she asked me for a copy of *Debrett's Peerage*. She read that until 12:19. I must say it engrossed her rather much. For luncheon, I brought her a tray upon which Cook had placed a chicken pie—Miss Sara's favorite, you know—a salad with six walnuts, two slices of—"

"Hargraves—" he warned.

"I wanted to make you aware of exactly what was given to her, because she didn't touch any of it. And as you know, Miss Sara never does without luncheon—especially when it's chicken pie."

Jordan scowled as he began to pace again. "You can save the commentaries. I know she hasn't been eating well since our return." She hadn't eaten much aboard the ship either. And this morning, he'd watched her butter a slice of toast with listless movements, then set it aside and never touch it again.

Nor was that the worst of it. She slept only a few hours every night and spent the rest of it wandering the halls like a ghost. She avoided any contact with him, and when forced into it, she answered his questions in monosyllables.

Except when they concerned that devil of a pirate, that is. Then she told Jordan more than he wanted to hear, all about the man's dreams for a utopia and his kindness to children and a whole host of other "wonderful" qualities, until he was sick of hearing the name Gideon Horn.

But all that was over now. She'd agreed to go with him to this ball. Surely that was a sign she was getting over her infatuation for Captain Horn. And it couldn't happen too soon, if you asked him.

"After luncheon, Miss Sara went out," Hargraves continued.

Jordan whirled on him. "Went out? I told you she wasn't to go anywhere without me!" Ever since their return, he'd lived in constant fear that she'd charter a ship on her own to return to that deuced island.

Hargraves colored. "She . . . er . . . sneaked out without anyone seeing her." When Jordan began to glower, the servant added hastily, "But she came back only two hours later. She said she'd been to visit one of her friends in the Ladies' Committee. She looked quite well, and she asked for you immediately."

That must have been when she'd entered the library to tell him she'd be attending the ball. What had happened in those two hours to change her mind?

It didn't matter. She was coming around, and that was all he cared about.

A door opened upstairs, signaling that she was finally ready, and he gestured to Hargraves to be quiet. "You can tell me the rest in the morning," he said in an undertone as he turned toward the stairs. "Go fetch Sara's—"

He broke off as he caught sight of his sister standing at the top of the stairs. His mouth gaped open. Oh, my God—what insanity had brought this on? She was wearing an appalling gown. Cut low enough to reveal most of her breasts, it skimmed her figure, molding every curve. What's more, it was made of gold gauze and thin as paper, the kind of gown only French women—or one of his mistresses—dared to wear. He could almost see her navel beneath it, for God's sake.

Had she gone mad? Sara had never worn a gown like that! Even a married Englishwoman would refuse to go out in public so scandalously dressed, and certainly no respectable unmarried woman dared it.

"Where in the devil did you get that gown?" he growled as he approached the stairs. "Go back upstairs and change it this instant! You're not going to Merrington's in that!"

She flashed him a cool glance. "Whyever not? The whole purpose of your taking me to the ball is to find me a substitute for Gideon, isn't it? I'm merely cooperating with your scheme. In this gown, I should be able to entice some poor man to take me, don't you think?" She glided down another step or two. "But after I catch him, you'll have to find a way to deceive him about my ruination. Then again, he might not care. I do have a fortune, after all. That should buy me a presentable husband if the dress doesn't do the trick."

"Fortune hunters? Lechers?" he shouted as he stalked up the stairs. "Is that who you want for a husband?"

She shrugged, pulling at her neckline to make it even lower, if that were possible. "What does it matter? One man's as good as another, don't you agree? You must, or you wouldn't have taken me from the one I loved in hopes that I'd find someone better."

He halted on the stairs, eyes narrowing. "What is this, Sara, some trick to make me feel guilty for what I did?"

"Trick?" she said innocently. "Not at all. I'm merely trying to help you. Since you've appointed yourself to decide who I should or shouldn't marry, I'm doing my part to catch the man. What do you think?" She smoothed the impossibly thin material against her skin. "Will Lord Manfred like this dress? He's looking for a wife, I hear."

Jordan gritted his teeth. Lord Manfred was sixty years old and both a lecher and a fortune hunter. The bastard had been sniffing after Sara for years. Sara loathed him almost as much as Jordan did. "You've made your point," he ground out. "Now go up and change into a decent gown."

"Oh, but Jordan, I have nothing better for snagging—"

"This instant, Sara Willis! Or I swear I'll change it for you!"

"Well," she said offhandedly, "if you insist. But don't blame me if I can't catch a suitable husband right off." With a sniff she turned and walked back up the stairs.

"And don't think this excuses you from going to the ball with me," Jordan called after her. "I expect you down here in no more than half an hour!"

"Yes, Jordan," she said in entirely too smug a voice.

As soon as Sara got inside her room, she smiled to herself. *Take that, brother mine,* she thought as she hurried to where Peggy held the gown she'd actually intended to wear. The servant made no comment as she helped Sara out of the scandalous French gown Sara had borrowed from her friend in the Ladies' Committee. Good heavens, Sara had never felt so naked in all her life, and before Jordan, no less. But maybe now he understood how she felt about his insufferably arrogant behavior.

God knows he hadn't understood before. She'd talked herself blue on the *Defiant*. Nothing she'd said had changed his mind. For a man reputed to be the most notorious rake in all of England, he was behaving like a prude. It was enough to drive her insane, knowing that for every minute he kept her away from Atlantis, Gideon put another brick in his fortress of distrust against her, believing that she'd abandoned him as cruelly as his mother. She couldn't bear the thought!

She frowned as Peggy helped her into her other, more respectable gown. Oh, if only she could return to Atlantis on her own! But she dared not without Jordan's permission or he'd just follow her, and this time he'd surely bring the Navy with him to destroy the island and all its inhabitants. He was so infuriating!

This morning, when he'd had the audacity to propose that she attend a ball, as if nothing had happened in her life over the past few months, she'd decided to make him understand how unfeeling he was being. Maybe now he'd listen to her.

But first she had to attend this ball, and for a very important reason. This morning, it had occurred to her that as long as she was stuck in England, she might as well find something out about Gideon's family. That's why she'd taken out *Debrett's Peerage*. According to it, there was a duke's daughter named Eustacia of the right birth date to be Gideon's mother. What was more astonishing, however, was the fact that the woman was alive. She was the wife of the Marquess of Dryden. Best of all, Lady Dryden was supposed to be at the ball tonight, if

Sara's information from her friend at the Ladies' Committee proved true.

Of course, Lady Dryden mightn't be Gideon's mother, after all. The other things her friend had told her certainly didn't fit the woman she'd envisioned as Gideon's mother. Lady Dryden and her husband weren't the glittering center of society, but recluses who lived quietly on their Derbyshire estate. Philanthropists who gave generously to several charities, they likewise avoided the public acclamation that came with such generosity. And Lady Dryden was renowned for her affability and kindness.

It didn't make any sense. The woman was supposed to be spoiled and selfish. She was supposed to be *dead*, for God's sake. But Sara had read every page of the peerage and hadn't found another woman who fit Gideon's description of his mother so closely.

Perhaps Elias had lied about his wife's death. Or perhaps Gideon had misunderstood or misheard the name. In any case, tonight she intended to learn the truth. *After* she tormented Jordan a bit more, of course.

When she came downstairs the second time, he cast an approving glance over her gown before hurrying her out the door. It was only after they were riding in the Blackmore carriage that he spoke to her. "I don't understand what I've done that's so wrong. I only want to make you happy."

She stared straight ahead, unable to look at him. "By keeping me from marrying the man I love?"

"You only *think* you love him. After a while, you'll see it was just a momentary infatuation—"

"Thank you for that flattering assessment of my character."

He cast her a startled glance. "What the devil do you mean by that?"

A bitter smile touched her lips. "You really don't understand, do you? I know there *are* women of the sort of frivolous character you imagine, who fall in love, then change their minds with a change of scenery." She thought of Gideon's mother, who'd abandoned him without a thought. "But surely you didn't think I was one of them. If I do as you hope and forget Gideon after a few days back in England, won't that show me to have the most unsteady and unreliable character imaginable?"

"It would show you to be sensible," Jordan retorted, though he looked uncertain of his position for the first time since they'd left Atlantis.

"Sensible? I think not. A sensible woman doesn't give her heart, then snatch it away on a whim. It took me a week to see past Gideon's gruff exterior to the real man beneath, and three weeks more to agree to marry him. It wasn't a decision I made lightly. Don't you see? I *knew* you were coming to rescue me. If I'd wanted to resist Gideon, I could have." Her voice softened as she thought of how Gideon had looked when he'd asked her to marry him. "But I didn't want to resist him. I still don't. That's why I must return."

He gave a low, exasperated curse. "Ask of me anything but that, Sara, and I'll give it to you! For God's sake, I'll let you practice your reform efforts anywhere you wish, at any time. Just don't ask me to take you back to that place!"

She stamped her foot, making the carriage wobble on its springs. "I don't *want* anything else! What kind of woman do you take me for, to accept such things in the place of the man I love?"

Gritting his teeth, he stared out the window into London's foggy night. "Haven't you wondered why this pirate hates the nobility so much? How do you know he won't change his mind about you one of these days, thanks to his unreasonable hatred?"

"It's not unreasonable. It's . . . it's . . ." She stopped just short of telling him about Gideon's past, just as she had stopped short so many times before. And with good reason. Jordan would never believe the tale. He would think it some sort of lie Gideon had told to gain her sympathies. The very fact that Gideon had never sought out his mother's family would make the story spurious in Jordan's eyes. He would never believe a pirate could be too proud to risk the humiliation of discovering that his mother's family still didn't want him. That's why she had to find out the truth before she told Jordan anything.

She fiddled with the clasp on her reticule. "Just believe me when I say he has every reason to hate us."

They rode in silence a few moments before he spoke again. "So you're still as set on having this pirate for a husband as before."

"Yes. And that won't change, no matter how many balls you drag me to."

"Then why did you agree to come to this one?"

She avoided his gaze. "I have some . . . business to take care of."

"Business? What kind of business?"

She debated what to tell him, then decided she could reveal part of the truth. "I want to meet Lady Dryden, who's supposed to be in attendance tonight. I have something to discuss with her."

"Concerning the Ladies' Committee? I know she's quite the philanthropist."

Sara pounced on the excuse eagerly. "Yes. Concerning the Ladies' Committee."

"You may have trouble finding her. There's supposed to be quite a crush."

"It doesn't matter. I'll find her." Yes, she'd find her. Even if it meant accosting every matron in the place. Because one way or the other, she was going to find out if Lady Dryden was Gideon's mother. It was the least she could do for the man she loved.

Gideon boarded the *Satyr*, pausing as he passed the railing where he had kissed Sara the night of the fire. The night she'd given herself to him so sweetly.

A crushing weight descended on his chest, the same weight that had lain there ever since she left. How long had it been? Three weeks? Four? He hardly knew. The past month had been a blur of sleepless nights and frenzied days. He'd worked his men hard until Barnaby had finally come to him and begged him to let up. But Gideon had wanted the cottages finished, and then when they were all done, he'd thrown himself into having a schoolhouse and a church built.

There was only one purpose left in his life now: to make Atlantis perfect in every way. Then the world would hear of his utopia, of the place where men and women lived freely side by side without the tyrannies of an unjust government. The world would hear, and *she* would hear. She'd know that he'd succeeded despite her, and she'd curse herself for leaving.

He pounded his fist into the rail. Who was he fooling? She wouldn't care what happened to Atlantis. She was free of it, and that was all that mattered to her. Everything she'd said about wanting to rebuild it and help it grow . . . it had all been empty words to distract him from what she was planning. And he'd believed them! Like a lovesick fool, he'd believed every word!

He started to leave the rail, then caught sight of his own cottage. It was the only unfinished building on the island. He hadn't touched it since the day she left. What was the point? Without Sara, there was no reason for him to have a cottage. The only woman he'd ever wanted to marry was her, and now that she was gone . . .

Now that she was gone, it made no difference what his house looked like or when he ate or how many successes Atlantis realized. Nothing mattered.

Confound it, why couldn't he get the woman out of his head? Everything made him think of her. When he cut a bunch of bananas, he thought of how much she used to love them. Every time he saw a white embroidered blouse or a red head of hair, his heart leapt. Until he realized it wasn't her. It would never be her. She was gone, and no matter what she'd said, she wouldn't be returning. It would be stupid to dream otherwise.

He pulled her locket out of his pocket and stared at it. Why he'd kept it he didn't know. He turned it over in his hand, remembering how she used to play with it when she was talking to him, her slender fingers twisting the chain this way and that. He ought to toss the blasted thing into the ocean. It represented a lie, the lie that she would return, one of the many she'd told him to deceive him until rescue arrived.

He dangled it out over the rail and looked down at the water, which was deep enough for his purpose. All he had to do was drop it, let it slip from his fingers.

But he couldn't. Some foolish, sentimental impulse made him shove the locket into his trousers pocket instead, a low curse erupting from his lips.

With a scowl, he strode across the deck and through the entranceway into the saloon, headed for his cabin. Molly and her children still slept there at night, but he used it during the day. And just now he had a very specific purpose in going there. He wanted his bottle of rum. He didn't often indulge, but today he planned to drink himself into oblivion. For once, he wanted not to be plagued by thoughts of Sara.

Throwing open the door, he entered his cabin, only to hear a squeal and see a blond head disappear under the bed covers. "Come out, damn you, whoever you are!" he shouted. "What in blue blazes are you doing in here?" He'd dismissed his cabin boy from his duties the day they'd settled on Atlantis, so it couldn't be him, and he'd seen Molly talking earnestly to Louisa not long ago, so it couldn't be her.

It had better not be one of the other women either. He wasn't in the mood to deal with any of them just now. So help him, if it was that blasted Queenie, he'd throw her out on her ass.

Then he realized that the shaking lump under the bed

covers was decidedly smaller than any of the women. He groaned. Jane, Molly's five-year-old. It had to be.

He forced some gentleness into his voice. "Jane, is that you, girl? Come out. It's all right. I won't hurt you."

A blond head emerged slowly from beneath the satin, red eyes and nose first, followed by a pouting mouth. "You yelled at me! You said bad words, and you yelled at me!"

With a sigh, he moved to sit on the bed. "I know, sweetie. I shouldn't have done that. It's just that I've been grouchy lately."

More of her emerged from under the covers. She laid two chubby arms on top and stared at him with solemn eyes. "Because Miss Sara went away, huh?"

He stiffened. "Miss Sara's got nothing to do with it."

"Oh. I thought Miss Sara was gonna marry you."

"Where's your mother?" he asked, eager to change the subject. He'd come in here to drown out all thoughts of Sara, not to be reminded of her by a child. "Why did Molly leave you in here all by herself?"

"She said she had to talk to Miss Louisa. She told me to take a nap." Again she pouted. "I don't like to take naps."

Suppressing a smile, he reached over and ruffled her hair. "Yes, but naps are good for little girls. Why don't you just lie down, and I'll leave you alone to sleep, all right?"

She lay back obediently against the pillows, but he could feel her eyes follow him as he rose and walked to the desk. Opening the drawer, he took out the bottle of rum, wishing he had some way to hide it from her sight.

"Is that gin?" she asked in a querulous voice.

"No. Now go to sleep."

"My papa used to drink gin sometimes when he was sad. Then he would sing funny songs and make me laugh."

Gideon stared at her. Though Sara had told him some of the women had husbands back in England, he'd never thought much about it. After all, if they'd had decent husbands, they wouldn't have gotten involved in criminal acts in the first place, would they?

"I miss my papa," she said with a child's candor. "I miss him lots."

He felt a twinge of conscience. "Why didn't you stay with him in England?"

"He and Mama said I had to go with her. He said the men over the sea wouldn't bother her none if they saw she had me." Her eyes lit up. "Papa said he would come to be with us soon's he got the money." Then her face fell again. "Only . . . only Mama says he can't come to be with us, now that we live on the island. Mama says I gots to have a new papa now."

A bitter lump of guilt caught in his throat. He tried to ignore it. Molly's husband would most likely never have made it to New South Wales, and she might have been forced to take a new husband there anyway, if only to provide for her children.

But telling himself that didn't lessen his guilt. Little Jane didn't understand those fine nuances, did she? She only knew there'd been hope of regaining her father before, and now there was none.

For the first time, he understood what Sara had been trying to make him see. Not all the women were happy to be here. They weren't all delighted to be given new husbands without having any say in it. No, indeed. Some weren't at all happy. Some were having to face the fact that they were to lose their loved ones back in England forever.

And it was all thanks to him and his grand plans for utopia. Utopia? When he'd called Atlantis utopia in front of Sara long ago, she'd called it "a utopia where men have all the choices and women have none." That's exactly what it was—he had created it to be so. But he was fast discovering that a utopia where only half the people have choices wasn't much of one.

"Mama says I hafta be a big girl," Jane went on, tears

forming in her pretty green eyes. "She says I got to learn to like my new papa." She looked up at him, and his heart twisted inside him. "But I miss my own papa. I don't *want* a new papa."

Quickly setting the bottle of rum down on the desk, he moved to sit beside Jane on the bed. He laid his arm around her small shoulders and pulled her close. "Don't worry, sweetie. You don't have to have a new papa if you don't want one. I'll see to that myself."

She snuggled against his shoulder with a little sniff. "I wouldn't mind *too* much if you were my new papa. But you're gonna marry Miss Sara, aren't you? When she gets back."

She said it with such assurance it nearly broke his heart. "Yes, when she gets back," he repeated hollowly.

Suddenly, Barnaby burst into the cabin. "Cap'n, you'd better come quick. Molly's having her baby." He glanced at the child, then motioned Gideon to come to the door. As Gideon stood up to join him, Barnaby added in a low whisper, "And she's not doing too well either. It looks like she's not going to make it. She's asking for the child, so you'd better bring her along."

In that moment, Gideon forgot about the bottle of rum he'd come to get. He forgot about Sara's betrayal and his own hurt. With a sickening lurch in his stomach, he scooped up little Jane in his arms and followed Barnaby out the door.

Chapter 25

The prevailing manners of an age depend more than we are aware, or are willing to allow, on the conduct of the women; this is one of the principal hinges on which the great machine of human society turns.

—HANNAH MORE, "ESSAYS ON VARIOUS
SUBJECTS . . . FOR YOUNG LADIES"

Jordan had been right, Sara thought as she looked through the crowded rooms of the Merringtons' luxurious mansion. Finding Lady Dryden in this crush was impossible. Sara had spent the last two hours looking for the woman, with no success. Since Lady Dryden was not often in society, few people knew her. When Sara did succeed in finding someone who knew her and asked to have Lady Dryden pointed out to her, she was told she'd just missed her. The lady was as elusive as a breath of wind in the calms.

Feeling frustrated, she headed for the balcony to gain a moment of quiet. Unfortunately, a woman emerged on the balcony to join her only a few moments later. They acknowledged each other with polite nods, but respected one another's privacy by standing in silence for several moments more. The other woman had just turned to go back into the ballroom when the pendant around her neck caught the torchlight, garnering Sara's attention.

It was an onyx horse's head, ringed round with diamonds. Though smaller than Gideon's, it was a veritable copy of the one he wore as a belt buckle.

Sara's blood pounded in her ears. "Lady Dryden?"

The woman halted, casting her a startled look. "Yes? I'm sorry, do I know you?"

Sara surveyed the woman with building excitement. It was her. It had to be. She had the same jewelry, and even her coloring was right. With midnight hair threaded with gray and eyes the color of bluebells, Lady Dryden certainly *could* be Gideon's mother.

But how to begin? Sara had rehearsed this meeting a hundred times, yet now that it was here, she was at a loss. She mustn't let the woman leave, that was for certain.

"My name is Sara Willis. I'm the Earl of Blackmore's stepsister." Sara swallowed. "I-I was just admiring your pendant." Nothing like getting right to the point, she always said. "I saw a brooch very like it recently."

The woman stiffened. "Did you? Where?" Her voice was far from nonchalant. Indeed, she seemed suddenly very interested in what Sara had to say.

"This is going to sound strange, I know, but it was worn by a pirate. He'd had it made into a belt buckle."

"A pirate? Do you mean that to be a joke?" Lady Dryden asked, clearly disappointed. Before Sara could protest, Lady Dryden's expression altered and she added, "Wait, you must be the young lady who traveled aboard the *Chastity*. My friend in the Ladies' Committee told me about you. The ship was accosted by pirates and you narrowly escaped capture."

"Yes, that was me," she said dryly. Jordan's story had certainly spread widely. But perhaps it was time that someone knew the truth, especially this someone. "Actually, I didn't escape capture at all. I spent a month with the pirates on an island in the Atlantic. I got to know them very well, especially their captain."

Lady Dryden looked shocked and just a little surprised at the way a complete stranger was taking her into her confidence. "The Pirate Lord? You spent a month with the Pirate Lord himself?"

"Yes. Have you never heard his real name?"

Lady Dryden shook her head, clearly confused to have Sara ask her such a thing.

"It's Horn. Gideon Horn."

The blood drained from Lady Dryden's face. She looked as if she might faint, and Sara rushed to her side. "I'm so sorry, I've upset you. Are you all right?"

"Did . . . did you say 'Horn'? The man's name was Horn? You're certain?"

"Yes. I came to know Captain Horn quite well during my stay on his island." She hesitated to continue, given Lady Dryden's obvious distress. But the woman had abandoned her son, after all, and she deserved to be upset. Sara's voice hardened. "Indeed, I was surprised to learn he wasn't an American at all. He was born English, the son of a duke's daughter. Apparently his mother had run off with her tutor, an Englishman named Elias Horn, then had abandoned her child after her family asked her to return."

"No!" Lady Dryden protested. "That's not the way it was at all! I never—" She broke off, tears welling in her eyes. "So *that's* why my son never looked for me. All this time he must have thought . . ." She trailed off as confusion spread over her face.

Sara shared the woman's confusion. This wasn't the reaction she'd expected. "Lady Dryden, are you saying that you are indeed Gideon Horn's mother?"

The woman stared about her distractedly. "Of course! Surely you had guessed that or you wouldn't have spoken to me of him!"

Sara's heart thundered in her ears. She'd found Gideon's mother. "I wasn't sure. Elias Horn told Gideon that his mother was dead. But there was only one duke's daughter named Eustacia in *Debrett's Peerage*, and it was you. Then, when I saw your pendant . . ."

"You were sure." Lady Dryden gazed back into the dining room, tears coursing down her cheeks as she surveyed the crowded room. She seemed almost frantic as she grabbed Sara's arm. "Oh, Miss Willis, we must find my husband! He must hear this at once!"

Sara felt all at sea. Lady Dryden didn't look or act like a woman just hearing that the son she despised was a pirate. And why, after all these years of not caring about him, would she suddenly be so eager to hear about him? Or to tell her husband of her sordid past?

"Lady Dryden," Sara murmured with concern as the woman tugged her toward the door, "are you sure you want to tell your husband of this without any . . . preparation?"

"Yes, of course!" Then, as if the full import of Sara's question hit her, Lady Dryden darted a glance at her, eyes rounded in distress. "Oh, but you must think— If my son thinks it, then you must think— Never mind. It doesn't matter. You'll understand when you hear my tale. But Miss Willis, we *must* find my husband first! I assure you he'll want to hear everything you have to say. *Everything!*"

"Certainly, my lady," Sara said. She could hardly say anything else.

But she made herself one promise as she let the woman drag her into the ballroom. After the marquess heard what she'd told his wife, she was going to get some answers of her own.

Gideon paced the drawing room in Silas's newly built cottage. Molly was ensconced in Louisa and Silas's bedchamber and was screaming for all she was worth. Thank God one of the women had taken Jane off as soon as she'd seen her mother. He wouldn't have wanted the girl to hear her mother suffering so.

By God, he'd never dreamed that birthing babies was

this awful. He'd never had any dealings with a woman in labor before. The few minutes he'd been in the bedchamber had almost been more than he could stand. And when he'd hurried out as soon as Jane had been taken from the room, Louisa had mumbled something derogatory about the entire male sex.

He hadn't taken offense. How could he? Molly was screaming her blasted head off and enduring hours and hours of pain, all to bring forth a child without her husband. At the moment, he had the utmost respect for women and nothing but contempt for himself and his kind.

Ann slipped through the bedchamber door, a worried look on her face. "The baby is in the breech position, cap'n. That's why Molly's havin' such a hard time of it."

"Breech position?"

"When a baby comes, its head is supposed to come out first. But this one's wee behind wants to come out first, and that won't work. Louisa and I don't know enough about it to make it right, and there ain't a midwife amongst the women. We already asked."

"Surely there's someone who can help," Gideon protested. "There are fifty women or more on this island."

"That's true. But most of 'em have as much knowledge of childbirth as I do—enough to take care of a normal birth. For somethin' like this, we need a midwife, and we don't have one. Ain't you got a doctor at all on this island?"

He shook his head as guilt sliced through him. No doctor. No midwife. Eventually, of course, he'd intended to coax a doctor to the island, but he hadn't done so yet. Still, he should have thought to bring a midwife here for the women.

Suddenly a raucous voice came from the entrance to the cottage. "All right then, where is she? Where's the laboring mother?"

They both turned to find Queenie standing there, her sleeves rolled up and her face set.

"Queenie," Ann said in a firm voice, "you mustn't disturb Molly. Things aren't goin' so well. The baby is breech. She needs to be kept still while we figure out what to do."

"She needs a woman who knows how to help her, that's wot she needs," Queenie retorted. Another scream erupted from inside the bedchamber, and Queenie headed toward it purposefully. Ann moved to block her path, and Queenie scowled at her. "Get out of my way, country girl. Who do you think delivered all the babies in the whorehouse? Me, that's who. We couldn't risk a doctor turning us in to the magistrate, so I always done it. I've birthed more babies than you probably held in yer lifetime. And I'll birth this one, if you'll just let me by."

Ann hesitated, staring at Queenie as if she didn't quite believe the woman.

"Let her pass," Gideon ground out. "If she says she can do it, let her do it, by God. We've got no choice."

When Ann stepped aside, Queenie sniffed, then flounced into the bedchamber, leaving the door open.

"Queenie!" Louisa exclaimed from inside the room. "What in God's name do you think you're doing?"

"It's all right," Ann said as she entered behind Queenie. "She says she used to birth babies."

Louisa harrumphed. "She's probably seen more things going into a woman than coming out of one."

"That's true enough," Queenie said mildly. "But I know a thing or two about bringin' a child into the world. And you ain't got much choice just now, Miss La-Di-Dah."

Gideon went to stand at the doorway and looked in, but all he could see were Ann, Louisa, and Queenie crowding around the bed. Just beyond them, he glimpsed Molly's pale face and her hair matted with sweat.

Queenie settled herself on the edge of the bed with a murmur of distress. He couldn't tell what she was doing, but when she finished, she wiped her hands on her apron and announced, "Aye, the baby's breech, all right. We'll have to turn it."

"Turn it? Can it be done?" Louisa asked anxiously.

"Aye, it can be done. Sometimes. I've tried it a couple of times before." Queenie sounded grim. "It worked only once, though. Sometimes you can't turn the baby."

"Do whatever you have to!" Molly's high-pitched voice rose above the others' murmuring. "Just get the baby out of me, damn it!"

Suddenly, Ann and Louisa moved away from the foot of the bed, both going around to help comfort Molly, and Gideon got his first sight of Molly's parted legs. He gasped. Blood and water smeared her thighs nearly to her knees.

"By God, do something!" he choked out.

"I'll take care of it, Cap'n," Queenie retorted. "You go fetch us some boilin' water, all right? And have Silas make extra for tea. The poor girl's gonna need it after this."

She didn't have to ask twice. Gideon fled, cursing himself for his cowardice. Molly was so small, so fragile. How would she make it through this? And what would become of her baby and little Jane if she didn't?

He found Silas in their new communal kitchen and gave him Queenie's order. Silas already had a pot boiling. He took it off the fire, then came up next to Gideon. "You're lookin' green around the gills, Cap'n. She's havin' a rough time of it, eh?"

Gideon looked at the older man with wild eyes. "She might die. The baby might die." He pounded his fist on the table, full of self-loathing. "And it's all my fault, do you hear? I should have brought doctors to this place and midwives. But what do I know about taking care of women? I don't know a goddamned thing! Sara was right. I didn't even consider their needs, not once! It's no wonder she left me!"

Setting down the pot, Silas patted Gideon's shoulder, then went to the cupboard and poured him a cup of whisky. "Here now, settle down and drink this. It can't be so bad as all that. And Miss Sara didn't leave you because you didn't bring doctors here. She left because she had to take care of family. But she'll be back. She said she'd come back, and I believe her."

"She won't," Gideon said grimly. "She hates me, as well she should."

"Stop talkin' that way. It don't do no good to think such things, most especially when they ain't true." He picked up the pot again. "You sit here and drink a bit while I bring this to Louisa. And maybe by the time I come back I'll have some good news for ye."

Good news? What good news could Silas possibly bring? Even if Molly lived, which looked doubtful, the poor woman was still trapped here, thanks to him.

And he was still without Sara. He had to get out of bed every day and move forward and work and eat and live, all the while knowing that Sara had not loved him enough to stay. For that matter, he didn't even know if she had loved him at all. She'd never said she did. Of course, he'd been equally silent on the subject, afraid to put into words something that might make him even more vulnerable than he already was. But he'd lost her anyway, and now it was too late to tell her that without her he was a ship without sails—dull, listless, emptied of meaning.

No wonder his father had drunk himself into a stupor every night after losing the woman he loved. It was one way of getting through the silent nights and the empty, cold days.

Gideon wouldn't do that, however. He had too much self-respect for that. No, he would just . . . exist. He would go on. But no matter how he tried, he would never succeed in driving her image from his mind.

With a groan, he dropped his face in his hands. If she had wanted to punish him for all his sins, she'd certainly found the way to do it. He hadn't realized how much she'd brought to his life until she'd taken it all away, not even giving him a chance to ask her to stay.

Rising from his seat, he thrust his chair aside in sudden anger, watching as it skittered across the new plank floor. That was what made it hardest. She hadn't waited for him, hadn't said a word, not even good-bye. She'd slipped away as if eager to take her chance to be rid of him.

And after all she'd said about wanting to help, after all she'd said that night on the deck of the ship . . . he remembered that night so clearly: the way she'd given him hope, the way she'd goaded him out of his despair by saying they could rebuild Atlantis—

Confound it, what had she said? *If you're willing to fight for it instead of letting it die.* Perhaps he hadn't fought hard enough for her either. She'd gone away, and he'd let her, so angry over her betrayal that he hadn't acted when he could have.

But now that he looked back on those weeks they'd had together—and especially the last two days—he couldn't believe she hadn't meant any of the things she'd said about wanting to marry him and help him rebuild Atlantis. No one had forced her to agree to marry him, after all. And if she'd known her brother was coming to rescue her, why hadn't she simply resisted Gideon's attempts at seduction until her brother arrived?

His blood ran cold. Perhaps he'd been too hasty in assuming she wanted to leave. He strained to remember what Ann and Petey had told him that night on the beach. Petey *had* hinted that Sara had been forced, before Ann had stopped him. And what had Ann said about Sara's begging her brother not to attack the island? Perhaps it hadn't been her brother she was concerned about.

He shook his head. He was pinning his hopes on a few chance words and misconstrued meanings.

Yet he couldn't shake the feeling that something else had gone on that day to make her leave without a word.

"Well, Cap'n," came a lilting voice from the door, "she's borne a fine baby girl."

He turned to find Ann standing there beaming. Relief swept through him, so intense it staggered him. "And she's all right? And the baby?"

"Both right as rain. Queenie surprised us all, she did, but she knew what she was doin' and took good care of them both."

"Thank God somebody knew what to do." He raked one hand through his hair wearily. "I certainly didn't."

Ann started to leave.

"Ann?" he called out.

"Yes, Cap'n?"

"I want you to tell me exactly what happened the day Sara left."

She dropped her gaze to the floor. "I . . . I already did."

"You didn't tell me everything, did you? You kept something back."

She drew a circle on the floor with her slippered foot. "It don't matter what happened that day, Cap'n. Miss Willis will come back soon as she can. I know she will."

"I can't wait for that." He drew in a breath and thought of how close Molly had come to losing her child and her life. "I'm going to England. I'm taking any women who wish to return. I won't have the blood of any more women on my hands." He paused, feeling more at peace than he had in a long time. "And I'm going to find Sara, and make her see that her place is here. I have to find her. I must tell her that I need her . . . that I love her."

Her gaze flew up to his, fraught with worry and fear. "Oh, but Cap'n, you can't! You mustn't! If you go after her, what she did will all be for naught! She'd never forgive me if I let you go! Never!"

He went still. "What do you mean?"

Clapping a hand over her mouth, she stared at him with round eyes.

"Ann, tell me the truth. Why wouldn't she forgive you? Does she . . . does she hate me?"

"Oh, no, Cap'n! How could she ever hate you?" Ann twisted her hands in her apron as if debating something. Then she sighed. "Her brother—the earl, that is—he told her he'd raze the island if she didn't go back with him to England. She feared he'd do it, too. He'd brought plenty of men and guns to do it and was sore determined. He relented only when she agreed to leave with him."

So Sara hadn't betrayed him. Sara had done what she always did—sacrificed everything for the ones she loved. Anger filled him—anger at Sara's brother, anger at Ann and Petey for lying to him . . . and most of all, anger at himself for believing that Sara would ever willingly abandon him.

"Why did you let me think she *wanted* to leave?" he said in a voice raw with pain as he took a step toward her. "Why would you do that, knowing how I felt about her?"

Guilt shadowed Ann's face. "I didn't want to do it. I had to. She made me promise not to tell you the truth, because she was afraid of the very thing you're speakin' of. That you'd go to England after her, and get yourself hanged. She feared for your life too much to risk it."

"As if I have any kind of a life without her," he bit out. "Now I *have* to go. I can't leave her there with her beast of a brother."

"No, you can't go after her! It would break her heart if you were caught! She said she'd do whatever she could to return, and I know that she—"

"Do you really think he'll let her come back here? A man who'd threaten to destroy everything she loves to get her to return with him?" He clenched his fists, wishing he could use them on Sara's brother. "He won't let her go. *I* wouldn't if I were him."

"Oh, Cap'n," Ann wailed, "if the English take you, they'll hang you!"

"The English haven't caught me before this," he said fiercely, "and I certainly won't let them catch me this time."

"But—"

"I'm going to England, and that's the end of it, Ann. Tell the women that I'll take anyone who wants to return with me. Or if they fear returning to England, I'll take them to Santiago and pay their passage to wherever they wish."

Ann's face mirrored her astonishment. "There are some who would go, but I think most would prefer to stay."

He softened his tone. "If any of them want to stay, we'll be happy to have them, of course, whether they choose to marry or not. But I'm done with the business of finding wives for my men. From now on, they'll have to find wives of their own . . . *willing* wives, if I have anything to say about it."

Stepping nearer, Ann reached up and pressed a soft kiss to his cheek. "You're a good man, Cap'n Horn. I know that Miss Willis would be here with you if she could."

"She *will* be here with me. She'll be here if I have to scour all of the confounded British Isles to find her."

Chapter 26

With a crisp snap, the *Satyr's* snowy sails caught the breeze, and the ship pulled away from Sao Nicolau. Standing at the helm, Gideon steered the ship toward England with building impatience. It had taken him nearly three weeks to get this far. The ship hadn't been in any shape for a long journey, so they'd wasted valuable time in careening it and tarring the rigging before they could even leave Atlantis. Then once they'd reached Santiago, they'd had to lay in supplies and a cargo that would help them pass for a merchant ship when they sailed into English waters.

They'd also had to see to the needs of the eleven women, and their children, who'd chosen to leave Atlantis. Eight of the women had wished to take passage elsewhere from Santiago. He'd had to find them lodgings and arrange passage on other ships. All of that had taken time.

The other three were aboard the *Satyr.* They'd insisted

on returning to England despite the risk of being caught again. Among them were Molly, little Jane, and Molly's newborn. He fully intended to see that Molly was reunited with her husband, no matter what it took. She wanted to bring her husband back to Atlantis, and he'd agreed to that, as long as the man wanted to come.

He was gratified that in the end, only eleven women had wanted to leave. Most had been content with the island, despite the bad beginning he'd given them. And of the ones who'd stayed, most had taken husbands.

Screening his eyes from the morning sun, he gauged the distance around the island's peninsula and tacked into the wind. He hoped to make England in no more than two weeks, despite having to travel against the trade winds. The *Satyr* was traveling light, after all, with just a token cargo and a skeleton crew. He hadn't wanted to risk any more of his men than necessary if he or the ship were captured in England. The few men who'd agreed to sail with him hadn't minded the risk. They were men of daring who for one reason or another had wanted to see England. A couple even intended on finding wives to bring back to Atlantis.

"It feels good to be sailing again, doesn't it?" Barnaby said at Gideon's side. Gideon glanced at his first mate. Barnaby was one of those who'd come because he enjoyed danger. Sometimes Gideon doubted the man would ever really settle down.

"Yes, it does feel good," Gideon replied, but only half meant it. Although he loved the sea as much as any sailor, he'd grown to love Atlantis more. Already he missed the grainy feel of sand beneath his bare feet, the chatter of the children playing in the stream, and the woodsy scent of the forest.

But perhaps he missed those things only because he'd shared them with Sara. And it was Sara he missed most of all.

"What do the men think of my changing the rules concerning the women?" Gideon asked. None of his men had been courageous enough to broach the subject, especially during his foul mood after Sara had left.

Barnaby leaned against the rail with a thoughtful look on his face. "The men are as soft-hearted as you, apparently. They actually seem to approve. I guess they decided you were right—that a lifetime with an unwilling wife wasn't a pleasant prospect."

"I wish I'd realized it sooner." Before he'd driven Sara beyond his reach. Before he'd fallen in love with a prickly reformer who'd probably rather have him thrashed for kidnapping the women than marry him.

No matter. He could endure a thrashing if he had to—as long as she married him afterward.

And if she didn't? If she proved to be fickle after all? If she threw his proposal of marriage back in his face and announced that she thought herself well rid of him? What then?

The possibility had tortured him throughout the past three weeks. He'd continually plagued Petey and Ann with requests to recount what had transpired between Sara and her brother, yet despite their constant insistence that she'd been forced, he didn't feel completely easy. Even though her brother had forced her to leave, a great deal could have happened in the two months since she'd been gone. Once away from the island and back among her social circle, she might have decided that her life on Atlantis had been a disturbing dream and nothing more. She might not want to see him at all.

Yet he had to risk it, even if it meant ending up like his father—tormented by memories of lost love every waking hour.

Barnaby suddenly let out a low whistle at Gideon's side, jarring him from his dark thoughts. "Look there, Captain. 'Tis a shame that we aren't roving anymore. Now there's the perfect prize. An English merchantman."

Gideon followed Barnaby's gaze. A large ship was sailing into the Cape Verde Islands under an English flag. Sitting low in the water, she looked sweet and plump, ready for the picking to anyone interested in chasing her down. "Aye, a pretty prize indeed. But not pretty enough to tempt me. I'm done with piracy, Barnaby. For good."

"Are you?" Barnaby's eyes narrowed. "This ship may change your mind."

"Nothing will change my mind," Gideon said dismissively as he turned back to the helm.

"Don't be so hasty. Look at the ship's name, and then tell me you don't want to board this particular ship."

With impatience, Gideon scanned the side of the ship. There, in plain gold letters, was written the name *Defiant*. He straightened at once and reached for the spyglass.

"Wasn't that the name of the Earl of Blackmore's ship," Barnaby muttered, "the one that took Miss Willis away?"

Gideon nodded as he scanned the ship's hull, then swept the glass over the decks. He saw nothing to indicate it, but he couldn't suppress the hope that it bore Sara. Could she already be—

No, not so soon, he realized. Not with a brother like hers. "I doubt there are two *Defiants* that have reason to sail in these waters. It's got to be his. I'll wager that bastard Englishman has come back to finish where he left off the last time he was at Atlantis. Since Sara wouldn't let him level the island then, he probably left her in England and came back to do it without her." A grim smile touched his lips. "He's in for a surprise, isn't he? I'll take his ship before I let him go within a mile of Atlantis."

"Take his ship? With what? We scarcely have any crew to speak of."

"When have desperate odds ever stopped us?" Gideon surveyed the other ship's crew through the spyglass, wondering why there were so few of them. "We have plenty of cannon, and his ship doesn't look that well manned. We can take him in a sea battle, I'll wager. If he refuses to come to and let us board him, I swear I'll blow fifty holes in his hull until I flush the coward out of hiding. If he's aboard, I'll make him tell me where she is. If he's not, I'll hold the ship for ransom until he gives her to me. Either way, I *will* take his ship."

"You're quite mad, you know," Barnaby said, most sincerely. Then he shrugged. "All the same, I must say I miss a good fight at sea."

Catching sight of the *Defiant*'s English flag, Gideon muttered, "It's a shame we destroyed our old Jolly Roger."

There was a long silence before Barnaby stammered, "Um . . . we didn't exactly . . . that is . . ."

Gideon held the spyglass aside as he stared at his first mate. "I thought I ordered it destroyed at the end of our last voyage."

"You did. But . . . well . . . I thought you might change your mind, so I kept it. It's in my cabin."

Gideon suppressed a smile. "I ought to sentence you to sanding the decks for a week for disobeying orders, Mr. Kent. But I suppose I can overlook your transgression this time." He returned to observing the *Defiant* through the spyglass. "Tell me, have we ever taken one of Blackmore's ships that you know of?"

Barnaby grinned. "I don't recall ever hearing that name spoken by any of the crews we've . . . er . . . entertained."

"Then it's high time we took one, don't you think?"

"Aye, aye, Captain. Mustn't let the good earl get too cocky about his prowess at sea."

"Indeed." Gideon set down the spyglass with a determined smile. "This earl definitely needs taking down a peg or two. And you and I are just the men to do it."

Sara sat at breakfast in the saloon of the *Defiant* with Lord and Lady Dryden and Jordan. She picked absently at her food, too excited to eat. They were nearing the

Cape Verde Islands, only two days' sail from Atlantis. She could hardly believe Jordan had finally agreed to transport her to the island. But he'd had little choice, once the marquess and his wife had brought pressure to bear on him. If he hadn't agreed, the marquess would have chartered a ship himself to go to the island, taking Sara with him. And Jordan never liked relinquishing control of a situation.

Sara had come to like Lady Dryden a great deal on this trip. And her husband, too. Although the man was obviously several years older than his wife, Lord Dryden had none of the pretensions that men of his rank and age often possessed. Indeed, his regal bearing, aristocratic features, and warm smile reminded Sara very much of her late stepfather.

So here they were, the four of them, traveling to Atlantis. The other three were conversing on some subject that might have been of interest to her if her mind hadn't been preoccupied with thoughts of Gideon. He was almost within her grasp. She had so much to tell him, so much to say that she could hardly contain it all.

Her only fear was that he wouldn't give her the chance to speak. Oh, if he refused to see her, to hear her out, she would never be able to bear it. Never.

The door to the saloon swung open, and the first mate rushed in. "My lord, there's a ship to starboard, gaining on us fast! And she's flying the Jolly Roger!"

As Jordan let out a curse, Sara leapt up from her chair so quickly she knocked it over. She ran into her cabin. The others came in behind her as she gazed out the porthole, straining to catch a glimpse of the ship that was well on their heels. Then she saw the figurehead. It was the *Satyr*. There was no mistaking it.

"Gideon," she breathed, her heart pounding faster.

Lord and Lady Dryden started murmuring behind her as Jordan came to her side. "I thought you said the Pirate Lord had given up piracy."

"He has." She faced them all. Lord and Lady Dryden

looked concerned and Jordan looked positively livid. She crossed her arms over her chest stubbornly. "He has," she repeated more firmly. "Of course he has."

"Then why is he here," her brother asked, "chasing after us and flying the Jolly Roger?"

"I don't know." She tilted her chin up. "But he must have a good reason for it."

"We'll find out soon enough, won't we?" Whirling away, Jordan strode past Lord and Lady Dryden out of the cabin and into the saloon.

Sara rushed after him as her other companions followed. "What are you going to do, Jordan?"

"I'm going to determine just how 'honest' and 'kind' your pirate captain really is."

"What do you mean? What—"

She broke off as the captain entered the saloon, his face mottled with fury. "It's the Pirate Lord, or so one of my sailors tells me. They've ordered us to 'heave to.' With your permission, my lord, I'd like to fight. I think we can win, even though we've not as many men as I'd like."

"No!" cried three voices at once.

When the captain stared at her and her companions in astonishment, Jordan grimaced. "I'm afraid fighting is out of the question, captain. You see, my sister intends to marry the Pirate Lord, and Lord and Lady Dryden are here to make sure it happens. Much as I'd like to order you to blow the *Satyr* out of the water, I can't. If I do, one of them is liable to murder me in my sleep, and then you'll have no one to pay your wages, will you?"

The captain cast his employer an incredulous look. "So you want us to heave to?"

"Yes." Jordan's voice held an edge. "But have your men armed and at the ready, hidden from the pirates. If anything goes wrong, we should be prepared."

With a curt nod, the captain left. Jordan turned to

Sara. "I want you to stay here until I've spoken with him."

"No!" she protested. "You'll shoot him, Jordan, and I won't have that!"

"Sara, I've agreed to all of your terms until now. The least you owe me is the chance to determine if your pirate captain's intentions are honorable. This attack on my ship doesn't give me confidence in his supposed willingness to 'retire.' And I'm not going to simply hand you over to him unless I'm sure he'll treat you well."

"But Jordan—"

"He's right," Lord Dryden interrupted. "I think we should all stay below until we're sure there's no danger."

Sara might like Lord Dryden, but she certainly didn't appreciate his interference just now.

Apparently, neither did his wife. "That is my *son* out there, Marcus, and I shan't sit in here twiddling my thumbs when I finally have the chance to hold him in my arms again!"

"I share your feelings completely, my dear. But no matter what we feel, we don't yet know this man. He's unpredictable, and according to Miss Willis, very bitter. I think it's best to test the waters, so to speak, before we reveal ourselves."

"Then we're in agreement," Jordan told the marquess. "You'll stay here with the ladies? Look out for them if anything goes wrong?"

"Nothing will go wrong unless you *make* it go wrong!" Sara protested, but both Jordan and Lord Dryden ignored her words. When Lord Dryden gave his agreement, Jordan walked out the door.

"Jordan!" she shouted after him. "Don't you dare hurt him!"

Coming up beside her, Lord Dryden patted her shoulder. "There now, Miss Willis, it will be all right. Your brother may be hot-tempered, but he does care about you."

"If he lays one hand on Gideon, I'll strangle him," she said fervently.

"Don't worry," his lordship interrupted with a faint smile. "If he lays one hand on Gideon, my wife and I will hold your brother down while you do."

Gideon stepped aboard the *Defiant* with several of his men, uneasiness in the pit of his stomach. This had been too simple. They'd ordered the ship to heave to, and it had complied without a murmur of protest. He motioned to Barnaby, who boarded the ship out of sight of its captain, accompanied by fifteen more of Gideon's best men.

Then he gripped the hilt of his saber as he faced the ship's captain, a sea-roughened raisin of a man who stood beside the main mast.

The man looked oddly unafraid. "We carry no cargo of any use to you and your villains, sir."

"I'm not here for cargo. I seek the Earl of Blackmore. Is he aboard?"

"He's aboard," came another voice from beyond the main mast. A man stepped forward, a pistol in his hand. "I'm the Earl of Blackmore."

Gideon scanned his enemy with cold eyes, looking for signs of the weak coward he'd expected to find. But though the man was finely dressed and younger than Gideon had expected, he looked nothing like the noblemen Gideon had dealt with in previous captures. There was a hardness about him, an edge of stubborn pride, that Gideon couldn't help but admire.

And he was leveling the pistol on Gideon as if he itched to fire it. "What do you want with me? Is it gold you want?"

"There's only one thing I want of you, and that's Sara," Gideon said bluntly, ignoring the pistol. "I want my fiancée. Either you take me to her, or I hold you and your ship captive until you do."

"Or I could shoot you and your cursed pirates. Even

now my men have yours under their guns and can pick them off at will if I command it."

Gideon sneered at him. "Barnaby!" he shouted. "How fare the earl's men and their guns?"

Barnaby and the fifteen other men emerged from behind the forward house, pushing a group of disarmed and disgruntled sailors ahead of them. "Oh, they fare quite well, Captain. As for their guns, let's just say we've added to our arsenal substantially this day."

The earl scowled as Gideon faced him with a thinly veiled smile. "I've been a pirate for many years, Lord Blackmore, too many to fall for such paltry tricks."

"I still have you under my own gun," the earl retorted hotly.

"Aye. And my men have you under theirs. Now, about your sister—"

"Jordan, you fool, put that gun down at once!" shouted a familiar feminine voice. Sara ran out from beneath the quarterdeck to stand in front of Gideon, facing the earl. "Don't you dare shoot him! Don't you dare!"

Gideon's breath stopped in his throat as he took in the flaming hair and lithe form. "Sara!"

She turned to him, her face glowing. "I told you I would return. I told you."

He gave her no chance to say more. Throwing down his saber, he caught her to him and crushed her against his chest. She was here. She was really here! "Sara, my Sara," he whispered into her hair, "you have no idea what I've endured without you."

"No worse than I've endured without you." She drew back from him a little, her tear-filled eyes scanning his face with tender concern. "You look far too pale and thin, my love. I'm so sorry. I didn't want to leave you. Truly I didn't."

"I know." He ran his hands over her waist and ribs, scarcely able to believe that he held her in his arms. "That's why I'm here. I was on my way to England to fetch you when I spotted your brother's ship."

Sara's expression turned irate. "Ann told you what happened? Oh, just wait until I see *her* again—"

"You mustn't blame her for telling me, sweetheart. I'd already decided to go to England to carry the women who didn't wish to live on Atlantis."

Shock spread over Sara's face. "You . . . you what?"

"You were right about so many things," he said solemnly, "but especially about the women. I finally learned that. What kind of a paradise is there where people are not free?"

"Oh, Gideon," she said, her voice choked.

He went on haltingly. "So I . . . decided to take the women back to England, those who wished to go." His voice grew earnest. "And once I was there, I intended to find you and beg you to return. That's why Ann told me the truth about why you left. She was trying to keep me from coming after you. She said if I got caught, all your sacrifice would've been for nothing."

"You should have listened to her," Sara protested. "Didn't you believe I would return? You should have, especially after she told you the truth."

"It wasn't *you* I was worried about." He looked beyond her to where her brother stood. The earl no longer had his pistol trained on Gideon, but he was scowling at him darkly enough to kill. Gideon's voice hardened. "I feared that your bastard of a brother would never let you go."

The earl crossed his arms over his chest, an impudent glare on his face. "The thought did cross my mind, Horn."

"Hush, Jordan," Sara said when Gideon stiffened. She lifted her face to Gideon. "What he did was awful, I know, but you must forgive him. He is my brother, after all."

"Not by blood," Gideon growled, his gaze still fixed on the earl. "And the man certainly doesn't deserve to call you his relation."

"I've known her longer than you have and taken care of her much better," the earl snapped. He stepped forward, his fists clenched, only to find Barnaby's pistol aimed at him.

Sara glared at Barnaby. "Put that thing down now, Barnaby Kent, or I shall never speak to you again!"

Barnaby glanced at Gideon, waiting for confirmation of her words. When Gideon hesitated, Sara faced him once more with a scowl. "You are *not* going to have my brother shot, Gideon, much as you may wish to. I know he behaved badly, but so did you. I wouldn't let him shoot you for kidnapping me, so I'm certainly not going to let you shoot him for the same thing. Do you hear me?"

Gideon suppressed a smile as she stuck her chin out at him. She was as stubborn and demanding and loyal as he remembered. Thank God some things never changed. "All right, sweetheart. I won't let Barnaby shoot your stepbrother. Besides, it wouldn't do to kill an earl just when I've decided to retire from piracy, would it?"

When she beamed at him, then reached up to brush her lips against his, he caught her to him and kissed her long and deep, despite the strangled sounds coming from her brother. When at last he managed to tear himself away from her mouth, Barnaby still held the pistol on his lordship, though a grin split the first mate's face from one end to the other. "Put the gun down, Barnaby," Gideon said jovially. "It appears that Sara has come back to me despite Lord Blackmore's machinations. So there's not much point in shooting him now, is there?"

"I suppose not." Barnaby stuck the pistol in his waistband.

"I take it that all the talk of shooting is over now?" a new voice asked.

Whirling around, Barnaby exclaimed, "Who the bloody hell are you two?"

Gideon looked to where an older couple had emerged from the doorway beneath the quarterdeck and now stood at Barnaby's back. Their eyes, oddly enough, were on Gideon, although there was no hint of fear in them.

Twisting her head to one side, Sara looked at them, then at Gideon. A sudden uncertainty seemed to cross her face. "Um . . . Gideon, I've brought some people with me whom I think . . . I hope . . . you'd like to meet."

The well-dressed couple were surveying him in a way that made him uncomfortable. "Oh?"

Stepping back from him, Sara swept her hand in the direction of the older couple. "Gideon, may I present Lady Dryden, Eustacia Worley. Your mother."

Thunderstruck, Gideon looked beyond Sara to the slight, dark-haired woman standing there. "My mother is dead, Sara."

The woman flinched and started forward, but the tall man beside her held her back.

"She's not dead," Sara said gently, forcing Gideon's attention back to her. "She's very much alive." Sara drew in a ragged breath. "Elias Horn lied to you all those years ago. The only true thing he ever told you was that he was your mother's tutor and that she was briefly infatuated with him. But everything else he said was a lie. When he pressed her to run off with him, she refused. She never eloped with Elias Horn. She married your father instead."

Gideon was still reeling from the knowledge that Elias had lied to him, when her last words arrested him. "Did you say my father?" His gaze returned to the couple standing behind Barnaby, and this time he surveyed the man who stood there, so proud and unflinching . . . the tall, gray-headed man with blue eyes . . . and Gideon's own face.

Gideon's heart began to pound as he clutched Sara's arm with painful tightness.

"Hello, son," the man said in a strained voice, his eyes bright with unshed tears.

Shaking his head, Gideon staggered back from Sara. "There must be a mistake. My father is dead. My mother is dead."

"Your mother is standing right here," Sara said firmly. "After she met Lord Dryden, she realized that Elias Horn wasn't the man for her. She'd already noticed his propensity for drink, so she told him as gently as she could that she didn't wish to marry him." Sara's voice hardened. "Apparently that didn't satisfy Elias. After she married Lord Dryden, he sent her notes, trying to get her to meet him. And when Lord Dryden put an end to that, he struck back at them both by stealing you away shortly after your birth. One day when the wet nurse brought you to the park, he waited till she turned aside for a moment, then he snatched you."

"No, it can't be," Gideon said hoarsely. "Elias was an unfeeling man sometimes, but he wouldn't have . . . he couldn't have . . ." His mind raced through a thousand memories, trying to reorient them according to this new information, yet failing. To be told that he had both a mother and a father, that Elias had lied—"But what about the brooch she left behind?" he said as he touched his fingers to his belt.

"I had pinned it to the inside of the basket you lay in, the day you were taken," said the woman who claimed to be his mother. "It sparkled so much that you used to love to look at it."

There was so much sincerity in her voice that he could almost believe her. Almost. "No, I saw the letter from you to my . . . to Elias. What about the letter?"

"Letter?" Lord Dryden echoed, his gaze flitting to Sara. "What is he talking about?"

But Sara seemed not to hear him. "You were ten years old, Gideon. Did you think to look for a postmark? Any identifying marks? Of course not. Elias wrote a fake letter and showed it to you, because you were making trouble for him by asking questions at the consulate."

"Oh, my God," Gideon choked out. He felt like a boat turned topsy-turvy by a tempest. If this was the truth, then everything he had thought, everything he'd believed about Elias and his mother, was totally wrong. "This is impossible."

"Think, Gideon," Sara said, her face full of sympathy. "If Elias had truly been your father, why would he have tortured you by reading you a letter that was calculated to wound? No caring father would willingly tell his son that his mother didn't want him, that his mother's family thought he was dirt beneath their shoes. He did that because *he* felt like dirt beneath their shoes, and he wanted to put you down there with him. No doubt he thought to taint Lady Dryden's marriage by stealing her son. Only he didn't know what to do with you once he had you."

Gideon's hands formed fists as he thought of all the times Elias had cursed him for being as proud and haughty as his mother. He thought of all the beatings he'd suffered, the lack of familial affection he'd sensed in Elias even from the beginning. Rage boiled up in him, a wild rage that needed an outlet.

He turned to his parents. "If you knew Elias had taken me, why didn't you look for me? Why did you leave me to that . . . that monster?"

"Oh, my dear boy, we *did* look for you!" Lady Dryden cried. "But we never dreamed he'd taken you to America. We didn't think he had the money. Besides, the war with America was still going on, so we assumed he would never take you there."

Lord Dryden stepped forward, his eyes stark with pain. "We searched through Ireland and England and Scotland. We even searched the Continent. Every time there was a report of an abandoned baby that matched your description, we traveled wherever it was to determine if it was you. We never believed he would keep you. Why should he? He knew nothing about babies."

"He certainly didn't," Gideon said bitterly. He looked at his mother. "I think he kept me only because I was a link to you. He always loved you, you know. And maybe some part of him came to believe that he really *was* my father." His tone grew harsh. "Knowing Elias, it's more likely he thought to punish you by punishing me. He always said I was like you, every time he—"

"Gideon, no," Sara said in an undertone as she came up beside him. "You musn't tell them all that. They've suffered endless tortures wondering how you were being treated, and it's not fair to heap more upon them now."

He looked at Lord and Lady Dryden and realized she was right. Never had he seen two people look more anxious. They weren't to blame for the actions of a man who'd never completely been right in his mind. And to tell them the full extent of Elias's perfidy would probably destroy them.

His parents. Confound it, they were *his* parents. How would he ever get used to the idea of having real parents?

"Son," his mother said in an aching voice as she came nearer. "I've been . . . waiting thirty years to hold you in my arms. Do you think . . . you could . . . indulge an old woman?"

Tears misted his eyes as he looked down into the face of the woman he hardly knew, the woman he had hated all his life with no reason. And suddenly, he wanted desperately to know her. "Mother," was all he said through a voice choked with emotion.

Then somehow they were embracing.

Sara watched them together, her heart near to bursting. She couldn't be angry at Jordan now for forcing her to return to England, not when it had come out like this.

Next it was Lord Dryden's turn to hold his son, his eyes red with unshed tears as he clutched the younger man to him. When after several moments his parents released him, Gideon had the look of a boy who'd just been given the key to a sweets shop. "A mother *and* a father. I can hardly believe it." Pulling away from his parents, he turned to Sara. "And it's all thanks to you. You found them, didn't you? You did that for me."

She ducked her head shyly. "I . . . I just never could quite believe that Elias's tale was true. It didn't make sense that a woman could abandon her child with so little thought."

Clasping her about the waist, he drew her close. "You always did have a better opinion of people than I did. It seems you were right this time. Think of all the years I might have had with them, if I hadn't been so ready to believe Elias." He tipped her chin up with one finger. "Maybe I would have met you sooner."

Her eyes glowed as she looked up at him and touched her hand to his cheek. "Those years are past. What matters is that we have each other now."

"And do I have you?" he whispered. "You'll marry me? You'll come back with me to Atlantis?"

"To Atlantis?" Lord Dryden broke in. "But son, you're my heir. You belong in England."

When Gideon looked taken aback, Sara added mischievously, "Yes, Gideon. It seems the Pirate Lord actually *is* a lord, one of those awful noblemen he always delighted in tormenting. You're the Earl of Worthing. You have a title and great lands in England."

His face clouded over as he looked at her. "I don't care about all that, Sara. It means nothing to me." His voice grew strained. "But I know it . . . counts for something with you. If you don't wish to live on Atlantis—"

She touched her finger to his lips to silence him. "Don't be foolish. Atlantis is the only place where I truly belong. How could I live anywhere but there?"

With eyes glittering, he murmured, "I love you, Sara. I love you so much that I'll willingly go to England and be the . . . the . . ."

"The Earl of Worthing."

"Yes, the Earl of Worthing, if that's what you want. If that's what it takes."

Her heart swelled to hear him offer to make such a precious sacrifice for love of her. "And I love you, Gideon. Which is why we will *not* go to England until you're ready . . . if ever."

"Am I to lose my son so soon then?" Lady Dryden asked in a plaintive voice. "Just when I have found him?"

Tucking his arm around Sara, Gideon turned toward his mother. "You won't lose me, Mother. I swear it." He smiled. "I'm a ship's captain, after all. I imagine Sara and I will be making a great many trips to England in the future."

"They'll hang you if they catch you," Barnaby put in sourly.

"Not *my* son," Lord Dryden retorted. "I assure you that between Lord Blackmore's influence and mine, we can ensure a pardon for the Earl of Worthing."

When Jordan snorted loudly, everyone broke into laughter.

"Do you hear that?" Gideon told Barnaby. "I'm to be pardoned and set up as an earl. Quite a fitting end for the Pirate Lord, don't you think?"

"Brought down by a woman," Barnaby grumbled. "They'll never believe it when we tell the tale on Atlantis."

"Oh, they'll believe it," Sara said as she stared up at her husband-to-be, her joy so intense she felt lightheaded. "After all, every one of those pirates has been brought down by a woman of his own."

"Aye, they have at that," Gideon murmured as he pulled her close for another kiss. "And if you ask me, it's not a bad comeuppance for a bunch of scurvy American privateers. Not a bad comeuppance at all."

Epilogue

March 1819

The ballroom at the Dryden estate in Derbyshire was crammed with people curious to glimpse the marquess's long-lost heir. His lordship had thrown a lavish costume ball to welcome his son, and now Sara and Gideon strolled about the room, having already been introduced to what seemed like every inhabitant of the county.

Thank heavens they were in costume, for it gave them something to talk about with people whom Gideon barely knew. Thinking it would be a grand jest, Sara and Lady Dryden had coaxed Gideon into dressing as Sir Walter Raleigh to match Sara's Queen Elizabeth costume. They'd even let him wear his earring. As Lady Dryden had said, "He looks like a pirate even in civilized clothing, so he might as well dress the part." With his black mask, tanned skin, and newly cropped dark hair, Sara thought he was by far the handsomest man at the ball, and she'd noticed more than one woman eyeing him with interest.

He was completely unaware of it, however. Never had she seen him look so uneasy, not even when he'd first set foot in England two weeks ago. Then he'd merely been curious and somewhat amused to find himself now a respected member of the very nobility he'd plagued for so many years.

Tonight, however, he seemed very conscious of what was expected of him as heir to the Marquess of Dryden. "Must the women keep curtsying to me as if I were some deity?" he grumbled.

"Yes. It's due you because of your rank." An impish smile crossed her face. "You didn't even have to brandish your saber in front of them to get it. Fancy that. It must be a new experience for you."

He cast her a sidelong glance. "If you don't show me some respect, my dear wife, I'll have to brandish my . . . er . . . saber in front of you later when we're alone."

"Oh, you will, will you? And you think that'll gain you some respect?"

He grinned. "It's been effective in the past."

She struck him playfully with her fan. "You are entirely too naughty for polite society, my lord."

"Stop calling me that," he said with a scowl. "The words still leave a bad taste in my mouth."

"Well, you'd better get used to them if you're planning to spend any time in England."

"We wouldn't even be here if you weren't expecting our child." He glanced down at her rounded belly, only barely hidden by the fullness of her costume, and his expression softened. "After watching Molly give birth, I refuse to take any chances with our firstborn."

"That's not the only reason we came for a visit, and you know it," she said quietly. "You also wished to see what your life might have been like if not for Elias Horn, didn't you?"

He shrugged, gazing out over the crowd. "Perhaps."

She opened her mouth to say something else, but before she could speak, her stepbrother came to her side. He'd also been invited to the house party at the Derbyshire estate by the marquess and his wife, much to Gideon's chagrin.

As was typical of Jordan, he hadn't taken the time to find a costume, but like many of the men, merely wore a mask with his usual evening attire. "And how is the expectant mother? You mustn't tax yourself, you know. I don't want my nephew born early enough to raise eyebrows."

Gideon laid his hand in the small of her back in a

protective gesture she knew all too well. "Are you implying that I'm the kind of man who'd allow his wife to tax herself?"

"If the shoe fits—"

"Behave, both of you," she admonished as Gideon bristled and Jordan glared. "I swear, when you two get near each other, you act like school boys fighting over a half-pence."

"Oh, you're much more valuable than a half-pence," Jordan retorted. Before Gideon could say anything to that, he added, "And in any case, I didn't come over here to anger you, moppet. I merely wanted to let you know I'm leaving."

"Good," Gideon mumbled under his breath.

She swatted him with her fan before turning back to her brother. "What do you mean, leaving? I thought you came up for the entire week!"

"I don't mean I'm returning to London. I'm merely leaving the ball for a while. I've found someone who wants me to take her home."

"Her?" Sara said, curiosity getting the better of her. "I thought you didn't know a soul in Derbyshire except Lord and Lady Dryden."

He grinned. "I don't. But when an intriguing widow asks me to take her home, I always agree."

"Now, Jordan—" she warned.

"Can I help it if women find me devastating?" He nodded toward Gideon. "At least I'm not of your husband's ilk, snatching her away against her will."

Gideon glowered at him. "Look here, Blackmore, I've had just about enough of—"

"Hush, Gideon. Can't you see he's *trying* to irritate you?" Sara scowled at her brother. "As for you, if you don't behave yourself, I'll return to Atlantis *before* the baby is born, and you won't get to see it for a year."

Jordan eyed her suspiciously. "Lady Dryden wants to see the birth of her grandchild too badly to let you do that."

"I'll take her and his lordship with us. They've been longing to go back for a visit every since that first two weeks they spent on the island, after Gideon and I were married." No need to tell him that Gideon would never allow her to travel by ship so close to the baby's birth.

Jordan glared at her. "All right, I'll attempt to be civil." Then he glanced over his shoulder in the direction of the door, where a young woman stood, dressed in black bombazine. Jordan's expression altered subtly. "I can be civil to anyone tonight, as long as I'm allowed to go home with that beauty." Leaning closer to Sara, he whispered, "Good night, moppet, don't wait up." Then he turned and walked briskly back to the young woman.

He was scarcely out of earshot before Gideon exploded into laughter.

"What in heaven's name is so funny?" Sara asked.

"Your brother, sweetheart, has vastly misconstrued that *beauty*'s intentions, unless I miss my guess. He's about to receive a much deserved comeuppance."

Sara stared at him quizzically.

His eyes shone with amusement through the slits in his mask. "I met that young lady earlier. Do you know who she is? The rector's daughter, and no merry widow. She's mourning her mother, not a husband. She came here with her cousin, who was dressed in a similar manner to your brother, and I'll wager that when she asked him to take her home, she thought she was speaking to her cousin."

"Bother it all!" Sara exclaimed and started to rush after Jordan.

But Gideon caught her arm. "Don't you dare. He deserves a little humiliation after what he's put us through, don't you think?"

She hesitated, watching as her brother took the pretty young woman's arm and led her out. She dragged Gideon onto the balcony to see what would happen. Her eyes narrowed as Jordan handed the woman up into the

Blackmore carriage. A rector's daughter? A sweet, dependable rector's daughter?

She began to smile. "Perhaps a rector's daughter is just the sort of woman my brother needs."

"Are we speaking of the same man? The Earl of Blackmore, whom you've said yourself is a rakehell? I can't even *begin* to imagine your brother married to a rector's daughter."

"Yes, but you have poor powers of imagination." She turned away from the balcony to gaze fondly at him. "A year ago you wouldn't have dreamed Barnaby would be happily married to a prostitute like Queenie and eagerly anticipating his first child. Or that grouchy old Silas would be capable of fathering twins *and* presiding over Atlantis in your absence. Or even that you yourself would be married to the stepsister of an earl. You wouldn't have imagined any of that, would you?"

"No." A smile touched his lips. "All right, you win. I suppose if a bloodthirsty pirate could find a decent woman, your brother could." Without warning, he dragged her into his arms for a stunning kiss that left her swooning. When he drew back, his eyes were twinkling. "But if my few moments' conversation with that rector's daughter is any indication, your brother will have a fight on his hands."

As a slow smile edged over her lips, she lifted her arms to pull him back into her embrace. "All the better. It's like I've always said: the best women—and men— are the ones worth fighting for."

Author's Note

Although Gideon and Sara are my creations, the capture of the *Chastity* has a basis in history. In 1812, the *Emu*, carrying forty-nine convict women, was taken prisoner by an American privateer ship, the *Holkar*. The women were let off on St. Vincent and never heard from again, while the *Holkar* returned with its prize to America. A French pirate also captured a convict ship, although he released it when he found no booty.

As much as possible, my story reflects true conditions aboard convict ships in this period.

Atlantis is based on St. Helena and Ascension Island off the coast of Africa. The latter wasn't inhabited until 1815, despite being located off a heavily traveled trade route.

Look for *The Notorious Lord* in Spring 1999, and find out what happens when Emily Fairchild, a respectable rector's daughter, finds herself alone in a carriage with Jordan Willis, the Earl of Blackmore—and the most notorious rake in England.

After one kiss, they part. Until they meet again in London . . . where innocent Emily has been blackmailed into masquerading as Lady Emma Campbell. Will Jordan unmask her and bring about her family's destruction? Or will he seduce Lady Emma the way he'd wanted to seduce Emily—unraveling the dark threads of his past, and casting them into a struggle for the truth?

Don't miss the second installment in Sabrina Jeffries' trilogy about three captivating lords and the women who tamed them!

Dear Reader,

Coming next month from Avon Romance are terrific stories—historical and contemporary—beginning with *Perfect in My Sight*, the latest from bestselling author Tanya Anne Crosby. Sarah Woodard and her cousin Mary had vowed never to wed, but Mary breaks that vow. Now, she has died under mysterious circumstances, and Sarah travels to meet her dear cousin's husband for the first time. Sarah has no reason to trust Peter, but she begins to find it impossible to resist his charms . . .

If you like western settings, then don't miss Karen Kay's *White Eagle's Touch*, the next installment of the Blackfoot Warriors series. Katrina is a wealthy English socialite travelling west; White Eagle is the proud and powerful Blackfoot warrior who once saved her life. Together they find an unforgettable love that spans their two worlds.

For fans of Regency settings, don't miss Marlene Suson's *Kiss Me Goodnight*. The devilishly charming Marquess of Sherbourne never expected to be so entranced by radiant redhead Katherine McNamara, but her fiery kisses quickly ignite passion's flame in this seductive, sensuous love story.

And if you prefer a more modern setting, don't miss *Baby, I'm Yours* by Susan Andersen. The last place Catherine MacPherson ever expected to find herself was sitting on a bus, handcuffed to a sexy bounty hunter, with only a suitcase of her twin sister's shrink-wrap clothing to wear. Sam MacKade doesn't care how irresistible Catherine is, he doesn't believe for a minute that Catherine *isn't* her showgirl sister. Will Sam solve this case of mistaken identity and lose his heart at the same time?

Look to Avon for romance at its best! Until next month, enjoy.

Lucia Macro

Lucia Macro
Senior Editor

AEL 0498

Avon Romances—
the best in exceptional authors and unforgettable novels!

Avon Romantic Treasures

*Unforgettable, enthralling love stories,
sparkling with passion and adventure
from Romance's bestselling authors*

EVERYTHING AND THE MOON *by Julia Quinn*
78933-7/$5.99 US/$7.99 Can

BEAST *by Judith Ivory*
78644-3/$5.99 US/$7.99 Can

HIS FORBIDDEN TOUCH *by Shelley Thacker*
78120-4/$5.99 US/$7.99 Can

LYON'S GIFT *by Tanya Anne Crosby*
78571-4/$5.99 US/$7.99 Can

FLY WITH THE EAGLE *by Kathleen Harrington*
77836-X/$5.99 US/$7.99 Can

FALLING IN LOVE AGAIN *by Cathy Maxwell*
78718-0/$5.99 US/$7.99 Can

**THE COURTSHIP OF
CADE KOLBY** *by Lori Copeland*
79156-0/$5.99 US/$7.99 Can

TO LOVE A STRANGER *by Connie Mason*
79340-7/$5.99 US/$7.99 Can